COMPLETE.

Price **6d.**

LEFT HANDED

The Terror of the School

JACK

Edwin J Brett Limited,   Hathaway House,
6, West Harding Street,   London, E.C.

LEFT-HANDED JACK;

Or, the Terror of the School.

"'TAKE IT OFF,' HE YELLED."—(See page 19.)

LEFT-HANDED JACK;

OR,

THE TERROR OF THE SCHOOL.

CHAPTER I.

FORBIDDEN FRUIT.

" I SAY, sir, I want to speak to you about your son—a very promising boy I must declare, very much so, indeed."

The speaker was a little, red-faced, choleric man, well-dressed, and of gentlemanly appearance.

His name was Sir Dando Titmarsh; he was a widower, with one son and one daughter.

His income was five thousand a year, and he lived at Glenalbyn Lodge, on the lower side of Windsor.

The daughter, named Ada, was a pretty girl of sixteen; the son, Septimus, was a haughty, overbearing boy a year younger, but withal a coward.

The gentleman he addressed himself to was Captain Massey, a retired officer of the army, with a small pension.

Captain Massey had one son, who was the idol of his wife and himself, who could see no fault in Jack.

It was about Jack Massey that Sir Dando Titmarsh had spoken to the captain.

They were neighbours.

Captain Massey resided at The Chestnuts, a cottage which adjoined the mansion of Sir Dando.

Glenalbyn Lodge had beautiful grounds leading down to the River Thames, with conservatories filled with flowers, and grapes, and pineapples.

The cottage called The Chestnuts had only a small garden, which was separated from Sir Dando's by a low brick wall.

Sir Dando Titmarsh was talking to Captain Massey over this boundary.

It was a fine day for the time of year, which was Easter.

The Masseys had lived in Windsor for years, ever since the captain had retired from the army.

But Sir Dando Titmarsh had only resided six months at the big house adjoining.

This was long enough, however, for Jack Massey to learn to love Ada Titmarsh, and to thoroughly hate her brother Septimus.

Jack was fifteen years old, and had never been to school, his education being conducted by a private tutor, to whom he went every day.

Septimus Titmarsh was at the near college of Eton; but, it being Easter-time, he was at home for the holidays.

Captain Massey was too poor to afford to send Jack to such an expensive school as Eton.

Septimus Titmarsh thought he was much superior to Jack, because he was an Eton boy.

"What have you to say about my son?" asked Captain Massey, calmly.

He had seen service on many a hard fought field.

Yet he knew how to keep his temper.

"I have in my hothouse some very choice black grapes, called *La Reine*," replied Sir Dando, "and I find that a bunch is missing, before I have ordered my gardener to cut away for my own table."

"You mean to insinuate that Jack took them?"

"I have proof positive."

"The matter shall be enquired into," said Captain Massey. "I can only express my regret, and offer you compensation. What are the grapes worth?"

"You would not buy them under five shillings," replied Sir Dando; "but I don't want your money."

"What then?"

"Just keep your boy off my grounds, or I'll have him up before a magistrate."

"Why have you such a prejudice against Jack?" asked the captain.

"Well, if you must know, he will not let my son Sep alone."

"Ah! they have been fighting again, I suppose?"

"No, sir. My son is too much of a gentleman to fight."

Captain Massey smiled.

He knew Septimus to be an effeminate coward.

"What does Jack do to your son?" demanded the captain.

"Why, sir, he comes running along like a locomotive, or a bull going into a china shop, and swings what he calls his steam arm about, striking Sep all over the body, making him run for his life."

The captain could not refrain from laughing.

Jack Massey was left-handed.

He possessed prodigious strength in his left arm.

It was a way of his to call it his steam arm.

He could swing it round and round, and strike out with a force that would fell a strong man to the ground.

There was not a boy in Windsor, years older than himself, who could stand up against him.

Left-handed Jack was well known and dreaded wherever he went.

At cricket he bowled like a demon, and many a batsman had to retire from the field.

In rowing he always pulled the boat round on one side.

The same strength did not exist in the right arm.

It was with his left that Jack Massey had made his name so much feared.

He had taken an especial dislike to Septimus Titmarsh, who put on too many airs to please hi—

Septimus had only been home from Eton for the Easter holidays two days, but Jack was on his track, as he phrased it.

Sir Dando Titmarsh had listened to his son's complaints, and had become very much angered.

In order to speak to the captain, whom he had seen in his garden, he had got on a three-legged rustic stool.

If he had not done so, his head would scarcely have reached above the top of the wall, for, as we have said, the worthy baronet was a little man.

His son Septimus resembled him in this respect.

"Don't laugh at me, sir," cried Sir Dando, furiously.

"I can't help it," replied the captain.

"You will find it no laughing matter, neither you nor your cub either."

"Moderate your language."

"I'll be hanged if I do!"

"Then I shall refuse to hold any further conversation with you."

"I—I'll go to law," shouted Sir Dando Titmarsh; "I'll go——"

His further utterance was cut short.

He had not time to say where he was going.

The rustic stool, being rather rotten from long exposure to the weather, gave way.

It wobbled—it broke beneath his weight.

The little baronet uttered a wild cry.

Then he disappeared from view, amidst a sound of crashing wood.

"Ha, ha!" roared Captain Massey.

Roused by the noise, Septimus, who was in the house, came out.

He ran to his father's assistance.

More irate than ever, Sir Dando Titmarsh rose to his feet.

He looked over the wall, trembling with passion.

"I'll let you know what kind of a neighbour you've got to deal with, sir," he said.

"I think I know pretty well already," was Captain Massey's quiet answer.

Septimus touched his father on the shoulder.

"Don't talk to him," he said, "such people are beneath our notice."

"True!" answered Sir Dando; "but I am not going to be imposed upon, or you either."

"Maintain your rights, but be calm."

"I can't. Captain Massey hasn't heard all yet. Didn't Jack call me Old D.T.'s, or Sir Delirium Tremens, because my initials are D. T., or Dando Titmarsh? Didn't he knock you about, and didn't he help himself to my grapes?"

"I saw him come out of the hot-house eating them," replied Septimus.

Sir Dando smiled triumphantly.

"There, sir, do you hear?" he exclaimed.

Captain Massey made no reply.

He only smiled, scornfully.

At that moment a handsome, well-built boy, with light curly hair, dressed in boating flannels, was seen coming up the garden.

Hanging on his arm was a pretty, dark-haired girl, who looked the picture of health and good temper.

They were Jack Massey and Ada Titmarsh.

Jack had taken her for a row on the river. They had been up as far as Boveney Lock together.

Landing at the garden stairs, Jack was seeing her to her house, intending to vault over the wall to his.

He did not suspect that her father and his were having an altercation.

But he had not advanced far before he saw that there was something wrong.

He squeezed Ada's arm.

"Don't be nervous," he said, "there is a row going on."

"What about?" she asked.

"I gave Sep a taste of my steam arm yesterday, and he has been making mischief."

"Isn't Sep dreadful? Although he is my brother, I cannot like him as I ought to."

"Don't my governor look wild?" continued Jack.

"And mine, too," said Ada, tossing her head.

"Sir D. T. gets easily excited. Come along, let us brave the storm."

"Certainly. Britons never will be slaves," replied Ada Titmarsh.

"Rule Britannia," cried Jack.

They walked on boldly, as if they thought nothing was going to happen.

"Father," said Septimus, "here's Ada with Jack Massey."

Sir Dando Titmarsh became purple.

The audacity of the proceeding was more than he could bear.

"Boy!" he exclaimed, "where have you been with my daughter?"

"I took her for a row on the river," replied Jack; "a jolly time we had, too—splendid! Take you for one if you like."

"Me! take me!"

"With pleasure; the boat is at the stairs. I'll row you like any young waterman."

"Not if I know it," said Sir Dando. "Why, I wouldn't trust myself in a boat with you."

"Why not?"

"You're a young jackanapes. Ada!"

"Yes, papa," she rejoined.

"How dare you go for a row with young Massey without asking my permission?"

"I did not think there was any harm in it."

"There is; I forbid it. You shall not speak to him at all. Go to your room, and stay there till I send for you."

"I'm sure I cannot!" exclaimed Ada.

"What, do you defy me?" screamed Sir Dando Titmarsh. "We have been talking about this fellow Jack."

"Easy over the stones!" cried Jack. "I'm not going to be called a fellow by anybody."

"You stole my grapes."

Jack's face flushed.

He walked angrily and excitedly up to the baronet.

"I did what?" he asked.

"You stole my grapes."

"You dare say that again."

"Ha! you threaten me. It is only what I expected. I'll go to law."

Ada held up her hand.

"Papa," she said, "it is disgraceful of you to make such accusations against a young gentleman—a neighbour too."

"Sep saw him eating the fruit."

"I gave it to him!" she exclaimed.

"You did?" replied Sir Dando, looking very much ashamed of himself.

"Yes," rejoined Ada, "you have often told me that what belongs to you, belongs to me."

"Well, yes, but——"

"Say no more. Sep has made mischief as usual," interrupted Ada. "I'm sure that Jack wouldn't take anything of yours without your permission."

"Oh! wouldn't he," remarked Septimus. "He's too poor to buy such things."

Jack turned a disdainful glance upon him.

"If I'm too poor, I'm honest," he said, "and only a cad would talk about his father's fortune."

"If you insult me, I will call the gardener to put you over the wall."

"What *are* you?"

"The son of a titled rich gentleman, and an Eton boy. What are you?" asked Septimus.

Captain Massey now interposed.

"Don't answer him," he said.

"With all due respect to you, father, I will," replied Jack, resolutely.

"It is not really worth while."

"If he is at Eton, he is a very bad specimen of an Eton boy, that's all I can say."

Septimus had beckoned to the gardener, who was sweeping a path a little way off.

He was a tall, vigorous, rough-looking Irishman.

"O'Grady!" exclaimed Septimus Titmarsh.

"Yu-, sorr," was the rejoinder, "shure, and I'm close forninst yez."

"I want you."

"What is it you pl'ase to want?"

"Throw this intruder over the wall, if he won't go of his own accord."

"Roight you are, sorr, over he goes," said O'Grady.

The gardener approached Jack in a confident manner.

"Look out, my boy," cried Captain Massey. "If you settle that rascal, I'll give you the Victoria Cross—that is, I would if I had the power to confer it upon you."

"Let him touch me if he dare," was Left-handed Jack's reply.

His lips parted with a half-smile, and he clenched his hands.

"Oh, begorra!" said the Irish gardener. "You may put up your fists, but it's me father's son that will knock the spots out of the loikes of you, ma bouchal."

"Touch me at your peril."

"That's aisy said, and aisy done. I'm a Tipperary man, and have had hard knocks at Donnybrook Fair."

"Touch me," repeated Jack.

"Aren't you over anxious to get a b'ating? Didn't yez hear the squire tell me to pitch yez into the middle of next week?"

"If you lay hands on me, you will commit an assault, breaking the law, and I shall know what to do with you."

"It's meself that will be afther breaking your head."

Saying this, O'Grady seized Jack by the shoulder.

With a jerk he instantly shook him off.

"I call you all to witness!" he shouted, "that this man has assaulted me by the order of Sir Dando Titmarsh."

"Give it him, O'Grady, or father shall discharge you!" cried Septimus.

Ada clung to her father's arm in affright.

She did not know what the issue of the contest would be.

To her simple mind, it appeared that the huge, hulking, Irish gardener would nearly kill her lover.

But she was mistaken.

Left-handed Jack swung his arm round three times.

Then he struck out.

He hit O'Grady between the eyes.

The Irishman staggered backwards about a dozen yards and fell.

Jack rushed after him.

"Throw me over the wall, will you?" he asked. "Get up and try again, my man."

O'Grady recovered himself sufficiently to rise.

"This bangs Bannager," he muttered; "but I'll have another go at yez, if you *have* got the ironclad fist."

"Where will you have it this time?" enquired Jack.

"I don't think you'll be able to hit me again. Be jabers, I'll stand like the Rock of Cashel."

"Your nose looks as if it wanted painting a little more."

"Arrah, be aisy, now; perhaps it's your own that will get the dose," rejoined the gardener; "an' if mine is painted, the whisky wasn't of your buyin', you spalpeen."

Again O'Grady endeavoured to grasp Jack, who stepped back and dealt him a terrific blow.

The left hand this time struck the man's nose, from which the blood spurted in a stream.

"Bravo!" cried Captain Massey, "you can hold your own bravely, my boy."

"Do you want any more?" asked Jack.

"Oh, bedad!" replied O'Grady, "it's the divil you are."

"Why did you not let me alone?"

"They don't call you Left-handed Jack for nothing. I'm a sick man, I am. I want to go home."

"Go, then," said Jack, "and let this be a lesson to you to let me alone in future."

The gardener slunk away—beaten.

He had had enough of it, and wanted to put his head under the pump.

"By the piper that played before Moses!" he muttered, "I'll die, shure, if I can't stop this nose bleeding."

He hastened his pace, and quickly disappeared.

So did Septimus Titmarsh.

He was afraid that his turn might come, as he was the cause of all the trouble.

Ada could not help laughing, and clapped her hands.

Jack sprang airily over the wall.

He stood on his own ground now, by the side of his father.

"When you have cause to complain of me again, be sure of your facts, Sir Dando Titmarsh!" he exclaimed.

"I am defied all round," replied the baronet, "both by you and by my daughter; but I will be revenged."

"So will I," cried Septimus in a shrill voice from an open window.

"Is it manly to talk to a mere boy in that way?" asked Captain Massey.

"I wish to hold no further conversation with you, sir," answered Sir Dando.

"The interview was none of my seeking."

Saying this, Captain Massey took Jack's arm and led him away to the house.

Mrs. Massey had gone out for a walk, and was in blissful ignorance of the scene which had been taking place.

"What a cantankerous, peppery little man the baronet is," remarked the captain; "but he has been in India, they say. A hot sun and too much curry do not improve the temper."

"To say nothing of brandy-and-water," observed Jack, laughing.

"You had better take care of yourself, or they may do you an injury."

"Why, yes. Septimus is mean enough for anything, but I will be on my guard."

"It's a pity you can't keep your left hand quiet, my boy."

"No use asking me to do that, it *will* strike out."

"Have you no control over it."

"Doesn't seem to me as if I had," replied Jack. "When anybody annoys me, away it goes into somebody."

"It will get you into trouble one of these fine days."

"Shouldn't wonder if it did," said Jack.

He became very thoughtful all at once.

Something was agitating his mind.

"Come, Jack, what is it?" exclaimed his father, who had been watching him. "You have an idea in that fertile brain of yours. What is it?"

"Send me to school, father," Jack replied.

"I would have done so long ago, but your mother wished you to be educated by a private tutor."

"I find I don't learn much that way."

"You know I cannot send you to Eton, as my income is too limited to afford it."

"I do not ask for it. I hope to go into the army and be a soldier like you when I am old enough, and I want to cram enough to pass my exam., or I shall never obtain a commission."

"That is true. When I entered the service I bought my commission. The abolition of purchase has altered all that."

"Besides," added Jack, "I should like to rough it with a lot of boys."

"That is only natural."

"Do you know what I thrashed Septimus Titmarsh for, yesterday?"

"How should I, when I wasn't there?" replied Captain Massey.

"He chaffed me about being tied to my mother's apron-strings," said Jack, "and I couldn't stand that, you know."

"It was rather hard."

"So the steam arm went to work, and he caught it nicely."

"Do you know of a school about here you would like to go to?" asked his father, after a pause.

"Yes," rejoined Jack; "there is one just out of Windsor, kept by Dr. Birchback; he takes fifty boys. There is a vacancy for one this next half."

"Who told you?"

"My chum, Dick Lambert. I shall see him presently."

"Where do you meet him?"

"At Signor Sarati's gymnasium, where I go to learn fencing. He teaches the Eton boys who want to learn Italian, and drawing, and singing. He visits Dr. Birchback's, too."

"If I am not mistaken, he instructs Miss Ada Titmarsh in singing twice a week. I have seen him going to the house."

"That is the man—tall, thin, dark as night."

"Then beware of him," exclaimed Captain Massey. "I think I have encounted that man before, though I cannot tell you all. He looks as if he had the evil eye, as they say in Italy."

"Does he owe you a grudge?"

"I am not sure. Some years ago I had a strange adventure in Naples. Sarati reminds me of a person I met there."

"Had that man reason to hate you?" asked Jack.

"He had cause to remember me until his dying day."

"Whew!"

Jack began to whistle.

"Take care of that man," continued Captain Massey. "I may be mistaken, but he has got treachery in his face."

"Your advice shall be followed. I will stay at home if you do not wish me to go to Sarati's, now."

"I do not forbid you to go; it was my intention to mention this before."

"It is my afternoon for gymnastics and fencing," replied Jack.

"Very well; come back to dinner. During your absence, I will arrange with your mother about your going to school; it will be the best thing you can do, though I should be sorry to lose your society."

"You think too much of me," said Jack, who was affected at this evidence of affection on the part of his father.

"Not at all. You are my only son. As a man grows old, he lives again in his children," replied the captain.

Jack put on his cap and left the house, taking the road to Windsor.

At one o'clock he was due at the gymnasium, to take his usual lesson in fencing from Signor Sarati.

The sky became clouded, as if an April shower was coming on.

It was a quiet, lonely road.

He had not gone far before he saw Septimus Titmarsh, engaged in con-versation with a rough-looking though powerful man.

From his appearance, he was one of the riverside men, accustomed to work on barges, and commonly known as bargees.

As Jack drew a little nearer, he saw the fellow's side-face.

Instantly he recognised him as Boler, one of the most desperate characters on the river, or in Windsor.

When not employed on a barge, he hung about the riverside taverns, picking up any odd job that came in his way.

He had been in prison several times for robbery, assaults, and poaching.

On one occasion, he had severely ill-treated and robbed an Eton boy who had rowed up to Surly.

The water bailiffs had caught him netting the river.

In fact, he was a very bad, reckless character.

Boler, the bargee, and Septimus were so earnestly engaged in talking, that they did not notice Jack.

The latter slackened his pace.

He wanted to hear all he could.

"There is a sovereign for you," said Septimus. "If you meet him on shore, give him a good hiding; if on the water, drown him."

"All right, sir. What's his name?" asked Boler.

"Jack Massey."

"D'ye mean Left-handed Jack, the army captain's son?"

"That's the fellow," answered Septimus.

"Timothy Titus!" cried the burly bargee, "he's a hard nut to crack. You can't drown him, for he's a regular water-rat, and he's bad to beat on land, but I ain't afraid of him. What's he done to you?"

"I'm his enemy."

"Bad blood between you, eh? Well, I'll put a polish on him."

Jack had heard enough.

Septimus was hiring Boler, the bargee, to do him an injury.

He stepped boldly forward.

CHAPTER II.

BOLER, THE BARGEE—A MEETING WITH DICK LAMBERT—THE GYMNASIUM
—SIGNOR SARATI—SEPTIMUS AT WORK AGAIN.

AT the sound of footsteps, the conspirators turned sharply around.

"By Jove! there he is," said Septimus Titmarsh, under his breath.

"I know him," muttered Boler. "We have met before."

Jack bowed, in an airy, jaunty manner.

"Good-afternoon, Sep," he exclaimed. "I am really very much obliged to you for the kind interest you take in my welfare."

Septimus looked greatly confused.

The bargee, on the contrary, drew himself up, and seemed inclined to bluster and bully.

"What do you mean?" asked Septimus.

"The wind was blowing in my direction, so I could not help hearing your amiable remarks," responded Jack.

"Listening, eh?"

"Call it so, if you like. Couldn't you get a better man than Boler to tackle me?"

"I was only joking. The fact is, I saw you coming, and——"

"That won't do," Jack interrupted. "If you *must* tell a crammer, invent a better one. You do not give sovereigns to a man by way of fun."

"You can go," said Septimus, addressing the bargee.

Boler touched his cap respectfully.

"Good-day, sir," he replied, "thankee for me."

He was about to walk off, but that was not what Jack wanted.

It was clear to his comprehension that he was to be attacked some time or the other.

It would be preferable to have it sooner than later.

"Stop, you overgrown lout," he cried. "If you want to fight me, now is your time. Step on the roadside, where the grass is soft."

"I'd rather not," replied Boler.

"No. You would rather surprise and take me at a disadvantage, but you sha'n't back out, I'm determined on that. If you won't defend yourself, I'll give you the biggest thrashing you ever had in your life."

As he spoke he stepped on one side.

Taking off his coat and vest, he hung them on the edge.

The bargee followed his example, facing him with a broad grin.

"I'm your man, young master," he remarked.

"You grinning chawbacon, I'll make you laugh on the other side of your face."

"Will 'ee? We've got to see about that."

The disparity between them in size and weight was greatly marked.

Left-handed Jack, however, had frequently put on the gloves at the gymnasium, and was not deficient in science.

Of the art of guarding, feinting, giving upper and lower cuts, Boler was totally ignorant.

He had to rely for victory on his brute strength alone.

Septimus looked on with a confident air, feeling sure that his champion would make short work of Jack.

The fallacy of this belief soon became apparent.

Jack let the bargee aim a blow at him.

Stepping back nimbly, he cleverly avoided it, and before Boler could recover himself, he hit out.

The terrible left hand struck the bargee under the jaw with such force that it was nearly dislocated.

His teeth rattled like castanets.

A sharp sensation of fierce pain shot up into his brain.

Quick as lightning, Jack struck him again, giving him a blow in the face, which tore his cheek open.

The blood streamed from the wound.

With a hoarse cry the bewildered ruffian returned the blows, only to have them parried or evaded.

A smashing hit settled the business for that time.

Boler stifled a curse, snatched up his clothes, and ran away as fast as his legs would carry him.

Greatly chagrined, Septimus would have done the same.

"Not so fast!" exclaimed Jack.

He grasped him by the collar of his jacket, and shook him.

"Please don't hurt me," he whined.

"You were very big just now, when you were backed up by a bully," replied Left-handed Jack.

"Let me alone, and I'll never do it again."

"You let *me* alone, or I'll teach you to. Your kind of revenge is cowardly."

"Don't hit me!" cried Septimus, in deadly terror.

There was a muddy ditch full of dirty water close by.

Jack gave him a push, which sent him rolling into it with a loud splash.

"Oh, dear! Oh, dear!" said Septimus, struggling out. "You've spoilt my best clothes, and I shall catch my death of cold."

"Serve you right, you sneak."

Septimus retreated, and did not venture to speak again until he was at a safe distance.

The muddy water dripped off him; his tall silk hat was in the ditch.

Altogether he presented a pitiable spectacle—wet and bedraggled.

"Massey!" he exclaimed, "I can tell you one thing."

"What's that?" asked Jack.

"Something you will not like to hear," continued Septimus Titmarsh, tantalisingly.

"Never mind. Out with it."

"You will not speak to my sister Ada again in a hurry."

"Oh!" said Jack, with an air of apparent unconcern, "why not?"

"You won't."

"What's to stop me?"

"Father has marched her off to a boarding school."

This was disagreeable news to Jack, as he was very fond of Ada.

It took him by surprise.

"Where has she gone?" he asked.

"Wouldn't you like to know? Ha! ha! I shan't tell you. Ho! ho! Good-bye. That is only a little bit of what we will do to annoy you."

Jack bit his lip, and Septimus ran off, highly delighted at the look of vexation on his enemy's face.

Putting on his clothes, Jack continued his journey.

A sudden change had come over his life, for he had hoped to see Ada on half-holidays, though he was going to school.

No more pleasant country walks would they enjoy, no more rows on the river, love-making in dead water among the lilies and the swans.

While he was wandering along, on melancholy thoughts intent, he heard his name called.

Raising his head, he saw his only chum, Dick Lambert, the son of a solicitor in the town.

Dick was enjoying a ten days' Easter holiday at home, his schoolmasters being as glad to get rid of him, as he was pleased to be away from them, for Dick Lambert was a troublesome boy.

He had a fatal facility for getting into mischief, though his intentions were always good.

It was not his desire to be mischievous, far from it, yet he was generally in some scrape or other.

"I am glad to see you," exclaimed Jack. "Whither away?"

"I was just going to look you up," replied Dick, "finding you were not at the gymnasium as appointed."

"You will be surprised to hear I am coming to your school."

"Never! That will be jolly. Manor Park School will be highly honoured at your presence."

"Don't chaff."

"Dr. Birchback will have a little more wrist exercise. What have you done to excite the paternal wrath?"

"Nothing," answered Jack. "It is my own wish, I assure you. I feel it will make a man of me."

"Glad to hear it," said Dick. "Your steam arm will make a commotion. We never had a left-handed fellow yet. It will be a decided novelty."

"I shall be all right if I am not interfered with."

"And if you are——"

"I mean to be a terror," replied Jack.

"You will have some bother with Slavin," remarked Dick, musingly.

"Who is he?"

"A big bully—cock of the school."

"Something like Septimus Titmarsh, perhaps?"

"Oh! he's a head and shoulders taller than that little Eton cad," answered Dick.

"I have quarrelled with him again."

"Not at all surprised at that. How could you help it? He is simply intolerable."

"He set Boler, the bargee, on to me just now, but I soon drove the ruffian off."

"That was a dastardly trick. How is the divine Ada?"

"Alas!" replied Jack, sentimentally, "her stern parent has sent the angel to a boarding-school."

"Things are not running smoothly for you, gentle youth," said Dick Lambert, in a mock compassionate tone.

"Quite the reverse. Will you jog along back to Sarati's? I am going to fence."

"With pleasure. I will do the horizontal bars, climb the long pole, and otherwise exercise my biceps," was the willing reply.

They walked arm-in-arm towards the gymnasium, little thinking what was going to happen.

Signor Sarati had a number of pupils, and attended several schools, being generally looked upon as well off.

He was very polite in his manner, speaking in an oily voice, but his black, piercing eyes, flashed occasionally.

This showed the dormant, hidden fire within.

The man evidently had a history which was buried in the past.

He always stated that he became an exile in this country for political reasons.

There were those, however, who had seen him start in his sleep, and heard him cry, as he held up his hands—"Blood! blood!"

Sarati was in his spacious hall; several boys were swinging on the bars. He received Massey and Lambert, smiling in his usual suave manner.

"You are welcome!" he exclaimed. "I am always glad to see a promising pupil come punctually."

"I am afraid you flatter me," replied Jack.

"Not in the slightest degree. You have only been with me a few weeks, but I can safely say you have made more progress than many boys would do in the same number of months."

He spoke English fluently, and with an excellent accent.

As Jack stripped to his shirt sleeves, a recently-taken photograph of his father fell from his pocket to the floor.

He was going to buy a frame for it.

With his accustomed and invariable politeness, Signor Sarati stooped to pick it up.

"Don't trouble," said Jack.

"On the contrary—a pleasure," was the reply.

"It is a photo of my dad."

"Ah! permit me to look, I have not the honour of the gentleman's acquaintance!" Sarati exclaimed.

"Certainly."

Jack regarded the Italian curiously.

He recollected what his father had told him previously to his leaving home a little while before.

Would Sarati recognise Captain Massey's photograph, and was there anything in the latter's suspicion?

Suddenly Sarati's face became darker, and his brow lowered.

The corners of his mouth twitched convulsively.

Although a man accustomed to exercise self-control, it was with difficulty that he mastered his emotion.

But his features cleared, and the smile came back to his thin, well-chiselled lips.

The exquisitely white teeth gleamed.

"It is a striking face," he remarked, "and one not easily forgotten when once seen."

"Do I understand that you have seen my father before?" asked Jack.

"Oh, no. I did not insinuate anything of the sort. It is the face of the handsome, well-born, travelled Englishman. I think he is an officer in the army—captain, is he not?"

"Yes—Thirty-seventh foot, retired on half-pay."

Sarati handed him back the *carte* as calmly as if he had not been momentarily betrayed into excitement.

Enough had occurred, though, to satisfy Jack that his father's suspicion was correct.

Captain Massey and the Italian had met before.

To Jack, the cause of their mutual antipathy must remain a secret.

"Take your foil," said Sarati, "and put yourself on guard. Ah! you would puzzle a Jew with that left hand of yours; it takes me all my skill to parry your lunges."

The fencing lesson began.

Frequently Jack caught the professor bestowing upon him looks of deadly hatred.

Never before had he so regarded him, or had his eyes such a peculiar, terrifying expression in their liquid depths.

When the lesson was over, Jack said:

"This will be my last visit, signor, to the gymnasium."

" How so, have I displeased you ? " asked Sarati.

" Oh ! no, but I am going to Manor Park School, to be one of Doctor Birchback's scholars."

" Then we shall meet again ; I teach the young gentlemen there."

" Send in your account, please, to my father, and he will send you a cheque."

" Excuse me ! " exclaimed Sarati, with the demeanour of a man who has made a sudden resolution.

" What is it, signor ? "

" I am so pleased with you, that I will accept no pay. Permit me to make you a present of the few lessons I have given. You have afforded me so much sincere gratification."

" As you will," replied Jack.

Sarati bowed, and retired to his private room.

" The humbug," thought Jack ; " he hates father so, that he will not take his money. I can see through him."

Dick Lambert swung himself off a bar, where he had been suspended like a monkey by one arm.

" I say," he cried, " what spiteful looks the Italian gave you."

" Did he ? " Jack rejoined.

" Every time he pinked you, he seemed to wish he was handling a real sword, so as to strike to the heart.

" Idle fancy, my dear fellow."

" I watched him, and I did not half like it," continued Dick.

" Merely zeal in his profession," added Jack, taking up a large dumb-bell in his left hand.

It was marked a hundred and twelve pounds, or just one hundred-weight ; by its side was another, which was two hundred pounds weight.

The first he lifted with ease to a level with his ear, then he passed it over his head, and let it slowly down.

Dick tried to emulate this feat, but could not get it higher than his knee.

" You are a wonder," said he ; " few professional athletes could beat you. Can you raise the other ? "

Jack smiled as he placed two fingers under it and brought it up to his chin.

This was really a very remarkable performance.

" Mind my toes," cried Dick, jumping quickly away.

" No fear," replied Jack, who moved it about, doing as he liked with it.

Several more pupils came in, and the two assistants, employed by the professor, were soon busy.

The signor himself did not appear, remaining in his private apartment.

" You will be a great acquisition to our school," observed Dick ; " we want a fellow who can fight—that is, fight in a just cause, and to protect the weak against the strong bully ; and I'll tell you more."

" What ? " enquirsd Jack.

" Our fellows are always getting licked by the Etonians," replied Dick Lambert. " They meet us out, or on the river, and call us private school cads. Most of our boys run away when they see a couple of Etonians together."

" I would not ; it should be the other way."

" You and I will go side by side to victory," continued Dick. " Manor Park School is getting a bad name for cowards."

" I will help to redeem it."

Just then Jack happened to glance in the direction of Signor Sarati's room.

To his profound astonishment, he saw Septimus Titmarsh walk rapidly towards it, knock at the door and enter.

The door he left slightly open.

" There's that cad Sep," he said, " he is in the professor's room. Whether it is ungentlemanly or not, I'm going to hear what he has to talk of, for I feel sure that it is about me, and with spite in his heart."

" Sep and Sarati were always great friends. Sep takes him out in his boat ; they go up to Monkey Island and dine together," answered Dick.

" Ada can't bear him," added Jack ; " he had the cheek to tell her he loved her once, when teaching singing. She threatened to inform her father if he did it again, and he has kept quiet since."

" What a piece of impertinence."

" Hold on here for a few minutes," Jack said, as he glided away.

Dick waited while his friend took up a position close to the door of the private room.

If Jack had been dealing with any-one else, he would not have done such a thing, but he could see that it was open war between Septimus and him-self, even for his very life.

In love and war all things are fair.

" I have come to tell you," he heard Sep say, " that Ada has been taken to a boarding-school. She was going a little too far with Jack Massey."

"Ha!" exclaimed Sarati, "the captain's son?"

"Yes; how I hate him!"

"It may sound strange to you, but I have my reasons for disliking him."

"You! bravo! we can work together," said Septimus. "I want you to marry my sister."

"It was so arranged between us the last time I lent you money."

This fact was a revelation to Jack.

He had known all along that Sarati loved Ada Titmarsh, and that he had the audacity to hope to make her his wife, but he was not aware that Sep had borrowed money from him.

Yet this was not surprising, for he had heard that Sir Dando was very close-fisted, and even niggardly in money matters.

His son Septimus was exactly the reverse.

He treated his Eton friends to champagne and expensive dinners in Windsor, at the principal hotel; he made bets on horse and boat races; he played cards for money, and though his gambling was for small amounts he generally contrived to lose.

Therefore it was not surprising that he was often glad to come to Signor Sarati for a ten-pound note.

"By Jove!" remarked Septimus, "I want you to be my banker to-day for a fiver. I will give you an acknowledgment."

He scribbled an I O U on a sheet of notepaper, which the professor accepted, giving him in return a five-pound note.

"Where has your sweet sister gone?" he asked.

"Keep it a secret from Left-handed Jack," replied Septimus, "or they will find means to communicate. While I have been at school they have been always together. My idea is, if we separate them she will forget the cur."

"He is going to school, too."

"Who told you?"

"Himself, not an hour ago. He is to be a pupil of Dr. Birchback's Manor Park School."

Sep threw himself back in his chair.

He indulged in an immoderate fit of laughter.

"Ha! ha! a private school," he cried. "Won't I chaff the life out of him, if I ever meet him. Our fellows think nothing low of a private tutor, but a private school—bah!"

"Where is Miss Titmarsh?" enquired Sarati.

"At Sappho House, Miss Mac-Foozle's academy for young ladies."

"It is not far from Dr. Birchback's establishment for young gentlemen, only a little way across the road."

"That makes no difference. Miss MacFoozle is widely known as a dragon of virtue, and chief of strict disciplinarians, and all her governesses are as strict as she."

"So I have heard," replied Sarati. "I must apply to teach Italian and singing there."

"Ada shall come home from Saturday to Sunday, and I will invite you to dinner," said Septimus.

"I thank you very much."

"It shall be made all right for you, but you must lend me more money shortly."

Jack gnashed his teeth.

"If Ada goes home, so will I," he muttered; "and I could tell them another thing—a dozen MacFoozles won't keep me from seeing her."

Septimus spoke again.

"I say," he exclaimed, "if you can do Massey an injury, or get him into a row, don't omit."

"That is well understood. I shall do it for my sake, too," replied Sarati.

"Why for yours?"

"I cannot tell you. That must remain my secret."

Jack had heard enough to make his ears tingle.

He moved away.

Silently he rejoined Dick Lambert, looking grave and somewhat annoyed.

This change in his demeanour his chum did not fail to notice, but though he questioned him, he could not get Jack to relate what had passed between the professor and Septimus Titmarsh.

"Don't press me," was all Jack replied to his interrogatories. "It is a private matter which would not interest you."

When they left the gymnasium they parted, going to their respective homes; Jack being puzzled whether he should inform his father of what he had heard or not.

After some consideration, he determined to do so.

Captain Massey was occupying the half-hour before dinner in walking in the garden.

He started when he saw Jack looking extremely solemn.

"What has happened?" the captain demanded.

"I have something to tell you," replied Jack.

"Has Sarati spoken to you, or you to him about me?"

"Neither. You shall hear."

Plainly Jack related the episode of the photograph, the altered appearance of the Italian, and the subsequent conversation between him and Septimus Titmarsh.

The captain was deeply agitated.

"It is the same man," he exclaimed; "I can no longer doubt the fact."

"What shall I do?" asked Jack.

"Say nothing; be on the watch. I am afraid there is danger and trouble ahead of us."

"Do you fear Sarati?"

"That is not his name, he is an Italian nobleman. Yes; he works with revenge in secret. I am in fear of him."

"Why?"

"I wronged him; it is many years ago, before you were born. I did him a great wrong, and he is not the man either to forgive or forget."

"Will you not tell me the story, father?"

"No, I will not; it is best that you should be ignorant of it," replied Captain Massey.

"Let us move away from here."

"It would be of no use. He knows me now, and would follow me. I feel sure of it, and I have another dread."

"What is that?"

"He may strike at me through you, my poor boy."

Jack laughed proudly.

"I am strong, father, and, thank goodness, can take care of myself," he said. "Depend upon it, I shall not eat my dinner with any worse appetite for what has occurred to-day."

Captain Massey shook his head, sadly. He had not the mercurial spirits of his son, and he reflected that the sins of the fathers are visited upon the children.

As for Jack, he thought of nothing but going to school.

His mother had, with some reluctance, given her consent, and the business of getting his box ready had commenced.

This task always exercises the mind and ingenuity of a mother, who wants her boy to look nice, and be provided with every requisite.

There was also the provision hamper to be packed, the ham to be boiled, the chickens roasted, and the cake to be made.

Septimus wisely kept out of Jack's way while the holidays lasted, though he grinned at him occasionally over the garden wall.

A clod of earth speedily made him duck his head.

Jack missed Ada very much, and wrote her a letter at Sappho House.

This was duly returned to him in an envelope, addressed by Miss Mac-Foozle's own hand.

The young ladies were not permitted to send or receive any letter that were not read by Miss MacFoozle.

"Bother the old cat," said Jack, as he tore up two sheets of satin note-paper, filled with his best English; "but I'll be even with her yet."

How he succeeded we shall see after his arrival at Dr. Birchback's establishment.

This important event will be duly chronicled in the next chapter.

CHAPTER III.

JACK'S ARRIVAL AT MANOR PARK SCHOOL.

AT mid-day a knot of a dozen boys of various ages and sizes were standing in the play-yard of Manor Park School.

It was an old red-brick building of large dimensions, facing the main road near the Windsor Home Park.

In the rear was the school room, the play-yard, and, beyond that, the field where football and cricket were played.

A giant-stride, some parallel bars, and a fives-court adorned the yard in which the boys were standing.

They had just come back after the holidays.

"There is a new fellow coming this

half !" exclaimed a tall, wiry boy with black hair.

This was Slavin, the leader of the school in athletics, though not the head in learning; the latter position being held by Gordon, who was as kind and gentle as the other was noisy and cruel.

"What a bore !" exclaimed a third-form boy named Targett, who was looked upon as more of a fool than anything else. "I hate new fellows. Who told you of it ? "

"Spoofer," replied Slavin; "he ought to know, as he is our general servant, and is ordered to lay so many knives and forks for dinner."

"Now, I like new fellows," observed Dawson, who, being also a bully, was naturally Slavin's great friend and ally.

"What for ? " asked Targett.

"Oh ! you can get such a thundering lot of fun out of them," answered Dawson.

"You won't out of this one," said Dick Lambert, who had been listening, much amused, to these remarks.

They were talking, of course, about Jack Massey.

Slavin turned his beetle brows on Dick directly.

"What do you know about him ? " he inquired.

"He is a particular friend of mine, about my own age, is the only son of his father and mother, has been educated by a private tutor, and, taken properly, is an all round, jolly, good fellow."

"What does he pay you to blow his trumpet ? "

"Nothing at all."

"You are singing his praises."

"Because he thoroughly deserves it. No one shall say anything against Jack Massey in my presence without my taking it up," replied Dick.

"Well said—that is plucky," cried Gordon.

"Shut up," exclaimed Slavin, "let Lambert finish his spouting. Why shan't we have any fun with this chap, Massey ? "

"Because he can take his own part."

"Does he fancy he can fight ? "

"I shall not say any more. You will find out in time," answered Lambert, with a quiet smile.

"Great Grundy !" said Slavin, "this man is coming to teach us how to behave, I suppose."

"Perhaps he's been told that our manners are bad," laughed Dawson.

There was a general merriment amongst the other boys who had as yet taken no part in the conversation.

"Look out, boys," cried Lambert.

"Who for—the great unknown ?"

"Massey himself—here he comes."

Dick pointed to the entrance of the house to the play-yard.

Left-handed Jack appeared, looking about him curiously, but not nervously.

In his right hand he carried an old hat-box.

Every eye was turned upon him.

Especially was he the object of Slavin's attention.

Dick Lambert stepped forward to greet Jack, which he did in a hearty manner.

Their hands met in a cordial grasp.

"Welcome to the old school," said Dick.

"Thank you," replied Jack. "I hope to be happy, and make everybody else so."

"Shall I do the honours ? "

"By all means. Introduce me to your friends."

Dick did so, mentioning the names of Slavin, Gordon, Dawson, and Targett.

They all shook hands with him except Slavin.

The tall bully held himself aloof.

"Don't you like the look of me ? " enquired Jack.

"No, I don't," answered Slavin, rudely.

"Please yourself; the feeling is mutual."

"Take off your hat to me, and pay your footing."

Jack stared at him.

"I'll pay for what is usual for a new fellow to buy, but I refuse to take off my hat to anybody except a master."

"We will see about that presently."

"When you please !" exclaimed Jack. "Depend upon it, I shall be at your service, Mr. Slavedriver."

"My name is Slavin."

"Oh ! pardon me, I heard indistinctly, but if you are not a slave-driver, you act like one."

"I'll make you my slave."

"Will you? You are very kind and very nice to look at."

"Stump up, and don't favour us with so much of your talk," said Slavin.

"Very well; didn't I say I was willing ? How much do you want from me ? "

"Five shillings. That will buy ginger-beer and cakes enough for us. The other fellows have not come yet."

Jack put his hand in his pocket.

He had some gold and silver.

"Your father isn't stingy," remarked Slavin.

"Perhaps yours is," replied Jack.

"Perhaps you will hold your tongue, and not give me any more of your cheek. What is my father to you?"

"As much as mine is to you," rejoined Jack. "Here is the five shillings, get what you like with it, and make your miserable life happy."

Slavin took the money.

He immediately handed it to Targett.

"Run and get a dozen bottles of ginger pop," he said, "and spend the rest in Bath buns, sausage rolls, and jam tarts."

"All right," replied Targett.

"If you aren't quick, I pity you."

He gave him a kick.

"Oh! ouch!" holloaed Targett.

"What did you do that for?" asked Jack.

"Isn't he a Targett, and isn't a target a thing to hit?"

There was a laugh at this joke.

"Bravo! you'll do," cried Dawson.

"Go up one, Slavedriver," said Jack.

"If you call me that again I'll give you a oner on the nose," cried Slavin.

"Say nasal organ, or proboscis, it sounds better."

Dawson began to sneer.

"Oh! you are one of the genteel division, I suppose," he remarked.

"He must belong to the upper circles of society," put in Slavin.

"Lives on a Bath bun," continued Dawson.

"Quite so, and sucks an acidulated drop when he's thirsty."

Even Gordon and Lambert had to smile at these sallies.

Left-handed Jack, however, was not in the least disconcerted.

"Keep it up lively, dear boys," he said; "it pleases you, and it doesn't hurt me. I shouldn't have thought Slavedriver had so much fun in him."

Slavin's face darkened again.

"You won't be advised," he cried, angrily.

"Not by you," said Jack.

"I shall have to thrash some of the impudence out of you."

"Of course you will; do try it. You are welcome to."

The quarrel which had been brewing

between them seemed destined to break out then and there.

It was postponed, however, by the advent of Targett.

This young gentleman had been speedy in executing his mission.

The sight of the ginger-beer and the tarts mollified the irascible Slavin.

Half-a-dozen other boys had by this time arrived, and as they claimed their share, the good things quickly disappeared.

When they had vanished, and the last bottle of "pop" was emptied, Slavin again turned his attention to the newcomer.

"Do you know what a cockshy is, Massey?" he asked.

"Rather. Ask me a harder one than that," was the reply.

"Take those ginger-beer bottles and stand them up on top of one another. Then get me a dozen round stones."

Jack stared at him superciliously.

"Only a dozen stones! Go on, anything more?" he enquired.

"That is all at present."

"Well, that's kind of you; but who made me your fag?"

"Never mind that," said Slavin, "are you going to obey my orders or not?"

"Your orders! Ha, ha! Slavedriver. Most decidedly not," was the firm answer.

The two stood and glared at one another.

It only required a spark to explode the magazine.

Dick Lambert did not really care whether there was a fight or not.

He rather liked to see the best man win.

Gordon, on the other hand, detested fighting, and did all he could to put a stop to it.

He was not altogether successful, but he checked the practice.

"Can't you two fellows leave off snarling at each other?" he remarked.

"Slavedriver snacks at me," replied Jack.

"I can't stand cheek from new fellows, and what's more, I won't," answered Slavin.

"Massey is fresh to the school," continued Gordon; "he does not understand our ways yet."

"I can't admit that as an excuse."

"You ought to show a stranger a little more hospitality."

"I don't keep it in stock," replied

"'IN YOU GO,' CRIED JACK."—(See page 39.)

Slavin; "I'm sorry to say I'm quite out of it."

"Civility and politeness, too, I should think," remarked Jack.

Slavin was about to reply when Gordon pointed to the hat-box which Jack still held in his hand.

"What have you there, Massey?" he queried.

"My property," replied Jack.

"Can't you tell us what it is?" exclaimed Slavin.

"I don't see what it has to do with anybody."

"We want to know," Slavin persisted.

"You are an inquisitive lot."

"Won't you inform us?"

"Inform you? No," said Jack.

"I'll bet it's a hat—a Sunday-going beaver. If so, we'll have a game at football with it. What do you say, boys?" cried Slavin.

There was a general chorus of approbation.

The proposition met with approval from all except Dick Lambert and Gordon.

"It is a shame to bait Massey like this," cried Dick.

"You shut up," cried Slavin.

"What have you to do with it?" chimed in Dawson.

"He is my friend."

"Let him go back to his mammy's apron-strings, poor dear," said Slavin.

Jack was growing very red in the face.

It was clear to Dick that he did not intend to stand much more bullying.

"If you want a hat for a game at football," he observed, "I'll provide you with one in a moment."

"Where from?"

"Wait till I get my steam arm ready."

"What's that?"

"You'll see if you live long enough."

Jack swung his arm about in his usual manner.

Everybody wondered what he was going to do.

They had not long to wait.

Suddenly he took a stride towards Slavin, and dexterously knocked his hat off without hurting him.

"There you are; kick away, boys," he said.

Slavin uttered a cry of rage.

He rushed at the hat-box, and with one kick knocked it over.

To his surprise a large bird flew out.

It was a brown owl of unusual size, which was a great pet of Jack's.

After circling in the air, it alighted on Slavin's head.

It stuck his claws in his thick, curly hair.

Then it bent over, and made its beak meet in his ear.

Slavin uttered a loud cry of pain.

All his efforts to dislodge it were entirely fruitless.

The blood dripped down his neck in a stream.

"Take it off!" he yelled.

"It is your fault," replied Jack.

"I am afraid it will attack my eyes."

"What did you let it out for?"

"For heaven's sake, take the beastly thing away, or I'll kill it!"

"If you do, you will be sorry for it," Jack said.

Frantic with pain and fear, Slavin put his hands over his head.

Then came a tussle between him and the owl.

He succeeded at length in grasping the bird tightly.

In pulling it off, he tore out by the roots a quantity of his hair.

This added fuel to the flames of his wrath.

With all his force he dashed the owl to the ground, where, after fluttering for a moment, it lay motionless.

The force with which it had fallen had broken its neck.

Jack Massey's pet was dead.

Jack took one sorrowful look at the poor bird, and then advancing to Slavin, said:

"That settles it; you will have to fight me, you spiteful coward and bully."

"He has been asking for it all along," remarked Dick.

"No he has not, he has done right," replied Dawson, "and Massey shall have a hiding."

"I'll mill the pair of you at once." Jack continued. "Stand up together, or I'll knock the one down that hesitates."

They did so.

The boys formed a ring amid great excitement.

No one had for a long time disputed Slavin's supremacy.

After him came Dawson.

All thought that Jack would be easily conquered.

These two had won all the battles they had fought.

"I'll give you one chance," said Slavin.

"In what way ?" asked Jack.

"Beg my pardon, and I will let you off a hiding this time, but don't venture to exasperate me again."

"Not I. What do you take me for—a coward ?"

"Dawson and I are the two cocks of the school."

"Look out, then," exclaimed Jack, "I am going to lower your colours. I'm ready."

Jack smiled confidently.

The next moment he rushed at them, parrying their blows with his right, and striking each in turn with his left hand.

The result was as immediate as it was unexpected.

Down they both went on their backs, like two poplars in a storm.

For fully a minute neither of them could move. They were completely stunned.

The boys looked on with wonder.

Slavin, being the harder of the two, was the first to recover himself.

With a tender care, which was his special characteristic, the captain of the school raised him.

"How do you feel ?" asked Gordon.

"Somewhat confused," was the reply; "he came at me like a battering ram or a cyclone."

"It was very neatly done."

"Ah ! but how did he do it ?" enquired Slavin.

"With his left hand. You didn't know he was left-handed."

"He is a terror. Where is Dawson ?"

"By your side, as you see," answered Gordon.

Slavin looked curiously at his friend, who was still lying on his back insensible.

He was bleeding from his nose and mouth.

"I don't think he will come to time," continued Gordon. "Are you going to stand up again ?"

"No, I am hanged if I do. I may as well own that I am licked first as last. Another blow like that would knock me out for a month," replied Slavin.

Jack advanced in a kindly manner.

He was not a boy to bear malice.

"You know me better now. Will you shake hands ?" he asked.

"Thank you ; I decline. I shall always hate you, and I will never be friendly with you," rejoined Slavin, sulkily.

"The row was entirely of your own making."

"That does not matter ; and I can wait for my turn."

Jack could see that he would always hate him for lowering his pride.

He had made enemies of him and Dawson before he had been an hour at his new school.

But that did not make much difference to Jack.

Fortunately, he was able to take his own part.

Presently Dawson recovered consciousness, and was as much bewildered as Slavin had been.

He looked at Jack with a bitter, spiteful expression.

Jack advanced with a smiling face, and enquired if he should repeat the dose.

Dawson was undesirous of continuing the contest, and simply answered :

"No."

One sledgehammer blow like the one he had received was quite enough for him.

The boys were really delighted to think that the bullies had met their match at last.

They had too long lorded it over and oppressed their schoolfellows.

"Three cheers for Massey !" cried Targett.

"Hurrah for Left-handed Jack !" exclaimed Dick.

The tide of popular opinion ran in his favour.

"Hurrah ! hurrah ! hurrah !"

Three cheers were given with a will and a force of lung power that brought Spoofer, the man-servant, out.

"Blest if there ain't been a fight," he muttered, "and the new one's got the best of it."

Spoofer was in the right.

From that time forth Jack's position was assured at Manor Park School.

Slavin and Dawson had found their level, and were not destined to rise above it as long as Left-handed Jack remained there.

Jack picked up the dead owl, and walked away with Dick Lambert to bury it in the field.

Soon afterwards Slavin and Dawson slunk off together, as they did not want to listen to the uncomplimentary remarks that were being made respecting them.

Everyone was loudly singing Jack's praises.

He was the hero of the hour.

Fresh arrivals were taking place every five minutes, and all the boys would soon be back.

Nothing was talked of except the way in which Jack Massey had dethroned the bullies from their pedestals.

The two walked into the schoolroom and sat down, looking very disconsolate.

"We have gone down considerably," remarked Dawson.

"Curse that fellow, Massey," replied Slavin, grating his teeth, "I wish I had let him alone."

"He is as strong as a giant. Who would have thought it? Not I. Why, I thought a cannon-ball had come at me out of an Armstrong eighty-pounder."

"It is that terrible left hand of his," said Slavin; "but we must be revenged. I shall have no peace until we have driven him out of the school."

"How is it to be done?" asked Dawson.

"That is the problem we have to solve."

"I wish it was as easy as a simple equation, or the first problem in the first book of Euclid."

"Never mind. Revenge is our motto," said Slavin, savagely.

So absorbed were the two boys in their conversation, that they had not noticed a gentleman enter the schoolroom.

It was Signor Sarati.

The Italian had come to pin a paper on the green cloth of the notice-board, which hung on the wall near the master's desk.

It was to this effect:

"Notice. — Fencing and Boxing. Summer Term. Three o'clock each Tuesday. Drill, four o'clock, Thursday. Sarati, Professor."

While pinning this *affiche* on the notice-board, he had heard Slavin talk about revenge.

Turning round, he exclaimed:

"What has disturbed your mind?"

"Good-day, signor," replied Slavin. "it is only a personal matter."

"Of course it is so," said the Italian, "we do not take up revenge for other people."

"Not usually," answered Dawson.

"We are not Crusaders, and they fought the Saracens on a religious question. Hate is a human passion, like love. Of hate, born, we will suppose, of a sense of injury or wounded pride, comes the offspring—revenge."

"That is true."

"It is as natural to hate as to love. Now, who is it you want to be revenged upon?"

"A new fellow," answered Slavin.

"He has left his mark on your face. His name?"

"Massey."

The eyes of the Italian, usually so soft, flashed.

He clenched his hands, and the corners of his mouth twitched nervously.

His agitation, however, was only momentary.

As a rule, he could control himself at will.

"This boy! What has he done to you?" he enquired.

"Knocked us both down. In common parlance, floored us. Made us ridiculous before nearly the whole school," replied Slavin.

"Ah! I perceive. Is he not left-handed? I have a pupil of the name of Massey who is."

"That is the identical individual."

"And you wish for revenge?"

"I would die for it," cried Slavin.

"You shall not die, you shall live," said Sarati, with an oily smile. "Listen to me, now."

"Yes, signor."

"We will admit that he hits hard, wonderfully hard, but his success consists principally in the quickness of his attack. I assure you his attack, whether with the fist or the foil, is simply magnificent."

"What can I do to avoid it?"

"Step back, feint, fall. You shall challenge him to box."

Slavin smiled.

"Thank you, I would rather not," he said.

Sarati lowered his voice.

"I like you two boys, and would help you. Can I trust you?"

"Certainly, signor."

"If I help you to your revenge, you will not betray me after?"

"Is it likely?" asked Slavin.

"Very well. I will supply the boxing-gloves when I come on Tuesday for my lesson—one pair for him, one for you."

"But I can't stand up against him."

"Hark you. I will put lead in the

knuckles of your gloves. You shall crush him—disfigure him for life. How now, will that do?"

Slavin jumped at the offer.

"Will you really, signor?" he asked.

"My word is my bond," answered Sarati.

"Then I will challenge him to box me next Tuesday He will not refuse."

"Good."

"And you will guarantee that I shall beat him?" continued Slavin, eagerly.

"Have I not told you that you shall smash him? It will be like a knuckle-duster on his face. I will teach you some new tricks. Good-bye, we must not be overheard; it is a compact. You shall disfigure him for life."

With a reassuring nod of the head, the Italian glided away.

The bargain was made, and a disgraceful one it was.

To stuff the knuckles of the boxing-gloves with lead, was as bad as to load the top of a stick with the same heavy material.

Slavin and Dawson felt slightly encouraged by the interview with Sarati.

The crafty Italian was evidently on their side.

They went into the lavatory and washed the blood off their faces, after which they proceeded to the playground.

"How do I look?" asked Slavin.

"Bad. I expect I look like a battered wreck," replied Dawson.

"Like an old warrior who has seen service on many a gory field."

He caught sight, as he spoke, of Jack and Dick.

They had buried the bird, and come back to the playground.

A dozen or more boys were talking to them, and feasting on tarts and buns, for Jack had generously stood treat again.

The willing Targett had gone a second time for a supply of good things.

"Look," said Slavin, jealously, "that fellow Massey is getting his name up."

"Quite a popular favourite," answered Dawson.

"They will put him in the first eleven, and won't he bowl with that left hand of his?"

"That little beast, Targett, is making up to him."

"Trust him, when there is any feed going on," replied Slavin. "Shall I go and challenge him now?"

"Why not? No time like the present."

"All right, I'll do it."

Slavin walked boldly forward.

As Targett had his back towards him, he did not see him approaching.

If he had done so, he would not have talked so loudly.

"How are the mighty fallen?" he was exclaiming. "The cock of the walk won't crow so loud now. What a lark it was to see him stretched out on the ground like a dead frog. Slavin won't sing 'Rule Britannia' as he used to."

"He got what he deserved," remarked Dick Lambert. "He was a little too uppish; in fact, he put on side till he got unbearable."

"That is bad form," replied Jack; "but I never wish to talk about a man in his absence."

"That is true," said Targett. "Yet if you want to talk about anybody, and you dare not do it before his face, you must do it behind his back."

"There is no necessity to talk at all. I licked him, and there is an end of it, as far as I am concerned."

"He won't think so."

"Why not?"

"Because he is frightfully vindictive. I hate him, and I move a vote of thanks to you," cried Targett.

Slavin now stepped between him and Jack Massey.

He seized Targett by the ear and drew him aside.

"Oh, heavens! my poor ear," cried Targett.

"Why are you at your spiteful tricks again?" demanded Jack.

"I have come to move an amendment," answered Slavin; "before you obtain any vote of thanks for hitting me, as that little disgusting wretch suggests, I want to be heard."

"There is no objection to that. Spin your yarn."

"I won't fight you again with naked fists."

"No; I should think not," cried Dick Lambert.

"But I will fight with boxing-gloves."

"When and where?" enquired Jack, eagerly.

"On Tuesday next, in this playground, and when Signor Sarati comes to give his usual lesson, he shall supply the gloves, and I will fight you."

Jack's face clouded.

"Sarati," he repeated, "did you say Signor Sarati?"

"I did."

"Have you seen him?"

"Dozens of times, but not since the holidays. Will you accept my challenge or not?"

For a moment Jack hesitated.

A suspicion crossed his mind that all was not right.

"Take him," whispered Dick, nudging his elbow.

"Very well. I accept," exclaimed Jack, "and you will find that I will give you as big a hiding with the gloves as anyone could wish for."

"You agree to fight? I shall hold you to your agreement."

"By all means. I am not likely to back out. When you are ready, you will find that I am face to face with you."

"Everyone here is a witness."

"That will do—act, don't talk," cried Jack, impatiently.

Saying this, he took Dick's arm and went to the house, at the back door of which Spoofer was standing, cleaning some plate.

"Are we going to have any dinner to-day?" he asked.

"No, sir," replied Spoofer. "The young gentlemen don't come in at any fixed time on the first day of the half, so we provide them with a high tea."

"At what time?"

"Five o'clock, punctual. I say, excuse me, sir," added the man, laughing, "but you did polish off Mr. Slavin."

"What has that to do with you? But you seem pleased."

"Many a sly kick I've had from him, sir."

"Then it pleased you. Well," said Jack, "you will see the performance repeated next Tuesday."

"Glad I am to hear it, sir."

"Do you know where Miss Mac-Foozle's school is?" inquired Jack.

"I do well," replied Spoofer. "It is on the other side of the road, about a furlong off."

"Sappho House it's called."

"That's the shop, sir. Seminary for young ladies, and kindergarten, as they term it, which, I believe is French or German for a babies' school. A proper old dragon is Miss Mac-Foozle."

"Indeed!"

"They say she treats the young ladies very harsh, and their screams at times are something awful."

"Perhaps that is exaggerated."

"It's what I'm told by the house-maid, sir, when she and me meets occasional."

"She is your sweetheart, I suppose?" said Jack, laughing.

"Me and she's courting, sir. I takes her out when she gets a few hours off, which isn't often. It's usual when you are keeping company with a young woman."

"What's her name?"

"Eva Jane," replied Spoofer.

Jack held up half-a-crown.

"Do you want to earn this?" he asked.

"Will a duck swim, sir? Try me with a half-a-dozen. Make it gold, if you like to, sir."

"I can't afford any more, but it is yours if you will go over to Sappho House for me."

"With the utmost pleasure in life. What am I to do?" answered Spoofer, cheerfully.

"Ask Eva Jane to give a note to a young lady boarder, by name Miss Ada Titmarsh."

"I'll go to the kitchen door, and it will be all right."

"Miss MacFoozle must know nothing about it," continued Jack, "or I don't know what the consequences might be to both of us."

"Very particular is Miss MacFoozle, sir."

"So you told me before."

"The old lady, sir, once locked a young lady in the cellar for looking over the wall at her lover. When found the next morning, she was stone cold and stiff."

"Dead?" asked Jack.

"Not quite, but it took two physicians, three surgeon doctors, and a veterinary to bring her back to life."

"That's rather a strong story."

"It's true, sir, because Eva Jane told me. It's nothing to what they did to a young gentleman, though, who looked over the wall at the young ladies."

"What was that?"

"He was caught waiting to see one of the young ladies as he was sweet upon."

"Well?" ejaculated his listener.

"Miss MacFoozle and Miss Curley—she's the assistant mistress, and an out-and-outer, wuss than t'other—they bound him with ropes, and flattened him out with the garden roller, so that he was put through the gate like a living skeleting, and his clothes wouldn't fit him for six weeks, hanging on him like sacks."

"That is not a very nice look-out."

"Keep away, sir," continued Spoofer, "don't you never look over the wall or go into them grounds, or the she-dragon will be after you."

"I'm not afraid. Here is the letter. I have it written."

"Well, I'll take the note and go now, before I'm likely to be called for, and thank'ee for me, sir."

Spoofer put the plate in the pantry, stuck his hat on his head, and went off.

Dick Lambert was curious to know what Jack was going to do.

It seemed as if he was determined to seek an interview with Ada, to whom he was so much attached.

If he wanted to do anything, Jack did not count the cost.

"Are you going to try and see Ada?" asked Dick.

"Why, yes," replied Jack; "I don't mind making a confidant of you, because you are my chum, and I'm sure that my confidence will not be misplaced."

"Never. I say that emphatically, old boy."

"To begin, I must tell you that I have just found out there is a fued of long standing between Signor Sarati and my father."

"How is that?"

"Sarati was injured in some manner, how, I do not know. He is going to have his revenge."

"What is that to do with you or Ada Titmarsh?" replied Lambert.

"I am coming to it; he will strike my father through me, if he can."

"The villain!"

"You may well call him that. Septimus Titmarsh is hand and glove with him."

"I thought they were leagued together."

"Up to the hilt. Sarati lends Sep money, and Sep has promised that he shall marry his sister."

"It sounds incredible."

"Fact, I assure you," said Jack. "I want to put her on her guard against the Italian."

"I can perceive your drift. But won't you run a great risk in going to the school?"

"If so, I do not care. I have, in my letter, asked her to meet me at the garden gate in an hour's time, and shall get over the wall in some manner."

"Should you not turn up at tea-time, I shall know where you are. You may be captured by the enemy, to wit, Miss MacFoozle, the she-dragon. What shall I do?"

"Tell Doctor Birchback, and ask him to come after me," replied Jack.

"I wish you were not going."

"Really I feel I must, and there's an end of it."

"You will be punished by the doctor."

"I'll chance that," said Jack; "the dear girl shall not be coerced by her brother Sep, or preyed upon by that wily foreigner."

Dick Lambert did not attempt to argue the point further.

They waited until Spoofer came back, which he did in a few minutes.

"Well, how did you succeed?" demanded Jack.

"First-rate, sir," answered the servant. "I saw Eva Jane taking in the milk, and I gave her the note."

"What did she say?"

"That the young lady should have it the moment the school was over."

"When will that be?"

"In half-an-hour."

"Then I am off up the road," exclaimed Jack, "to reconnoitre the wall, and see how I can get over it into the garden."

"It ain't a high wall, sir," replied Spoofer, "there's a tree near the gate, outside, on the path; climb up that, get on the wall, and over you go."

"Thanks for the tip, that's a wrinkle worth knowing, but how shall I get back?"

Spoofer shook his head gravely.

"You'll have to engineer that yourself," he said.

"Once inside, I'll get out. Good-bye, Dick."

"I wish you luck," rejoined Lambert.

Jack smiled, though his heart beat a little quicker than usual, and strode off to meet his sweetheart Ada.

CHAPTER IV.

MISS MACFOOZLE IS ALARMED, AND SO IS JACK MASSEY.

EVA JANE, the parlour-maid at Sappho House, was a kind-hearted, intelligent girl, who was in love herself, and could make allowance for others who felt the tender passion.

Consequently, she treasured up the letter Spoofer had given her, and waited until school was over.

The girls were not allowed at that time of the year to go into the garden in the afternoon.

There was an interval of an hour, at the expiration of which time tea was ready.

That space was spent in a large apartment called the recreation-room, where they could talk or read.

When the young ladies filed out of the schoolroom, Eva Jane stood in the passage.

As Ada came along, she touched her arm.

"A note for you, miss," she whispered.

Ada trembled.

"Who from?" she asked.

"I don't know, miss. It was given to me by my young man, who is servant at the boys' school, near by."

Ada took the letter, and crumbled it in her hand.

Who could it be from?

She passed with the others into the recreation-room, and sat down by the window.

Her particular friend was Fanny Meadows, a girl about her own age.

No sooner had she opened the letter, than Fanny came up.

"What are you reading, dear?" she asked.

So engrossed was Ada with the epistle that she did not hear her.

Fanny Meadows took the liberty of looking over her shoulder.

"Dearest Ada," Jack had written, "I want to see you at once. When the clock strikes five I shall be in your garden, near the gate. Come and meet me. Yours ever, Jack Massey."

"Oh!" thought Fanny, "isn't this awful? I must tell Miss MacFoozle, or dear Ada will be eloping. I shan't be her true friend if I don't tell. She must be protected."

This was a curious idea of friendship, but Fanny had never had a sweetheart, and was propriety itself.

To her mind, Ada was on the brink of destruction.

The honour and good name of the school were involved.

Besides, how Miss MacFoozle would thank and reward her for the important information she had to reveal.

With cat-like tread, Fanny Meadows retreated to another part of the room.

Ada had been unconscious of her presence.

Her little heart was fluttering dreadfully, and her agitation made her draw her breath quickly.

She looked at her watch.

It was nearly five o'clock, and if she would keep her appointment, she would have to make haste.

Accordingly she slipped out, took her hat down from a peg in the passage, and proceeded to the garden door.

Fanny Meadows followed her.

"It is a shame to betray her," she muttered, "but it is my bounden duty. I really must do it."

She tried to persuade herself that Ada would thank her for it in the end.

Watching Ada go out into the garden, she hurried to Miss MacFoozle's private room.

The schoolmistress was old, wrinkled, and of a crabbed disposition.

She had been disappointed in love when young, and had affected to despise the whole male sex ever since.

Man was her solemn detestation, except he came in the form of a clergyman or a doctor.

Her spectacles were on her rather short, snub nose, as she read the daily newspaper.

Miss Curley, her assistant, who was a tall, gaunt female with a strident voice, had gone out to do some shopping.

"Come in," said Miss MacFoozle, as Fanny knocked.

"Oh! ma'am," cried Fanny, bursting into the room, "so awful—so utterly dreadful."

"What is it?"

"I don't think I can summon up courage to tell you."

"Speak out, if you please, at once."

"Yes, ma'am. The fact is, Miss Titmarsh has gone into the garden to meet a man."

The paper dropped from Miss Mac-Foozle's hand, the spectacles fell from her nose.

With a look of petrification, she rose and confronted Fanny.

"A man!" she echoed, in a sepulchral voice, "don't tell me anything so terribly dreadful."

"It may be a boy."

"How do you know?"

"I looked over her shoulder, ma'am. as she was reading the letter, which requested her to be at the garden gate at five; it was signed Jack Massey."

Just then the ormolu clock on the mantel tinkled out the hour in silvery tones.

"One is as bad as the other," said the schoolmistress. "How truly horrible! What a disgrace for Sappho House. Can it be true?"

"Indeed it is, ma'am."

"And she has gone?"

"I saw her go with my own eyes. Oh! please ma'am, save her, for she is my friend, and I would not have believed it of her," replied Fanny, with tears in her eyes.

"You shall come with me," replied Miss MacFoozle; "unluckily, Miss Curley is out."

"I am afraid, ma'am——"

Miss MacFoozle regarded her sternly.

"Of what?" she demanded, "of a man? Be brave. I will freeze him with a single glance. We will hasten to the gardener's lodge. Jacobs shall make him a prisoner, and we will hand him over to the police."

"Perhaps he means to rob the house and murder us all."

"Let us hope not. Give me my bonnet, and shawl, child."

Fanny attempted to get them from the back of a chair, but she burst out crying, and sank on the floor.

"Get up," cried Miss MacFoozle.

"I can't, I'm fainting. Oh! I know I shall die if I accompany you, I am trembling so."

"Then I must go alone."

"Don't leave me, ma'am, for heaven's sake," pleaded Fanny.

"Tush! no harm can befall you here."

"He may have accomplices—partners in crime. Perhaps he means murder."

Miss MacFoozle bestowed a contemptuous glance upon Fanny, who continued to sob as if her heart would break.

Then, with a majestic tread, she left the room, and letting herself out into the garden, hastened to the gardener's lodge.

The gardener was an aged, decrepit man, who was lame of one leg, and suffered from chronic rheumatism in the other.

His name was Jacobs, but some people declared that he was a distant relative of the schoolmistress, who had provided for him in his old age by making him the custodian of her garden.

He had his meals in the house with the other servants, but slept in his lodge.

When Miss MacFoozle knocked at his door, he was smoking the pipe of peace in his little parlour.

"Jacobs! a man or boy is in the garden," she exclaimed, "I know not which."

The gardener quickly made his appearance.

"Is it a flirtation, or a contemplated robbery?" he asked.

"I have private information that he is talking to one of the young ladies," she replied.

"What do you want me to do with him?"

"It mustn't be a police case. If it gets into the papers, the school is ruined."

"Shall I chase him out?" continued Jacobs.

"Yes, yes; beat him well with a stick. I will punish the girl; she shall have bread and water for a week, and locked up in her bedroom."

"Very well, ma'am. Will this do?"

Jacobs took down from a nail in the wall a formidable-looking dog-whip.

"The very thing. Come along," said Miss MacFoozle.

They walked together to the gate, where they saw Jack and Ada standing close to some laurel bushes.

"I beseech you," Jack was saying, "to beware of that man Sarati. He is capable of carrying you off to Italy."

"He is my great aversion," replied Ada. "Oh! Jack, I want only your love."

"That you can always depend upon,

but I don't want to be robbed of you by a dastardly foreigner."

"Sep ought to be ashamed of himself; he was always a bad boy, and never cared for me."

"We will defeat them yet, dear Ada."

At this moment, Jacobs, who had crept up unobserved, brought the lash of his whip down on Jack's back with a swish.

"Nice goings on," said Miss Mac-Foozle.

Jack clenched his hands and looked savagely at the gardener.

"How dare you strike me?" he demanded.

"You are trespassing. Be off or I'll call a policeman and lock you up."

"Do it. I give you permission, but wait a moment while I speak to this lady," continued Jack.

Miss MacFoozle waved him back.

"Horrid creature, I don't want to listen to you," she said.

"But I insist upon telling you the facts. I came here——"

"The facts speak for themselves. What right have you here?" she interrupted.

"The right of an old friend to warn this young lady against a bitter and designing enemy."

"Dreadful creature! I daresay you would like to turn it off that way," said Miss MacFoozle, sarcastically.

"Dear madam," interposed Ada, "it is true, indeed it is. Jack Massey would not tell a falsehood."

"Massey! that is the person your respected father, Sir Dando Titmarsh, specially instructed me to keep you away from. I intercepted a letter from him, and sent it back whence it came."

Jacobs raised his whip again.

"Are you going, or not?" he asked. "The gate opens from the inside. I have not locked it yet."

"Not at your bidding," answered Jack.

"We will see about that, as sure as I grow geraniums."

"Touch me if you dare," cried Jack, defiantly.

The gardener's only reply was another stinging cut on the shoulders.

"What! am I to be whipped like a dog by a clod such as you are?" shouted Jack.

"Punish him! whip him! teach the horrid thing a lesson!" exclaimed Miss MacFoozle, holding Ada.

Jack made a spring at the gardener, and gave him one of his left-handed blows.

Three teeth were knocked out, and he rolled into a holly-bush, pricking himself all over.

"Oh! I say—help! Who's chucking bricks? That ain't fair," yelled the gardener.

"Help, help! Murder! fire! thieves!" screamed Miss MacFoozle.

"Hold your tongue, my dear woman," said Jack. "Do you want to compromise your school and this young lady?"

"You do; and don't presume to call me a woman, you horrible creature."

"I was wrong. You are a gorgon."

"Oh! the wretch, to go to the heathen mythology to find a name for me. I shall faint, I know I shall."

"I'll be off at the double," muttered Jack.

There was no one to bar his passage.

Jacobs had had enough of it. One blow of Jack's usually settled the business; it was like the man in Bret Harte's ballad—"When the chunk of old red sandstone stretched him senseless on the floor, the subsequent proceedings interested him no more."

But he was destined to be interrupted unexpectedly.

As we have said, Miss Curley, the assistant schoolmistress, had been out.

Jack had no sooner opened the door, than he was confronted by her.

She had heard the cries, and was tugging violently at the bell.

"Help!" again screamed Miss Mac-Foozle, dismally.

"Police! police!" cried Miss Curley, whose corkscrew ringlets began to sway to and fro in her agitation.

Fortunately for Jack, there was no constable to be seen.

Yet another stoppage was in store for him.

A stalwart lifeguardsman was passing by on his way to the cavalry barracks.

"What's the matter, ma'am?" he asked.

"Thieves! murder! We are all dead except me," replied Miss Curley. "Seize him, for goodness' sake."

"Here, young fellow," exclaimed the soldier, "you are my prisoner."

"Am I?" answered Jack. "Don't you touch me, you lanky horseguards blue."

"Come along with me; I'll take you to the station."

Jack struck at the lifeguardsman.

For once his left hand failed him.

The soldier was six-feet two in his boots, and he could not reach his face.

The blow struck him on his tunic, just on his chest.

The next moment, Jack felt a hand on his jacket-collar, and he was hurled violently to the ground.

His head struck the gravel, and he saw the big soldier standing over him.

Seeing that Jack Massey was lying prone on the ground at the mercy of the tall lifeguardsman, Miss Curley determined to improve the occasion.

It is the custom of the world to hit a man when he is down.

This was her idea.

She carried a sunshade with a long handle, and a knob at the end, which the irreverent term a "husband beater."

Raising this, she rushed upon Jack and dealt him a blow. Another one followed.

"You wretch!" cried Miss Curley. "How dare you enter our premises, you vampire?"

"Leave off, you horrid cat!" said Jack; "I have done nothing wrong."

"Yes, you have. Why, you just called me a cat, I will punish you severely."

The lifeguardsman intervened.

"Leave the vicious young cub to me, ma'am," he exclaimed. "I'll walk him off double quick."

"Take him away, then."

"Now then," continued the soldier, Jack having got upon his feet; "eyes right, dress."

"Touch me again, if you dare," Jack replied.

"Mark time."

"Get out," said Jack. "It is no business of yours."

"Isn't it? I'm a self-constituted guardian of the public peace."

"Bosh! I'll report you to your colonel."

"Do it, and welcome. My character will stand that. Now, come along, or I will make you, in a brace of shakes."

"You meddling fool," retorted Jack. "You overgrown weed, you pig-headed longshanks."

"Nice language. Do you think I'm going to stand that?"

"Have a few inches lopped off."

The lifeguardsman stooped down to hold Jack, but the latter, seeing his movement, struck out.

Using a naughty adjective, he stepped back.

Seizing his opportunity, Jack ran into the garden of the ladies' school.

He thought he would be safer there for a little while than in the street.

At least, he could hide in the bushes.

The gardener had limped behind a tree, deeming discretion the better part of valour.

Miss MacFoozle still stood on the grass, holding Miss Titmarsh in a tenacious grasp.

Wonderingly she watched the scene that was being enacted outside the gate.

"Hi, hi!" shouted Miss Curley, as Jack ran, "stop him!"

"Right you are," replied the private in the horseguards, "I'll pursoo the villain."

"No, no, soldier," said Miss Curley, "you must not enter the forbidden precincts."

"Bless you, ma'am, I shan't do any harm."

"Forbear, man, I entreat you."

The soldier pushed her gently on one side, and followed after Jack.

His temper was roused by the blow he had received.

He did not intend to be foiled by a boy if he could help it.

When he entered the garden, Miss MacFoozle was quite as much horrified at the intrusion as her assistant.

"Back, back, man! oh, man, go back!" she screamed. "A lifeguard red in the grounds of Sappho House! What shall I do? Go back, you horrid-looking, long-legged man!"

"I won't hurt any of you, ma'am." he answered. "I want to hide that young villain."

"It is too—too awful! A common soldier, too!"

"I'll catch the young imp. Just you wait."

"Go back, I implore you, dreadful man."

"Leave it all to me, ma'am."

"Just think of the scandal. I cannot bear it. I shall faint. Oh! where is my vinaigrette? Give me sal volatile."

"I don't know where she is, ma'am."

The soldier thought she spoke of a pupil, or a servant.

He caught sight of Jack, who was scaling a tree.

After him he darted.

Miss MacFoozle sank to the ground and fainted dead away.

Ada Titmarsh began to scream, and hastened to the house, while Miss Curley arrived on the scene.

She opened her sunshade and

fanned her superior with it in a very vigorous manner.

"Don't give way, dear, don't," she pleaded, "pray do not."

Miss MacFoozle was unconscious of her sympathy.

The apparition of a lifeguardsman on her premises had been too much for her sense of propriety.

Meanwhile the soldier had reached the foot of the tree.

Jack was quietly seated on a branch at least ten feet above his head.

"Come down!" cried the soldier.

"You are too big for your boots, aren't you? How do you live on a shilling a day? Borrow Sarah's wages, I suppose," replied Jack.

"If you sit up there defying me and giving me cheek, I'll chuck stones."

"Brave man! You'd run if you saw an enemy."

"I served in Egypt, and was in the charge of Kassassin!" said the soldier, with a great show of indignation.

"Fighting the poor Egyptians, who ran like a flock of sheep," taunted Jack, in a sarcastic manner; "gallant Egyptian butcher."

"Look here, I can't stand it."

"Sit it, then."

"Are you coming down, that's the question?"

"When it suits me, not before."

It is very annoying for a big man to be irritated by a boy; all the more is it so when he cannot be got at.

The soldier was white with passion.

He picked up some gravel stones, which he threw at Jack, striking him several times about the body.

In this kind of warfare he had decidedly the advantage.

"Now will you come down?" he demanded.

"No, you red-coated lamp-post," was the rejoinder.

"It's my duty to take you to the police-station."

"What for?"

"Being on these premises with a felonious intent; didn't the old lady say so? You can't get out of it."

"I am a thoroughly respectable young gentleman at a school close by."

"That's all my eye," replied the soldier, with a wink.

"I'll give you my card. I am a son of Captain Massey, who was in the army, now on the retired list."

"All right; show me your card."

Jack felt in all his pockets.

To his dismay and consternation he could not find a card anywhere.

He must have put his card-case in his box when packing up.

Cards were articles that Jack prided himself upon very much, for he had his name engraved in a neat copper-plate hand, and the cards themselves were gilt-edged.

"By Jove!" he exclaimed, in a tone of annoyance, "I have left the beastly things at home."

The lifeguardsman grinned consumedly.

"Ain't got 'em, eh?" he queried.

"Haven't a paste-board about me. Awfully sorry, you know, full private blank; but, of course, you'll take my word for it," said Jack.

"Of course I shan't do anything of the sort."

"Don't you believe me?"

"Not a ha'porth. You're a young burglar, qualifying for penal servitude or the gallows."

Jack drew his breath with difficulty.

"You insolent scoundrel!" he exclaimed, "how dare you insult a gentleman? You will soon find out your mistake."

"It shall be the other way, for I'll wait here till you do come down," answered the soldier.

Jack was about to reply in the same defiant manner, when a terrible screaming turned his attention in another direction.

Ada Titmarsh had roused the house.

She had rushed in amongst the girls, declaring that Miss MacFoozle was in a fit.

The consequence was that the young ladies ran into the garden, making a noise like a flock of frightened parrots.

Jack got to the end of the bough to see what it was all about.

The garden was full of girls, some dark, some fair, screeching at the top of their voices.

It was a very remarkable scene.

"What fools girls are," he muttered.

Miss Curley seeing the incursion of the scholars, left her superior to kick on the greensward, and ran with upheld hands to send the girls back to the house.

In his eagerness to see what was going on, Jack had gone too far.

The bough broke off short.

With a cry he fell out of the tree, right on the top of the overgrown lifeguardsman.

Bump! thud!

The soldier broke his fall, so that he was uninjured, but he did not manage to escape, any more for that.

He felt himself caught up by the collar, and he was half-pushed, half-dragged out of the grounds of Sappho House.

The shrill chorus of the young ladies faded away in the distance.

Miss Curley saw him depart, and speedily shut and locked the gate.

When he was in the road, the necessary policeman made his appearance.

As usual with the members of the force, he was a full quarter of an hour later than required.

"What's up?" he asked, "anything wrong?"

"I was called to the girl's school to arrest this young man for being unlawfully on the premises," answered the soldier.

The policeman frowned as if he thought his authority had been usurped.

"You've no right to arrest anybody," he continued; "let him go, he's my prisoner, not yours."

"You are welcome to him."

Jack was instantly released, and again collared by the policeman.

The lifeguardsman stalked sulkily away, glad to get rid of Jack.

"What have you been a doin' of?" the policeman enquired; "tell the truth, or it will go hard with you. Though I'm bound to warn you that you needn't say anything to criminate yourself—that's the lore."

"Oh! lor', is it?" replied Jack, mocking him.

"Don't give me none of your sauce, or I'll run you in, though I have the option of taking your name and address, so as the parties injured can proceed by way of summons."

"Do as you please," said Jack, "I only went to the school to see a young lady friend. The governess caught us talking. I ran, she shouted, and the bold lobster of a soldier interfered without any right."

The policeman rubbed his stubbly chin thoughtfully.

It is a way that country policemen have.

"You admit being guilty of trespass?" he remarked, with a blush of conscious pride in his legal knowledge, "and that's agi'n the lore."

"It is a case for a civil action, then," replied Jack.

"Not if you were in search of game."

Jack laughed aloud at this sapient abservation.

"There is no game there," he said, "unless you call young ladies game, and perhaps they are fair game, in a case of love. My sweetheart is very fair, in fact, quite a little fairy, and fond of a game, too."

The policeman looked puzzled.

"Are you chaffing me?" he demanded. "You must respect the majesty of the lore, as represented in my person, you know."

"Certainly," answered Jack, touching his cap. "I salute you as a highly intelligent guardian of the police. Now take your hand off my jacket, and I will wish you good-bye."

"Not so fast," said the policeman, as his rather muddy eyes opened wide at a sudden thought. "I think I ought to take you to the inspector for enquiries to be made."

"Let me go, I have had enough of it," cried Jack. "First the old woman at the school, then the big coward of a lifeguardsman, and now you. It sounds like a joke on All Fools' Day."

The policeman shook his head gravely.

"I'm afraid that you will find it anything but a joke," he rejoined. "No more of your jore, we must observe the lore. Come!"

Fortunately for Jack, his trouble with the guardian of law and order was to come to an end.

Dick Lambert and Dr. Birchback were seen approaching, side by side, at a rapid pace.

As Jack had not made his reappearance within what Dick deemed a reasonable time, the latter reluctantly sought the doctor.

To him he told his story, and together they repaired to the sacred precincts of Sappho House.

On their way they encountered Jack and the policeman.

Dr. Birchback was very wrath.

His brow lowered and his nostrils dilated.

Anyone who knew him could see that there was a storm brewing.

CHAPTER V.

PRIVATE SCHOOL AND PUBLIC SCHOOL.

UP to the present Jack had not had the pleasure of seeing the head-master of Manor Park School.

But when he noticed the flowing gown and the four-cornered, flat-topped, mortar-board cap, he guessed who was coming.

It was an unlucky encounter.

He ardently wished the interview could be avoided, but that was impossible, thanks to the imbecility of the thick-headed constable.

"Is that Massey?" asked the doctor. "I have only seen his father, who is a very nice gentleman."

"Yes, sir, that is my rash friend," Dick Lambert answered. "Don't be hard on him. He has only been to see his sweetheart, as I had the honour to inform you."

"Boys have no business to think themselves in love."

"Look over it this time, sir."

"Silence!" cried the doctor.

They had now come face to face with the policeman and his captive.

"What are you doing with that young gentleman?" demanded the doctor. "Come, speak out."

"He is under suspicion of being on private premises for an unlawful purpose," was the rejoinder.

"Nonsense! he is one of my pupils. Let him go."

"If you will be answerable for him to come up for judgment if called upon——"

"Rubbish! Who gave him in charge?" interrupted Dr. Birchback.

"Nobody. I took him, hearing that——"

"Not another word," again interfered the doctor. "You are a dolt, an idiot. Be off about your business, or I'll report you to the watch committee."

This threat was sufficient.

The policeman released Jack, and walked away with all the rapidity he considered consistent with his injured dignity.

Then Dr. Birchback assumed his severest scholastic voice, before which generations of boys had trembled.

His eyes, fixed upon the culprit, seemed trying to read his innermost thoughts.

"John Massey, my new pupil, I presume?" he said.

Jack bowed in his politest and most winning manner.

"Dr. Birchback, I believe?" he replied.

"Yes, sir; and the birch will soon make an intimate acquaintance with your bare back if you cannot satisfactorily explain the meaning of your escapade in Miss MacFoozle's garden. A nice letter of complaint I shall have from her. What do you intend by running after a young lady? Shameful conduct!"

"Affection for an old friend and neighbour must plead my excuse, sir. Her brother is plotting to marry her to an Italian."

"What has that to do with you?"

"I love her."

"Ridiculous! Young men of your age should only love their studies and their sports; that is enough for them. You were caught, I suppose, together?"

"We were, and I fear the dear girl will get into trouble."

"There is no fear but that you will. I shall expect you in my study in half-an-hour for punishment."

"But sir, it is my first fault," objected Jack.

"I can make no allowance in this case," the doctor replied.

He turned away without another word, and began to retrace his way to the school with slow and majestic strides.

Dick Lambert and Jack followed.

"I intended to get you out of a row," said Dick.

"And you have got me into one," replied Jack.

"It was far from my thoughts."

"Save me from my friends. I should have been all right," continued Jack; "however, I am in for it, and it is of no use crying. What did the doctor say to you coming along?"

"Such pranks were detestable, and he was determined to put a stop to them."

"Thank him; perhaps he won't be able to."

"He also said he would begin with you as he meant to go on."

"Good old Buzfuz! Isn't that the nickname you call him?" exclaimed Jack.

"Yes. He is always Buzfuz out of school," replied Dick; "he isn't a bad fellow, but he prides himself on being a strict disciplinarian of the old school. We have plenty of lessons and plenty of liberty. By the way, where shall we go to-morrow afternoon?"

"Is it a half-holiday?"

"The second afternoon of the half always is, from immemorial custom. In the morning we dust our books, arrange our desks, and are formed into classes, while the course of study is settled."

"Then I vote we go on the river."

"We may have a row with the Eton fellows, they are fond of quarrelling with private school boys," said Dick.

"All the better. I should like it," answered Jack. "I'm not afraid of them, if they are like Sep Titmarsh."

"But they are not; don't be led away by that idea."

"We will go on the water, any-how."

"The Eton men think the river belongs to them."

"Let them see that it is a mistaken idea. Hullo!" added Jack; "what's that noise?"

He had suddenly become aware of a sound of many feet, as of people running.

Then arose the alarming cry of "Mad dog! mad dog!"

This is always enough to frighten the most courageous.

Hydrophobia seems to stare the hearer in the face, and the blood runs cold at the very thought.

Looking up the road Jack saw several men and boys running as fast as they were able.

Behind them was a huge retriever with a curly black coat.

His tongue was lolling out of his mouth, and his chops were flecked with foam.

His eyes rolled in a frenzy, which plainly bespoke the existence of rabies in the animal in its worst form.

Woe betide the hapless wretch who was bitten by that dog.

Dr. Birchback had stepped into the middle of the road to cross over to his own house.

He, too, saw the mad dog, and appeared undecided how to act.

It looked, Jack thought, as if he had lost his nerve.

A terrible scream arose.

The dog had bitten a boy, who fell down in agony.

Its poisoned fangs had met in the fleshy part of the boy's thigh.

This momentary stoppage enabled the other people it was pursuing to turn round and run the other way.

There was no one before the animal now but Dr. Birchback, who made no attempt to get out of the way.

He was as if rooted to the ground.

"Good heavens!" cried Jack, "the doctor will surely be bitten. I must run to him."

"Keep back, you are too bold," said Dick.

"No; I must go, hinder me not."

"You will be bitten. Stop, for heaven's sake!"

"No. I'll save the doctor, if I can. I'm off."

Setting his teeth firmly together, he darted forward.

There was not more than fifty yards to run, but the dog on the other side of the doctor had less than that to go to reach his intended victim.

Dr. Birchback did not see anything of Jack, because his back was turned towards him.

His eyes were riveted on the ferocious retriever.

The impassive attitude he maintained led Jack to believe that he was fascinated by the dog.

Or, if that was not so, his faculties were paralysed by the magnitude of the danger he was in.

Jack could see the slime dropping from the envenomed fangs.

He redoubled his efforts.

Breathless he arrived in front of the doctor, a brief space before the dog.

The creature halted, growled, raised itself on its hind legs, and made a spring at Jack's throat.

Now was the cool courage of Jack Massey fully demonstrated.

He stood erect.

Not a muscle of his face moved as he drew back his left hand, and dashed it at the side of the dog's head.

The terrific blow he dealt took effect under the ear.

Without a yelp or a howl, the dog fell on its side, quivering all over, but unable to move.

It had received a concussion of the

"YOU ARE NO BROTHER OF MINE,' HE YELLED."—(See page 57.)

brain, which rendered it powerless for further mischief.

The wretched brute's life was passing away.

The doctor now recovered from the stupor into which he had been plunged.

He held out his hand to Jack, who warmly grasped it.

"My dear boy," he said, in a choked voice, while tears trembled in his eyes, "under heaven's blessing you have saved me from a great danger, perhaps from the most horrible of all deaths. Receive my sincere thanks."

"I was only just in time, sir," replied Jack.

"Never did I see anything more promptly or pluckily done. As for myself, I confess I became a coward. Not hand nor foot could I move. But what force must you have in your arm."

"I am left-handed, sir, and considered pretty strong," said Jack, smiling.

"Another Samson! a young Hercules!" said Dr. Birchback, admiringly.

"I believe I could floor anything at a blow, except a tree, or a lamp-post, or a long-legged horseguard," replied Jack.

"Why not the latter?"

"Because their legs are so long, and their heads so small, that I can't get at them."

"A good and sufficient reason'; but I thank you again. You risked your life to save mine."

"I am glad I succeeded, sir."

"You—er, need not come and see me in half-an-hour," continued Dr. Birchback.

Jack knew what he meant.

He was let off the promised whipping.

A smile of satisfaction wreathed itself round his mouth.

"Thank you, sir," he answered, "I will try not to get into trouble again."

"Good boy. Adhere to that resolution and we shall be always good friends."

Saying this, Dr. Birchback crossed the road and entered his house by the private door, of which he carried a key.

This was Jack's hour of triumph; but now that the danger was over he felt weak and nervous.

The reaction came when the danger was past, for he fully realised the nature of it.

Dick Lambert shook his hand cordially with genuine admiration.

"By Jove, old fellow!" he said, "you are quite a hero—one of those chappies we read of in books, like 'Jack the Giant Killer,' and 'Guy of Warwick,' who slew the dragon."

"Don't overwhelm me," replied Jack, modestly.

"It ought to be written in letters of gold."

At that moment Spoofer made his appearance from the house, handling a wheelbarrow.

"This here affair is to be perpetooated, as the doctor calls it!" he exclaimed.

"What's that?" replied Jack.

"Which of you gents was it as killed the mad dog?"

"I am the humble individual."

"Very good; read that."

He presented him with half a sheet of notepaper, on which was written:

"This dog, in a rabid state, was about to bite Dr. Birchback, when Mr. John Massey, one of his pupils, with marvellous courage and strength, rendered the brute senseless with one blow of his fist."

Then followed the date.

"What are you going to do with this?" enquired Jack.

"I'm to take the dog to the stuffers and have him preserved. This here inscription is to go on the glass case," answered Spoofer.

"That is rather more honour than I deserve."

"The doctor is going to apply for a gold medal for you," continued Spoofer.

He gave the dead dog a kick.

"Ugh! you brute," he went on. "I suppose there is no bite in you now, so I'll kick you again."

"No fear," rejoined Jack. "He is as harmless as a dried snake, or a frozen elephant in the wilds of Siberia."

"How did you do it, sir?"

"Oh! I just gave him a gentle tap on the head."

"Not to hurt him, of course," said Spoofer, with a grin.

"Oh, no! I wouldn't on any account hurt a dumb animal."

"Regular society for prevention man you are. Tapped him, eh, same as you did Mr. Slavin and Mr. Dawson? Ho! ho! I shouldn't care about one of your taps—not me," laughed Spoofer.

Then he wheeled the barrow to the side of the dog.

"Come here, you beast," he remarked, as he took him up. "You've picked your last bone, barked your last bark, and bit your last victim."

Spoofer went on his mission after this philosophic observation, and the friends walked in just in time for tea.

Jack did not say anything about his adventure, but Dick Lambert was not so reticent.

In glowing colours he represented the gallant deed to several, and it was soon all over the school.

The consequence was that Jack was warmly congratulated by many boys.

This occasioned great annoyance and vexation of spirit to Slavin and Dawson.

Jack was rapidly attaining a position that made them very envious.

Their mean and narrow minds could not tolerate it with equanimity.

"I wish the dog had bitten him," said Slavin.

"So do I," answered Dawson. "Wouldn't it have been fun to see him strapped down, barking, and shuddering at the sight of water?"

The evening passed quickly.

That night Jack's sleep was disturbed by vivid dreams, in which he was fighting whole armies of mad dogs and packs of howling, ravenous wolves, urged on by soldiers and policemen.

In the morning Jack was examined by the assistant-master, Dr. Syntax, and placed in the second class.

The first was the highest, and the third the lowest.

He had the satisfaction of finding that Dick Lambert was in his class.

This was all the more agreeable, as they would be able to get up their lessons together to their mutual advantage.

After dinner they donned their boating flannels, and put on straw hats, which had a band round them with the inscription "Manor Park School."

The doctor insisted upon this, though the boys did not like it.

Not that they were by any means ashamed of their school.

Far from it.

It often got them into conflict, however, with the Eton boys.

One glance at the riband on the hat, showed that they belonged to the private school.

Fights were of common occurrence in consequence.

When dressed, Jack produced a medium-sized luncheon basket, and took from his hamper a pigeon-pie, some cut ham, and a fowl.

"What are your intentions with regard to all that grub?" asked Dick.

"We will have a little picnic by the banks of the river, all by our dear selves," replied Jack.

"How jolly, if the Etonians don't interfere with us."

"I'll take care they do not. All we have to do is to buy some rolls and bottled beer. Here is salt and a corkscrew."

"Capital. We are sure to be hungry after a spin," said Dick.

They sallied forth, procured what they required, and going to one of the rafts belonging to a boat-house near Windsor Bridge, obtained a pair-oared skiff, and rowed up past the Brocas Meadows.

The leaves on the trees were of the most delicate green, and the grand old river was as pellucid as a pond.

It was early in the afternoon, the Etonians had not come up town yet, and there were scarcely any boats on the river.

They passed a barge heavily laden with bricks, drawn by a horse, laboriously toiling along the towing-path.

When they shot the railway bridge, they saw a grassy, tree-sheltered spot between what is called Cuckoo Weir and Lower Hope.

Running their boat ashore, they decided to have their picnic there.

Everything seemed to invite comfort and repose.

Dick did not think they were destined to get it, in spite of Jack's confidence that no one would dare to interfere with them.

A newspaper served them as a table-cloth, plates, and knives and forks had not been forgotten.

As they sat down, they saw the Eton eight and the ten-oar go by on the way to Surley.

In a short time the small boats would follow.

"Will you have barndoor songster, or dove tart?" asked Jack.

"Fowl and ham first, pigeon-pie to follow," responded Dick.

"Draw the beer, then, and I'll attend to your requirements."

They were soon engaged in eating vigorously, demonstrating how soon boys can enjoy one dinner and be ready for a second.

Their serenity was disturbed in a not altogether unexpected manner.

A boat's nose was run up alongside their own.

Two boys stepped out on to the tow-path, and began to regard them rudely.

One, who was stoutly built, and wore a gold rimmed eyeglass suspended from a cord, said :

"Private school cads having a tuck in."

"Yes," replied his companion ; ".Manor Park—come away."

"Why should we ? "

"I know one of them."

"Are you afraid of private school cads ? I am not ; let us take their grub away, it will be a lark."

"No, no ; come away."

Hearing voices, Jack looked up, having been absorbed in the important operations of eating and drinking.

He nudged Dick Lambert.

"Look," he said, "there is Sep Titmarsh and another fellow."

"So it is. I know the other, he is often at Sarati's gymnasium."

"Who is he ? "

"An awfully insolent, exclusive fellow, by name Lord Goldenhurst."

"Ah ! that's like Sep ; nothing under a lord for Sep. I wonder what they are going to do," said Jack. "Shall I wind up my steam arm ? "

"Not yet ; don't interfere with them if they let us alone," answered Dick.

"All right. I have no wish."

They were not left long in ignorance of Lord Goldenhurst's intentions.

The young nobleman stepped up close to them.

Septimus, more prudent, remained by the boat, wishing they had not landed at that particular spot.

He had his own reasons for not wanting to challenge Jack to an encounter.

Lord Goldenhurst had never heard of Left-handed Jack, and simply looked upon him as he would have done on any other boy.

There was nothing specially remarkable in his appearance.

"You'll know me again the next time you see me, I should think," said Jack.

"I do not think I shall take the trouble to preserve in my memory your plebian features," answered his lordship in an affected tone.

His manner was arrogant and offensive to a degree.

Jack took an instantaneous dislike to him.

"You are very rude to stare at people when they are eating," he said.

"I like to see the beasts feed," was the cool reply. "It is as good as going to the menagerie, or the Zoo."

"Do you apply that remark to me ? "

"I don't want to talk to private school cads, it is not my custom," exclaimed Lord Goldenhurst. "I intend to have some of that pie, and a bottle of beer."

Jack laughed quietly.

"Don't you wish you may get it ? " he replied.

"I am Lord Goldenhurst, of Eton College. You, perhaps, are the son of some successful shopkeeper, and through your father cheating his customers, have escaped the workhouse."

With difficulty Jack kept down his rising temper.

Nevertheless, he got up and began to swing his left arm about.

Dick chuckled inwardly.

Full well he knew that this action meant mischief in the near future.

"Is that all ? " asked Jack, calmly.

"All ! what more do you want ? " Lord Goldenhurst demanded.

"I only thought you might have been a Knight of the Garter, or a Commander of the Bath at least."

"I am not old enough for that ; those distinctions will come when I grow up, and take an active part in politics, as I intend to. Keep the common people down, will be my great motto."

"Mind they don't down you."

"Impossible. Now I shall trouble you to bring me that pie and a bottle of beer. Do it at once."

"Keep on, I like a speech ; isn't it clever, Dick ? "

"Awfully," replied Lambert, who was choking with laughter, and nearly swallowed a chicken bone.

"I could listen all day to such eloquence," continued Jack ; "why don't you take off your hat, Dick ? That is the great Lord Donkeyhorse."

His lordship frowned darkly.

"Goldenhurst is my name, if you please," he corrected.

"Beg your pardon, it is a pity you are not more so."

"More what ? "

"Asinine. You'd win a prize at a donkey show."

" You are insolent, you Manor Park cad."

" Now," said Jack, "you wouldn't believe it, perhaps, but I am a Commander of the most honourable Order of the Bath."

" You are. Pooh! don't talk like that."

" I can give anybody a bath, free gratis for nothing. For instance, if you say much more to me I will give *you* one."

" Give me a bath ! "

" Certainly. I will souse you in the river, and you may get out the best way you can, my boy."

Dick rolled on the grass, roaring with laughter.

In a profound rage, Lord Goldenhurst turned to Septimus.

" My dear Titmarsh," he exclaimed, "do you hear what this disguster is saying to me ? "

" You need not appeal to him," cried Jack. " Sep and I are well acquainted already, aren't we, Sep ? "

There was no reply to this query.

" What cheek ; he calls you Sep, and swears he knows you," exclaimed his lordship; " surely you would never, never associate with a private school cad like that ? "

" His father lives next door to my father, Sir Dando," said Septimus, who felt it incumbent on him to say something.

" Surely you are going to remove to a more congenial locality."

" We are looking about for another house."

His lordship had let his glass fall; he put it to his eye again, and once more focussed Jack.

" I say," he exclaimed, "are you going to give me some of that pie, which, I must confess, has an appetising smell, or shall I take it ? "

" Take it if you want it," rejoined Jack.

" Get out of the way, then, or I might be tempted to—er—box your long ears, don't you know."

Jack stepped on one side.

" Come away ! " shouted Sep, " he will hurt you."

Lord Goldenhurst smiled, contemptuously.

" Hurt me ? No, I think not," he said. " It will be very much the other way if he provokes a conflict."

" You don't know him."

" Bah ! I can always lick a cad like this fellow."

His lordship made this remark with studied insolence, which was his chief characteristic.

He was a young aristocratic cub who wanted, as the saying goes, a good deal of licking to lick him into shape.

Septimus Titmarsh was one of his friends, because his father was a baronet ; he would not walk up the town with a commoner.

Jack allowed him to cut a piece out of the pie and taste it.

" How do you like it ? " he enquired.

" Don't talk to me while I'm eating," Lord Goldenhurst replied ; " it is very bad form, don't you know."

" I don't mean the pie, but where would you like to be hit ? "

" Eh ? what ? hit me ? "

" Yes, I have given you warning ; defend yourself. I'll knock you down first, and give you a bath afterwards."

His lordship put down the piece of pie.

" Oh ! that's your game, is it ? " he said. " Come along, Mr. Private Schoolman, I have learnt boxing from Sarati, and will thrash you well."

" Indeed ! I can show you a trick or two Sarati does not know ! " cried Jack.

Lord Goldenhurst put himself into a fighting position.

He struck out at Jack, who received the blow on the chin.

The next moment his lordship felt as if he had been struck by a cricket ball between the eyes.

He saw as many stars as there are in the firmament on a clear frosty night, and went over on his back.

" Very neatly grassed," was Dick's comment.

" There is plenty more where that came from," replied Jack.

" How are the mighty fallen ! " cried Dick.

Jack turned round to look at Septimus, who was as white as a sheet.

" Sep," he cried, "why don't you come and help your friend ? "

" It is his own fault," answered Septimus Titmarsh. " I told him to leave you alone, and now, I suppose, he has got half killed for his folly."

" Do you want to have a round with me ? "

" You know jolly well I don't."

The prostrate lord groaned, and sat up, rubbing his forehead.

" What did you hit me with ? " he asked.

"The fist, that's all; what do you think?"

"I never felt anything like it. I'm quite faint, 'pon my soul I am."

"It was one of his left-handed blows," said Septimus; "I really think he could fell an ox."

"Quite fair, was it?" continued Lord Goldenhurst.

"Oh! yes; there is no doubt about the fairness of it. I have seen him knock down a bargee."

"Well, I don't feel equal to any more of it. The next time I meet him, I shall give the Manor Park prize-fighter a wide berth."

"I am no prize-fighter," cried Jack; "if you say that again I'll pound you to a jelly. Apologise this moment."

"Not to a cad. I am descended from the Plantagenets."

"My father is Captain Massey; how dare you keep on insulting me?"

Lord Goldenhurst rose to his feet, scowling and crestfallen.

"Put our boat in the water," he said to Septimus.

Jack faced him.

"Apologise!" he exclaimed.

"No; really couldn't think of it," replied his lordship. "Can't, you know."

Jack wasted no more words on the sprig of nobility, who did not know how to behave himself.

He seized him by one arm and the nape of the neck, running him ignominiously across the towing-path towards the brimming river.

"I say, this won't do," cried Lord Goldenhurst; "my dear Titmarsh, will you not help me? really, it is too bad."

"In you go," said Jack.

"Titmarsh! I say, oh!——"

Splash! Dash!

His lordship went head-first into the Thames and disappeared like a stone; after the fashion of a bad half-penny, he turned up again.

Septimus had got into the boat, which he pushed with an oar into the stream.

He thought it would be safer to be afloat, as he might be treated in the same unceremonious fashion.

Lord Goldenhurst swam to the boat and climbed in, none the worse for his ducking.

He sat on a thwart and looked daggers at Massey.

"I'll remember you!" exclaimed he; "a nice pair of black eyes I shall have; you shall regret it bitterly, I promise you."

"Whose got the best of it, public or private school?" replied Jack. "Go and play. You are only fit for the nursery."

"The private school conquered this time, but wait till we next meet," hissed his lordship through his tightly-clenched teeth.

Jack poured out a glass of foaming Bass.

"Here's to our next merry meeting," he retorted, mockingly.

Lord Goldenhurst turned his back, and seized an oar, and he and Septimus began to pull leisurely up stream.

"Another enemy," said Dick. "It seems your fate to make them."

"And conquer in the end," answered Jack.

"Don't be too cock-sure of that. The pitcher goes to the well often, but gets broken at last."

"By George! didn't the Plantagenet look savage? If he could, he would clap me into one of the lowest dungeons in his ancestral castle."

"Aye, and put you to the torture," replied Dick. "I told you what the Eton fellows are, they look upon us like dirt."

"We are as good as they are. Let them try a football or cricket eleven against our school eleven."

"Bless your simple, innocent heart, they are much too high for that. They will only play Oxford, Cambridge, Harrow, and Winchester."

"Not Rugby, Marlborough, or any like Westminster, or Charterhouse, or Cheltenham?" asked Jack.

"Not one; they are not good enough."

Jack whistled as if he could not quite understand these nice distinctions, nor the assumed sense of superiority.

They finished their repast, packed up what was left, shied stones at the empty beer bottles as they floated in the water, and finally re-embarked.

Jack took the rudder-lines to steer, and Dick consented to scull, they having provided themselves with a pair.

Slowly the skiff was propelled up stream, past upper Hope and the rushes, towards Boveney Lock.

It was not their intention to go through the lock, as they had come out for amusement, and not for a hard row.

Jack steered alongside of the long eyot on the Windsor side, and Dick took it very easily.

Suddenly Jack became aware of a boat in which were two people coming down with the stream at racing speed.

They had no coxswain, and did not seem to be aware that another boat was right in their course.

"Hi! hi!" he shouted, "look out! Mind where you are coming!"

No attention was paid to his warning.

There was no doubt that the boat had been lying to, or hiding under some willows, or he would have seen it before.

It must have darted out of its place of concealment very suddenly indeed.

Was it a trap?

Jack was inclined to think so, and the conviction grew into a certainty as he drew out into the stream and the boat followed.

The bow had looked over his shoulder.

It was no other than Septimus Titmarsh.

Of course, the one who was rowing stroke was Lord Goldenhurst.

Animated by a cowardly spirit of revenge, and guessing that the Manor Park boys would come up soon, they had been lying in wait for them.

Their manifest intention was to run them down, smash up their boat, and swamp them.

"Scull hard, Dick," cried Jack. "Scull for your life, or we shall have the Plantagenet into us!"

"You don't say so," replied Lambert, exerting every muscle.

"Hang that fellow! When I get hold of him again I'll make him feel worse than a boiled bloater."

Dick smiled in spite of himself, for the figure was so ludicrous.

Those in the other boat knew, that to get out of the way, Jack would have to turn the head of his boat.

They would then be able to strike him amidships, or take him broadside on, as a sailor would say.

Therefore, the sharp bow of their boat would cut his in half almost, or, at any rate, do it irreparable damage.

"Look out! do you want to run into us?" cried Jack.

No notice was taken of his exclamation.

On came the boat with the speed of an arrow.

Jack was nearly in midstream now, but the other boat followed, with the current in its favour, which gave it an overwhelming advantage.

By the towing-path a barge was coming up.

All at once there was a shock and a crash.

Jack and Dick were capsized, their craft filled, and they were struggling in the water almost before they could realise that they were upset.

Both were expert swimmers, and struck out for the shore.

How it was, Jack did not know, but he felt a blow on the head which made him dizzy.

He floundered about without being able to see where he was going.

Then there was a rushing noise, like that of a thousand shuttles, in his ears, and all was a blank.

CHAPTER VI.

LEFT TO PERISH.

THE cause of Jack's insensibility was a cowardly blow dealt him by Septimus Titmarsh, who struck him with an oar from behind while he was swimming.

The next instant, both he and Lord Goldenhurst sprang into the water, overturning their boat as they did so.

This was to make the affair look like an unfortunate accident.

A collision in which both boats are swamped and one of the occupants injured is not an uncommon or improbable event.

In fact, it is an event of frequent occurrence on the river.

All had been arranged beforehand between the confederates while they were lying-to under the willows of the eyot.

Jack's body floated under the lee of

the barge when it came to the surface —for he had sunk after being hit.

The bargeman, who was assisted by a boy, the latter being engaged in steering, having seen the whole affair, took up a long-handled boat-hook.

As the body drifted by, he caught the hook in the flannels, and hauled him on board.

Jack was saved from drowning.

This act was unnoticed by Lambert, who was on his way to the shore.

Septimus uttered a cry of rage at being baffled in this unexpected manner.

He had made sure that his revenge on his enemy was complete and final.

The barge had not stopped, but the bargeman ran to the stern, near which Septimus now was.

"Meet me in the lock cut," said the bargeman, hoarsely.

Septimus alone heard the request, and looked up in surprise.

It was Boler who spoke.

Being remarkable for low cunning, Boler recognised both Titmarsh and Massey, and he had not forgotten what the former had told him at the time he had encountered Jack at Clewer.

Septimus held up his hand and nodded his head to signify that he understood.

The barge swept on its way, and the three boys gained the shore, the first to land being Dick Lambert.

"Hold your tongue," whispered Septimus to his lordship, as they were climbing up the banks; "leave all the talking to me."

"I have seen and heard nothing," replied his lordship, with a ghastly smile.

"That is right."

When they got on the path, Dick was eagerly searching the surface of the water for his friend, who was nowhere to be seen.

He could not understand it at all.

They had both struck out together, and that Jack could swim he knew well, as they had often bathed together.

"That was a dirty trick you served us," said he.

"Quite an accident, I assure you," answered Septimus. "We did not see or hear you till we were into you."

"That won't do; but where is Jack?" asked Dick, in perplexity. "I can't see him anywhere."

"Good heavens!" cried Septimus, with well-affected surprise, "he can't be drowned?"

"Poor fellow!" said Lord Goldenhurst; "seized with a sudden cramp, perhaps. The water is awfully cold."

Dick glared at them.

"Heaven help us!" he exclaimed; "if he is drowned, you are his murderers, and I shall tell everyone so."

"Come! that is going a little too far," replied Septimus. "One skiff runs into another, and——"

With a wild cry, Dick dashed his fist into Septimus's face, which effectually cut his eloquence short.

Then he ran up and down the bank like a madman, looking for his lost friend.

His face was the aspect of despair, and he wrung his hands wildly.

Presently he came back.

"Cowards!" he cried, "what have you done?"

"Nothing at all; it was a sheer accident," replied Septimus; "you can't make it out anything else. The river must be dragged for the body."

"I will run for a waterman," said Lord Goldenhurst; "there is always one at Cuckoo Weir. Shall I meet you anywhere, Titmarsh?"

"Yes, at Goodman's raft. I will go up to the lock and tell the keeper. It is an awful thing."

"I would not have had it happen for a thousand pounds," replied his lordship.

"Nor I for twice that sum," rejoined Septimus.

The two hypocrites separated, going in different directions.

Dick Lambert threw himself on the grass, completely overcome, and wept bitterly.

The shock had completely unmanned him; every nerve in his body was quivering with uncontrollable emotion.

Meanwhile, Septimus, who was really bad at heart, secretly rejoiced, as he ran up to the lock.

His dastardly intention had been to kill Jack by a blow on the head with the oar, and Lord Goldenhurst made no objection.

What to do with Jack now would depend upon the conversation he was to have with Boler, who he knew from experience would be his ready tool in any villainy.

It was simply a question of money with the bargee, and his lordship, who was very rich, would have to pay.

He was as deep in the mud as Septimus was in the mire.

Septimus had acted with cold-blooded calculation, born of a long-rooted enmity.

His lordship had consented to the foul deed on a sudden impulse, arising from wounded pride, and the stinging indignity of a blow.

Now that the vengeance was perpetrated, he was sorry for it.

Yet, whatever his accomplice chose to do, he could not prevent.

It was too late to go back.

The barge had come to a standstill in the approach to the lock, the horse was cropping the grass, the driving-boy smoking a pipe, while Boler and his assistant, a carroty youth of seventeen, were standing on the deck, eating some bread and bacon, and drinking beer out of a stone jar.

"Barge ahoy!" cried Septimus.

"Come aboard, master," replied Boler, "I'll give you a hand up. This is only my boy, Rumbo, one as I picked off the streets; he's an orphan, and never opens his mouth to nobody, 'cepting me, do you, my chappie?"

"Not me," answered Rumbo.

Septimus climbed on board; the barge was close to land, in the still water of the cut.

He could see no sign of Jack Massey.

"Where is——" began Septimus.

The bargee cut him short.

He held up his finger, warningly.

"Hush!" he said; "he is below."

"Alive?"

"He breathes as right as rain, though he ain't come to yet. Saint Christopher! that was one on the nob you give him."

"I meant it, and the thing would have been all serene if you had not come along with your ugly barge."

"How could I help that?" asked Boler.

"What did you want to fish him up for?" asked Septimus.

"I thought I saw a bit of money in it, that's the reason, young master."

"You will not get much out of me, unless you complete your work."

"Walker!" replied Boler. "I must be paid for holding my tongue. If you haven't got the money, your father, Sir Dando, has."

"He never parts with money."

"This time he will have to, or see his hopeful son go to prison for attempted murder."

Septimus Titmarsh turned deathly pale.

He began to realise what he had done, and that he was in the power of this common man.

Before this, Boler would not have dared to talk to him in such a way.

"Well," he exclaimed, after a pause, "I will get you the money on certain conditions, which I will name presently."

"That's the way to talk," responded Boler.

"How much do you want?"

"A hundred and fifty pounds. There is a little public-house in Windsor called the Royal Harry. It is free for beer and spirits, long lease, low rent, garden, fowl-yard, and piggeries, all at the sum stated; for months I have had my eye on it. I'm tired of barging, and want to settle down as my own master, that's the long and the short of it."

"The gentleman who was with me in the boat to-day will find that."

"Who is he?"

"Young Lord Goldenhurst."

"Rich?"

"As Crœsus," replied Septimus.

"Oh! if he is a rich lord, I must have two hundred and fifty," said Boler, who thought there was nothing like opening his mouth wide while he was about it.

He saw his chance, and did not mean to let it slip.

It might not occur again in a lifetime.

"Agreed," answered Septimus, who had not time to drive a bargain; "now for my terms."

"Name them."

"Jack Massey must die! It is for you to finish what I began."

Boler looked hard at Septimus and shook his head.

"No, thank you," he exclaimed; "not for me. I might be found out, and murder is a very dangerous thing. I've seen the inside of a prison, and I've seen a man hanged. Never shall I forget the pinioned wretch; his legs shaking under him as he was conducted to the scaffold. There was the tolling of the bell—boom, boom—the praying of the parson, the cap over the head. Ugh! it makes me shudder to recall the horrid scene."

"I did not think anything would affect you."

"That did."

"Will you bind him firmly, and, when it gets dark, put him on an island as you go up the river, and leave him to die ?"

"I don't mind doing that."

"It is a bargain, then ?"

"Right. Where shall I come for the money ?" enquired the ruffian.

"When will you be back in Windsor ?"

"To-morrow night. I am only going up as far as Marlow."

"Then I will meet you on the following day, after twelve, in the Long Walk, Windsor Park, and pay you."

"Good. If you fail, I shall go straight to your father, Sir Dando, and tell him all ; so keep faith with me and I will with you."

"You can depend on me."

"Enough said. I do."

Septimus shook his rough, horny hand and sprang on to the towing-path.

It was not safe for him to be seen talking to Boler.

There were several boats going through the lock, and it was time for him to be moving.

Indeed, there was nothing more to be said, the brutal compact was made.

But Rumbo had been an attentive listener.

Not a word had escaped Rumbo's ears.

"The brass is what I want," muttered Boler ; "but I'm not such a fool as to put my neck into a noose to get it."

He watched Sep go up to the lock-keeper, and guessed he was telling him about the accident.

Soon after, he saw a water-bailiff join them.

The drags were taken from the lock-house, and the bailiff and Sep got into a boat and went down stream.

Jack's body was to be dragged for.

There was no doubt that Septimus was acting his part in a very clever manner.

"Rumbo," cried Boler.

"Yes, guv'nor," replied the boy.

"Start the barge, take the tiller, and we'll be getting up river. I'm going below for a few minutes."

"Right you are."

The horse was quickly put in motion, and the lumbering barge was once more on its way up the winding Thames.

Boler descended the wooden ladder to the hole which was dignified by the name of a cabin.

He had to stoop when he got there,

or he would have knocked his head against the roof, for it was barely five feet high.

There was a stove, not lighted, a couple of three-legged stools, two bunks for sleeping, one on each side, a locker containing a little crockery, a frying-pan and a gridiron, as well as a saucepan for making stews.

It was inconceivably dirty, this cabin, and reeked with foul smells, which was not surprising, as it had not been cleaned out for years.

A pig would have disdained such accommodation, and a dog would not have lived in it if he could help it.

Jack was lying in one of the bunks with his eyes open, looking pale and wan.

He had come to at last.

The wound on his head had stopped bleeding, no fracture of the skull had taken place, and he was only suffering from weakness and shock to the system.

"Where am I ?" he asked, when he saw Boler.

"On a barge," was the reply. "I saw you swamp, and picked you up. We are on the way to Marlow."

"Something knocked me on the head," continued Jack. "What was it ?"

"I don't know."

Jack looked at him in the imperfect light which came down the hole where the ladder was.

"Haven't I seen you before, somewhere ?" he demanded.

"Not as I knows on, master."

"Yes, I have. You are the bargee I licked at Clewer, when Sep Titmarsh set you on."

Boler uttered a curse.

"Suppose I am, what then ?" he replied. "Haven't I just saved your life ? doesn't that sound friendly ?"

Jack looked extremely sceptical.

"I don't know," he said ; "it is odd to be picked up by you, of all persons in the world, just as Titmarsh had capsized my boat. Give me a drop of brandy, and put me on shore at once."

At this request Boler laughed loudly, as he took a seat on one of the three-legged stools.

"Think you're at a hotel, don't you ?" he answered. "Want to be a swell in full bloom when you haven't a shilling to pay for it."

"Not at all. Your class of men live on stimulants and tobacco. You would always be tipsy if you could afford it. As a rule, you have generally some kind of liquor stowed away."

"True, I've a drop of gin, but I mean to drink it myself. None for you, my young master," said Boler.

"That makes little difference; it shows bad feeling, however, and I cannot trust you, or believe anything you say."

"Did I ask you?"

"Hold your noise," cried Jack, impatiently. "Stop this old water-hearse of yours, and put me ashore."

Boler nodded.

"Yes, it is a hearse," he said, "that's in the manner of speaking, and I'll put you ashore presently."

"At once. I demand it at once," exclaimed Jack, in a peremptory tone of voice.

"Don't be in too great a hurry."

"You scoundrel, if I did not feel so weak, I'd punish you as I did once before."

Boler grinned until his big mouth yawned like an abyss.

He fumbled in his pocket.

Suddenly he drew forth a knife of the clasp order, which opened with a patent spring.

"Where should I be if I allowed you?" he asked. "What price me, mister gentleman? I'm not in Windsor now. This isn't the high road; you are in the cuddy of my barge."

"Yours?"

"If it isn't mine, I'm the captain of it, and can do as I like in it, youngster."

"What do you mean?"

"The time has come for us to understand one another," said Boler, fiercely.

Jack crouched back in the bunk.

For once in his life he was fairly startled.

It was evident to the meanest capacity that he was in the power of an unscrupulous ruffian.

If his life had been saved, it was for no good purpose.

"Ah! I see, it is a plot between you and Septimus Titmarsh," he exclaimed; "but beware how you trifle with me."

"I never trifle," replied Boler. "When I undertake to do a thing it is done thoroughly, as you will find out."

"Do you intend to take my life?"

"Not quite. Offer no resistance to what I am about to do, and all will go well with you."

He got up, and groping in the locker, produced a coil of rope.

It was growing dark now.

The sable shades of night were stealing over river, meadow, and upland.

From the water a white mist was rising, which threatened soon to hide everything from view.

"Now, the first thing you must do is to put your hands behind your back," said Boler; "I must bind them."

"What for?" asked Jack.

"Do as you are told, or——"

The wretch held up the knife.

His manner was too significant to be mistaken.

Jack felt too weak to resist, so smothering a cry of impotent rage, he obeyed the instructions given him, and was rendered helpless.

He was not strong enough to fight.

There was treachery written in the villain's face, and cruelty stamped on every lineament.

Boler made him sit on a stool while he drank nearly a tumblerful of some evil-smelling, vitriolic spirit which he poured from a case-bottle.

This deep potation sent the blood flying to his already rubicund face.

"Stay there," he said, "until my return; if you dare to move I'll floor you, bound as you are."

"That's a brave threat from a strong man," sneered Jack.

"I'll do it."

With a menacing look, the bargee went on deck and took in the surroundings.

Every bit of land on each side of the river was known to him.

He had been familiar with the scenery and currents for years, almost since he was a child, in fact.

The dim outline of an island was visible in the thickening mist.

"Stop the horse," he holloaed, "and you, Rumbo, steer close in shore, to get out of the stream's headway as much as you can."

The barge was at once stopped, and drifted in shore.

Then Boler called Jack Massey on deck.

"I'm going to land you," he said. "Come to the stern, when I will help you into the dingey."

"It will be dangerous, unless I am unbound," replied Jack.

"Not it."

"Can I trust you?"

"By heaven! you must, because you've no choice, my hearty."

Reluctantly Jack allowed himself to be guided to the stern and dropped into the little boat.

Boler followed immediately.

He slipped the painter, took up the sculls, and rowed across the river, the boat being watched by Rumbo as long as he could see it.

What was passing in the boy's mind was not easily discernable in his features.

He was calm and impassive, apparently engaged in watching the bats fly about over the water in eccentric circles.

Boler rowed to the island, fastened the boat to a willow bough, and put Jack on the shore.

"This is the Berkshire side," remarked Jack, "or I am mistaken."

"It is neither," answered the bargee, bluntly; "you are on an eyot."

"What's the good of that to me, when I can't swim with my hands tied?"

"No good at all, I should say, if you ask me."

"Is this a vile trick?"

"Now," exclaimed Boler, "ain't you hard on a feller? Didn't you ask to be landed, and here you are."

"But you admit that I am on an island," replied Jack. "Night is coming on; I may holloa myself hoarse and no one will hear me"

"No, they won't."

"Why not?"

"Because I'm going to tie your legs together and stuff some grass so tight in your mouth that you can never holloa."

This threat almost petrified Jack with horror.

It was equivalent to a sentence of death—death by lingering starvation.

Better, far better, would it have been if Boler had suffered him to drown, or killed him with his knife on board the barge.

"You surely cannot be so inhuman," he remarked through his chattering teeth.

"It's business with me," rejoined Boler, "and good biz, too."

"My father will pay you anything in reason if you let me go free."

"I am paid already."

"Then I know who is at the bottom of this outrage. I have to thank Septimus for it. If I live, a day of reckoning shall come."

"If!" repeated Boler, with a coarse laugh; "dismiss that idea from your mind. I won't shed your blood, but I'll do for you all the same. Step on a bit further. You'll be out of sight among these osiers."

"Wretch!" cried Jack; "I hope you will not die in your bed. May the hangman strangle you, villain that——"

His further utterance was cut short by Boler catching hold of him, flinging him on the ground, and stopping his mouth with dry grass.

"Stop your jaw!" hissed the ruffian, "I can't abear the word of hangman, it always makes my flesh creep."

A hollow groan died away in Jack's throat.

He felt as if he were already passing through the Valley of the Shadow of Death.

Boler hurried him along to a clump of osiers, pushing him down on the ground and passing a piece of rope round his feet.

Unable to move or speak, Jack could not have been in a more pitiable condition.

Those who might happen to be on the river the next day, could neither hear nor see anything of him.

As it was not the picnicing season, no one was likely to land on the island.

"You'll do," muttered Boler. "Now we are square for that smack on the mouth you gave me. If you get out of this fix I'll eat my head."

Lighting his pipe, the bargee walked back to the dingey, got in, and returned to the barge as silently as he had left it.

The island died away in the mist.

"Now, boy, on we go!" cried Boler.

An unusually dark night set in.

Rumbo was ordered to light the lanterns, and Boler expressed his intention of stopping to daylight at the next lock.

This was not more than a mile off.

Meanwhile Jack Massey was left to perish.

His only companions were the water-rats, the bats, and the screech-owls.

CHAPTER VII.

THE RESCUE.

IN due time the barge reached the lock, and was safely moored in smooth water.

The horse was turned into a piece of meadow land where it could graze, the boy in charge crept behind a haystack to sleep, Rumbo crawled into a bunk, and Boler sat in the cabin smoking and drinking by the light of a lantern.

He could not rest.

His mind was ill at ease, and bitter thoughts tormented him.

The spirits he was imbibing getting into his head, did not improve his already irritable temper.

He talked to himself, cursing and swearing.

Rumbo began to snore loudly, which angered Boler, who took up a stool and threw it at him.

It struck him on the forehead, raising a bump as big as a pigeon's egg.

Of course, the pain arising from the blow was considerable.

"Hullo!" he cried, "who's that chucking bricks?"

"It's me, you hard-snoring young whelp," replied Boler. "What do you mean by it, eh? tell me that."

"How could I help it? Suppose I rolled over on my back."

"You did it a-purpose."

"No I didn't," answered Rumbo, "and you've no call to hit a chap like that."

"I'll do it again if you sauce me, and worse to," threatened Boler.

"Will you? I'll let you see I've got a spirit as well as you, though you've never thought so."

Boler glared at him, astonishment being mingled with anger.

He was half-maddened by the vile gin he had been drinking.

In his temper he felt as if he could commit murder.

Was this the quiet youth who had never dared to contradict him, or go against his will in any way?

"Don't rile me," he said, "I'm not myself to-night, and I don't want to hurt you."

"Liar!" retorted Rumbo, who was fairly roused; "it's always been a kick or a blow first with you, and a word afterwards."

"Ain't I treated you kind, you fool?"

"Far from it. My life has been one long misery with you."

"Didn't I take you off the streets when it was snowing, and you freezing with cold, without a bit of boot to your foot?"

"It would have been better to let me die in the snow," replied Rumbo.

"There's gratitude for you," exclaimed Boler; "blowed if ever I do a stroke of good ag'in to anybody."

"What do I get from you?" asked Rumbo.

"Vittles and shelter."

"The coarsest of food, the hardest of work, vile language, beatings, and no pay; it won't do any longer."

"Look here!" said Boler, "didn't I tell you that you were to be my apprentice for three years, and then I'd give you a shilling a day, with a rise in the screw every year?"

"The time is up."

"When?" asked Boler.

"To-day. For three years have I been your drudge. I'll have no more of it. Get another lad who'll stand it as I've done."

The bargee lowered his tone at this speech.

He did not want to lose Rumbo, who was very useful to him.

"Why, you ain't talking of leaving me, are you?" he replied. "I'll treat you up to the nines in future. Your pay shall begin, and I'll give you the same food as I have myself."

"It's too late," answered Rumbo. "You've had me for a fool and a slave long enough."

"D'ye mean that?"

"As sure as I'm sitting up in this bunk, old man," rejoined Rumbo. "You'll have to get another to do your work."

The ruffian uttered a terrible oath.

He took a long drink out of the bottle.

The veins on his forehead swelled, and his bloodshot eyes nearly started from their swollen sockets.

"I ain't to be defied," he exclaimed. "You ought to know me well enough by this time, and if you don't keep quiet and snooze again, I'll kill you."

Rumbo sprang out of the bunk.

He was very thin, owing to bad, insufficient food and everlastingly hard work, but well-made and agile.

"Will you?" he remarked. "Come and try it, old man. I'm game for you."

Boler hesitated.

"I can't make it out," he muttered; "it's a puzzle that fairly staggers me. What's come into the chap? He can't have been drinking."

"I've been thinking, not drinking," said Rumbo, who caught the words. "Yes, thinking what a fool I am."

"Of course you are, to quarrel with your best friend. Now you're talking sense. Let it drop."

"Not me. I shall leave you to-morrow, as soon as it's light. Don't you trouble after me, as you've no claim, and I sha'n't never come back," said Rumbo, who seemed terribly in earnest.

He was a realisation of the proverb that "Still waters run deep."

For a long time he had hated Boler, longing to get away from his tyrannical thraldom.

Rumbo moved towards the ladder.

"Where are you off to?" asked Boler.

"I'm going to pitch on deck," was the reply.

"Don't risk your precious life a-sleeping in the fog."

Rumbo laughed harshly.

"A lot you've thought about my precious life," he said. "If I hadn't as many lives as a cat, I'd have been dead long ago through your rearing."

"Didn't I rescue you?"

"We've heard enough about that."

"I won't let you go; I'm your keeper. Look here."

Boler drew out the knife he had shown to Jack Massey, whereupon Rumbo made a dash up the ladder.

It was very dark as we have said.

In a moment Boler plunged after him.

"I'll stick him," he roared. "I'll settle him this night; he knows me. I'm not to be defied."

He stumbled half-way up the ladder and fell in a heap.

This did not disconcert him.

Putting the knife between his teeth, he seized the ladder with both hands, and succeeded in getting up.

By this time he was frantic with rage.

Nothing was to be seen of Rumbo.

"Where are you?" he yelled. "Answer me, you devil's imp, and I'll mark you for life."

There was a sound of mocking laughter on the other side of the barge.

"Come on, old man," said Rumbo.

A tarpaulin covered the cargo.

With difficulty Boler climbed over it.

He took up a lantern which was hanging to the side of the barge, and holding it aloft, looked around him.

Here, there, and everywhere, he peered and pried.

At last he saw Rumbo standing erect and fearless.

"Are you going below?" demanded Boler, hoarsely.

The reply was in the negative, given distinctly and firmly.

"Look out, then, it's you or me this time."

As he spoke, Boler, with the knife upraised in his hand, rushed upon the boy, who was dimly visible in the light of the lantern.

Suddenly Rumbo stepped lightly on one side.

The impetus Boler had given himself was too great to be stopped.

He went blundering over the side of the barge into the cold, inky water.

There was a loud splash.

This was followed by a piercing cry for help.

Rumbo remained perfectly motionless.

If he had had any desire or inclination to assist his cruel task-master, he could not have done so, the darkness was so dense.

He listened attentively for further sounds.

The cries for help continued, but they grew fainter and farther off till they died away altogether.

There was little doubt that the bargee had failed to find the land, and was being carried down the river by the stream.

How long his strength would endure, Rumbo could not tell, but that he would finally be drowned, if not rescued, he had no doubt.

In this sad termination to an ill-spent life, the boy certainly had borne no active part.

Boler had been the aggressor all through.

He had brought his fate on himself entirely.

Rumbo, as he stood motionless on the deck of the barge, could feel his heart beat wildly.

Was he to be delivered from worse than Egyptian bondage, or become once more this man's slave?

At last his idea that Boler was drowned became a certainty.

If the wretched man had gained the shore, he would have instantly returned to the barge.

To Rumbo's great delight, the mist began to roll away before a breeze which sprang up.

The stars became visible, and the moon rose.

Going aft he got into the dingey and sculled to the shore.

There was no necessity for him to go into the cuddy for his clothes, as all he had were on his back, and the only change of linen he possessed was with the washerwoman at Windsor.

When he landed he sought the driver-boy, who had previously informed him that he was going to sleep under the haystack.

Waking him up, he said:

"Dick!"

"What is it? time to move? Seems to me I've only just closed my eyes."

"I've bad news for you."

"Don't say it. Has the old tub been run into and sunk?"

"Worse than that."

"Anything wrong with the master?" Dick enquired.

"That's just it. He's got drunk and fell overboard. I'm afraid he's drowned, but I'm going to look for him."

"He'll be no loss if he isn't never found."

"You mustn't talk like that. I'll do my best to find him. If I don't I shall go on to Windsor."

"What shall I do with the barge?" Dick asked.

"Stay by it. I'll acquaint the owner and he will send help to take it up the river to Marlow," replied Rumbo.

"I shall be awfully lonely, and I ain't got not a coin to buy any food."

"Here's sixpence for you, it's all I possess. The lock-keeper will talk to you. Bear up, I may be back with Boler."

"No," said the driver-boy, "I can see from your manner that you think he's gone to the mole country. However, I'll finish my nap, for I'm dead for sleep."

It was not to be wondered at, poor fellow.

Driving a barge horse is killing work, and the boy was wasted away almost to a shadow.

There must be people for every vocation, or the world's work would come to a standstill.

Yet, surely, driving a barge horse from early morn to dewy eve, in all weathers, sunshine and storm, is the worst of all.

Rumbo, having given this timely intention as to the state of the affairs to Dick, once more entered the dingey.

It now became apparent what his purpose was.

He sculled down the stream by the aid of the silvery moonlight, not stopping until he arrived at the island which Boler had taken Left-handed Jack.

Although he kept a good look-out, he could see nothing of the bargee.

Securing the dingey, he stepped out and whistled shrilly.

There was no answer.

"Hi!" he cried, "is there anybody here?"

Still an awful repelling silence, and a solitude which seemed to make itself felt.

Then a soul-chilling fear took possession of the lad.

"He has killed him, as he would have done me," he murmured.

Rumbo was in search of Jack Massey.

He had hoped to find him alive, but now he dreaded lest he should only discover his corpse.

Almost in despair, he walked up and down, looking under trees and osiers, calling out occasionally, and stopping for a reply.

Hark!

He heard what resembled a smothered groan.

With a palpitating heart he hurried forward.

A joyous exclamation escaped his lips.

In front of him was the prostrate body of Jack Massey.

The movement of the latter's lustrous eyes, which followed every motion of the boy, sufficiently proved that he still lived.

Producing a knife, Rumbo cut the ropes which bound him.

Jack's first act was to raise his hand

"'PARDON ME; BUT WHAT DO YOU KNOW ABOUT IT?' ASKED SARATI."—(See page 67.)

to his mouth and take out the grass which had acted as a gag.

He then rose to a sitting position with difficulty.

Lying on the damp ground had cramped him.

For a brief space he was unable to speak, for his mouth seemed set.

A vigorous rubbing enabled him to move it, and he said :

"I don't know who you are, or how you found me ; but, from the bottom of my heart, I thank you."

"I am Boler's boy," replied Rumbo.

"Ah ! yes ; now I recollect. I saw you on the barge. You were steering, I think ? "

"Yes, sir."

"How is it you have come to my help, and where is Boler ? " asked Jack.

The blood began to circulate again, till he felt it tingling at his finger-tips.

"Boler is dead," Replied Rumbo.

"Heaven's vengeance has been swift upon the ruffian."

"You may well say that. After he left you here, he got drunk and attacked me, and while trying to stab me, he fell overboard, and I have every reason to think he is drowned."

"Can you account for his conduct to me ?" continued Jack.

"Oh! yes. A young gentleman came on board at Boveney, offering to pay him well to finish you."

"To kill me ? Great heavens ! What was he like ? "

Rumbo gave an accurate description of Septimus Titmarsh.

"My enemy! And has he taken at last such desperate means for revenge ? I can understand it all now," said Jack.

"Boler thought me very quiet, timid, and foolish," added Rumbo ; "but I listened and took in all that was said between them. I have long been tired of Boler's villainy, wishing to get away."

"What did they say ? "

"The young gentleman had hit you on the head with his oar as your boat capsized."

"I thought as much."

"Boler fished you out of the water, on to the barge with a boat-hook, and carried you below for his own revenge."

Jack saw now that Septimus tried to drown him under the disguise of an accident ; that Boler, in passing, saved him for his own ends, and that Septimus had made a bargain with the bargeman to put him out of the way for a money reward.

"Have you anything else to tell me ?" he queried.

"Boler was to have met the young gentleman about twelve o'clock, the day after to-morrow, to receive the money promised him."

"Where ? " demanded Jack, eagerly.

"In the Long Walk, Windsor Park, sir."

"Good ; I will be there. He will think it my ghost—ha ! ha !—that will be a rare bit of sport. I'll punish him in my own way," said Jack.

"I had made up my mind to help you, sir, if I could, from the first," continued Rumbo. "I'm only a poor boy without friends or home, but I'm honest, and know what's right and just."

"You have never been a thief, or mixed up in Boler's rascally transactions ? " enquired Jack, eyeing him searchingly.

"Never, sir ; I swear it. My character is all I've got in the world."

"In that case, I engage you."

Rumbo's face lighted up with undisguised pleasure.

"You engage me, sir ? "

"Yes," added Jack, "you shall be my boy in future. I will get you a place in my school, and when I go into the army, after growing up, you shall join the same regiment."

"Thank you ; I wish nothing better," replied Rumbo.

"We must walk back to Windsor. I shall stay to-night and to-morrow at my father's house, and keep dark ; everyone shall think I am dead."

"If you are weak, I can row you in the dingey."

"Very well, that will be better. We can land at the bottom of my father's garden, and get in unperceived."

This being settled, they walked to the boat, got in, and proceeded down the river.

Jack could not help chuckling to think how he would turn the tables on Septimus Titmarsh in a few hours.

What a surprise was in store for him.

The tables would be turned with a vengeance.

"I will drive him from the country," muttered Jack ; "he is like a pig in clover now, but he shall yet learn what it is to starve in the stubble."

CHAPTER VIII.

THE MEETING.

As they glided down the river in the stillness of the night, Jack and Rumbo exchanged confidences.

Jack told his new friend all about Septimus's hatred for him; he spoke also of Ada and Sarati.

In return, Rumbo related what he knew of his own life.

He recollected travelling with some gipsies in a caravan; but before that he had a vague remembrance of something better and brighter, of a big house, numerous servants, and kind parents.

It might be a dream, but he did not think so.

The gipsies were sent to prison for a robbery, and he was transferred to the workhouse, where the early days of his boyhood were passed.

At length he ran away, and was found in the streets, half perished with hunger and cold, by Boler.

Up to now he had been the obedient slave of the latter.

A new era seemed about to open before the boy, and he brightened at the prospect of better days.

"Perhaps you were stolen," said Jack.

"That is what I have always thought."

"Have you no clue to your parentage?"

"Only a very slight one, sir."

"What is that?"

Unbuttoning the collar of his flannel-shirt, Rumbo showed him a gold ring, suspended round his neck by a piece of faded riband.

It had a stone in the centre, on which was engraved the letter T, over which was a crest representing three swallows flying.

Reaching over, Jack deciphered the crest and monogram by the aid of the moonlight.

"How long have you had that?" queried Jack.

"Ever since I can remember. Certainly before I lived with the gipsies," replied Rumbo.

"It is a wonder they did not take it away in the workhouse."

"I never allowed anybody to see it."

"Do not part with it on any account," Jack exclaimed, looking at it with wonder.

"I did not when I was starving, and I am not likely to now I am under your protection."

"It may lead to the discovery of your identity. The three swallows represent a gentleman's crest. I will apply to an heraldic office."

"After all these years, would my father recognise me?" asked Rumbo.

"If you are a lost or stolen child, perhaps a fortune awaits you. Who can tell?" Jack answered.

These remarks set Rumbo thinking.

It would be strange, after all his vicissitudes, if a high destiny awaited the poor despised waif.

During the remainder of the journey Jack had great difficulty in keeping his eyes open.

The wound, added to the excitement and fatigue he had been subjected to, had almost overcome him.

His head nodded, his chin fell on his chest, and if he had not sat in the bottom of the boat, he would have gone overboard.

It was the dawn of day when the garden of his father's house was reached.

"There you are; pull to the right," cried Jack, who had roused himself, as if by instinct, on arriving at his home.

To his astonishment, he saw Captain Massey standing at the top of the steps looking wistfully at the river.

As the nose of the boat touched the steps, he sprang up and seized his father's hand.

The latter started, and the pallor of his careworn countenance vanished as if by magic.

"You!" he exclaimed. "You, Jack! Can I believe my eyes? Is it you in the flesh, alive and well, or does a ghost mock me?"

"I'm all right, dad," replied Jack. "Wait till you see me eat my breakfast, then you will see how much ghost there is about me."

"It is all over the town that you were drowned."

"Who told you?"

"Lambert—your friend, Dick; and Septimus has been expressing his deep regret that he and Lord Goldenhurst had run into you."

"The humbug."

"What?"

"They did it on purpose," said Jack; "And Sep hit me on the head with an oar. Do you see this scar?"

He pointed to his head, which was bare, his hat having been lost when he was plunged in the river.

"I do, indeed; you will carry it to your grave. Did young Titmarsh do that to you?" asked Captain Massey.

"Yes. I have a lot to tell you."

"So I should imagine."

"Tell the servants to say nothing to anybody about my turning up. I want it to be believed, for a day or two, that I really am drowned."

"What is your object?"

"I will inform you presently," replied Jack.

"It seems like a dream. Men were dragging the river for you till dark yesterday. I have offered a hundred pounds reward for your body," remarked Captain Massey.

"Isn't it more than I am worth, father?" asked Jack, with an arch look in his expressive eyes.

"You rogue," replied the captain, laughing. "You know the answer before you ask the question. You are worth your weight in gold to me."

Jack beckoned to Rumbo, who approached.

"Who is that?" enquired his father.

"My new boy. Real name unknown, parentage uncertain, but supposed to be a prince in disguise, or at least a long-lost nobleman."

"That sounds very romantic."

"I am going to find out the secret; he saved my life. If it had not been for his sagacity, I should have died miserably," Jack replied.

"Come inside, both of you," the captain said.

They followed him into the house, where an excellent breakfast was prepared for them with all rapidity.

Jack's supposed death by drowning had been kept from his mother, so that when she saw him she imagined he had come home from Manor Park School for a brief holiday.

While he satisfied his hunger, Jack related his adventures, which caused his father as much indignation as surprise.

"I should not have believed it of Septimus," he observed; "though he has a facial expression that denotes evil."

"When I see him, I shall speak plainly," replied Jack.

"You could have him arrested."

"I shall be satisfied if he will leave the country. England isn't big enough to hold him and me."

"Perhaps that will be the best plan. Shall I accompany you?"

"Thank you; no. I would rather do the business myself," answered Jack. "I have no fear of him."

This settled the matter, Captain Massey having every confidence in his son's judgment.

After breakfast Jack went to bed, and slept for ten hours without awaking.

Rumbo was accommodated in the servants' hall.

Jack's return home was kept a profound secret, according to his expressed desire.

He spent a pleasant evening with his father and mother, and after another long rest, felt as well as ever.

A strip of plaster on his head alone indicated that he had sustained any recent injury.

It was rather a dull, cloudy morning when Jack and Rumbo (the latter having got quite used to his new life already), started to meet Septimus Titmarsh.

The sun showed its face at intervals, but quickly retired, as if ashamed at being seen so early in the summer.

In the Long Walk the glorious old trees, the pride of Windsor, were in the full panoply of their attire.

About a quarter of a mile up Jack saw a youth whose figure resembled that of Septimus.

Nor was he mistaken in his surmise that it was he.

Septimus was waiting, agreeably to his appointment, to see Boler, for whom Lord Goldenhurst had procured the required sum of money by writing to his agent.

The cash was in bank-notes, secreted in Septimus's pocket.

He walked up and down, ever and anon looking eagerly for the bargee.

Suddenly Jack Massey burst upon his view, as he turned round expectantly.

He could not believe the evidence of his senses.

Had Boler deceived and played him false after his express agreement?

"Good morning, Mr. Titmarsh!" exclaimed Jack. "Are you in your usual health? What makes you tremble so?"

In fact, Septimus was trembling like a leaf.

He looked as if he was about to drop on the ground with terror.

His eyes rolled fearfully, and his mouth twitched convulsively.

"Good heaven, Massey, is it you?" he managed to reply. "I am really so glad to see you."

"Hypocrite as well as coward."

"I thought you were drowned, you know."

"What you mean is, that you hoped so; or, failing that, you expected I was put out of the way somehow by Boler."

"No, no. If he has t-told you so, do not credit him. It is a pack of falsehoods," stammered Septimus.

Jack laughed coldly.

"Don't trouble yourself to make excuses, my good fellow," he said. "I know all about it, and have Boler's boy here as a witness."

"His boy?"

"Yes. I was put on an island, bound, and left to perish; this lad saved me. You are in my power."

Septimus fell on his knees in an agony of apprehension.

He, in fancy, saw himself condemned to a long term of imprisonment.

In reality, he did not feel sure that the hangman's rope would not be put round his neck.

"Pardon, pardon!" he cried.

"You cannot expect any from me," Jack replied, sternly. "Your conduct has been too dangerously base for any forgiveness on my part."

The wretched youth held up his hands in supplication.

"Mercy, mercy!"

"There is but one chance for you," rejoined Jack.

"What is that?"

"Consent to leave the country within twenty-four hours and never return to it, or I hand you over to the police."

"I will go. Oh! yes, let me go. My father, Sir Dando, has been talking of sending me to Italy or Russia."

"I care not where you go; that is a matter of indifference to me. Do you accept my terms?" said Jack.

"A thousand times yes," answered Septimus; "and I give you a million thanks for you clemency."

"It is more than you deserve."

"I know it. You are acting like an angel."

Jack turned away in disgust.

"Don't talk in such a sickening manner," he cried, "you know you do not mean it."

"Indeed I do," replied Septimus, rising.

He felt as if an incubus had been removed from his mind.

"Am I to tell Sir Dando all?" he asked.

"If you do not I shall make it my business to do so," Jack answered.

"It will be a great blow for my father, who is far from well; he has been confined to his bed for some days," said Septimus.

"You should have thought of that before you plotted against my life, you villain. I have a good mind to give you a parting blow."

Septimus cowered before him.

"Don't, please, hit me with that terrible left fist of yours," he exclaimed.

As he spoke he held up his hand.

A ring on the third finger attracted Jack's attention.

"Let me have a look at that ring, if you please," he exclaimed.

Septimus removed it from his finger.

"You can have it, if you like," he said; "it is our crest and monogram. I make you a present of it."

Eagerly Jack took it, and his eyes opened with astonishment.

"You can go now," he continued. "Mind, our compact is made; break it at your peril, and you go to prison, perhaps for life."

Bowing his head in token of acquiescence, Septimus slunk away like a whipped hound.

His doom had gone forth.

Henceforth he was a fugitive, an exile, an outcast from his country.

Though his punishment was hard to bear, he had well merited it.

When he was gone, Jack asked Rumbo to let him see his ring.

It was instantly produced.

Jack carefully compared the two.

"My boy," he exclaimed, "Providence has thrown something of the utmost importance in our way."

"How is that, sir?" enquired Rumbo.

"We are on the eve of a great discovery," replied Jack.

The boy looked at Jack with the utmost astonishment.

"What have you found out, sir?" he asked.

"Just this," replied Jack; "these two rings are precisely similar; look for yourself."

Rumbo did so.

On each ring were the three swallows and the initial T.

"Septimus admitted that this was his family crest," continued Jack, "and it is my impression that you are a Titmarsh."

"Is that good for me, or bad?" inquired Rumbo.

"Time alone can tell," answered Jack. "Sir Dando is very rich; let us go and see him."

"Perhaps you are mistaken after all."

"If so, no great harm will be done," Jack replied. "Come!"

Jack was elated at the discovery he had made, and Rumbo was greatly excited.

They walked quickly to Sir Dando's house.

Septimus had arrived before them, and was looking out of the window.

Raising his hand, Jack beckoned to him.

Opening the door, he admitted his unwelcome visitor, wondering what he could want.

The unlucky youth dreaded that there was more trouble in store for him, nor was he mistaken.

CHAPTER IX.

THE SECRET OF THE RING.

"CAN I see your father?" Jack asked.

"Yes," replied Septimus. "He is reclining on the sofa in the morning-room. Do not excite him, he is very shaky."

"I fear that I cannot help causing him some excitement."

"It may prove fatal to him at any moment."

"Why so?"

"His heart is affected," answered Septimus.

"Have you told Sir Dando about your going abroad?" inquired Jack, "and, if so, what does he say?"

"If it be really necessary, and for my good, I might go to-day, if I like, and he will make me an allowance of two hundred a year. When you knocked, I was trying to persuade him to make it three."

"It may be, you will not get so much as two, when he hears what I have to say."

Septimus looked at him with spite in his eyes.

"Don't make mischief," he exclaimed. "I am willing to leave you alone, but I can still be your bitter enemy. Recollect, when my father dies, I shall be Sir Septimus Titmarsh, with plenty of money; and, in this age, money can do almost anything."

"I am not so sure of that."

"What do you mean?"

"Wait a little while, and you will find out, my dear fellow. Show me in. Come, Rumbo."

Septimus looked contemptuously at the poorly-dressed boy.

"You cannot take that beggar's brat into my father's room," he said.

"That is just what I intend to do," Jack replied.

"Are you mad?"

"Not by any manner of means. Lead on, or I go without you."

Greatly disgusted, and filled with surprise, Septimus did as he was requested.

Sir Dando, looking very pale, thin, and ill, was reclining on a lounge.

He raised his head as the three entered.

"Massey wishes to speak to you, father," exclaimed Septimus.

"I wish he would spare me the interview, unless it is very urgent," answered Sir Dando in a faint voice. "You have told me what has occurred; it is extremely regrettable, but I have arranged for you to go away in accordance with his request."

"Pardon me, Sir Dando," replied Jack, "I have come on another matter, and shall feel glad of a few minutes' conversation."

"Then oblige me by being brief."

Rumbo, cap in hand, was standing near the door.

The baronet took no heed of him; indeed, he did not seem to have noticed his presence in the room at all.

"Did you lose a child in its infancy?" Jack asked.

"Yes, I did," was the quick answer. "How did the fact come to your knowledge? My wife never recovered from the shock; it was my eldest son, and he was supposed to have been stolen by gipsies. I offered a large reward, but never got any tidings of him. I had been hard on the gipsies. I prosecuted them as vagrants, and for poaching. The deed was supposed to be done out of revenge."

"Would you be surprised to hear that your eldest son is alive?"

Sir Dando started up.

His eyes flashed with an unwonted fire.

"Good heavens!" he cried, "you do not mean to say you have found him after all these long years?"

"That is my meaning," rejoined Jack.

"There was one clue to the boy," continued Sir Dando, "and that was my signet ring, which his mother, Lady Titmarsh, had hung round his neck, attached to a piece of riband."

Jack beckoned to Rumbo.

"Come forward," he said.

The boy immediately presented himself.

A striking likeness between him and Sir Dando was at once perceptible.

Anyone could have seen that they were father and son.

"Here is the ring!" exclaimed Jack, pointing to the one Rumbo wore.

The baronet examined it carefully, and asked a number of questions, all of which were answered promptly and truthfully.

He was told how Jack and Rumbo became acquainted, and the names of the gipsies were given among whom Rumbo had lived, which the baronet recollected perfectly.

"His face is like what I recollect mine to have been when a boy. There is little doubt he is my son," said Sir Dando, "the heir to my title and my property, which, years ago, was settled on the first born. Give me your hand, boy. What are you called?"

"Rumbo," was the reply.

"That is something near your real name, for you were christened Dando after me. You are two years older than Septimus, your brother."

The boy's eyes filled with tears.

His recognition by his father, the sudden change in his position and condition, the knowledge that he belonged to a good and rich family, overcame him entirely.

He sank into a chair, covering his face with his hands.

"Bear up," said Sir Dando; "you will find that I shall do my duty by you."

At hearing these revelations, Septimus became furious.

His face was convulsed with rage, and he trembled in every limb.

Sir Dando had taken his long-lost son by the hand, which he was holding in an affectionate manner.

Rushing forward, Septimus separated them rudely.

"You shall not recognise this impostor," he said; "it is a plot of Jack Massey's. Are your title and money to go to a beggarly scamp who worked on a barge? I will not suffer it."

"Calm yourself," replied Sir Dando. "I believe he is my eldest son. I have my doubts about you, but you shall be provided for."

"I can go abroad and starve."

"If you have to become an exile, you have only your evil passions to thank for it."

"And Jack Massey," said Septimus; "but I will be revenged. He is not going to get rid of me so easily as he thinks."

Jack now thought it was time to interfere.

"I have accomplished the task I took in hand," he exclaimed, "which was to restore to you your son, and I will retire. If you wish him to stay with you, he can do so; if not, I will care for him, but rest assured that I will protect his rights."

"There is no occasion to do so," rejoined Sir Dando; "he shall stay with me, and fill the vacancy that Septimus's absence will cause."

"I will not allow it," cried Septimus.

"You cannot help yourself," said Jack. "One word from me will consign you to a living tomb, for such is a convict's fate."

"Am I to be robbed of title, home, and money?"

"Yes; that is your just punishment."

Young Dando—for such we shall call him in future, that being his real name—had recovered from his emotion.

"Father," he exclaimed, "I am deeply sensible of your kindness, and am quite ready to let my brother share with me."

"Brother!" replied Septimus, scornfully, "you are no brother of mine, and I will not admit such a thing."

"Your father is satisfied, why are not you?" asked Jack.

"It is an outrageous swindle, and you are at the bottom of it."

"Don't call me a swindler."

"Bah!" hissed Septimus, in a venomous manner, "you and this fellow, Rumbo, or Jumbo, or whatever you call him, ought to be prosecuted for conspiracy to defraud me of my rights."

The baronet held up his hand, which trembled as if with the palsy.

"Do you want to hasten my death by quarrelling?" he asked. "If you persist in showing this vile temper, I will disinherit you, and you shall work for your daily bread."

"Thank you," sneered Septimus, "I have a friend who will provide for my wants."

"He means Sarati," said Jack.

"What does it matter to you who I mean?" demanded Septimus, angrily. "I do not ask you to keep me. Before I go, though, I will settle accounts with this usurper."

His temper had now got entirely beyond his control.

The blood rushed to his head.

He seized a heavy stick which stood in a corner, and ran up to Dando.

"You are no brother of mine!" he yelled; "I will never call you so. Never, never!"

Jack endeavoured to step between them, but before he could do so, Septimus felled Dando to the floor.

The blow was delivered with all his strength.

Dando sank like a log, insensible, covered with blood.

"Wretch!" cried Sir Dando, "what have you done?"

"I should not care if I had killed him," was the callous reply.

"Never let me see you again."

"You will all hear of me—yes, even to your death."

With these defiant words, Septimus ran to the door, and rapidly made his way out of the house.

Jack was about to follow.

"Let him depart; it is better so," exclaimed Sir Dando. "I have been cherishing a viper. My heart is broken!"

"If you have lost one son, another is brought to you," replied Jack, as he raised Dando.

It was with difficulty that he stanched the flow of blood.

A great gash was visible on his forehead.

The scar was one which he would carry with him to the grave, if he survived the injury.

"I think you had best get a doctor, Massey, if you will be so kind," said Sir Dando. "This is my only son, now. I discard the other."

"He is coming to," answered Jack.

"Yet, a doctor's care he needs. Ring the bell."

Jack rang the bell, and a domestic was despatched for a neighbouring surgeon.

"I am very grieved and vexed to know that my unworthy son, Septimus, has treated you so badly," remarked Sir Dando.

"All that I can afford to ignore."

"But not forgive, eh?"

"Well, sir," said Jack, "to be candid with you, I cannot forgive, because I know that Septimus will do me all the harm he can."

"He is going abroad, you know."

"To Italy?"

"Yes, or Russia. Dear me! Perhaps he will become a brigand."

Jack laughed.

"Under Sarati's leadership, he ought to be a big success," he replied.

"Ah! me," sighed the old man, "I have tried to be a good father in the absence of his mother, but he has turned out a bad son."

Tears coursed down his face.

He was terribly agitated by what had occurred.

"Shall I call him back, sir?" asked Jack. "You have only to say the word, and I will put my feelings in my pocket."

"No, no. It is best he should go."

At this juncture the doctor arrived.

He made an examination of the wound on Dando's head.

His face became very grave as he proceeded.

"Is there any hope, doctor?" asked the baronet, anxiously.

"He will live," was the reply.

"What is it?"

"Concussion of tho brain."

The baronet uttered a cry of agony.

"Do not tell me that," he said; "it was his brother who did the deed, and——"

The doctor interrupted him.

"I must tell you the truth," he exclaimed, "however painful it may be to hear it."

"Well?"

"It is a terrible blow. I fear that he will be an imbecile for life."

"Heaven help me!" groaned Sir Dando in a tone of anguish; "both of my sons are lost to me!"

It was a terrible prospect.

Septimus had fled, the newly-found boy was threatened with idiocy.

With a heart-broken cry, Sir Dando fell on the floor, and Jack, who had done all that he could, went to his father's house to inform him of what had happened.

He did not intend to return to school till the next day.

Sir Dando and his son were left in the doctor's hands.

CHAPTER X.

THE GLOVE-FIGHT.

SLAVIN and Dawson had lingered in the schoolroom after the other boys had sought the cricket-field and the playground.

It had just struck the hour of twelve.

Three days had elapsed since Jack was reported to be drowned.

"I say," exclaimed Slavin, "we have got rid of Massey without much trouble. He will no longer be a terror to the school."

"As far as I am concerned, I am not sorry," replied Dawson. "His left-handed blows were a caution. I suppose he really is drowned, though they have not found the body?"

"Of course he is. The body is lying in some hole, and will not rise to the surface for seven days."

"Who told you so?"

"Spoofer; he heard in the town that this was the general opinion."

"Then your glove-fight will not come off?"

"It does not look like it, although I am disappointed; because, with Sarati's help, in putting lead in the gloves, I should have knocked him out of time easily."

"You might have been bowled out."

"What?" laughed Slavin, "with Sarati at the back of me? not much."

"How was it to be managed?"

"In the simplest manner. After I had knocked him senseless in the first round, I was to throw the gloves on the floor. Everybody's attention would be centred on Massey. Sarati would then take up the loaded ones, and put another pair in their place."

"A good dodge."

"Rather. What do you think?"

"I wish the event had come off," Dawson said.

At this moment Dick Lambert came into the schoolroom, looking very ill and disconsolate.

Since Jack's disappearance he had been thoroughly miserable.

The friendship existing between them had been of a very firm and enduring character.

He went to his desk and took out a book.

"Have you heard any news of Massey?" asked Slavin.

"None whatever. I wish I had," replied Dick; "he was the best fellow that ever came to this school, or any other."

"That's your opinion."

"And I mean to stick to it," said Dick Lambert, with flashing eyes. "I will fight anyone who dares to say a word against him."

"If you fought me you would get the worst of it."

"Try it," replied Dick. "I'll stand up as long as I can."

Slavin walked up to him in his rude, insolent, overbearing manner.

"Aren't you getting very cocky?" he demanded.

"Give it him," replied Dawson; "he hasn't got his left-handed friend to protect him now, and it is about time he was taken down a peg."

"So I think," said Slavin.

The schoolroom was not a good place to fight in, as it was encumbered with forms and desks.

This did not matter in the least degree to Slavin.

"Mind yourself," he added.

Dick put himself on the defensive, but Slavin got within his guard and delivered a blow which knocked him down.

He rolled over a couple of forms, making a great clatter.

"Ha, ha!" laughed Slavin, "you are a pretty fellow to fight."

"I can't help it if I am not as strong as you," answered Dick.

"Come on again."

"Not if I know it. It is not fair to fight in a place like this."

"You're a coward. If you can't fight, don't talk."

"If poor Massey were alive you wouldn't dare to threaten me."

"Oh, indeed! shouldn't I? Who cares for him?" asked Slavin.

"You did, and you would again, if he were here," retorted Dick, who got up and wiped the blood away from his face.

Slavin walked up to the blackboard.

He took up a piece of chalk, and drew a rude picture of a donkey with prodigiously long ears.

Underneath he wrote — "Jack Massey, Nature's masterpiece."

"There is your friend's epitaph," he said. "What do you think of it?"

Dick's face glowed with honest indignation.

"What do I think of you? ought to be the question," he rejoined.

"Well, I should like to know," said Slavin.

Dick looked steadily at him.

"You are a low-minded beast to insult the dead," he exclaimed. "I wonder Jack Massey's ghost does not haunt you."

"Ghosts are all nonsense."

"Are they? Guilty consciences are often tormented by shadows."

"Oh! go and muzzle yourself," said Slavin. "Get out of here; I wish to talk to Dawson, and we don't want listeners."

"I came for a book."

"Take it and go, or I'll paste you again."

"The shoolroom is as much for me as it is for you," rejoined Dick Lambert.

"Throw a book at him," suggested Dawson.

"I'll throw a library at him if he does not make himself scarce."

Dick was overweighted in the contest, as he had two against him.

He did not care to be knocked about any more.

Consequently, he determined to curb his temper and take his departure.

As he moved towards the door, he was astounded to see a pale, ghastly-looking figure standing on the threshold.

No one had hitherto observed the ghostly-looking form.

A sheet enveloped it from the head to the feet, only the face being visible.

Dick Lambert could scarcely believe the evidence of his senses.

The face he saw was that of Jack Massey, whom he believed was lying dead at the bottom of the river.

Slowly the figure walked up the room to where Slavin and Dawson were standing.

The countenance was as stony as if it had been cut out of marble.

"Who are you?" demanded Slavin, in a shaky voice.

"I am the spirit of Jack Massey," was the reply in a sepulchral tone.

Slavin sank to his knees, the picture of abject terror.

The effect on Dawson was to make him crouch in a corner, while Lambert sat on a form.

What did it mean?

He was utterly at a loss to occount for the apparition, which had a terrifying effect on all three of them.

"Go away," said Slavin; "don't come here to torment me. What have I done to you?"

"Weren't you rejoicing in the fact of my death? Get up and face me," was the reply from the sheeted form.

"I dare not."

"You don't believe in ghosts, you know. Didn't you say just now they were all nonsense?"

"I—I do n—now," said Slavin with chattering teeth.

"In me you behold an avenger. Reflect on the past, and repent."

"I will, if you go away and leave me."

"Take that first," exclaimed the ghost, raising its left hand.

Slavin received a blow on the head which sent him rolling, half-stunned, on the top of Dawson.

The bully was unable to move for a time, and his toady did not dare to do so.

Dick Lambert rushed forward with outstretched hand.

His face beamed with smiles.

"Thank Heaven!" he cried, "ghosts don't hit out like that. Jack old fellow, how are you?"

The figure discarded the sheet, and Massey stood revealed before him.

"Alive and well, my dear boy," answered Jack.

"How did you escape? Where have you been——?"

Jack interrupted him.

"You shall hear all in good time," he said. "I have just come back to school, and did this for a lark. I saw you three in the schoolroom, ran up to the dormitories, chalked my face, got a sheet, and enveloping myself in it, stole upon you unawares."

"I am so glad to see you; words cannot express my feelings," replied Dick. "Oh! if you only knew how miserable I have been. Let us leave these curs; come out into the field, where we can have a talk."

"With pleasure."

They quitted the schoolroom.

The boys were playing cricket, but they did not go near them, as they wished to have a quiet conversation all by themselves.

Jack knew that his return would be bruited about soon enough.

That he would receive an ovation, he did not doubt, because he had already made himself popular.

Yet he did not care about that kind of thing.

While they walked under a row of trees, Jack told Dick everything that had occurred since he had been picked up by Boler and put on the barge.

"What a blow for Sep," said Dick; "he is nobody now."

"Not if his brother lives," replied Jack; "and if he dies, he will hardly dare to show his face in England, for he will have been guilty of manslaughter, and liable to be put in prison."

"So you think we have seen the last of the treacherous little beast?"

"Candidly, I do," answered Jack; "but I still fear Sarati, and am anxious about Ada."

Scarcely had he finished speaking than he noticed the Italian approaching arm-in-arm with Septimus Titmarsh.

They were closely engaged in earnest conversation.

So engrossed were they that they did not observe Jack and Lambert.

"Quick," whispered Jack, "get behind a tree; the villains are plotting."

"Right," answered Dick, "we may hear something to your advantage."

They rapidly ensconced themselves behind a large chestnut tree, which effectually hid them from observation.

It happened that Sarati and Septimus stopped close to their place of concealment.

"This is serious news you tell me," observed the Italian.

"After the attack on my newly-discovered brother I must fly," replied Septimus. "I might have baffled and defied Jack Massey. But this last affair is too serious to be treated lightly."

"Very true; it is unfortunate, indeed."

"But you do not blame me?"

"Not in the least; it was maddening to find yourself disinherited by a nobody, an outcast pauper."

"I would to Heaven this unwelcome brother would die," said Septimus in a bitter tone.

"Have you heard of his condition?" asked Sarati.

"Yes. I met one of our servants, and he informed me that he had concussion of the brain, and may never be quite sane again."

"But he will live."

"That is the worst of it. He will live to enjoy what would have been mine—to rob me of property and title."

"You have one consolation," said Sarati.

"What is that?"

"If he becomes imbecile, he cannot have any real enjoyment; all must be a hideous blank to him."

"Let us drop that subject," exclaimed Septimus, impatiently.

"At your pleasure," replied the Italian, in his suave manner.

Apparently, nothing irritated him, for it did not appear on the surface that he was annoyed, no matter what happened.

Yet there was a deep current of rage and plotting treachery running within his mind.

"Have you the money you promised me?" enquired Septimus.

"One hundred pounds," said Sarati.

He took from his pocket a bag of gold and handed it to him.

Septimus's face lighted up with a satisfaction he could not conceal.

This sum, with the two hundred Lord Goldenhurst had given him to pay Boler, and which he had retained, made him feel rich.

"You can have some more within a reasonable time," added the Italian; "but if you are going to paint, you must sell your pictures, and I think you have some talent that way, from what I have seen of your art."

"Thank you; that is understood. I shall not be always a drag on you," replied Septimus, biting his lip.

"When do you start for Naples?"

"To-night, by the express."

"Very well," continued Sarati; "go direct, on your arrival, to the 'Hotel Rè Galantuomo,' Number 19 in the Strada di Popolo."

Left-handed Jack made a note of this address.

It might be useful to him in the future.

"Are the people of that hotel friends of yours?" Septimus asked.

"Of long standing. I will join you in a week or two. There is something on foot in connection with our mutual enemy, Jack Massey."

"I am glad to hear that."

"Where you failed, my friend, I hope to succeed."

Jack clenched his hand.

"You cold-blooded villain!" he muttered.

He did not, however, disclose himself, though he felt inclined to do so.

There was more to be heard yet.

Of that he felt confident.

"Now we will talk about your charming sister, Ada," exclaimed the Italian, whose dark eyes sparkled as he mentioned the name of the girl he loved in such a passionate manner.

"I took her away from the school yesterday, when I left home," replied Septimus.

This was more news for Jack.

He was hearing something that interested him very much.

By learning the secrets of his foes, he might be able to foil them yet.

"Good," said Sarati. "How did you manage it?"

"I forged a letter in my father's hand-writing, stating that she was to come to his bedside, as he was very ill."

"Where is she now?"

"We went straight to London. She is at a hotel, awaiting my return. I told her that father was in Naples, and we were to join him at once."

"Excellent. Did she speak of Massey?" asked Sarati, rubbing his hands.

"She was anxious to bid him farewell, but I persuaded her that there was no time to be lost, and she would be back in a month," replied Septimus.

The Italian smiled benignantly upon him.

"I have great hopes of you, for you are a capital organiser for one so young," he observed.

"Now all is settled," said Septimus, "I will go back to London."

"How did you come?"

"By train to Staines, where I hired a horse and rode over to Windsor, coming here to see you, as I knew it was your day at the school, and that I should not find you at the gymnasium. I was afraid to be seen at the railway-station."

"Clever again. Where is your horse now?"

"In the road. I gave a boy sixpence to hold him. You must write to me. I shall be very anxious to hear about my brother, and how you get on in your operations against Massey."

"Depend upon me. My love to Ada. Speak well of me, and try to influence her in my favour!" exclaimed Sarati.

"She shall be your wife," answered Septimus. "I have told you so before, and I mean to keep my word."

"You will not find me ungrateful. *Santa Maria!* I will be a prince to you, and to her also."

They shook hands in the most friendly manner.

The field was separated from the road by a brick wall, in which was a door, which happened to be close by.

To this Septimus advanced, intending to leave by that way.

He had his hand on the handle, when Jack Massey stepped forward.

"Stop!" he cried.

Septimus cast a look of deadly hatred upon him.

"You here!" he replied. "What do you want with me? Was it not agreed upon that I was to go abroad? and I am going."

"I recall that promise I gave to you."

"What on earth do you mean by

playing fast and loose with me?" demanded Septimus.

"You shall only go if you restore Ada," said Jack.

"Ha! You know that she is with me?"

"I do. Give her up."

Septimus laughed scornfully.

"To you?" he cried. "Never!"

"Then, by Heaven, I will make you!" retorted Jack.

He rushed forward.

Septimus presented a pistol at him.

"Back!" he shouted, "or I will put a bullet in you."

At this threat Jack hesitated.

He knew that Septimus was desperate, and would not stop at anything to effect his escape and accomplish his ends.

Was it worth while to risk his life in the encounter?

A moment's consideration told him that it was not.

Taking advantage of his hesitation, Septimus Titmarsh turned the handle of the door and flung it open.

Then he dashed into the road.

His horse was standing close by.

In a moment he had seized the reins and was in the saddle.

"Villain," exclaimed Jack, "you will find that I shall triumph in the end."

Septimus deliberately presented the pistol at him again.

He pulled the trigger with a malignant scowl.

Bang!

Jack pressed his hand to his side, and staggered against the wall.

With a yell of savage triumph, Septimus gave his horse the rein, and was soon out of sight.

Sarati had discreetly vanished at the commencement of the altercation.

Seeing his friend fall, Lambert ran to his assistance.

"Heaven help us!" he cried. "Are you hurt again by that wretch?"

"I felt a shock," Jack answered, "but I am in no pain."

Dick hastily unbuttoned his waistcoat and examined his shirt.

There was no sign of blood on it.

"By Jove! I can't understand it!" said Dick.

Jack put his hand in his waistcoat-pocket and produced his watch.

The glass was smashed, and it was severely indented.

"My ticker stopped it," he exclaimed.

"Look here, at my feet, is the bullet. What do you think of that?"

"A most providential escape," said Dick. "You bear a charmed life, old fellow; but aren't you going to send the police after him?"

Jack shook his head.

"No use," he rejoined; "he will get to Staines long before the police can, and take the train for London."

"Still, you know his future address in Naples."

"That is where I will have him. I'll follow Sarati when he goes after Ada."

"Will you have the pluck and determination to do that?" asked Dick.

He gazed at him with admiration.

"You ought to know me well enough by this time," said Jack. "Haven't we been friends for years?"

"Certainly we have."

"Did you ever see me show the white feather?" continued Jack. "I tell you I will hunt that treacherous coward down, by following Sarati, and save Ada, who is the victim of an atrocious plot."

"Have you thought of the perils attendant on such a course of action?"

"Yes, but nothing shall stay me. I am determined to rescue Ada, and punish her foes and mine."

"Will you let me come with you?" asked Dick.

"It would not be fair to involve you in my danger; besides, it would cost money. My father is not rich; again, your parents might object to your going."

"Not they, if I state the case fairly."

"I can get money for myself and chance it," said Jack.

"So will I, if you will let me go."

"Very well, that is settled. I have no further objection to offer, but you will have to rough it."

"That I am not afraid of," replied Dick. "You will find me a faithful friend, and a good companion."

While talking, they had strolled towards the boys who were playing cricket.

Jack was at once recognised, and several of his schoolfellows crowded round him, congratulating him heartily.

He was asked how he had managed to escape from drowning.

In reply, he stated that he had been picked up, insensible, by a bargeman, and it was some time before he had recovered sufficiently to come back to school.

Gordon, the captain, was especially glad to see him.

"Give three cheers for Massey, boys," he exclaimed.

These were given with a will.

Slavin made his appearance, green with envy and rage.

He had got over his fright at the apparition of the supposed ghost.

"Here is Massey back again among us," exclaimed Gordon. "We have been cheering him with all the honours."

"Quite a dramatic surprise," replied Slavin; "got up on purpose, I suppose?"

Jack turned rather fiercely upon him.

"Why do you say that?" he demanded.

"A telegram only costs sixpence, and you might have relieved our alarm and anxiety at your reported death. The suspense we have been in has been something awful."

He put his handkerchief to his eyes and pretended to cry.

Dawson imitated his example.

Some of the boys thought this very comical, and began to laugh.

Jack was greatly enraged at this turn in affairs.

He could not bear to be ridiculed.

"Stop chaffing me," he exclaimed, "or I shall be under the painful necessity of punching your head."

"You need not do that," replied Slavin.

"Why not?"

"You have already accepted a challenge to box with the gloves."

"Ah!" said Jack, "so I have. I had forgotten that."

"Your memory is rather treacherous, I should imagine. Perhaps you are not so good with the gloves as you are with the naked fist?"

"That remains to be seen. I'm ready to face you whenever you like," replied Jack.

"If you wish to back out of it, I'm agreeable."

"Not I. Lambert shall be my second. What are the terms of the contest?"

"The one who gets the best of four rounds to be the winner," said Slavin. "Place—the school-yard; time—now. Signor Sarati, who is now at the school, to be referee. Is that fair?"

"I would rather not have Sarati—he is a villain who bears me no good will," answered Jack; "but no matter. I shall knock you out in one round."

"One round! You are over-confident in that steam arm of yours, as you choose to call it."

"I have never found it fail me yet."

"What a prize-fighter you would make," sneered Slavin.

"My dear fellow, I am a gentleman, and that is more than you will ever be."

Gordon touched Slavin on the arm.

"Don't quarrel here," he said. "It is bad form when you are going to have it out in another place directly."

"He treats me as if I knew nothing at all," was Slavin's answer.

"Come along, there is time for the glove-fight before dinner. We will all come and see it."

Slavin did not seem to relish this proposition.

"Thank you!" he exclaimed, "I don't want a lot of fellows. The seconds and the referee are quite enough for me."

"I have no objection to everyone witnessing the fight," remarked Jack. "Everything is fair as far as I am concerned."

"So it is with me; yet I do not want to make a public exhibition of myself, and if you insist upon it, why, the match is off."

"Come on," cried Jack, "you shan't sneak out of it that way. I can see what your game is."

"Don't talk in that absurd manner," Slavin retorted. "If you mean business, you will find me in the school-yard in ten minutes."

Taking Dawson's arm, he walked hastily up the field.

Knowing that he was going to attempt foul play, he did not want all the school to be on the spot.

Someone with quick eyes might see how it was done, and disclose the baseness of which he intended to be guilty.

"All right," observed Gordon, "we will go on with our game. I wish you every success, Massey, for I am sure you deserve it, as from what I have seen of you, it isn't in your nature to kick up a purposeless row with anybody."

"Indeed, it is not," replied Jack. "I always want to live in peace and amity with everyone."

"See you later. Don't imagine you will be hurt much by that big boaster."

"Don't trouble about me," said Jack, laughing lightly.

He and Lambert walked after his opponent, and the boys resumed their cricketing.

Our hero and his friend saw in the distance Slavin and Dawson sparring, while Sarati was looking on.

It seemed as if the Italian was teaching them something.

"Slavin is taking a lesson," remarked Dick.

"I don't care how much he learns," replied Jack. "I am sure to knock him out in two rounds, if I do not in one."

"If you do not lick him, I shall be disappointed."

"Don't fear for me," Jack said.

When they arrived on the scene of action, Sarati looked askance at our hero.

He did not know how much of his conversation with Septimus Titmarsh had been overheard.

He inclined to the opinion that Jack had come upon them suddenly, and heard nothing of any importance.

He determined to be civil, at all events.

"So glad to see you, Massey," he exclaimed; "it is quite refreshing to know that you are in the land of the living."

Jack bestowed a look of unmitigated disgust upon him.

"I don't suppose I should have been much loss to some people," he replied.

"We mourned you as one dead."

"It is a wonder you did not buy a black hat-band."

"Ah! you love your joke," said Sarati, with a smile. "Very good; shall we begin this little harmless fight to see who is best man?"

"As soon as you like."

"Here are the gloves. One pair for you, and a pair for Slavin. Now pitch in, as you boys say, and give one another the postman's knock—one—two."

The combatants were soon ready.

They donned the gloves and faced one another.

"He looks pale," remarked Sarati, alluding to Jack.

"So would you if you had gone through what he has," replied Dick.

"He is not strong."

"Think of the blood he lost when he got that cut on the head from the scull."

"I will bet five shillings on Slavin."

"Done. I take you," said Dick.

The fight now began in real earnest, after a little preliminary sparring.

Jack Massey, always impetuous, forced the fighting.

He broke down Slavin's guard and struck him on the chin, making his teeth rattle.

Sarati was eating an orange, and seemingly by accident, he threw the peel on the ground near Jack, who placed his foot on a piece.

This caused him to slip.

Before he could recover his balance, Slavin got at him.

With his right hand he struck him on the forehead, but fortunately the hit was more of a graze than anything else.

Yet it tore away the skin, and made the blood flow in a remarkable manner.

It was extraordinary for a glove to do a thing of that kind.

"Time!" cried Lambert.

"No, no," exclaimed Sarati, "the round is not yet over. I am the referee, and my decision is final."

"I will not allow it to go on."

"And why not, pray?"

"There is something unfair about this," continued Dick Lambert, "and I want to examine the gloves that Slavin is wearing."

"Monstrous," said Serati.

"Not at all. As a second, I demand an inspection, for I am under the impression that the gloves are unequal, and I want them weighed."

"What do *you* say, Massey?" asked Serati.

He had become ghastly pale.

"I place myself, unreservedly, in the hands of my second," was the prompt reply.

When he heard this, Dick manfully threw himself on Slavin.

With a clever trip, that would have delighted a Cornish or Cumberland wrestler, he threw him to the ground.

Slavin was unprepared for the attack.

He was half-stunned by the sudden fall.

Dick Lambert pulled off the glove on the bully's right hand.

He held it up.

Several pellets of lead fell to the earth.

"I have found out the trick," he cried. "Bully Slavin is a despicable coward! Treachery has been at work!"

"WHEN HE CAME TO HIMSELF A MAN WAS BENDING OVER HIM."—(See page 90.)

No. 5.

CHAPTER XI.

THE SECRET OF SIGNOR SARATI'S ENMITY TO CAPTAIN MASSEY IS REVEALED.

EVERYBODY present seemed to be astounded at the revelation made to them by the astuteness of Dick Lambert.

It was certainly a complete surprise to Jack and Dick, though the astonishment of the others was pretended.

"This requires explanation," exclaimed Jack. "I have been grossly deceived by somebody, and I want to know who is the culprit."

Slavin rose to his feet with an air of unconcern.

"I know nothing whatever about the matter," he replied.

"You must admit that the knuckles of the gloves were filled with lead."

"Perhaps Lambert put it there," Slavin said, coolly.

"That is ridiculous," answered Jack, "he had no time to do so."

"We have heard of conjuring tricks before now; sleight of hand, and all that kind of thing, you know."

"Don't talk such nonsense. I am going to get to the bottom of this affair, which, in my opinion, is simply imfamous. You have been unmasked by the quickness of my friend. The question is, who supplied the gloves?"

Slavin made no answer.

It was incumbent on the Italian to say something.

"It was a pair among many," he exclaimed. "I took them, promiscuously, from the school for fencing."

"Do you, as a rule, fill up the fingers of your gloves with lead? If not, who did it?" asked Jack.

"I cannot tell."

"Because you won't."

"It is an unfathomable mystery to me. No one can regret such a deplorable incident more than I do, and I will discharge all my attendants."

Jack looked puzzled.

Whom could he accuse of the foul play of which he had nearly been the victim, after the denial of Sarati and Slavin?

He had positively nothing to go upon, yet it was fair on his part to presume that one, if not both, were guilty.

Suddenly the door of the schoolroom opened.

A tall, majestic-looking form, clad in cap and gown, stepped forth.

It was Doctor Birchback himself.

"I will decide this question," he exclaimed.

"You, sir?" cried Sarati. "Pardon me, but what do you know about it?"

"Everything," answered Doctor Birchback, frowning at him. "I have watched the scene from my window, and overheard the conversation."

"I wash my hands of the whole affair," said the Italian, with one of his oily smiles. "It was a friendly set-to between the boys."

"You supplied the gloves, sir, and there was lead in one which was given to Slavin."

"How am I to blame for that?"

"Massey might have been seriously injured, and I hold you responsible."

The Italian shrugged his shoulders.

"I deny that you have any authority over me," he cried, "and I tell you plainly, that I shall not come to your school again."

"It is not necessary to tell me that. I am privately informed that you have sold your gymnasium and your connection in Eton and Windsor, and that you give up possession in a fortnight."

Sarati became livid with rage.

"Saint Geronimo!" he said, "you know too much."

"I intend to know a little more," replied the doctor, "before I have done with you."

"We have always been friends; why this hostility?" asked Sarati, in a deprecatory tone.

"Because I take a great interest in Massey."

"I cannot see that that is any reason why I should be unjustly suspected. But, pardon me, I must be going."

The Italian moved away.

"Stop!" shouted the doctor. "If you are a man, you will hear me out. If not, I shall brand you as a scoundrel all over Windsor."

Sarati halted.

"Say on," he exclaimed; "I am willing to listen."

Doctor Birchback called Slavin to his side.

The bully came reluctantly, and Dawson looked on with evident trepidation.

"Please, sir," said Slavin, "it was not my fault. I am entirely innocent in the matter."

"Tell me the whole truth, or I will first flog you and then expel you from the school, for, to my mind, this is a very disgraceful transaction, whoever may be at the bottom of it."

For a moment the bully was almost unable to say anything.

"Speak!" thundered the doctor, who was terribly in earnest, "or I will birch you at once in a way that you will remember to the day of your death. By the weight of the glove, you must have known that it was loaded."

"Please, sir," answered Slavin, very humbly, "Signor Sarati put me up to it."

"How did the plot originate?"

"The signor heard me complaining to Dawson that Left-handed Jack had beaten me in a fight."

"Who is Left-handed Jack?"

"Massey, sir. They call him Left-handed Jack because with his left hand he can give such awful blows."

"Yes, I know," said Doctor Birchback. "I have reason to be thankful to that same hand, but I was not aware that he was so nick-named. Proceed."

"Signor Sarati proposed that I should challenge Massey to a glove-fight, and he would put us on equal terms by placing lead in one glove."

"Sir!" exclaimed the doctor, turning to the Italian, "will you be good enough to explain your hostility towards Massey?"

"Yes," was the reply, "I do not care about keeping the secret; but there is no necessity for all the world to know it."

"Do you object to Massey knowing it?"

"Not at all."

"Fall back, Slavin, Dawson, and Lambert."

The three mentioned walked away out of hearing, and there remained only the schoolmaster, the Italian, and Massey.

Jack's heart was beating wildly.

He was about to hear the secret to which his father had darkly alluded when he had left home to go to school.

"Now, sir," continued the doctor, "we three are alone, and you are at perfect liberty to speak. I need not tell you that whatever you may choose to tell me, will be received in strict confidence."

The Italian bowed.

"My name is Count Sarati di Mora," he began. "I belong to the nobility of Calabria, and years ago was living in Naples—rich, happy, and married. My wife, Anita, was the pride and joy of my life, but a snake crept into my Paradise; his name was Massey, an Englishman."

"My father?" asked Jack.

Sarati nodded.

"Massey," he went on, "became acquainted with me at a Neapolitan club; he was making the tour of Europe. I invited him to my house. Why should I dwell on the miserable story? Anita eloped with the handsome young English officer, and died of fever, shortly afterwards, at Capri."

He paused.

His eyes filled with tears, and his frame shook with emotion.

"From that day, until a short time ago, I lost sight of the man who robbed me of my wife, though I had vowed an eternal revenge," he proceeded. "When I found out that this boy was the son of the man who ruined my happiness for ever, I vowed to strike the father through the son, and, by Heaven, I will do it yet."

Doctor Birchback had listened attentively.

It was a sad and pitiful story, the truth of which Jack had no reason to doubt, after what his father had admitted to him.

Yet he could feel no compassion for the Italian, and for this reason:

They were rivals in love.

Sarati had Ada Titmarsh in his power, through the instrumentality of her brother Septimus.

They could never be anything else but implacable enemies.

"It is a painful story you have told me, Count di Mora," said the doctor.

"You have not heard all yet," replied Sarati.

"I am here to listen."

"Maddened by the loss of my wife, I plunged into the wildest dissipation, and became a gambler. What did I care? Had I not lost the stay of my life?

"In a few years, I had lost all my fortune. I came over to England and established myself as a fencing-master. Finally, I settled in Windsor, where I have succeeded beyond my most sanguine anticipations. There is nothing more to tell. I have only to say that I can never forgive Captain Massey for the wrong he did me."

"You must not forget," exclaimed the doctor, "that to err is human, to forgive, divine."

"Mere platitudes, my dear sir."

"What has the son done to you, that you should vow such deadly enmity against him?"

"I will answer you in your own language—the sins of the fathers shall be visited upon the children."

"But——"

"Farewell," interrupted Sarati, "you will see me no more. I return to my own country, after a long absence."

"Let me speak," cried Jack.

"No, no. I have nothing to say to you," was the reply.

The Italian hurried away, and Jack was left alone with the schoolmaster.

"Is all this true?" asked the latter.

"I fear so, sir, from what my father has let drop," answered Jack; "but this man is a villain. You do not know all."

"Is there more behind? Keep nothing from me. I will be your friend and adviser."

Encouraged by his kindly tone, Jack told Doctor Birchback about the intrigues of Septimus, and the taking away of Ada to Naples.

"Then you have two desperate enemies," said the doctor. "Yet, you being here, and they in a foreign country, they cannot harm you."

"I intend to follow them," replied Jack.

"That surely would be madness."

"I must save the girl I love from their vile machinations."

"I am sorry for you," said the doctor, "yet, I can do no more in the matter. It will be best for you to go at once to your father and tell him all. I am no prophet, if the Count di Mora will not try to do him an injury before he leaves England."

"Do you think my father is in danger, sir?"

"Most decidedly I do. You should inform Sir Dando Titmarsh, too, about his daughter, whom, of course, he does not know has left school, being deceived by her brother's story."

"Shall I go now, sir?"

"At once. Believe me, I am very, very sorry for you. I had hoped that you would be one of my most promising and cherished pupils."

"If I have to go abroad, sir, I shall return."

"I hope so. Let me hear from you after you have seen your father."

Jack promised that he would comply with the schoolmaster's desire, and, shaking hands with Doctor Birchback, hurried away without saying a word to anybody.

He was anxious to see his father and Sir Dando Titmarsh.

That the doctor was right he had not the slightest doubt.

There was danger in the air.

As Sarati was going away, he would endeavour to injure Captain Massey before he went.

Nor would he allow the grass to grow under his feet.

Jack had not gone a hundred yards down the street before he encountered Spoofer, the man-servant.

"Hullo! young gentleman," exclaimed Spoofer in a thick voice, which denoted that he had been indulging in liquor.

"Don't stop me," replied Jack; "I'm in a hurry."

"It's my dooty so to do. You're running away; I can see it written in your face and eyes."

"Fool! you are intoxicated."

"Intossicated, am I?" said Spoofer. "Only a glass with a friend. The master sent me to pay a cheque into the bank."

"You are drunk, I tell you."

"No—hic—'tossication 'bout me. I know myself and character better. Come back with me."

He laid his hand on Jack's shoulder.

"Let go," cried Jack, angrily.

"You are one of our boys up at Manor Park School."

"What of that?"

"A lot. You're a bolter, and my orders are to stop and bring back all bolters. Ain't you been away three days on the spree, shamming as how you'd been drowned?"

"You idiot!"

"No; I ain't nothing of the sort. I ain't no ijot. Who are you calling names?"

"I shall hit you with my left hand if you don't let go."

"This day," replied Spoofer, "England expects every man to do his dooty."

"Let go, do you hear me ? "

"Them's the words of the immortal Nelson, and I'm going to do my dooty."

"Fool! " cried Jack.

"Come back with me, and I'll report that I've captured a runaway. The doctor will say ' Spoofer, get out the birches,' and, while I hold you down, you'll holler as loud as the rest of them."

Jack, with a vigorous jerk, shook him off, and gave him a left-handed blow, which sent him sprawling into the middle of the road.

The impression on Spoofer's mind was that he had received a galvanic shock.

Never had he had such a blow before.

A policeman was close by.

He had witnessed the assault, which was, to his mind, utterly unprovoked.

"What did you do that for ? " he asked.

"Mind your own business," replied Jack. "What is it to do with you ? "

"I can't see a person knocked down and not interfere. What did you do it for ? "

"Find out."

"I mean to ; it's my dooty."

"Oh, hang your duty! To-day you all seem to have got duty on the brain," replied Jack.

"Give an account of yourself, or I'll run you in !" exclaimed the policeman, drawing his truncheon.

"You can have my name and address."

"Thas isn't sufficient. Come with me to the station."

"What for ? "

"To give an account of yourself to the inspector. I've had enough of false names and addresses. You look like an Eton boy out of bounds, and I know what *they* are."

"Touch me if you dare," cried Jack.

"If you try to assault me, I will hit you with my truncheon. Come quietly, and it will be all right."

Jack groaned inwardly.

He was to be arrested entirely through Spoofer's tipsy stupidity, and what a loss of time it would be before he could send for Doctor Birchback to explain the matter.

He ground his teeth with impotent rage.

It was no use to think even of fighting the guardian of law and order.

When he arrived at the police-station, he made his statement to the inspector.

"I am sorry," was the answer ; "but I must detain you until I have sent to the school to verify what you have said."

"The policeman is a fool," cried Jack.

"There are always fools in the force. We can't make policemen to order."

"I want to go home to see my father on important business."

"It can't be done until your school-master comes to explain the matter," said the inspector.

Jack chafed at what he thought was gross injustice.

Nevertheless, he was detained while the inspector sent for Doctor Birchback.

In the meantime, what was Sarati doing ?

This will be explained in the next chapter.

CHAPTER XII.

SARATI'S NEXT MOVE—THE DUEL TO THE DEATH.

WHEN Sarati left the school after revealing the secret of his life to Doctor Birchback and Jack, he walked as quickly as he could to Captain Massey's house.

His dark eyes flashed with the light of fierce determination.

He evidently meant to do something desperate.

People looked as him as if he was a madman as he passed them in the street, talking to himself and swinging his arms about.

Arriving at Captain Massey's house

he knocked at the door, which was opened by the servant.

"Is the captain at home?" he asked. "If so, be good enough to tell him that a gentleman wishes to see him."

"What name, sir?" enquired the domestic.

"Never mind the name. I am an old friend. Conduct me to him."

"The captain is in the library, sir. Mrs. Massey is out on a visit to a friend, but will return shortly."

"Which is the library?"

"The second door up the hall, sir."

"Thank you very much. I wish to introduce myself. Take no more trouble," said the Italian.

He walked in the direction she had indicated, and entered the library, closing the door after him.

Sarati burst suddenly on the astonished view of Captain Massey, who was reading a book, and smoking a cigar.

If a thunderbolt had fallen in the room he could not have been more amazed.

In a moment he recognised the man he had so cruelly wronged.

"Di Mora!" he cried. "You here!"

His face became ashen pale, and he trembled violently.

"Ha! you know me;" replied the Italian, with a vicious smile. "I thought you would, and that is why I did not send in my card. No necessity for an introduction, eh?"

"Good Heaven! What have you come here for?"

"Have you not been expecting me?"

"I must admit that I have thought of you as a possible intruder; but let the past be buried," exclaimed Captain Massey.

"Never!" replied Sarati, emphatically, "the sky shall fall first. I have sought you for years."

"Well, you have found me. What next?" asked Captain Massey, summoning his courage to his aid.

"You must render me an account for the wrong you did me years ago."

"Recollect that there were extenuating circumstances. You were always a man of violent temper. You spent your time and money with gay companions in Naples. You beat your wife, she sought protection, and——"

"Enough of that, she fled from my home with you." interrupted Sarati.

"I admit it."

"What right had you to be her protector?"

Captain Massey moved his hand in an impatient manner.

"Let the subject drop, and leave my house," he said.

"I refuse to do so," replied Sarati. "It is your life or mine."

"What do you mean?"

"I challenge you to a duel to the death."

"But, madman that you are, I am unarmed," replied Captain Massey in alarm.

The Italian drew from his pocket a brace of hair-trigger pistols, which he placed on the table.

"Take your choice, I give you a chance for your life," he said.

"You know very well that duelling is illegal. If I kill you, I shall suffer the penalty of the law, and *vice versa*."

"That is a secondary consideration."

The captain stretched out his hand to the bell.

It was his intention to ring for assistance, as he fully believed the Italian to be out of his mind.

Sarati snatched up one of the pistols.

"Touch that bell and you are a dead man!" he cried.

"Will you murder me in cold blood in my own house?" demanded Captain Massey.

"Craven hound! defend yourself, or I fire."

"Be it so. I will fight you."

"Good!" ejaculated Sarati, with a demoniacal grin.

He felt he had his enemy in his power now.

The long hoped for revenge was coming at last.

"Anita! beloved wife of my youth. This is for you—for you; may your spirit direct my hand," he muttered.

The captain seized the remaining pistol.

"What are the terms of the duel?" he enquired.

"We will stand back to back; at the word 'Go!' which I will utter, each will take six paces forward, turn sharply, and fire."

"Will one shot satisfy your sense of honour?"

"Yes," replied Sarati, grimly; "these are single-barrelled pistols, and I shall not require more than one shot."

"Very well," said Captain Massey.

It seemed to him that his last hour had come, and that he was already traversing the gruesome Valley of the Shadow of Death.

"One moment!" exclaimed Sarati.

"What now?"

"There is one preliminary we have forgotten."

"Name it," said Captain Massey.

"Let us each write a letter, stating that the writer has committed suicide; it may be of use to the survivor."

"By all means."

They both sat down at the table, on which there were pens, ink, and paper.

The captain wrote to this effect:

"I hereby declare that, being tired of my life, I have determined to commit suicide — JOHN MASSEY, late Captain of Her Majesty's Land Forces."

Sarati's letter was couched in nearly similar terms.

This formality being disposed of, they rose, and grasped their pistols again.

They stood back to back, touching each other.

"Go!" said Sarati, in a sepulchral voice.

They took six paces forward.

Each man turned simultaneously.

The Italian did not stop to take aim.

He made what is called a snap-shot.

Before Captain Massey could pull the trigger of his pistol, the bullet of his opponent struck him in the region of the heart.

With a hollow groan, he fell heavily to the floor.

"Enough! I have avenged Anita's wrongs," hissed Sarati.

He put his pistol in his pocket, snatched up the letter he had written, and rapidly left the room.

Passing through the hall without encountering anybody, he let himself out into the street.

Then he walked quickly up the road.

Strange to say, neither of the two servants, who were in the kitchen below, had heard the shot fired.

A short time afterwards Mrs. Massey came home and knocked at the door, which was opened by the house-maid.

Mrs. Massey was a delicate little woman, who had been in failing health for some time.

The doctors had recommended her to live a retired life in the country, and that was why she and her husband had come to live at Windsor.

A shock to her nerves was especially to be deprecated.

Not the slightest suspicion had she of the ghastly tragedy.

"Where is your master, Jane?" she asked.

"In the library, ma'am," replied the servant. "A strange-looking, foreign-like gentleman called half-an-hour ago."

"What was his name?"

"He did not give any, ma'am."

"Has he gone?"

"I have not heard him go," answered Jane.

Mrs. Massey walked on, and entered the library.

A horrible spectacle presented itself to her terrified gaze.

Near the door, stretched at her feet, was the corpse of her husband.

The carpet was saturated with his blood.

The face was contorted with a dying spasm, and the eyes glared wildly.

In the right hand was tightly clenched a pistol.

A loud, piercing scream echoed through the room, and Mrs. Massey sank into a chair.

Alarmed at the noise, the housemaid came up, and she, too, succumbed to the terror of the scene.

Her cries, joined to those of her mistress, brought up the cook, and soon the three women were screaming.

At length Mrs. Massey went off into a dead faint, and the servants ran out into the street.

At this juncture Jack came up.

He had been liberated after a detention of an hour, by a visit to the inspector by Doctor Birchback.

That hour had made a considerable difference in Jack Massey's family affairs.

His encounter with Spoofer was a most unfortunate occurrence.

If it had not been for that, Sarati would not have had his revenge.

CHAPTER XIII.

TOO LATE!

JACK was surprised at the action of the servants.

"What is all this hullabullo and rumpus about?" he asked.

"Oh, sir, it's awful!" said the cook. "Enough to make your hair turn grey in a single night, as the saying is."

"It's given me the cold shivers and creeps," replied Jane.

"Explain yourselves."

"Oh! Master Jack, I shall never get over it, and I'm afraid to go into the house alone."

"But what on earth is it?" demanded Jack.

"Oh, sir, I can't tell you! Oh, Master Jack! Oh, that I should live to see this day!"

Jack took hold of her arm and shook her.

"Speak, girl!" he cried, angrily.

"Master's been and shot himself, if he hasn't been murdered by the foreign-looking gentleman," said Jane at last.

"My father?"

"Yes, sir; he's stone dead."

Jack looked bewildered and horror-stricken.

"Come inside. Don't make a fuss in the road!" he exclaimed. "Surely there must be some mistake."

"I've seen him, poor, dear man," replied Jane.

"So have I," said the cook; "there's a pistol in his hand, sir. Oh, it's right enough!"

Jack waited to hear no more.

He had got all he could out of the two domestics, and now he had to go and investigate the awful mystery for himself.

The women followed him into the house.

Jack's presence had somewhat reassured them, but they halted on the threshold as if fearing to go into the chamber of death.

One look at the body was quite sufficient to show our hero that the unhappy officer was quite dead.

"My father!" cried Jack, in a wailing voice.

He knelt down and affectionately kissed the pale, marble-like forehead.

Then he rose, his brow rapidly knit, and the corners of his mouth drawn down in a determined manner.

His eye caught sight of the open letter on the table, and he read it.

"I cannot believe it," he said. "Why should he commit suicide?"

There was more in it than appeared on the surface.

He determined to unravel the mystery.

Calling the housemaid to his side, he enquired about the gentleman whom she had mentioned.

The description she gave him satisfied him at once that it must be Sarati.

In his opinion it was a case of deliberate murder.

Mrs. Massey had now revived, and she began to cry and bewail her fate.

With the assistance of the servants he removed her to another room, where restoratives were applied.

She was very weak, and seemed to be sinking lower every minute.

Jack went out, calling first upon a doctor, and then giving information to the police.

"Too late," he kept on muttering to himself, "too late!"

How the remainder of that day passed he scarcely knew, for his brain was in a whirl.

He saw his mother carried upstairs in an unconscious condition; he talked to police-inspectors and doctors, giving all the information that it was in his power to supply.

He saw crowds of curious people in the street, who assembled as soon as the news spread.

It was within his recollection that Sir Dando Titmarsh came to the house and spoke words of sympathy and kindness to him.

Then came a state of collapse.

He fell on the floor exhausted and brain-weary, and knew nothing more until the next morning, when he awoke in his own bed.

The sun was shining brightly, the birds were gaily singing, and it was one of those days which no one can fail to enjoy, except those whose minds are oppressed.

His heart was as heavy as lead.

There was only one hope that kept him up, and that was the hope that he would be able to run Sarati to earth, and rescue Ada.

He resolved firmly that the villainous Italian should not escape him.

"How strangely quiet and still the house is," he thought, as he went down the stairs.

The clock struck the hour of eleven.

In the breakfast-room, to his great delight, he saw Dick Lambert, sitting near the table, which the servant had not forgotten to lay neatly.

"This *is* kind of you!" exclaimed Jack, wringing his friend's hand.

"I only heard the news this morning," replied Dick, "and got leave from the doctor to come over at once. I am so grieved for you, old fellow."

Jack could not help bursting into tears.

"You did not know him as I did," he said in a broken voice; "so good, so kind."

"Can I talk about the terrible affair? Will you have breakfast first?" enquired Dick. "Perhaps I had best leave the subject alone for the present."

"Not at all. I must face it, and bear it like a man."

"That's right."

"I will ring for some tea and toast, which is all I want, and enquire after mother."

His wants were soon supplied by the servant, who informed him that his mother was much better than the doctor had expected to find her.

This was good news, and Jack began to brighten up a little, for he was very fond of his mother.

After he had eaten a slice of toast, and drank a cup of tea, Dick asked why the captain had committed suicide.

"It is nothing of the kind," replied Jack. "My father was not the man to do a thing of that sort."

"That's what I thought," said Dick. "But how did——"

"Sarati killed him," interrupted Jack.

"How do you explain away the letter?"

"That is a mystery I cannot fathom. It may be a forgery. Perhaps he wrote it under coercion."

"What do you intend to do?"

"There must be an inquest, of course; the funeral will follow. When that is over, I will see my mother comfortably settled, take some money, and start for Naples."

"Remember your promise to me!" exclaimed Dick. "I am not to be left behind."

"Certainly not. Your company will be of great service to me in tracking the villain to his death."

"I saw Sir Dando Titmarsh as I came into the house," remarked Dick, "and he reports very favourably of your boy Rumbo."

"No longer Rumbo, but Sir Dando's son and heir. How is he?"

"Progressing favourably. Sir Dando has had a specialist from London to see him. He will be well and hearty again in three months or less."

"I am very glad to hear that, for it puts another nail into Septimus's coffin."

"Sarati and Septimus will have to stand or fall together," remarked Dick.

"Yes. I shall be compelled to fight the two."

"Use the plural instead of the singular, say ' we.' "

"So it shall be. We will fight side by side, until those dastardly villains are finally routed," cried Jack.

The servant knocked at the door.

Entering, she handed him a card, on which was written :

"Detective Spark, Scotland Yard, London. Criminal Investigation Department."

"Show the gentleman in," Jack said.

A thin, wiry, elderly man, with grey hair, entered.

He was shabbily dressed, but there was an air of intelligence about him, and a far-away look in his eyes, as if he was used to thinking.

"Which of you young gentlemen is Mr. Massey?" he asked.

"I am," replied Jack, "this is my friend Mr. Lambert."

"Accept my sympathy, sincere and heartfelt," continued Spark. " This sad affair has been put into my hands at headquarters, and I have lost no time in coming down. It is a poser to the local police."

He paused to smile.

The local police were always despised by him, wherever they might be located.

"Have you made any investigations?" said Jack.

"I've had a look round and a chat," was the careless reply. "You, I am told, accuse a Signor Sarati of the murder. The locals laugh at that idea, and the doctor thinks the wound consistent with suicide."

"They may all say what they like. They cannot prove that my father was not foully murdered. I am after the Italian as soon as the funeral is over."

"Do you know where to find him?"

"Yes. I know more than you do. You have a lot to learn yet, Mr. Spark; but if you intend to work this case up in the interests of justice against Sarati, I will tell you a great deal that you will find of importance."

"My orders are to follow it to the bitter end."

"Then we operate together. Well and good," replied Jack.

"Let me ask you one question, Mr. Massey."

"A score if you like."

"To your knowledge, did your father keep a pistol in the house?"

"Never. I am sure."

The detective produced one, and held it up.

"Have you seen this before?" he asked.

"Decidedly not," replied Jack, examining it closely. "Why, what is this," he added, "I see the letter 'S' on the butt."

"Precisely. I noticed it. That should stand for Sarati. I think, at the inquest, we shall get a verdict against the Italian for wilful murder, and if you like to help me in my quest for him, I shall be glad of your company and assistance, sir."

"Agreed," Jack cried, eagerly. "You, Dick, and I, will work together. We shall have two against us, but we ought to win the battle."

"Tell me all," said the detective; "there is more at the bottom of this than I am acquainted with."

Jack related everything unreservedly.

In half-an-hour Mr. Spark was aware of the cause of Sarati's hostility to Captain Massey, of Septimus Titmarsh's conduct, and of Ada's journey, under false pretences, to Naples.

Nothing was kept back.

"I will see Sir Dando!" he exclaimed. "Await my return, please."

He was gone some time.

When he came back, he said:

"Sir Dando Titmarsh is very indignant at his son's conduct. He insists upon Miss Ada being brought back, and will spare no expense; I have a cheque on account from him already in my pocket."

"What do you think of the campaign?" asked Jack.

"We shall win; yet we must not under-rate the importance of the enemy. Sarati is a very dangerous man to deal with."

"That is my opinion."

"The country round about Naples is very disturbed and unsettled; brigands still exist. We cannot tell what kind of friends Sarati may have. The dagger is still an institution in Italy, as well as the poisoned bowl."

Jack brought his hand down heavily on the table.

"I will dare any peril!" he cried, "so that I avenge my father and rescue Ada."

"And I," said Dick Lambert.

"My head, perhaps, may be useful," remarked Spark. "I've done some clever things in my time, and I'm not too old to work yet. Trust to my professional skill, and obey my orders."

"We will," replied Jack. "You shall be the captain of the expedition, and we must all pull together. I feel that Septimus Titmarsh and Sarati are doomed!"

CHAPTER XIV.

ADA'S PERPLEXITY—THE STRANGER.

THE "Ré Galantuomo Hotel," so called after the late King Victor Emmanuel, faced the splendid bay of Naples, commanding a magnificent view.

It was to this hotel that Septimus and his sister went.

Not finding her father there, as he had informed her she would, her suspicions were excited, but he allayed her fears by telling her that, by the advice of his doctor, he had gone for a short sea voyage.

Still the girl was very much perplexed.

Her brother was strange in his manner; he had the English paper every day when the mail came in, giving it her to read afterwards; but one day he turned pale when he was perusing the *Times*, and put it in his pocket.

"I'm going out," he said; "when I come back, in an hour, I will take you for a long drive."

"Cannot I have the paper?" she asked. "It is so far away from home, and though I learnt Italian at school, the news here does not interest me."

"I want it," he replied, gruffly.

"When will papa come?"

"Don't ask questions."

"I wish you would be frank with me," Ada exclaimed. "I begin to fear that I have been brought here for some bad purpose. What is it?"

"You will find out in time."

"Give me the money, and I will go back alone. I distrust you, Sep. You were never my friend."

"Silence! You are in my charge."

"But I insist——"

"Silence, I say!" Septimus interrupted. "If you dare oppose my will, you shall be put in a convent, and kept there."

Ada burst into tears.

"Oh! how foolish I was to come with you to this strange place," she moaned. "What could have possessed me to do so?"

"It is too late to grieve now," cried Septimus. "You are in my charge; that is quite sufficient for you to know."

Saying this, he put on his hat and left the room, slamming the door after him.

Ada ran to the balcony—their rooms were on the second floor—and saw Septimus quit the hotel, and walk up the street.

Then she rang the bell and asked the servant for the English *Times*, which, in a brief space, was brought to her.

She felt assured that there was something in it which her brother did not wish her to see.

Nor was she mistaken.

It was just as she had imagined, for she came across the following paragraph:

"MYSTERIOUS TRAGEDY AT WINDSOR.

"Yesterday, in the afternoon, the body of Captain Massey was found in the library of his residence, shot through the heart.

"A letter, in his handwriting, was on the table, stating that he intended to commit suicide.

"Various rumours are afloat. One is to the effect that he was visited shortly prior to the lamentable occurrence by Signor Sarati, the well-known fencing-master at Windsor, between whom and Captain Massey a feud existed.

"Sarati has left the neighbourhood, and although the police are said to possess a clue to his whereabouts, they are very reticent about the matter.

"An inquest will be held on the body to-morrow.

"This sad affair has cast quite a gloom around the vicinity in which the deceased officer was well-known and highly respected.

"Latest—It is stated that Signor Sarati has gone to Italy."

Ada was greatly shocked and alarmed at reading this.

How full of peril and menace to herself was the announcement that Sarati was coming to Italy!

She was sure now that she had been the victim of a plot.

While she was gazing blankly at the paper, Septimus suddenly returned.

"Ha!" he cried, "what are you reading?"

"I know all," she cried. "Let me go home at once, or I will demand protection from the proprietor of the hotel."

Septimus burst into a loud fit of laughter.

"My dear girl," he exclaimed, "he is a particular friend of Sarati's, and would not listen to you."

"Why am I to be kept here? It is infamous."

"You are here in order that Sarati may come and claim you as his own fair bride."

"But the paper says the detectives are on his track," replied Ada.

"They will never find him," said Septimus. "I had a telegram from him last night, dated Marseilles, in which he states that he is on his way here. We may expect him shortly, and then we shall go further."

Ada clasped her hands in the extremity of her grief.

"I will ask for help," she cried, sobbing. "I am sure somebody will aid me."

"If you dare to call out I will

declare you are mad, and lock you up in your bedroom," replied Septimus.

The poor girl almost fainted.

"Heaven help me," she murmured. "What shall I do?"

"Be a sensible girl. Sarati is rich, and——"

"Do not mention that man's name to me," she interrupted. "You cannot make me marry him; he is more hateful to me now than ever, because he is a murderer."

"You don't know that. It appears that Captain Massey commited suicide. I wish his hopeful son would do the same."

"You need not sneer at Jack, for you are not worthy even to name him," retorted Ada, passionately.

"Mind I don't make him humble himself before I have done with him."

Ada did not reply, for she saw that it was hopeless to defy her brother.

She determined to resist all Sarati's advances, and to take the first opportunity of escape that offered.

Septimus looked out of the window.

"By Saint Januarius, as they say here," he exclaimed, "the mail steamer is in. I wonder if Sarati has come by that boat?"

Ada trembled like a bird in the presence of a snake.

The danger was coming very near to her now.

A quarter of an hour passed, during which Septimus talked to her about the futility of resistance, and expatiated on the good qualities of, and the advantages of a match with, the fencing-master.

She listened in silent disdain.

Suddenly a footstep was heard upon the stairs.

The door opened and the form of Sarati appeared.

"Welcome," exclaimed Septimus, shaking his hand. "We have just been reading about you in an English paper."

"Ah! I thought you would see it," Sarati answered. "I am not guilty; it is Left-handed Jack who has put that story about."

He advanced to Ada and smiled affably.

"May I hope," he said, "that you are glad to see an old friend, Miss Titmarsh, who is an ardent admirer of your charms?"

"You cannot expect a favourable rejoinder from me, signor," she said,

"for I own, frankly, that I cannot ever regard you as a friend."

"What have I done that I should be so coolly received by you?"

"I have been lured here on the pretence of seeing my father, when, in reality, it was to meet you, but I will not be compelled to marry you."

Sarati drew himself up haughtily.

"I have not asked you to do so yet," he replied, with a curl of his thin lip. "When I do—if I do at all —perhaps I shall receive a different answer."

"My brother told me I should be forced."

"I care not what anyone tells you. I am my own spokesman when the occasion requires it, and never woo my deputy."

"Will you allow me to go home?" asked Ada.

"You are in your brother's care, not mine, miss. I am simply his travelling companion for a time, and yours. I consider you under the control of Septimus."

He bowed in a polite manner.

Ada did not know what to make of him; but, after a moment's reflection, she came to the conclusion that he was acting a part.

However, so long as he did not pester her with his hateful attentions, she was satisfied.

"You were not long coming," observed Septimus.

"No. I did not allow the grass to grow under my feet. Travelling from London to Paris I found myself in the same carriage with a rich English lord, from whom, at cards, I won a thousand pounds."

"Luck follows you."

The Italian shrugged his shoulders, and smiled.

"It is a way I have," he went on. "One night I spent in Paris to visit some old haunts, then on to Marseilles, where I stayed long enough to partake of some *bouillabaise,* and then steam to Naples over the deep, blue sea."

"Do you intend to stop here long?"

"Not a day," answered Sarati, with a fox-like look. "I have wired to an old friend to meet me at the 'Café di Roma.'"

He looked at his watch.

"*Cospetto!*" he added, "the time is up. We will lunch there. Miss Titmarsh will favour us with her company, I hope."

"If she does not I'll know the reason why," replied Septimus. "Put on your things, Ada, and look sharp. I can promise you something super-excellent at the 'Café di Roma.' It is a tip-top place."

Ada had determined to make her life as happy as she could under the circumstances.

Accordingly she dressed herself.

"I'll cry no more," she murmured. "I will be brave, self-reliant, and watchful. I am eighteen, and at that age, one is not a child."

She quitted the room with her brother and Signor Sarati.

The street was gay with a crowd of people, none of whom seemed to be in a hurry.

In Naples, people take life as it comes, and the lazzaroni, or beggars, are happy if they can only obtain a little maccaroni and a glass of iced-water as their diurnal fare.

They had not far to walk to the café, and during the walk Sarati took little notice of Ada, addressing his conversation on indifferent subjects to her brother.

In a short time they arrived at the café, and seated themselves at a table.

Signor Sarati ordered a lunch in the first style of elegance.

Scarcely was it placed upon the table than a tall, handsome man, not over thirty years of age, well dressed, and having the incontestable air of the well-born gentleman, entered the restaurant, and advanced to Sarati.

The latter at once rose and extended his hand.

"My dear Count Casati," he exclaimed, "you have, I see, received my telegram."

"Count di Mora, friend of my youthful days," was the reply, "I have the pleasure of being here, at the rendezvous, exactly at the appointed time."

A clock struck the hour.

"That is so," said Sarati.

"The gentleman called you Count di Mora," remarked Septimus.

"That has been the title of my family for centuries. We are one of the most ancient nobles in Calabria," rejoined Sarati.

"Will you not introduce your friend?"

"I was about to do so. You will find him an excellent fellow. He speaks English and French as well as he does Italian. His wealth is great, and his hospitality unbounded, though he does not take a fancy to everybody."

Sarati looked at the handsome stranger.

"Permit me to have the honour of introducing you to my young friends, Ada and Septimus Titmarsh. Very well born, very rich, children of Sir Dando, in the English nobility."

The count bowed low.

"I am proud to know Signor Titmarsh and the signora," he replied.

"Be seated, count, I pray," continued Sarati.

"Many thanks. Your kindness is only equalled by your intelligence."

"Allow me to return the compliment, and say that your heart is as large as your purse."

After this exchange of compliments the waiters removed the covers of the first course, and the meal commenced.

The vintages of Italy were supplemented by those of France and Spain.

Ada had a good opportunity of observing the Count Casati.

His was a massive head, covered with short, black, curly hair; his classic features resembled the portrait of one of the Roman emperors on an old coin. The chin was square, showing great determination, and the eyes—dark, flashing, restless—could exhibit a pitiless tenacity one moment, and laugh at you, in mirth, the next, or glow with the light of love.

The Count Casati was no ordinary man.

Anyone could see that at a glance.

Ada was a good judge of character, and she was sure that the well-made Italian had a secret.

There was more in him than appeared on the surface.

Every now and then she found the count regarding her in a manner that denoted admiration.

Her maiden modesty caused her to lower her eyes.

"How do you find the lunch?" enquired Sarati.

"It is excellent. I shall not get anything like it at my country house, whither I go to-day," replied the count.

"How much I should like to accompany you," said Sarati.

"Indeed! Your wish is easily gratified. My carriage will be here in an hour. Come! bring your friends with you."

"I am agreeable. What do you say, Septimus?"

"Perhaps the country will agree with our health for a time," answered Septimus.

He grinned feebly, as if he thought he had said a good thing.

"You have not asked the young lady," remarked the Count Casati.

"Oh!" rejoined Sarati, "where we go, she also goes."

Ada gave him a look of hatred.

"It is not because I like either of you," she retorted, "but I am, unhappily, compelled to do so. I am under my brother's care."

"Hush!" said Septimus.

He clenched his hand and held it up warningly.

"Let her speak out," cried Sarati; "what matters it?"

"Yes, I will speak to this gentleman!" exclaimed Ada. "I have been brought over here on false pretences, signor, and I am detained against my will. If I had money I would run on board a boat and go to London."

"You are with your brother, signora," the count replied.

"He is a wretch, and I think he is playing me false."

Septimus turned up the whites of his eyes.

"There's ingratitude for you," he observed, "after all my kindness to her. I swear that no girl ever had a better brother. By Jove! I was made to order, I think. I have done everything for her."

"He wants to marry me to the Count di Mora," said Ada.

"Do you not like my friend, Sarati?" asked Casati.

"No; and he shall not make me marry him."

"I admire your independent spirit, signora, but, at the same time, I must declare that you are hard to please. Sarati di Mora is of noble birth, pleasing carriage, and rich in wordly goods."

"I love another," cried Ada. "My sweetheart is Jack Massey, Left-handed Jack they call him. He could knock you down with one blow of his terrible fist, signor."

"*Santa Maria!* he must be a wonder."

"He is, indeed. I should not be surprised if he found out where I had gone, and came after me, and punished those that detain me."

"Like a knight of old, to rescue his ladylove."

"He is as brave as one."

"I shall be glad to make his acquaintance, signora," said the count, with a smile, which seemed to her to be full of meaning.

"Let the subject drop," exclaimed Sarati. "I mean the lady no harm. I will woo her fairly. If she will not have me, I must even put up with a broken heart."

"That is well expressed. Let us be cheerful. You are going to be my guests for a few days. It shall be a labour of love on my part to make you all happy and comfortable."

His tone was friendly, and Ada felt reassured.

She had an idea that the Count Casati would protect her against the wiles and cunning of Septimus and Sarati.

The waiters now placed the dessert on the table.

While they were eating the luscious grapes an agent of police entered the café.

He was dressed in full uniform.

Going to the wall close to where our party were seated, he took a printed bill from his pocket.

It was an ordinary *affiche*, or police notice.

This he pinned on the wall.

Everybody looked at it with evident curiosity.

It was worded as follows:

"5,000 SCUDI REWARD.—The above sum is offered by the municipality of Naples for the apprehension of Possilippo, the brigand, and will be given for him, dead or alive.—Signed MADIA, Chief of the Police, Naples."

The count beckoned to the man, who approached him.

"Will you take a glass of wine with me, my friend?" he asked.

"Two, if you like, signor," was the reply.

He was immediately given a tumbler filled with well-matured Chiazi.

"What is your name?" continued the count.

"Sparghetti, at your honour's service."

"Are you going to capture this brigand?"

"I mean to have a try. They say he lives in the hills, towards the north. If I find him, let him look out."

"They say he is a very terrible fellow, and not to be trifled with, though it is stated to his credit that he never robs or ill-treats the poor."

"That is so, signor," answered Sparghetti, "he flies at high game; only this morning he stopped the Duke of Calabria on the old Roman road, and took from him all his money and valuables."

"A daring robber!"

"The scandal is becoming grave, signor. For the credit of the Neapolitan police and the safety of the citizens, he must be caught."

Saying this, Sparghetti bowed, drank up his wine, and departed.

"How romantic," exclaimed Ada; "I did not know that you were blessed with brigands in this locality."

"This man, Possilippo," replied Casati, "is a most remarkable individual. He has been defying and laughing at the authorities for two years, on and off. Sometimes he is not heard of for months, then he breaks out and does the most audacious things."

"Is he a ferocious ruffian, steeped in blood?"

"On the contrary. They say he avoids deeds of violence if he can, and is a most polished gentleman."

"Oh, I should like to see him," exclaimed Ada.

"Don't say that. We are going on the northern road, which is his favourite ground, and we may be stopped by him," answered the count.

"If he is what you describe him to be, he would not hurt a lady."

Casati gave her a meaning look.

"He would be a brute, indeed, if he injured you," he rejoined.

The time had been running on while they were talking. A servant came to the table and announced that the count's carriage was at the door.

"Shall we go?" asked Casati.

"By all means," replied Sarati, who had been settling the bill for the lunch.

Septimus rose from his chair with a yawn.

The good things he had been eating, and the wine he had imbibed, had made him feel sleepy.

Ada, on the other hand, was wide awake.

"Shall we stop at your hotel for your luggage?" said Casati. "Miss Titmarsh will not be happy without her trunk, I am sure, though I entertain nobody but yourselves."

They went out and got into a closed carriage drawn by two horses, the driver of which was a long-bearded, truculent-looking ruffian.

He received orders to stop at the hotel, which he did, Septimus going upstairs for the two boxes which belonged to his sister and himself.

While they were waiting for them to be brought down and placed upon the coach, Casati noticed Sparghetti, the police agent.

He had been home and changed his clothes for those of a civilian, and was standing on the steps of the hotel.

Casati, who had an eye like that of a lynx, recognised him in an instant.

Yet he did not pretend to do so, for he went on talking to his companions in quite an unconcerned manner.

The air was still and calm, an ominous hush reigned everywhere, and the heat was very oppressive.

A cloudless sky hung over the beautiful blue water of the lovely bay, whose placid surface was undisturbed by so much as a ripple.

Casati glanced furtively occasionally at Sparghetti.

The police agent held in his hand a piece of paper, which he consulted as if for instructions.

Then he looked at Casati, as if making notes, or drawing comparisons.

In a few minutes Septimus came back and reseated himself. The boxes were put on the coach by the hotel porters, and with a smack of the whip the driver started the horses.

The Count Casati looked out of the window.

Sparghetti was in the roadway, following behind the carriage.

At this Casati smiled, but said nothing.

In half-an-hour they were out of the city, leaving Mount Vesuvius on their right.

The road went through an open country, principally devoted to vine cultivation, the sides of the road being dotted with villas here and there.

Suddenly a brilliant and exciting spectacle burst upon their view.

For days past the volcanic mountain had been emitting clouds of smoke, which hung over it like a pall.

In a moment a magnificent mass of flame shot up in the air.

The smoke rolled away.

An ominous rumbling, as of distant thunder, accompanied the phenomenon.

"Ha!" cried the count, "you are, indeed, lucky. Vulcan and his Cyclops

"THE CAPITANO SNATCHED HIS WEAPON OUT OF HIS BELT."—(See page 95.)

are at work. The mountain is in eruption."

"Is there any danger?" asked Ada.

"We may have an earthquake somewhere; but nobody thinks about that here. We are used to such little affairs. Wait until night, then you will see the active volcano in all its grandeur," said Casati.

Ada called Septimus to witness the scene; but he was asleep, overcome with the effects of too much eating and drinking.

At last she succeeded in rousing him.

"Look at the burning mountain, Sep!" she exclaimed.

He took a glance and closed his eyes again, growling, "Let her burn; I don't care."

"I am afraid your brother does not appreciate the wonders of Nature," remarked Casati.

The carriage continued at a fair rate of speed until the road became uneven, owing to the hilly nature of the ground.

At the top of a hill the driver stopped to rest his panting horses, which were covered with foam.

"Let us alight," said Casati; "we shall obtain a splendid view of the city and bay from this eminence."

"With pleasure," replied Sarati.

Septimus woke up again.

He rubbed his eyes in a drowsy manner.

"What is it?" he enquired; "stopping for refreshments?"

A burst of laughter greeted this question.

Disregarding the merriment of his companions, Septimus curled himself up and went to sleep again.

Casati got out first, and extended his hand to assist Ada to alight.

Seeing this, Sarati pushed by her, and helped her out himself, occasioning the count to stand on one side.

This proceeding caused a cloud to gather on the brow of the count.

With the quickness of feminine perception, Ada noticed it at once.

The malignant scowl soon vanished from Casati's face.

"You see how polite we Italians are," said he. "I resign in favour of Di Mora, who has more right to protect you than I."

"That's a right I do not admit," answered Ada. "I would just as soon accept your polite attentions as his."

Sarati took no heed of her answer.

Nevertheless, she could see spite and malice in his eyes.

They gleamed, snake-like, with internal rage and fury.

He was evidently seriously annoyed at the marked attention which Casati paid the young English beauty, but he wanted Casati's aid and protection.

In addition to this, he was afraid of the handsome count.

Why he was in dread of him will be revealed in the next chapter.

CHAPTER XV.

A REVELATION—THE EXECUTION OF A SPY—THE STRONGHOLD OF THE BRIGAND CHIEF.

THE flames cast up by Mount Vesuvius increased in volume every minute.

They entirely dimmed the splendour of the sun.

Casati did not busy himself any more with the eruptive vagaries of the volcanic mountain.

His thoughts were intent on something of a far different nature.

"Signora!" he exclaimed, "are your nerves strong?"

"I hope so," Ada replied. "Why do you ask?"

"Something terrible is going to happen; at least, it will be terrible to you, if not to me and Sarati."

This speech aroused Sarati's attention.

He turned round sharply on his heel.

"What do you mean?" he demanded.

"Perhaps an earthquake is coming," said Ada.

"Oh, no; nothing so bad as that," replied Casati. "I am only going to kill a man."

He laughed lightly, as if he had spoken of killing a fly.

"Is it I who have incurred your resentment ?" enquired Sarati.

"You ! an old friend ! absurd !" was the reply. "You ! ah, ah !"

"I wish we were at your country house, and you would cease joking."

"I am not joking."

"It looks to me like it."

"I have no country house."

"Where are you taking us, then ?" asked Sarati.

"You will find out in a short time. Did you not telegraph to me from Marseilles, stating that you were in fear of the police, and request me to shelter you and two friends ?"

"Certainly I did. Fifteen years ago we were like brothers, and you vowed you would always do the best you could for me."

"I admit it."

"In my hour of trouble and danger I sought you."

"Shelter you shall have, and protection, as far as I can give it you," replied Casati.

"There is an air of mystery about you," observed Sarati.

"You find me altered since you saw me last ?"

"Strangely so."

"My friendship for you has not changed, although a great change has taken place in me, as you will know, presently."

As he spoke, the count drew a six-chambered revolver from his pocket.

Ada with difficulty restrained herself from screaming, for she was beginning to get frightened.

"In heaven's name," said Sarati, "let me know what this secret is that you are hiding from me ?"

"Very well. In the first place, I know that we are followed by a police spy."

"How can that be ?"

"Sparghetti, the agent, who posted, in the 'Café di Roma,' the bill offering a reward for Possilippo, the brigand, is seated on the springs behind our carriage."

"Ha ! is it so ?"

"I have quick eyes, my friend, and saw him follow from your hotel. My instinct tells me he is there."

"But why, in the fiend's name, should he follow us ?"

"It is not you, but me, that the rascally spy is following," said Casati.

"That makes the matter all the more perplexing. You are a rich Italian nobleman," replied Sarati.

"I was rich, I was a gentleman ; but I spent my fortune, and now——"

He paused abruptly.

Ada kept her eyes riveted on his expressive face.

"Again I ask why the police should follow you," exclaimed Sarati.

He seemed sorely perplexed.

Casati drew himself up to his full height, and a proud smile curled the corners of his well-chiselled lips.

"Because," he answered, "I am Possilippo, the brigand !"

Sarati was now perfectly astounded.

"Impossible !" he ejaculated.

"Nothing is impossible in this world," was the calm reply. "In Naples, at my house, the Villa Borghese, I am the man of fashion, Count Casati."

"Well ?"

"In the hills, I am the man of blood, Possilippo, on whose head a price is set."

Ada became deathly pale and alarmed at hearing this.

She trembled in every limb.

"You will not hurt me ?" she queried, in a quavering voice.

"Not a hair of your head carissima," the brigand chief rejoined.

This promise greatly relieved her mind.

She felt she could trust him still, though she now knew his true character.

The man lived a double life.

This accounted for the Neapolitan police becoming so greatly puzzled about him, and for their inability to arrest him.

Possilippo, as we shall now call the Count Casati, walked to the rear of the carriage.

As he had expected, he beheld Sparghetti, who was crouching on the springs.

The man had received a description of the brigand, and his suspicions had become excited.

Casati certainly resembled Possilippo according to secret information received by Madia, chief of the police of Naples.

Sharghetti had determined to follow the carriage to its destination.

He had heard all that passed.

The poor wretch was trembling with fear.

He felt that he was doomed !

Sparghetti had not dared to run away, for he knew that he would be shot down.

The discovery he had made was very important.

He had discovered that the Count Casati and Possilippo the brigand were one and the same person.

Madia, the chief of the police, would have given anything for that information.

Promotion would have been sure for Sparghetti.

Also he would have secured the large sum of money offered as a reward.

But he was threatened with death, and the knowledge he had acquired was not likely to avail him much.

Possilippo faced him, pistol in hand.

"Get down from there, my man, and give an account of yourself," exclaimed the brigand.

The man did as he was requested.

His right hand sought his pocket.

"Hold up your hands," shouted the brigand, "or you die at once."

Sparghetti raised his hands above his head and suppressed a curse, for he, too, was armed.

He had intended to draw his pistol, but his design was frustrated.

He was now completely at the mercy of Possilippo, who was notorious for showing none to his enemies.

"Pardon, noble signor," he exclaimed, "I was going to see a friend in the hills, and I thought there would be no harm done if I rode behind your carriage. The roads are dusty, the way long, and the heat tiring."

"You lie!" thundered Possilippo.

"Why should I tell you a falsehood?"

"To save your life, cur that you are."

"Excellency, I swear——"

The brigand cut him short.

"Prepare to die," he said. "Down on your knees and say your prayers, if you know any. I will give you time to make your peace with Heaven."

The near prospect of death threw the man into an agony of apprehension.

Instead of falling on his knees and praying, he threw himself into the road and writhed in the dust.

"Coward!" said Possilippo, "you would betray me to the scaffold, and you cannot contemplate your own end with patience."

Sarati stood by with folded arms.

Pale, trembling, deeply agitated, Ada looked like one fascinated.

"Let the poor wretch live," she pleaded, "he is not fit to die."

"How can I, signora?" replied the brigand. "Gladly would I comply with you request, were it possible; but if I spare this man my own doom is sealed."

"How is that?"

"He will go to the chief of the police in Naples and betray me."

"Moreover," continued the brigand, "they will hunt for my stronghold in the hills, and run me down. No, no, I cannot spare him, though I would gladly do so at your request. Turn your eyes away, you are young to see bloodshed."

Ada put her handkerchief to her eyes.

The next moment there was a loud report.

A bullet whistled to the left of her, where the brigand was standing.

But it was not Possilippo who had fired.

Sparghetti had, while rolling in the dust, got hold of his weapon.

Taking aim as well as he could in his excitement and hurry, he discharged the pistol at the brigand chief.

Fortunately for the latter the ball went wide of the mark.

"Ha! traitor!" cried Possilippo. "You should die twenty deaths, if I had the power to mete them out to you!"

Before he had finished speaking the messenger of death was on its way.

Sparghetti uttered a horrible cry, clutched wildly at the dirt, and rolled over on his back.

His features were awfully convulsed, and his teeth tightly clenched.

The blood flowed from a wound in his side in a profuse manner.

"So may all spies perish!" exclaimed the brigand.

He walked to the body, took it by the legs, and dragged it to the side of the road.

There were no signs of life in the unlucky police agent.

"Our horses are rested," continued Possilippo. "Will it please you, signora, to re-enter the carriage?"

"It is my fate," she replied, and with trembling limbs she entered the carriage.

Sarati and he followed; the driver cracked his whip, and a fresh start was made.

Septimus woke up.

"Time for refreshments?" he asked.

"I'm awfully thirsty. It is a long time between drinks, I say."

Possilippo handed him a flask of sherry, which he put greedily to his lips, and went off to sleep again.

The remainder of the journey took place in silence.

Sarati was by no means satisfied with the company he found himself in ; but he could not retreat.

He had been deceived in the character of his old friend, whom he knew to be unscrupulous, but did not expect to find a brigand.

The latter had him in his power.

At last a hilly region was reached and at the foot of one of the highest hills, in a grassy valley, the carriage stopped.

A small stream meandered through the valley.

Trees and brushwood abounded, making the spot resemble a sylvan paradise.

The driver of the carriage was one of the brigand's band, which numbered over a dozen members.

When the party had alighted, he said :

"Any orders, signor ?"

"Go back to the Villa Borghese," replied Possilippo. "If you hear any news, Guiseppe, saddle a horse and ride out to the cave at once."

"*Si, signor.*"

"Be careful that you are not followed."

"They will not catch me napping," answered the man, remounting the box and driving off.

Possilippo led the way to a winding path that looked like a sheep walk, which was very steep, and went in a zigzag fashion up the hill.

Ada followed with Septimus, to whom she explained what had happened, at which he was surprised but not alarmed, and Sarati brought up the rear.

Occasionally, when they came to a steep or difficult part, the brigand graciously assisted Ada in the ascent.

"I like brigands," observed Septimus. "They are jolly fellows; they have plenty to eat and drink, and they play cards. I think I shall join the band."

"That would just suit a low mind," replied Ada. "I shall make my escape as soon as I can."

"Don't you wish Left-handed Jack would rescue you ?" sneered Septimus.

"Perhaps he will yet. More wonderful things than that have happened."

"Not he. You will only go away as Sarati's wife."

"That shall never be," said Ada.

They had now ascended about two hundred and fifty feet.

This brought them to a broad plateau fringed with flowering shrubs.

From behind these a hideous, truculent-looking dwarf sprang up, armed with a rifle.

"Who goes there ?" he demanded in a squeaky voice.

"Friends," was the reply.

"Captain, is it you ?" said the dwarf. "Welcome back to the cave. We have been exceedingly dull without you."

"My lieutenant, Tito," exclaimed Possilippo. "A better fellow for the post never breathed."

"By the holy cross, you are right there !" answered the dwarf. "I was born to be a bandit ; the restraints of civilisation never suited me."

"Go, Tito, and tell my old housekeeper, Bianca, that I have company— one of whom is a young lady. We shall want wine and dinner as soon as possible. The lady will be accommodated in Bianca's cave."

"Your orders shall be obeyed, signor."

"Send two men into the valley to bring up the baggage of the visitors. Quick ! away with you."

Tito vanished among the bushes.

"*Diavolo* !" he muttered, "the captain was always fond of a pretty face. The women have been the ruin of him. Bah ! I can see nothing in them."

Possilippo moved on again.

Behind the bushes was the entrance to a cave, or rather a series of caves, in which the brigands had located themselves.

It was a well-situated place, and free from observation.

From the plateau, the side of the hill to the summit was a sheer precipice, down which no one could get.

To reach the caves, the winding path must be ascended.

Some one of the brigands was always on guard, and a splendid view of the valley and its approaches could be secured from the elevation.

"I cannot offer you first-class accommodation," said Possilippo ; "but as far as my poor hospitality will extend I bid you heartily welcome."

"Any port in a storm," replied Sarati.

"Enter, then. My wines are good, my cook is excellent, and provisions are plentiful."

They walked into a spacious cavern in which a dozen rough-looking men were seated at tables playing cards and drinking a kind of light sherry.

They rose and saluted Possilippo, who shook hands with some and spoke to others.

This cave was lighted from the doorway, but the next one they entered was rendered light by oil-lamps hanging from the ceiling by long chains.

It was rudely furnished.

"Be seated, gentlemen," exclaimed the brigand, "I will introduce the signora to my faithful Bianca."

He took Ada by the hand, leading her to a third aperture in the rock.

"Ho, Bianca!" he cried.

An aged woman, whose features were sharp and pinched, made her appearance, bearing in her hand a lamp.

At the same time the dwarf, Tito, came along with bottles and glasses, which he put before Sarati and Septimus.

"Bianca," continued Possilippo.

"What is your pleasure?" answered the old crone, regarding Ada with a compassionate air.

"Look to this lady; she will sleep in your apartment. Let all her wants be instantly supplied."

"Is she a prisoner?"

"On the contrary, a favoured guest."

Bianca gave Ada her hand, conducting her through a passage into a cave where a fire was burning, the smoke of the wood finding its way out through a fissure in the rock.

Beyond this was a cave in which the hag slept, a mattress supplying the place of a bedstead.

"Heaven help you, my child!" said the old woman, feelingly.

"Of what am I in danger?" asked Ada.

"You have come into the wolf's lair. For the Virgin's sake get away as soon as you can, for you are in the power of a bad man."

"Will you help me?" asked Ada, thoroughly alarmed.

"Alas! I cannot, he would kill me."

"Why do you serve him?"

A look of intense piteousness came into the woman's face.

Her eyes filled with tears, and her bosom heaved with emotion.

"Because I am his mother," she replied.

"You! his mother?" ejaculated Ada.

"I cannot war against my son, my only child; for, with all his faults, I love him," continued Bianca.

A brigand now arrived with Ada's box.

She then went into the second cave, fortified by a promise from Bianca that she would help and guard her as much as she dared.

Septimus had gone to sleep again in a chair after drinking more wine.

In fact, he seemed to have given himself up entirely to drink lately, as if he did not care what became of him.

His brain was becoming softened, and his system soddened with the drink.

Possilippo and Sarati were quietly smoking cigarettes of Turkish aromatic tobacco, and talking earnestly.

"Join my band," said the brigand. "'Tis an exciting and romantic life, this of ours. We are free as the eagle in his eyry."

"When the fowler comes the eagle is sometimes caught and caged," replied Sarati.

Possilippo was emboldened by long immunity from capture.

He laughed scornfully, in the manner of one who felt perfectly secure.

"I defy Naples and all the secret police!" he exclaimed. "When they catch me, they will only have one more to get hold of."

"Who is that?"

"The foul fiend himself!" answered Possilippo, recklessly.

The banditti in the outer cavern burst into a roar of laughter, as if enjoying some exquisite jest.

"Hark at them," said the chief. "They are a set of jolly dogs, I'll warrant, and would one and all lay down their lives for me."

"They are making merry."

"Aye! 'tis always their wont. Tito is a comical fellow, and can always make them laugh. They sing and gamble; but they can fight like demons, if need be. Come, be one of us."

"What does Ada say to it?" asked Sarati, looking at her. "I should prize your opinion highly. You know you are to be my own fair bride soon. How would you like to be a brigand's wife?"

"I will never be yours!" said Ada, in a spirited tone. "I would meet death rather."

"By Heaven, you shall be my wife!" retorted Sarati. "I have ascertained that one of the bandits is a fully ordained priest; he shall marry us. I give you a week to consider the matter."

"Join the band, by all means," exclaimed Ada.

"Ha! is that your advice?"

"It is. You will stand a chance of being shot or hanged, and I and Left-handed Jack would be avenged."

Sarati grew livid with rage.

A malediction escaped his quivering lips.

"You mock me," he cried. "I will make you repent this levity."

Possilippo stepped between them, for it really seemed as if in his passion Sarati was going to strike her.

"Hold!" said the brigand. "You seem to forget that this young lady is my guest."

"What have you to do with her?"

"While she is enjoying my hospitality, it appears to me that she is under my protection," was the rejoinder.

"But I have known and loved her for a long time; her brother favours my suit."

"No matter; she must be treated with respect."

Sarati gnashed his teeth with rage.

But he saw the wisdom of keeping quiet.

It would never do to show his teeth to the brigand chief while he was in his lair.

He must, perforce, bide his time.

If he had known at first what he did now, he would never have sought the help of Possilippo.

"Well, well," he replied, curbing his temper, "do not let us fall out. The girl is mine, and I will treat her fairly, but I intend to stand no nonsense from anybody."

"Are you going to be one of us?" enquired the chief.

"No!" said Sarati, decisively.

"In that case, you must consider yourself a prisoner."

"This is an outrage."

"Call it what you like," returned Possilippo, coolly; "I am master here."

He raised his voice.

"Hi, Tito!" he added, "you are wanted. Tito, I say!"

The dwarf instantly made his appearance from the outer cave.

"Master," he replied, "you called."

"I did."

"What is your pleasure?"

"Conduct this man to our prison. If he is insubordinate, take him to the plateau, and hurl him down the rocks into the valley below."

Sarati was completely dumfounded at this unexpected order.

The chief was acting with a high hand.

"Stop!" he exclaimed. "I have reconsidered my determination, and, rather than have any unpleasantness, I will be a member of your band."

Possilippo smiled.

"I thought we should bring you to reason," he answered. "Swear to obey my commands, whatever they may be, under pain of death."

"I swear," said Sarati, in a husky voice.

"Good! You can go, Tito; your services are not required."

"Bah!" growled the dwarf. "I had hoped that he would have shown fight, and I should have the pleasure of throwing him down the rock. By the saints! that is the kind of fun I can enjoy. How they shriek! how they roll! how they bump! and then go dashing with a thud to the bottom! It is a sport fit for a king!"

He grinned with delight as he thought of it.

"Do you remember the rich merchant we captured on the Roman road?" he went on. "He tried to shoot, and we cast him down! Ha, ha!"

"Peace, fool."

Tito rubbed his hands gleefully.

"Ho, ho! More to come. Ha, ha, ha!" he roared.

"Go with him, Sarati," said Possilippo. "He will introduce you to your companions. Give them some money. They always expect it from a new recruit."

"Am I to herd with such as they?" asked Sarati in a tone of the most ineffable disgust.

"You can live with me. I will make you my second lieutenant."

"That is better."

Jingling some gold and silver in his pocket, Sarati followed Tito into the robbers' cave.

Loud acclamations soon showed that he was being well received.

"Signora!" exclaimed Possilippo, when he was alone with Ada, "it is my intention to protect you from that man."

"I thank you most cordially," replied Ada.

"May I have the pleasure of kissing your white hand."

Before she could prevent him, he had raised it to his lips.

There was no doubt now that he was enamoured of her, and jealous of Sarati.

Here was a new danger.

Her path was blocked by more than one peril of no ordinary magnitude.

"I go to Naples to-morrow," he continued, "and will bring you a diamond bracelet fit for a princess to wear."

"No, no; a silver ring would be enough—any trifle that a brother might give a sister."

"May I not be something more than that to you?"

"No," replied Ada.

"Ah! I understand. Sarati told me of a girlish affection for a mere boy— a stripling at school."

"He is my sweetheart."

"In this land of sun and flowers, you will learn to forget him," said Possilippo; "but I will not urge you further now."

She was grateful for this relief.

"One thing let me impress on you," he continued. "If Sarati insults or persecutes you during my absence, complain to Tito."

"The dwarf?"

"Yes; the one you saw just now. He will know how to act."

"I will not fail to do so," Ada replied.

At that moment Bianca came to make preparations for dinner.

Septimus heard the noise of knives and forks, and roused himself from his sottish lethargy.

"Good," he said; "time for refreshment. I'm getting hungry. What have you got for dinner, count?"

"You will see in a short while. It will be half-an-hour yet," rejoined Possilippo.

Septimus helped himself to a goblet of wine.

"Oh! in that case," he answered, drowsily, "I'll go to sleep again. When the banquet is ready, call me."

In another minute he was again snoring.

CHAPTER XVI.

A MARVELLOUS EFFORT—ARRIVAL OF LEFT-HANDED JACK IN NAPLES—ON THE TRACK OF THE BRIGAND.

FOR once in his adventurous career, the brigand chief had made a mistake in his calculations.

Though to all appearance the police agent, Sparghetti, was dead, in reality he was not so.

He had been dangerously wounded, and was bleeding profusely.

In spite of his terrible injury he preserved consciousness, being fully aware of all that was going on around him.

Not a sound escaped him, though he was suffering the most acute agony.

He remained perfectly impassive and motionless until the sound of the carriage-wheels had died away in the distance.

Then he sat up in the road, and pressed his hand to his wound.

He withdrew it covered with blood.

His face was ghastly pale.

Not a traveller or a peasant was in sight.

He got up, tottered a little way, and with a cry, wrung from him in spite of his heroic fortitude, fell down in the dust.

By his side he saw a white silk scarf, which Ada had let fall when she alighted from the carriage.

He grasped it eagerly, and tearing open his clothes, contrived to press it tightly on the wound.

Then he managed to fasten a leather belt he wore over the scarf, so as to hold it in its place.

He would not bleed to death now, he thought.

A terrible fainting-fit, however.

attacked him, and he sank like a corpse on his side.

The blazing sun streamed down upon him.

For half-an-hour he remained in this position.

When he came to himself a man was bending over him, and chafing his hands.

A cart filled with fruit was drawn up by the side of the road.

It was a peasant proprietor, who was going to Naples to sell the produce of his garden.

He had seen the body of Sparghetti lying in front of his cart, and had pulled up just in time to prevent running over him.

When the police agent opened his eyes, the man exclaimed :

"Jesu ! that is better. Have you fallen amongst thieves, my friend ? "

"I have been shot by brigands," replied Sparghetti.

"Ha ! Was it Possilippo's famous band ? They are a terrible lot."

"I know not," said Sparghetti thinking it wise to keep silence on the point, as the peasantry went in mortal dread of Possilippo.

"Are you from the city ? I am going that way. Shall I take you to a priest ? You should not die, if die you must, without being shriven."

"I will give you ten scudi if you will drive me to the headquarters of the secret police."

The peasant looked nervously around.

"Are you sure those accursed brigands, whom Heaven and our Lady confound, are not coming back ? " he asked.

"They have gone up the road long ago ; fear not."

"Come, then, I will take you. Lift up, lean on me. You can sit at the back of the cart, and quench your thirst with a few of my peaches."

"May the saints take you into their holy keeping," replied Sparghetti with great thankfulness.

It was with the utmost difficulty that he got into the cart, groaning all the time.

So weak was he, that the carter had to make him fast with a rope, for fear that he would fall out.

To add to his troubles, the jolting of the conveyance made his wound break, and commence bleeding again.

It was in a very exhausted condition that he arrived at the police office.

Two men who were on duty outside recognising a *confrère*, assisted him inside.

He requested to see the head of the bureau, Signor Madia, and was conducted into his presence.

"What has befallen you, my poor fellow ? " enquired Madia.

"I wish to speak to you alone," was the reply.

Madia motioned everyone to retire.

He placed a chair for the wounded man, and bade him tell his story.

This Sparghetti did in a circumstantial manner, omitting no detail.

It took him some time to complete the narration, for he had to stop at intervals to gasp for breath.

When he had finished, he was so weak as to be scarcely able to articulate.

Madia was surprised beyond measure.

But, on the other hand, he was intensely elated.

The intelligence he had received was of the very first importance.

He went to a cupboard, and taking out a bottle of brandy, gave Sparghetti some in a tumbler.

This enabled him to rally for a brief space.

The sound of blood falling drip, drip, on the sanded floor, startled Madia.

"Good Heaven ! man," he exclaimed, "why did you not tell me that your hurt was not properly bound up ? "

"My duty, signor, was to speak first for the public good, and think of myself afterwards," replied Sparghetti.

"That is magnanimous, but risking your life."

"Are you satisfied with me, signor ? "

"Perfectly. I shall recommend you for promotion."

A sickly smile crossed Sparghetti's wan and pallid face.

"I fear," he replied, " that I shall not require it."

"Tut, tut ! don't talk like that," said Madia.

Then he did what ought to have been done at first.

He rang his bell, and despatched a messenger for a doctor.

"Let me recapitulate what you have told, so that there can be no mistake," exclaimed Madia.

"Proceed, signor."

"The Count Casati, of the Villa Borghese, and Possilippo, the brigand chief, are one and the same person ? "

Sparghetti nodded.

His utterance was beginning to fail him; his jaw fell, and his eyes rolled fearfully.

"Casati has gone in a coach to the hills, with a countryman you heard called Sarati, and a young Englishman and lady, from the 'Hotel Ré Galantuomo'; their names, you ascertained, being Ada and Septimus Titmarsh? At least, that is what the hotel clerk told you?"

Again Sparghetti's head moved like that of an automaton.

"Good. We shall soon have the fish in our net," concluded Madia.

His face was illuminated with a smile of satisfaction.

All Naples would, before long, be startled with a veritable sensation.

Suddenly Sparghetti gave a lurch, and fell forward on his face.

Madia rushed to his assistance, but arrived at his side too late to catch him, or break his fall.

"Help, help!" he cried, ringing his bell furiously.

The door opened, and the doctor who had been sent for entered in hot haste.

He raised the police agent, and put his hand to his heart.

It had ceased to beat.

"Well?" exclaimed Madia, anxiously.

"The man is dead," replied the doctor.

The chief pretended to be profoundly affected, and expressed his deep regret.

Inwardly, he was thanking Fate that Sparghetti had lived long enough to tell his precious secret.

At a sign from him, two policemen who had entered at the same time as the doctor removed the body.

Another came with a can of sand, and sprinkled the bloodstains on the floor.

"What is it—a street affray?" asked the doctor.

"Some drunken sailors," answered Madia, carelessly. "A trifling affair, though it has cost me the life of one of my best men. Good-day."

The doctor bowed and retired.

Madia despatched this message to the central police-station:

"Let the house of Count Casati, the Villa Borghese, be carefully watched at once, day and night. When the count shows himself, arrest him promptly."

He resumed his seat.

"The trap is set," he muttered, "and only awaits the coming of the fox."

Then he went on writing at his desk as if nothing had happened.

Five minutes later the messenger entered, and announced that three Englishmen wished to see him on business.

He presented their cards.

They severally bore the names of Mr. John Massey, Mr. Richard Lambert, and Mr. Sparks, Detective, Criminal Investigation Department, Scotland Yard, London.

"Show the strangers in," said Madia.

He was an accomplished linguist, and could speak English and French as well as his own language.

Jack Massey, Dick Lambert, and Sparks, the detective, entered, and were accommodated with seats.

They had not been many hours in Naples.

Their first visit was to the hotel in the Strada Popolo, where they expected to find Septimus and Ada, if not Sarati.

Ascertaining that the birds had just flown with their luggage, they decided to call upon the head of the secret police.

It was easy to discover the address of his office.

"In what way can I be of service to you, gentlemen?" asked Madia.

"I have a warrant for the arrest of a person named Sarati, long domiciled in England, but now supposed to be in this city—that is, if the information I have received is correct," replied Sparks, "and I thought, as you keep a register of newcomers, you might kindly give some assistance."

Madia smiled.

"Sarati arrived in Naples this morning," he said.

"Ah; you are well informed."

"It is necessary that I should be so."

"Where is Sarati now?"

"He has joined a well-known brigand named Possilippo, who has a stronghold in the hills to the north of the city."

Madia took down a map from the wall, and pointed out the hilly region in question, and the road that led to it.

"Here is the district," he remarked.

"Why do you not put a stop to his depredations?" enquired Jack.

"In the first place, I do not know the exact locality of his hiding-place; secondly, he is no ordinary man; thirdly, I believe it would take two or three regiments of soldiers to dislodge him; and fourthly, I have laid a trap to catch him shortly in this city, the particulars of which I cannot disclose to you or anybody."

"Do you know anything, sir, of a young Englishman and his sister, named Titmarsh, who were staying at the 'Ré Galantuomo Hotel'?" continued Jack.

"Yes," replied Madia, carelessly.

"You are marvellously informed."

"Passably well."

"Where have they gone—I am much interested in them?"

"I am credibly informed that they, in company with Sarati and the brigand, Possilippo, who appear to be old friends, have gone to the hills."

Jack gasped for breath.

"Can it be true?" he asked.

The idea of Ada being in the power of the brigand and Sarati was almost more than he could bear.

It took his breath away for the time.

Yet it was nothing more than he had expected from the first, as he had always imagined Sarati to be the associate of bad and lawless men.

"Cannot we arrest Sarati at once?" he said.

Madia smiled again.

"Certainly you can," he replied, "whenever you can find him, but I can render you no assistance at present."

"You mean that I may do it alone and unaided?"

"If—you—can."

The words were spoken slowly and deliberately.

A look of disappointment crossed Jack's face.

"Should you succeed in capturing Possilippo, you will be entitled to a large sum of secret service money, offered as a reward," added Madia.

"Bother Possilippo," said Jack; "I want to rescue Ada Titmarsh, and bring Sarati to the gallows."

"What for?"

"Killing my father."

"You have a difficult task before you, Signor Inglese," exclaimed Madia. "If you can find out the hiding-place of Possilippo, and assure me it is possible to take it by assault, I will promise to make the attempt."

"Brigandage seems to be an institution of this country."

"You in England have your garotters, your burglars, and other choice characters."

"True," replied Jack. "Pardon me, I spoke hastily. You have been very kind in giving me the information you possessed."

"Do not mention it."

"I will follow this man, Possilippo, to the bitter end, and show you that an English lad can teach the Neapolitan police something."

"If so, you will be very clever," answered Madia, sarcastically. "Should I capture this man, and I am sanguine enough I shall, his band will melt away. It is always thus. The brigands are nothing without a head. Better leave the task to me, and be patient."

"No," said Jack, sternly; "I go and rescue the girl I love."

"I will go, too," cried Dick.

"What can two youths like you do, though you boast of being English?"

"You will see shortly."

"Be advised and wait," exclaimed Sparks. "I shall stop here."

"Take your own course," replied Jack, "my mind is made up. Whatever the risk, I mean to be on Possilippo's track before this night is over."

"Then we part. We shall be good friends, I hope?"

"Why not? You do your work in your way, I will do mine in my own. It is only a difference in temperament and judgment, or perhaps courage."

"I will co-operate with Signor Madia," replied Sparks.

"With pleasure," replied the Italian police officer, "I shall be glad of your assistance. We may trap Sarati and Possilippo together."

"Good-day," said Jack; "Dick and I will try our luck, and perhaps trap the villains first."

"If you are wise, and value your lives," remarked Madia, "you will stay here."

"No, thank you. I intend to follow up the brigand. If I come to grief, that is my look out. Come, Dick, now to save Ada, and show these Italian villains we English lads know how to risk our lives, and fight for those we love."

Jack shook hands with Sparks and bowed to Madia, after which he and Lambert quitted the office.

He had gained all the information he could, and it was quite enough for his purpose.

Sarati, Ada, and Septimus were with Possilippo, the brigand, somewhere in the hills.

It was his self-imposed task to find them.

The dangers to be encountered were innumerable, but he was not afraid to face them. His love for Ada urged him on.

He knew he could rely on Dick to the last drop of his blood.

They went to a small hotel near the railway station, where they had left their luggage.

As they sipped their wine, and looked out seaward, in the direction of Capri's wonderful grotto, they confessed that the bay was very lovely.

But they had other things to occupy their minds, besides the beauties of Nature.

"I did not think our travelling companion, Sparks, had much fight in him," observed Jack, "but I didn't expect he would leave us in the lurch."

"He will not risk his life out of the city," replied Dick.

"Of course. It is a good job," continued Jack, "and he wants to prolong it. He gets so much a day and expenses."

"We can do without him."

"I should hope so," said Jack, with a smile.

"How do you propose to begin?" asked Dick.

"Before I left England I foresaw that we should have to rough it, so, in London, I bought a couple of knapsacks and water canteens. We must provision ourselves for a week."

"When will you start?"

"To-night. The moon will be up, and we can do several miles before we curl up under some old wall for a sleep," replied Jack.

This decision being come to, they lost no time in making their preparations.

The knapsacks were got out of the portmanteau and filled with such articles of food as were deemed necessary, sure to keep, and easy to carry.

Each wore a belt instead of braces.

In this belt was stuck a formidable-looking knife and a brace of pistols—seven-chambered revolvers.

"Shall we do?" enquired Jack, as he put on his canvas sun-helmet.

"We look ready and fit to march anywhere and do anything," replied Dick.

"Then off we go. This is the opening of the campaign to hunt down Sarati."

Side by side they walked up the street, their martial bearing and manly appearance attracting universal attention.

People turned round to look at them.

"Ah! name of Mary!" was the general exclamation. "English on a walking tour. Labour for pleasure. Bah!"

The ease and leisure-loving Neapolitans could not understand a person walking when he could ride, or, what was better still, sit down and not undergo the fatigue of moving.

The sun was setting when they quitted the precincts of the city.

This caused the temperature to fall, and the air was rendered more agreeable by a cooling breeze which came up from the sea.

But the sandy, gritty dust was all-pervading, assailing the traveller in clouds, and getting into the pores of the skin in a most irritating manner.

Vesuvius kept on vomiting smoke and flames, and occasionally stones shot into the air, falling on the sides of the mountain.

This strange sight reminded them of the destruction, by lava and scoria, of Pompeii, two thousand years ago, which is so well described by Pliny.

Jack had a guide-book and compass with him.

By the aid of these useful companions, he steered direct for the hills.

They persisted in their self-imposed task till close upon midnight.

"I shall have to cry a go," exclaimed Dick, "for I never felt so tired in my life before."

"Same here," replied Jack.

"Isn't that a house on the right? There is a light burning," continued Dick.

The road had been very lonely for some miles.

Not a house, not a man, had been seen.

"Yes," answered Jack, a few yards further on, "it's a queer-looking crib, but a house it is."

"An inn," cried Dick, delightedly; "that is more than I expected. It will be better to sleep there than pitch under a hedge."

"I don't mind, and if the place is open I should not object to some supper."

Dick Lambert was right about the dwelling being an inn.

There was a sign over the door representing a man in a red shirt.

"There is, to my mind, something uncanny about the place," remarked Jack.

"It looks as if it were all glued up," replied Dick.

"I'll knock and see," continued Jack. "My dad, you know, lived here, poor old chap, and he taught me enough Italian to get along with."

"Give them two or three rousers," said Dick. "If there is any chance of comfortable quarters I don't want to lose it."

"Bear one thing in mind, Dick."

"What's that, old son?"

"Don't let out what our little game is. The brigands may have friends all round here."

"That's correct," replied Dick. "We are in their territory now. Trust me, I will not be indiscreet."

Satisfied with this promise, Jack knocked loudly at the door.

They had been going uphill for some time past.

At the elevation they had gained the air was quite cool.

Consequently the doors and windows of the inn were all closed.

The noise of footsteps was heard coming up the passage.

"Who knocks, and what do you require?" asked a gruff voice.

"We are two English travellers on a pedestrian tour," Jack answered. "What we want is a bed and some supper, if it be not too late."

"Sleeping accommodation you are welcome to, as sure as my name is Geronimo, and that of the partner of my joys and cares, Teresa, but if my patron saint were to come here to-night, I would not cook for him."

"That does not matter."

"Yet if you can be satisfied with maccaroni and parmesan, you can eat your fill," added the landlord.

"Excellent! I would not ask for better fare."

The bolt was shot back.

A somewhat unusually ponderous door for an inn was thrown open.

"Enter, and be at home," said Geronimo.

He had an oil-lamp in his hand, and bidding them follow him, led them into a room in which a man, dressed as a shepherd, was seated at a table, facing the host's wife.

She was an elderly woman, with a vicious, hawk-like face.

Geronimo was not a prepossessing person, Jack thought, when he obtained a good look at him.

He was thin, sallow, and had an extremely avaricious eye.

In fact, greed was stamped in every lineament of his features.

"Capitano," said Geronimo, "these are two English travellers. They will not incommode you?"

"Not in the least," was the reply.

Teresa, after a few words from her husband, placed cold maccaroni and cheese, flanked by some excellent wine, before the guests.

They enjoyed the repast very much, and Dick ordered some more of the red wine which was stronger than he had any idea of.

It rapidly mounted to his head.

The stranger who had been addressed as capitano, watched them both narrowly.

"Pardon me," he said, "have you been long in this country?"

Jack Massey did not answer him.

He thought that there was something peculiar in the fact that a simple shepherd should be addressed by the innkeeper as "captain."

Then, again, there was that in his manner which stamped him as being above the lower order of men.

The capitano looked and talked like a gentleman.

In addition to this he spoke in English, which could not be the accomplishment of a peasant.

"A civil question ought to receive a civil reply," continued the capitano, bending his brows in anger.

"I am not in the habit of talking to persons I do not know," rejoined Jack. "Everyone is equal in the parlour of an inn."

"You may think so, but I do not."

Dick had finished his supper, and the bottle too.

He was just in the humour to talk, and although Jack gave him a severe glance, he would not be restrained.

"We only arrived to-day in Naples," he said.

"Oh, indeed. You are more amiable than your companion," answered the capitano. "What is your object in coming up the country?"

Dick winked at him.

"You want to know too much, old boy," he exclaimed.

"Are you art students going to Rome,

and too poor to pay the railway fare ? "

"Guess again."

" If it were so, I would help you on your way."

"You ! " laughed Dick. "I'll bet we have more money between us than you have."

The capitano looked confused.

He quickly recovered himself, however.

" If I am poorly dressed," he replied, "I own my sheep, which form a numerous flock. I have money. You should never judge of a man's circumstances by his dress, young man."

"Keep your money," said Dick, "and your sheep too. I only like sheep in the form of mutton."

"Will you hold your tongue, and come to bed ? " exclaimed Jack.

"Nò, I won't," rejoined Dick.

"I admire your independent spirit," remarked the stranger, forgetting his anger, and lapsing into a smile.

" If you want to know our business, I will tell you," said Dick.

" Please yourself."

Jack was in despair, for he saw it was impossible to keep Dick back.

"It is an awfully funny and romantic thing," said Dick, leaning back in his chair, and laughing with hilarity.

"What is ? " asked the capitano.

"Some would call it foolhardy," continued Dick.

"To what do you allude ?"

"Why, you see, we have started out brigand hunting."

The capitano and Geronimo exchanged glances.

"Who are you after ? " enquired the capitano.

"A fellow called Possilippo."

"What harm has he done you ? "

"Well, you see, he is harbouring a man name Sarati, who is our deadly enemy, and, if I meet with Possilippo, I mean to——"

He paused, and opening his jacket, touched his pistols.

"What ! " demanded the capitano, "what will you do ? "

"I mean to capture him or have his life," replied Dick.

With a quick movement the shepherd threw off the smock-frock he had been wearing.

He was seen, when bereft of his disguise, to be dressed in a handsome suit of velvet.

"Hullo ! " said Dick, "is this a transformation scene ? "

The capitano seized him by the arm and snatched his weapons out of his belt.

He was rendered powerless in a moment.

The next, he was hurled to the ground, and his head coming in contact with the brick floor, he became insensible.

Jack saw that he had stepped into a hornet's nest.

He prepared to defend himself, but before he could draw a pistol, the innkeeper was upon him.

"Back ! " shouted our hero.

Geronimo attempted to seize him.

Quick as lightning, Jack raised his fist, and dealt him one of his terrible left-handed blows.

With a groan, Geronimo measured his length by the side of Dick Lambert.

The capitano would have fared the same, had he not presented a revolver at Jack's head.

"Pause," he said, "or you are a dead man."

The pistol was on a level with Jack's heart.

He was, perforce, compelled to remain inactive, though he gnashed his teeth with rage.

"Who are you ? " he demanded, fiercely.

"Possilippo, the brigand, at your service," was the reply.

Jack was completely staggered.

"Be good enough to put your weapons on the table," continued Possilippo, "and no harm will befall you."

With a sigh of vexation, Jack removed the pistols and knife from his belt, laying them upon the table.

Possilippo at once took possession of them.

"Geronimo and I are old friends," he remarked. "In fact, he is one of my most trusty agents."

"I wish I had known it."

"You would have given the 'Garibaldi' a wide berth ? "

"Most decidedly."

"And you would have acted wisely," the brigand replied. "Geronimo always gives me instant information of the arrival and movements of travellers. I often come down from the hills and spend a night with him."

"I suppose I am your prisoner ? "

"What else can you expect ? You came to find me, and instead of that I have found you, Mr. Massey."

"Ha! you know my name."

"I have guessed who you are."

"How?" demanded Jack.

"By the blow of the fist you gave poor Geronimo. No one but Left-handed Jack could have done that."

"Who told you about me?"

"Miss Ada Titmarsh has spoken of you," answered Possilippo. "Signor Sarati, or the Count di Mora, has also told me a good deal respecting you."

"I have walked into a trap," said Jack, dismally.

"There can be no doubt about that," answered the brigand chief, with a self-complacent smile.

"At the same time, I think I can walk out of it."

"In what way?"

"I'll show you."

Saying this, Jack made a dash at the brigand, completely taking him by surprise.

He knocked his arm up, and his pistol exploded harmlessly in the air, making a big hole in the ceiling.

Before Possilippo could recover his position, Jack dealt him one of his famous blows.

The redoubtable brigand spun round like a teetotum, and fell across the body of Dick Lambert.

This roused Dick, who was not much hurt.

His senses were confused, however, by the wine he had imbibed, and the fall on the floor the innkeeper had given him.

With a wild cry, he rushed to the door and ran into the road.

"Dick!" cried Jack, "where are you off to? Come here, I want you."

There was no response.

Dick had taken himself off, possibly thinking that Jack had gone before him, as, for the time being, he was not exactly clear-headed, and did not understand what had happened, or what was going on.

Jack was about to rush after Dick, when Possilippo rose, and putting a silver whistle to his lips, blew it shrilly.

CHAPTER XVII.

CAUGHT IN A TRAP.

JACK MASSEY ran to the door, intending to follow his friend.

He hoped to be able to make his escape.

In this expectation he was signally disappointed.

A fierce-looking man standing outside presented a rifle at his breast.

With a cry of rage he retreated, and hastened to the window.

To throw up the sash was the work of a moment.

Here again he was baulked.

Two men faced him with their loaded weapons.

A peal of mocking laughter rang through the room.

"Signor Massey," exclaimed Possilippo, "you are fairly beaten. I think, as a sensible person, you will recognise the advisability of admitting it."

"A man cannot fight successfully against such odds," replied Jack.

"When I blew my whistle, it was a signal to my brave fellows. The house is surrounded by them. Shall I make you a prisoner, and subject you to the inconvenience and indignity of being bound?"

"I suppose you can do as you like."

"Will you give me your word of honour, as a gentleman, not to attempt to escape? If so, I will accept your parole."

"No," answered Jack, flatly.

"You refuse?"

"I'll get away if I can."

"Very well," said the brigand. "I have no alternative but to bind your arms. That left hand of yours might play havoc with my men, if they were taken unawares. *Cospetto!* my jaws will ache for days to come."

He beckoned to Teresa.

Accustomed to similar scenes, the inn-keeper's wife had sat perfectly still during the brief scrimmage that had taken place.

She contented herself with holding up a strong metal tea-tray, to protect herself from any bullets that might fly in her direction.

"THE KNIFE HAD STRUCK HIM IN THE THROAT."—(See page 115.)

No. 7.

"Some rope, Teresa!" exclaimed Possilippo.

"Is the skirmish over?" she asked.

"Yes, the enemy is hopelessly defeated."

"Has my good man sustained any injury, poor fellow?"

"Nothing worse than a knock-down blow, from which he will soon recover."

Teresa gave a grunt of satisfaction, and searching in a cupboard found some rope, which she handed to the chief.

The latter quickly bound Jack's arms behind his back.

"I am very sorry to be obliged to do this," he remarked, "but you have brought it on yourself by your own obstinacy."

"What do you intend to do with me?" asked Jack.

"To protect myself I must take you to the hills, and keep you there for a time."

"My life is safe?"

"Yes, I will guarantee that, though it is more than you deserve, because you started to hunt me down. You cannot deny it, for your friend, who has escaped, admitted as much."

"Until to-day I never heard your name. It is Sarati I want to catch, for I have reason to believe that he murdered my father."

"You are mistaken," replied Possilippo.

"I should be glad to think so."

"It happens that I have heard all about it."

"Perhaps you will have the kindness to explain the mystery," Jack replied.

"With pleasure. Many years ago, before you were born, your father came to Naples, and ran away with Sarati's wife, who died shortly afterwards, hence Sarati's long-standing grudge against Captain Massey. Sarati called at his house and forced a duel upon him. Your father fell dead."

"I call it murder, all the same; but, as Sarati is your guest, I must ask one favour at your hands."

"What is that?"

"Do not leave me bound and at his mercy. He hates me as much as he did my father, and would kill me if he could. With my arms free, I fear him not, but I certainly don't relish the idea of being murdered without a chance of defending myself."

"He shall not know that you are my prisoner. I will take you to the caves to-night, and put you in a secret cavern."

Jack winced at this.

He had hoped that he would be able to see and speak to Ada.

Yet a moment's reflection showed him that it was best he should be hidden.

If Sarati found him, he would surely be killed by the vindictive Italian.

"How long will my detention last?" he queried.

"I cannot tell, it depends upon circumstances," was the reply. "I have been driven to the life I am leading by the want of money. My fortunes were ruined. I have now replenished my coffers, and I have an intention of going away."

"You will cease to be the brigand chief?"

"That is my resolve. The life has its charms, but, at the same time, it possesses its drawbacks."

"One of which is the chance of a bullet; another, I apprehend, is the hangman's rope."

"I fear not that," replied Possilippo.

"Has death no terrors for you?"

"None at all; but a public execution I am adverse to. To avoid that, I always carry a deadly poison concealed about my person."

"Ah! you are thoughtful."

"The public would have the satisfaction of knowing that the dreaded Possilippo was dead; but the executioner would not kill me."

"Have you shed much blood?" asked Jack.

"How can I be what I am without having done so?" said Possilippo, shortly; "but a truce to this foolish talk. You will please to fall in between two of my men."

He whistled twice.

Half-a-dozen brigands crowded into the apartment.

Geronimo, the innkeeper, had recovered from Jack's knock-down blow.

He got up rubbing his head.

"Where is the scoundrel who hit me with a bar of iron?" he demanded.

"The boy struck you with his fist," replied Possilippo.

"Malediction! is that true?"

"I was floored in the same way," continued the brigand, "so I can speak from experience."

"Holy Mary! these English are

marvellous creatures. What strength! muscles of iron ! thews of brass !"

"Get some wine," cried Possilippo ; "We are going. Let each man have his pint."

When the men had partaken of the refreshment ordered for them they quitted the house, taking Jack with them.

Possilippo had gone on before.

Dick Lambert had succeeded in making his escape, and Jack felt there was hope in this, for he would doubtless return to Naples and inform Sparks and Madia of what had happened.

Dick was unlikely to leave any stone unturned to effect the rescue of his friend.

In the brigands' stronghold Jack would be close to Ada, which was an agreeable prospect for him to dwell upon.

He determined to invent some means of communicating with his sweetheart.

He did not falter in his resolve to avenge his father's death upon Sarati.

He did not really believe that he had fallen fairly in the duel.

He knew Captain Massey to have been a dead shot.

While he was revolving all these things in his mind, the ground was being rapidly traversed.

Not a word passed between him and his captors.

At length the foot of the hill was reached, and the ascent began.

The dawn was now breaking with glorious splendour.

Before the orb of day, Mount Vesuvius paled its fires.

Weary and footsore, Jack arrived on the plateau, and was at once marched to a small cave.

The entrance was so low that he had to stoop to get in.

Two men rolled a large stone against it, so that he could not escape, and by the light which came in over the top of the stone, he saw that his prison was about the size of an ordinary sitting-room.

A heap of dry grass piled up in a corner invited repose.

They had unbound him before he was incarcerated, and with a heavy sigh he threw himself upon the rude couch.

His eyes closed, and he was soon asleep, as exhausted Nature wanted recruiting after the fatigue and excitement he had gone through.

All his dreams were of Ada.

He thought she came to him, rolling the stone away from the mouth of his dungeon, and bidding him fly with her.

Suddenly a flood of light burst in his face.

He awoke with a start.

So tired had he been, that he had slept till midday.

A glance sufficed to show him that the stone had been rolled away.

But it was not Ada who stood before him.

Possilippo had come, attended by Tito, the dwarf, who carried a stone jar of Italian wine in one hand, and a cold fowl and some bread in the other.

These delicacies he placed on the floor.

"I had not forgotten you, Signor Massey," said the brigand. "Tito, my lieutenant here, has orders to look after you, if I happen to be absent. There is no enmity between you and me."

"I duly appreciate your kindness," replied Jack. "Can I have some books to read ? it would pass the time."

"You have asked me for what I cannot give you. My fellows have no mind for reading, and I have no time. There is not a book or a paper in the caves."

"Cigarettes, I suppose, are plentiful ? "

"Ah! yes ; we are well supplied with tobacco."

"Then I must be content to smoke and dream the hours away ; not a very pleasant prospect for an active mind."

"Beggars cannot be choosers," answered Possilippo, with a slight sneer.

Jack's face flushed.

He was quick tempered, and always ready to take offence.

"You would not talk to me like that if we were in Naples," he exclaimed.

"Peace," cried Possilippo ; "I wish to have no angry words with you. Be satisfied with good treatment."

"Throw the English hound down the rocks," said Tito.

"I will, if he provokes me too far, but not now. See to him, Tito, and his comforts. I am going away."

"Your wishes shall be attended to, capitano."

"Come, then ; I have nothing more

to say to the prisoner, who is too proud and insolent for me to be his friend."

Possilippo and Tito left the cave, the heavy stone was rolled back, and Jack was alone.

It was a lovely day, and the brigand sat down on a bench on the plateau, under a shady tree.

He gazed on the beautiful scene below.

In a few minutes he was conscious of someone standing near him.

Looking up, he saw that it was Ada.

Fastened to the rock, over his head, was a wooden pigeon-house, in which were a dozen or more birds cooing too one another.

Ada was watching the birds, and did not notice Possilippo until he spoke to her.

It had been far from her thoughts to seek him.

"Will you take a seat by my side, signora?" he said.

"Oh!" she replied, with a slight shiver, "I did not know you were here. I was tired of staying inside with Bianca, so I came out to enjoy the sunshine."

"It is your right. The sun belongs to everyone."

"You were out last night, Bianca tells me."

"We stopped a traveller on the Roman Road, and took from him a thousand pounds in English money."

"Did you injure him?"

"He lies behind a stone wall with half-a-dozen bullets in his body."

"How dreadful!" cried Ada.

"Bah! 'twas his own fault. He shot one of my men first. We could not show him much mercy after that."

"But you had no right to take his money," said Ada, simply.

"My dear signora, a brigand knows not law."

"It seems very strange, and very dreadful to me. How rich you must be. What do you do with all your money?"

"I buy diamonds—they are easier to carry or to hide than gold. I have diamonds worth a thousand pounds apiece."

"Many of them?" enquired Ada.

"Thirty, and a large number of smaller ones. These I can turn into money, when I want to, in any capital in Europe, or the United States."

While he was speaking, a pigeon, flying slowly, came from the direction of Naples.

It hovered over the plateau.

Possilippo whistled to it gently.

The bird, as if it knew him, fluttered towards the dove-cot, and finally settled on the ledge.

The brigand stretched out his hand and grasped it lightly.

"Oh! the pretty bird," cried Ada. "What are you going to do with it? Pray do not hurt it."

"I shall not harm it any more than I would you."

"Why have you taken it up?"

"This is my pigeon post; it comes from the city, and has brought me a letter," Possilippo replied.

It was true.

He kept a stock of carefully-trained carrier pigeons at his house in Naples, the Villa Borghese.

In his absence, the coachman, Guiseppe, and his wife, looked after the house, and were ordered to send off a pigeon to the hills if they had any important information to impart to their master.

The brigand unfastened a piece of tissue paper, which was tied with white silk round the bird's leg.

Then he allowed the pigeon to fly to the coop, where corn and water were waiting for it.

"See!" he exclaimed, as he unrolled the paper, "here is the letter. What news, I wonder? I expected none."

Possilippo's brow darkened as he read the letter.

His lips became compressed, and he drew his breath quickly.

"Ha!" he exclaimed, "Guiseppe writes thus:

"'Something is wrong. Since six o'clock last evening, the villa has been surrounded by men, who, I am convinced, are agents of the secret police. I can swear to it by their looks. They were on duty all night. This morning they were relieved by another lot. They even penetrate to the garden. Be warned in time, for your life is in danger.'"

"Who can have betrayed you?" enquired Ada.

"I know not. My secret has been divined by somebody. The police are evidently aware that Count Casati and Possilippo are one and the same."

"Will they attack you here?"

"It is not likely. In this fastness I am a match for all the police in Naples, and to employ soldiers to dislodge me would imply a weakness in the government—it would be a public scandal. Madia would be dismissed from his post. They would rather tolerate me than send the troops here."

"You will not be able to visit Naples again."

"Shall I not ?" answered Possilippo, with a disdainful curl of his lip.

"They will capture you, and then they will kill you," said Ada.

"Would that distress you, little one ?"

"I should not like to see you in danger. I am afraid of such men as you, but you have been kind to me. Keep away; give up this life."

"In a short time I intend to do so, but I must go to Naples to-day, for I have accepted an invitation to the Duke of Calabria's ball. If the police are looking for me at my villa, they will not think that I am at the Duke's palace. *Cospetto* ! how they will stare when they hear of it next day."

He laughed at the idea.

"Excuse me, now," he added. "I want to speak a few words to my trusty lieutenant, Tito, and then I walk to an inn, where I keep two fleet horses."

With these words he left her.

The sentry (one always was on duty day and night) paced up and down in a monotonous fashion.

Fiercely the sun beat upon his head, and ardently he longed for the time to come when he could rejoin his companions.

Tito was standing at the entrance to the outer cave watching the eruption of Vesuvius, which was assuming grand proportions.

From his sanguinary disposition, he had acquired the nickname of the Dwarf of Blood.

"Tito," said Possilippo, "I leave you in command, while I go to Naples."

"Don't go, master," answered the dwarf, "I had bad dreams last light."

"I *must* go."

"Have you had bad news from Guiseppe ?"

"Yes. Madia has surrounded my home with his spies."

"Malediction ! Where could he have got his information ?" asked the ill-shaped little monster.

"That puzzles me," replied Possilippo. "Of course, I shall not go to the Villa Borghese to dress. I shall change at some costumiers, as if I were going to a fancy ball at the opera."

"Is this a masquerade ball ?"

"No ; evening dress simply," replied the brigand.

"All the more danger. If you wore a costume and a mask you would be far safer."

"No matter, I intend to risk it. Keep the prisoner we brought in last night secluded from all. See that Sarati offers no insult to the young lady, and if I fail to come back by this time to-morrow——"

He paused abruptly.

"What then ?" asked the dwarf.

"Say nothing. Let everything go on here as if nothing had happened to me. The prison is not yet built that will keep me."

"Good."

Waving his hand lightly, Possilippo descended the path, and was speedily lost to sight.

In a short time his tall form was seen as he gained the valley, and walked to the Garibaldi, where his horses were stabled.

Feeling the sun's rays oppressive, Ada retraced her steps to the caves.

To do so she had to pass by the rock which blocked the entrance to the cave in which Jack Massey was confined.

She had no inkling of his proximity.

Passing by the lazy-looking, murderous brigands, most of whom were asleep, she entered the second cave.

Sarati was pacing up and down like a caged tiger, and an ominous frown was on his brow.

Having had his breakfast, Septimus had ordered Bianca to bring him a flask of wine, and had soon gone into a doze again.

He was always now, as the French say, between two wines.

That is, he was never really sober.

Being roused by the rustle of his sister's dress, he looked up.

"Time for refreshment ?" he asked.

"Not yet," replied Ada, with a look of disgust.

"Call me when it is. Ha! ha!" chuckled Septimus, "very good quarters these. Nothing to do, plenty to eat and drink, no payment asked for."

His head sank back, and he relapsed into a drunken stupor.

"He will kill himself if he goes on like this," remarked Ada.

Sarati stepped in front of her, his eyes flashing, his broad chest heaving.

He was evidently under the influence of great excitement.

"Where is your friend and admirer, Possilippo?" he demanded, with suppressed fury.

"I am not aware that he is either one or the other," she replied. "You are responsible for his introduction to me, or I should not be here."

"Answer my question."

"If you want to know, he has gone to Naples on a very perilous errand."

"How so?" asked Sarati.

"He is to be present at a ball to-night, given by the Duke of Calabria, but the danger consists in this fact—the police know that he and Casati are one and the same."

"Ha! his secret has leaked out."

"Yes, at last."

"I am glad of that!" cried Sarati, rubbing his hands with undisguised glee.

"His man, Guiseppe, sent him the news by pigeon post," continued Ada.

"*Sapristi!* I hope they will catch the brigand dog and hang him."

"Why should you desire that?"

"Because I do not like his familiarity towards you. I am jealous. The fellow means to rob me of you if he can."

"Small danger of that," replied Ada. "I would never marry him, nor would I marry you."

"This thing has gone far enough," Sarati exclaimed. "As Possilippo is out of the way, now is my time to speak. I do not intend to stop here."

"You are watched, escape is impossible."

"I will make all the rogues drunk to-night, and you and I will get away in the darkness. Come, answer me frankly, will you fly with me and be my wife?"

"You have had my answer already."

"Then, by Heaven, I will kill you!" Sarati shouted. "No other man shall call you his. I will have your life."

Ada was terribly frightened.

Nevertheless, she preserved her presence of mind.

The fact that Tito, the Dwarf of Blood, was not far away, somewhat assured her, for the brigand chief had given him strict orders to protect her.

Sarati drew a knife and seized her by the wrist.

She uttered a piercing shriek, which rang through the vaulted chamber.

"Help, help!" she cried.

Startled from his lethargy, Septimus sprang to his feet.

He saw his sister struggling in the grasp of the Italian, and the gleam of the upraised knife in the lamplight.

Rushing between them, he knocked Sarati's arm on one side.

This bold action saved Ada's life.

She sank fainting to the floor.

Another moment and the cruel knife would have been buried in her heart.

But the effort was to cost Septimus dear.

"This won't do," he said; "hang it all, what are you up to man, with the girl? She is my sister, you know, and I can't allow this kind of thing."

"Fool! go back to your chair. Why do you interfere?"

"It is my duty to do so."

"I mean to kill her, and if you do not get out of my way, by St. Peter! I will kill you too."

"Are you mad?"

"No matter. Stand aside."

"I will not," replied Septimus. "By Jove! you ought to be shot like a rabid dog. Where is my pistol?"

He fumbled in his pocket for the weapon.

Before he could find it, Sarati plunged the knife into his neck.

"Oh, Heaven! I am stabbed," was all Septimus could say.

He sank by the side of Ada, who, feeling the hot blood spurt on her cheek, shrieked again.

This time Tito heard her.

The Dwarf of Blood lost no time in penetrating to the second cavern.

"*Diavolo!* What is this?" he asked.

Sarati turned furiously upon him.

"Misshapen monster!" he exclaimed, "begone. I am settling accounts with my enemies, and unless you want to be included in the number, you will let me alone. I have warned you."

"Ha! is it so?" replied Tito. "Brigands to me! succour!"

The swarthy ruffians poured in from the outer cave in obedience to his summons.

Sarati was surrounded.

"Seize him!" cried the Dwarf of Blood.

The Italian endeavoured to defend himself, but after a brief struggle he was overpowered and borne to the ground.

"We shall have to make an example of you, since you cannot behave yourself," continued Tito. "I am master here, now, in the chief's absence. It seems to me that you are anxious to take a roll down the hill."

Sarati was completely sobered by this time.

His insensate passion, which had overcome his prudence, had died away.

"Respect my life, or you will have to answer to your master, whose old friend I am," he said.

"You deserve death."

"Remember, I am one of your band."

"That makes no difference. Our law is, a life for a life, the same as it is in a civilised and law-abiding community," answered the Dwarf of Blood ; "and, unless I am mistaken very much, you have settled the worldly affairs of this young man."

He took Septimus up in his long arms, and examined him closely.

The blood was pouring from a gaping wound in the neck.

No pulsation of the heart was to be discovered.

"Thousand fiends!" said Tito, "anyone could swear you were a Neapolitan, you have done your work so neatly."

Holding Septimus under the lamp, he gazed at the wound.

"Come here, boys," continued the Dwarf of Blood, "I never saw anything better done. It is quite a work of art."

The brigands, with the exception of the one who held Sarati, crowded round him.

"Holy Mary!" cried one named Maestro, "a surgical operation. What knowledge of anatomy to kill like that!"

There was a general chorus of approval.

"A man like that does not deserve to die," added Maestro, "he should live to kill more men ; besides, he is one of us."

Sarati saw his opportunity.

The tide of popular opinion was turning in his favour.

"Come!" he exclaimed, "what are you thinking about? To begin with, I am a compatriot, and one of your band. Shall I treat you to a couple of dozen bottles of wine? If so, I have money to pay old Bianca."

"Yes, yes!" cried the brigands, "he is one of us."

"Release him. We will have a grand carouse," said the Dwarf of Blood.

Sarati was set free.

A smile of triumph irradiated his saturnine countenance.

Ada had recovered from her brief fainting fit, and was leaning against the wall pale with horror.

Her brother's body was lying before her eyes, and the murderer was not to be punished.

"To the outer cave," cried Sarati, "let us drink and be merry."

The brigands moved off.

As Sarati passed Ada, he hissed in her ear :

"You have only escaped me for a time ; be mine or dread my vengeance."

She shrank from him as if he were plague-stricken.

"Wretch!" she rejoined, "I hate and defy you."

"Beware!"

Giving him a look of scorn and despisal, she glided into the cavern occupied by Bianca.

With a groan and a sob she sank upon the rude couch which did duty as a bed, and fainted again.

"Poor child," murmured Bianca, "this kind of life does not suit her. It is a pity she cannot go back to her friends."

Presently Tito came in, with money given him by Sarati to buy wine, for Possilippo made his men pay for all demands on his cellar.

Soon the sound of drunken revelry arose.

While this merriment was going on, the body of Septimus was conveyed into a cave adjoining the entrance cavern.

It was of large size, and partly open to the light and air.

This was set apart for wounded men and invalids, and was known as the infirmary.

An old man named Pincio, who had been a doctor, had charge of the cave.

He had a fair supply of medicines at his command, as well as surgical appliances.

Pincio examined Septimus, and, to the surprise of those who had borne him there, strapped up his wound.

"Is he not dead?" asked one.

"Shade of Cæsar!" said the other, "the knife went in far enough."

"No important artery is cut," exclaimed Pincio, "nor is the heart touched. I have hopes that I can cure him."

"If so, you are a marvel. I will tell his sister of this, for she thinks him dead," said the brigand.

"I cannot speak with certainty, but you may say that he lives," said the doctor.

The brigand sought Ada, finding her in Bianca's apartment, and the news he brought tended to console her.

Vile and despicable as Septimus was, and grossly as he had deceived and betrayed her, he was her brother.

She did not wish him harm.

Her nature was forgiving, her heart soft and womanly.

CHAPTER XVIII.

THE DUKE OF CALABRIA'S BALL.

WHEN Dick escaped from the inn, he ran down the road to a safe distance.

It was his idea that Jack would follow him.

His senses were somewhat confused.

He halted and sat down on a bank.

In a short time the cool night air revived him, and the fumes of the wine evaporated from his brain.

Then he stole back to the vicinity of the inn, and made investigations.

He found armed men standing in every direction.

Presently he beheld Jack taken away a prisoner, and knowing that he could do nothing to help him, he turned away with a heavy heart to walk back to Naples.

His only hope now was in Sparks, the English detective, and the Neapolitan police.

Madia might be urged into action.

Dick lamented his indiscretion, for Possilippo would not have attacked them, if he had not foolishly betrayed their secret.

He felt very sorry that Jack was suffering through his folly.

Regrets, however, were unavailing, and in a bitter frame of mind he retraced his steps to the city.

Weary, jaded, and footsore, he arrived at his hotel about nine o'clock in the morning.

After taking a cold bath, he ate a hearty breakfast and went to bed, ordering the servant to call him at five o'clock, which would give him about six hours' sleep, of which he stood greatly in need.

When he got up, he descended to the dining-room much refreshed, and ready to do justice to the *table d'hôte*, which was being served.

To his great satisfaction he saw that Sparks was there, and took a place by his side.

"Ha, ha!" laughed the detective. "I thought you boys had gone brigand-hunting?"

"So we did," replied Dick.

"You are soon back."

"Good reason why."

"What made you give it up so quickly?" asked Sparks.

"Possilippo made it too hot for us," Dick answered.

"Did you see him?"

"I regret extremely to say that we did."

"Where is Jack Massey?"

"Captured," rejoined Dick.

The detective dropped his spoon in surprise at this unexpected announcement.

"That's bad news!" he exclaimed. "How did it happen? I was afraid you fellows would run your heads into some trouble."

Dick related their adventure at the "Garibaldi Inn," at which narration the detective looked grave.

"He has run his head into the lion's mouth, and no mistake," he remarked.

"The question is," said Dick, "what will the brigand do with his prisoner?"

"Either put him to death or hold him to ransom."

"Cannot we rescue him?"

"Impossible. Madia will not lend us his men."

"Sarati is with Possilippo, and if he sees Jack we may as well look out for a funeral," replied Dick, in a melancholy tone.

"We are blocked," observed Sparks. "If Sarati had been in Naples, I would have captured him, but you cannot expect me to go to a brigand's cave single-handed ; besides, no one knows where the mysterious hiding-place is."

"Confound such police as they have here."

"That is what I say. They are a silly lot. Our men would not sit down and twiddle their thumbs."

Dick stuck his fork viciously into a piece of fish which the waiter had given him.

"What am I to do ? " he cried. "I can't sit still while Jack is a captive."

"You must wait. There are combinations of circumstances under which men are absolutely powerless."

"Where there is a will there is a way."

"Show me the way," replied Sparks. "My head is tolerably level, and I can't see my way."

"Is there no official in this city who is above Madia, and who can put him in motion ? He wants whipping up a bit."

"Let me see," said Sparks. "You see, the seat of government is at Rome, but I think I saw in the paper that the Minister of the Interior—that is the equivalent to our Home Secretary —is staying in Naples."

"What is his name ? " asked Dick.

"The Duke of Calabria."

"Is Madia under him ? "

"Of course he is," replied Sparks.

"By Jove !" exclaimed Dick, "I think I have a letter of introduction to him. That's fizzing ! Before we left Windsor, Sir Dando Titmarsh, who has lived in Italy, gave us some letters of introduction to tip-top swells. Jack handed them to me to keep, luckily."

"Look and see."

Dick took out his pocket-book, and, sure enough, among his letters was one to the Duke of Calabria.

Fortunately for Dick, the duke happened to be spending a short vacation at his villa in Naples.

"I'll call on him at once," said Dick. "Perhaps I may get an invitation to dine with him. Nothing like good society."

"If you do, take me with you," replied Sparks.

"How can I ? Excuse me, you are not a gentleman of society, only a detective, you know. If it were found out, I might get into trouble. These foreign grandees are awfully particular about the people they entertain."

"Say I am a friend of yours. Call me an army man, or anything you like. Military men can go anywhere."

"All right. I'll call you Captain Sparks, of the Rifle Brigade."

"That will do."

When he had finished his dinner, Dick enquired the way to the duke's villa, and, taking a carriage, was driven to the ducal residence.

It was beautifully situated, overlooking the bay.

He sent in his card, and the letter which Sir Dando Titmarsh had presented him with.

The Duke of Calabria received him at once.

"I am very pleased to make your acquaintance, Mr. Lambert," said the nobleman. "I well remember meeting Sir Dando in Rome."

"He mentioned as much, your grace," Dick replied.

"I give a ball and supper to-night. If not too fatigued with your journey, will you favour me with your company ? "

"Your grace honours me too highly. May I bring a friend with me, a travelling companion, Captain Sparks, of the British Army ? "

"With pleasure. Do you stay here long ? "

"It depends upon circumstances."

"If so, I hope you will be a frequent guest."

"I have come over here on very peculiar business, your grace," said Dick, "which I should like to explain to you."

"To-morrow, not now ; time presses."

"I thank your grace," replied Dick, with one of his politest bows.

He was annoyed to think that he was obliged to postpone his explanation, but pleased to find that he was received so graciously.

The next day he hoped to be able to render Jack some effectual assistance.

He felt sure that if the Minister of the Interior would consent to send a company of soldiers to the hills they would find and dislodge the brigands.

Returning to the hotel, he imparted the good news to Sparks.

They got their dress clothes out of their portmanteaus, and put on the conventional white tie.

At nine o'clock they appeared at the duke's residence, and being ushered into the ball-room, found themselves among a select and fashionable crowd.

This throng included all the rank, talent, and beauty that were to be gathered together in Naples.

Dancing was going on to the strains of a military band.

The duke and duchess received their guests as they arrived, with the utmost urbanity.

Then they were passed along and lost in the crowd.

The detective was very much impressed at what he saw.

"What a distinguished company," he remarked to Dick, as they halted near a group of orange and myrtle trees.

"The jewellery of the ladies is superb, and almost priceless," replied Dick.

"Did you notice the duke's diamond snuff-box?" asked Sparks. "He is a great snuff-taker, and offered me a pinch."

"Yes, indeed I did. It was studded with diamonds all over. An ordinary fortune would not buy it."

"I heard someone say it was worth twenty thousand pounds."

"That may be perfectly true, as I have heard that the duke is very rich," answered Dick. "What a prize it would be for a brigand."

"You are right," exclaimed Sparks. "But there is little chance of Possilippo venturing to show his face here."

"Is it likely?" replied Dick, laughing at the idea. "The man would not be such a fool as that."

"What kind of a fellow is he?"

"Very gentlemanly; he is fitted to move in the best society."

"Perhaps he is a decayed gentleman," said Sparks, "who has spent all his money on his friends, and now wants to revenge himself upon the spoilers."

Suddenly Dick clutched the detective's arm tightly.

"By Heaven!" he said in a hoarse whisper, "I never saw such a likeness."

"To whom?"

"Possilippo, the brigand, of whom we were talking. Look, do you see that tall man with a red camellia in the button-hole of his coat?"

"Yes; he wears a decoration also," replied Sparks. "It is the Order of St. Vincent de Paul, if I am not mistaken."

"Well, I could swear that he is the very man I saw at the 'Garibaldi Inn,' on the old Roman road, last night."

"That sounds incredible."

"Nevertheless, it is true. I'll swear to him," said Dick in a tone of decision.

At that moment a footman in gorgeous livery passed by on his way to the card-room.

Dick stopped him.

"Excuse me," he exclaimed, "can you tell me who that gentleman is over there, by the statue?"

"He is well known in Neapolitan society," rejoined the footman, "as the Count Casati."

"Are you sure?"

"Perfectly, signor."

The footman passed on.

"What can we do?" asked Sparks. "I have no right to arrest him. It is no business of mine. I am after Sarati."

"It is my duty to inform the duke."

"He will laugh at you. You must be mistaken. They say every man has his double. You are deceived by an accidental resemblance."

"Not I," replied Dick. "Have you got a pistol with you?"

"I always carry a revolver."

"Can I have it for a little while?"

"With pleasure, only let me beg of you to do nothing rash."

"Trust to my judgment. I am not likely to make a fool of myself."

Satisfied with this promise, Sparks gave him his pistol.

It was rapidly transferred to Dick's pocket.

No one noticed the action.

"What are you going to do?" enquired Sparks.

"You will see shortly," replied Dick. "Stay here."

Saying this he walked towards the spot where the Duke of Calabria was standing.

He saw a troubled expression upon his face.

"Can I speak with you for a moment, privately?" Dick said.

"Presently, Mr. Lambert," answered the duke. "I have to leave my guests for a short time."

"May I enquire what for?"

"I will tell you. The fact is, I have lost my diamond snuff-box, which is extremely valuable. It is unique, and worth a fortune."

"I saw it when I arrived," said Dick in astonishment. "Do you remember when you last had it in your hand?"

"A few minutes ago," rejoined the duke. "I offered the Count Casati a pinch, which he refused. I replaced it in my pocket, and, to my amazement, it has disappeared."

Dick felt sure that he knew who had stolen the jewelled snuff-box.

"What do you intend to do ?" he asked.

"My intention is to go to Signor Madia, the head of the secret police, and ask his advice."

"I can save you the trouble."

"How ? " ejaculated the duke.

"In the easiest manner possible."

"Explain yourself, signor."

"I will point out the thief," replied Dick.

"If you do that, you will be clever. I thought of having everybody here searched as they left the house."

"That would be an insult to the innocent."

"So it would. My friends would never forgive me. Yet, my dear sir, I cannot lose my diamonds."

"Your grace shall not lose them."

"Who is the offender ?"

"The Count Casati," replied Dick.

At the mention of this name the duke elevated his eyebrows.

He was evidently very much annoyed at the accusation.

Not for a moment did he believe there was any truth in the statement.

"Do you know the gentleman ?" he asked.

"I have met him under another name," said Dick.

At this juncture the music, which had ceased for a brief interval, commenced again.

The band played a seductive waltz.

Count Casati whirled past them, having for his partner a princess.

"Look !" exclaimed the duke ; "Casati is dancing with a lady of the house of Savoy."

"That makes no difference," answered Dick.

"He is one of my oldest friends."

"I persist in my statement."

"But, my dear sir, his character is above suspicion, and you suggest that he picked my pocket ?"

"Most decidedly, and I adhere to it."

"If you had not been introduced to me by Sir Dando Titmarsh, I should regard you as an extremely impertinent young man."

"Let me tell you who the Count Casati is," replied Dick ; "then you will not find so much fault with me."

"I cannot understand you," said the duke.

"He is Possilippo, the brigand."

The duke laughed.

To him the idea of such a thing seemed preposterous.

"My friend," he exclaimed, "I do not know whether you are joking or serious. If it is a joke, it is a bad one."

"I am in earnest," replied Dick.

"Then you are mad, for I am not in the habit of entertaining brigands. My visitors' list does not include that class of people, I can assure you."

The music ceased, and the dancing, for a time, was over.

"Will you send for the police," cried Dick, "and have that man arrested ?"

"I will order one of my servants to go for the police, but it is you I shall have taken in charge."

"What have I done to deserve such a threat ?"

"You are mad."

"Your grace," said Dick, almost in despair at his obstinacy, "I am telling you the truth. Do you wish to recover your diamonds ?"

"Of course."

"Then arrest that man."

As he spoke, the Count Casati walked by, with the princess leaning on his arm.

"Count," cried the Duke of Calabria, "a word with you."

Casati paused and faced his host.

When he saw Dick he turned pale.

With an effort he recovered his composure.

"As many words as you like, so long as they are not angry ones," he replied.

"Possibly, I may provoke you to anger."

"I could not quarrel with so old a friend as the Duke of Calabria."

"Well, I must risk it. This young Englishman alleges that you have my diamond snuff-box in your pocket."

The count trembled with rage.

"How dare you say such an infamous thing ?" he demanded, glaring at Dick.

"Because you are Possilippo, the brigand !"

The count's lips became livid.

"I will treat this youth with the contempt he deserves," he exclaimed, "and, to avoid further insult, I will, with your grace's permission, retire from the room at once."

"I beg that you will do nothing of the kind," said the duke.

"Permit me to do as I please."

"Mr. Lambert shall go, but you shall not. I request him to retire, and, at the same time, I apologise to you for the indignity to which you have been subjected."

The lady, with whom Count Casati had been dancing, had retired to a seat at the side of the room.

With admirable coolness, Casati bowed to the Duke of Calabria.

"I have the honour to wish you good-evening," he said.

Bestowing a malignant look upon Dick, he walked to the door.

His movements were hurried, as if he were anxious to get away.

This was certainly the fact.

Dick's presence at the ball had completely disconcerted him.

He had not anticipated anything of the kind.

Dick followed him into the hall.

"You shall not escape me," he exclaimed.

Possilippo turned upon him with a furious air.

"Do you value the life of your friend, Jack Massey?" he asked.

"I do," replied Dick.

"If you interfere with me he shall die."

Dick produced the pistol he had borrowed from sparks.

He presented the weapon at the head of the brigand.

"Surrender, or I fire!" he cried.

Possilippo grew livid.

He saw that the boy was a match for him.

"Let me depart in peace," he said, "and your friend shall be released to-morrow morning."

"That won't do," replied Dick; "I mean to break up your band, and I will begin with you."

Sparks had seen them leave the room.

He followed them into the hall.

Hearing Dick's last words, he exclaimed:

"I have a pair of handcuffs, and I will put them on you. If there is any mistake the police will rectify it, and I am prepared to take the consequences."

"Who are you, fellow?" asked Possilippo.

"A London detective. You can't play with me. Hold out your hands."

The brigand gnashed his teeth with rage.

"I am armed," he said. "Beware!"

"If you attempt to draw on us," cried Dick, "I will shoot you as I would a dog. Again I call upon you to surrender."

"Never!"

He made an effort to get at his pistol.

Seeing this, Dick hesitated no longer.

He fired.

With a cry of anguish, Possilippo fell to the tesselated floor.

"By Heaven!" he gasped, "am I beaten by a boy?"

The bullet had struck him in the left arm, which was limp and powerless.

Some servants who were standing near the door rushed in.

Thinking that a murder had been committed, they seized Dick, and held him tightly.

"Bravo!" said Sparks, "I'll run to the office for Madia. We will soon see who is right or wrong."

"Make haste," replied Dick.

"I will take a fly, and go as fast as the horses can gallop."

"My life may depend upon your speed."

"Rest contented. I know my book," the detective answered.

He was off in a moment.

The shot had not been heard in the ball-room.

A lackey, however, had hastened to inform the duke of the deplorable occurrence which had taken place in the hall.

The Minister of the Interior at once came upon the scene.

He was horrified beyond measure.

"What have you done?" he demanded of Dick.

"Shot the brigand," replied Dick, boldly.

"You will be hanged for this outrage on the noble and respected Count Casati."

"I tell you he is Possilippo."

"Maniac! I cannot listen to you. The friend of my youth a brigand? Bah!"

"Have him searched."

"What for?"

"To see if he has in his possession your gold snuff-box studded with diamonds."

"Yes, I will do that," answered the duke.

Possilippo had fainted.

The pain from his wound was

excessive, and he was bleeding profusely.

Kneeling down, the duke placed his hand in one of the pockets of the brigand.

He was successful at his first effort.

His fingers clasped the box and he drew it forth.

Like one dazed he looked at it.

He could scarcely believe the evidence of his senses.

It was more than a surprise.

To him it was a revelation, and, at the same time, a mystery.

But he was greatly rejoiced to recover his valuable property.

He extended his hand to Dick.

"Mr. Lambert," he said, "I am deeply indebted to you, and beg to recall the harsh words I uttered just now."

"Do not mention it," replied Dick, "I knew what I was about."

"Casati a brigand! I cannot understand it."

"Well, you see he is a thief."

"Undoubtedly; but, be he what he may, he must not bleed to death. There is a distinguished surgeon upstairs, one of my guests to-night. I will call him."

The duke walked rapidly away.

When he had shaken hands with Dick, the servants who held the young fellow in restraint released him.

In a few minutes the duke returned with the doctor.

After a brief examination, the latter took a handkerchief from his pocket, and, having stripped the brigand's wounded arm, bound it up.

"That will do for the present," exclaimed the surgeon.

"Is he much injured?" asked the duke.

"No. The ball has passed through the fleshy part of the arm."

"Is the bone injured?"

"Grazed, I expect. There is no fracture; he will be able to use his arm in a week or two, I think. What was the cause of the *fracas*?"

"We suspect that he is a brigand," replied the duke.

"Send for the police, and let them judge," answered the doctor.

"I have already done so," said Dick.

He had scarcely spoken, than Sparks came in with Madia.

"Good-evening," said the chief, saluting the Minister of the Interior; "I hear your grace has made an important capture."

"You know the Count Casati?" rejoined the duke.

"Yes, I know him as Possilippo."

"The brigand?"

"Your grace, they are one and the same."

"Are you sure?"

"My information on this point is correct. I have had his house watched for the last two days and nights," replied Madia.

"It sounds like a dream," said the Duke of Calabria. "Convey him to the prison of St. Angelo, and keep him closely guarded."

"I will take very good care of that."

"You will be held responsible for his safe keeping. Should he escape I will dismiss you from your post."

The chief of the secret police inclined his head.

"I accept the responsibility," he said. "Give the man some brandy to revive him, and I will take him away."

The spirit was sent for, and after it was poured down his throat, the brigand revived.

"You here!" he said, looking at Madia; "formerly you were my friend."

"I must do my duty," answered the chief of the secret police; "but I know you to be Possilippo."

"Do you rely on the word of that English boy?"

"No."

"Who is your informant? Who has dared to calumniate me?"

"Do you remember shooting one of my men on the Roman road?" replied Madia.

Possilippo made no answer.

"He was not dead, as you thought. The man was picked up by a carter, and brought to my office. Now you know the informer."

"You will have to prove all you say."

"Wait until your trial comes on."

With assistance, the brigand rose to his feet.

His face was distorted by a vile expression.

All the evil in him seemed to be coming to the surface.

If his left arm was crippled, his right was uninjured, and before anyone could divine his purpose, he drew a pistol and fired at Dick.

The bullet grazed the young Englishman's ear.

In a moment Possilippo was disarmed.

"Fiends take you!" he shouted, "you will suffer for this, and your friend Massey also."

"Don't make too sure," replied Dick.

"If I am captured and exposed, thanks to you, I am not without resources, and I swear to you, Signor Englishman, that I will hang you to the branch of a tree within a fortnight."

"Ha, ha!" laughed Dick, "that will be your fate, not mine."

"For heaven's sake do not prolong this scene!" exclaimed the duke. "The scandal is great enough already."

Madia had brought two officers with him.

At a sign they approached.

The brigand was seized by them, and hustled along the passage into the street.

A conveyance was in waiting.

Getting into the carriage with him, Madia said:

"To the Castle of St. Angelo."

This was the strongest prison in Naples.

When the redoubtable brigand was removed, Dick addressed the Duke of Calabria.

In a few words he told him his story.

"Will you send some soldiers to the hills," he asked, in conclusion, "to arrest Sarati, and rescue my friend Massey, and Ada Titmarsh?"

"The nest of brigands shall be exterminated," answered the duke; "but how are we going to find their hiding-place?"

"That is easy enough."

"I should like to know how."

"The landland of the 'Garibaldi' inn is in league with them."

"What of that?"

"Arrest him, and promise him his liberty if he will betray the brigands," replied Dick.

"That is a good idea," said the Duke, "I will telegraph to the Prime Minister at Rome for instructions."

"Cannot you act independently?"

"No. I must be guided by orders from headquarters. Casati has many influential friends in Rome."

"When shall you know?" asked Dick.

"In a few days. Casati, or Possilippo, is in custody, so there is no hurry. Come and see me the day after to-morrow."

"I want my friend rescued."

The duke shrugged his shoulders.

"I will do all I can," he replied; "but we move slowly in this country."

"So I should think. I wish your grace good-night."

Saying this, Dick took Sparks by the arm and walked out of the house.

He was disgusted with the sluggishness and want of energy displayed by the Minister of the Interior.

As they went down the street, the detective praised him highly for the way in which he had behaved that evening.

"You are entitled to the reward," he said.

"I mean to claim it," answered Dick, "but what interests me most at the present time is the fate of Left-handed Jack."

"Possilippo threatened him."

"Yes; and he may find a means of communicating with his band. If so, Jack is doomed to death."

"Perhaps the authorities will send the soldiers in time to save him."

"You heard what the Duke of Calabria said," exclaimed Dick; "things take time over here. What are we to do? Will you come with me and try to rescue him?"

Sparks shook his head.

"That would be sheer insanity," he rejoined.

"You refuse?"

"I do."

Dick bit his lip.

He was intensely annoyed at the detective's answer, but a little reflection convinced him that Sparks was right.

What could they do unaided?

"I suppose we must wait," he exclaimed, "until the Minister of the Interior thinks fit to move. Poor Jack! Heaven help him!"

"You can call on the duke to-morrow and urge him to action."

"I will keep on calling, and make him act."

"That is all you can do," replied Sparks. "If it would do any good, I would go to the hills with you to-night."

"Say no more. We must wait," answered Dick.

In a melancholy mood he entered the hotel and went to his bedroom, while Sparks walked up and down in front of the sea.

He smoked a cigar and talked to himself.

"This is a queer start," he muttered. "I did not expect work of this kind. By luck we have caught the brigand, but, it strikes me, we shall not get Sarati so easily. I've a good mind to throw it up and go home. Fighting brigands is dangerous work."

He paused for a moment.

"No," he resumed, "I'll stick it. There is money in the game, but I will keep out of danger as well as I know how."

CHAPTER XIX.

THE NEWS OF POSSILIPPO'S CAPTURE ARRIVES AT THE BRIGANDS' CAVE.

ON the day following Possilippo's arrest, a man arrived at the "Garibaldi" inn, riding a horse whose glossy black coat was flecked with foam.

The animal had been ridden hard.

Putting the horse in the stable, he entered the hostelry, and was cordially greeted by the host.

"Why, Guiseppe, my old friend!" exclaimed the latter, "it is good for my eyes to see you."

"I may say the same thing," replied Guiseppe, the coachman of Possilippo.

"Have you just come from the Villa Borghese?"

"As hard as I could ride."

"There is one in my parlour you will be glad to see."

"Who is that?"

"Our merry little Tito, the Dwarf of Blood. He came down from the hills this morning early, and has been drinking ever since."

"'Tis him I am anxious to meet."

"No bad news, I hope?" said the host.

"Come with me to Tito, and you shall hear. It is no use telling a story twice."

"There you are right, life is too short. Come."

They went together to the parlour, where they found the Dwarf of Blood reclining on a sofa, smoking a cigarette, and fanning the flies off his face.

"Ah, Guiseppe, my brave!" he cried, "is it you? What news from the city? You would not be here for nothing."

"Correct," replied Guiseppe. "Let me quench my thirst, and I will tell you."

"Nothing bad, I hope?"

Guiseppe poured out a glass of red wine from a bottle that stood on the table.

He drank it at a single draught.

"You were always a thirsty soul," remarked Tito; "you will drink twice before you speak once."

"It runs in the family."

"How is that?"

"My father died in a lunatic asylum through the effects of drink, and my mother drowned herself in the bay owing to her fondness for brandy."

"Bother your family history," cried the Dwarf of Blood; "tell us your news."

"The captain was captured last night."

Tito sprang from the sofa.

His little dark eyes seemed as if they were starting from his head.

"Is this true?" he asked.

"All Naples is ringing with the intelligence. Every paper has got it."

"Perdition to the traitorous man or woman who betrayed him! How did it happen?" asked Tito.

"It was at the Duke of Calabria's ball that he was seized," replied Guiseppe; "full particulars are not given, but 'tis said he is shot in the arm."

"Ah! he would defend himself to the death. I know him."

"They have lodged him in the Castle of St. Angelo."

"By the saints!" cried the Dwarf of Blood, "this is bad news. I am captain of the band now."

"As such, I salute you with all due respect."

"Are you coming to the caves? If so, I will show you some sport."

"I may as well do so," answered Guiseppe; "there is nothing for me

"'HOLD,' SHE EXCLAIMED, HER EYES FLASHING; 'WHAT WOULD YOU DO?'"—(See page 122.)

No. 8.

to do in Naples; but let me tell you one thing."

"Name it."

"The papers talk of the soldiers being sent after you."

"Bah!" said the dwarf, "we have heard that talked of before. Let them come; we are prepared. They must find us first."

"Suppose they do?"

"St. Januarius! are we going to be caught like rats in a trap? I will be a terror to the whole country round."

"You can fight, we know that," Guiseppe said.

"Aye! and when it is of no use to fight, I have some barrels of gun-powder to blow the place up with. Ho, ho! they won't call me the Dwarf of Blood for nothing."

"Would you kill all your com-rades?"

"Every one."

"Then your mind is as deformed as your body," remarked Guiseppe, into whose head the wine was mounting.

The Dwarf of Blood scowled upon him.

"Do you intend to insult me?" he hissed, fiercely.

"I speak the truth," was the reply. "If you want to fight, I am as good a man as you are, any day."

"Bah! I don't fight with curs like you."

"What do you do then?"

"I murder them."

The innkeeper grew alarmed.

He stepped between them and held up his hands.

"For Heaven's sake, comrades!" he cried, "do not lose your head. Holy Virgin! my wine is too strong for you."

Tito gave him a push.

"Out of the way, you drivelling idiot," he cried, "or I'll murder *you!*"

The host stepped back.

He muttered part of the Paternoster, and crossed himself.

"Now," continued the Dwarf of Blood, "down on your knees and beg my pardon."

"What—*yours?*" answered Gui-seppe.

"If not, prepare to die."

"Oh! if it comes to that, I carry a knife like a true brigand."

"A fig for your knife, look at mine."

In an instant the dwarf drew his blade from his belt.

He rushed upon Guiseppe with an eagerness that was as irresistible as a mountain torrent or an avalanche.

Guiseppe had no time to defend himself.

The knife struck him in the throat.

As he fell to the floor, the blood spurted out in a stream.

Tito laughed demoniacally.

"That's the way to do it," he said. "What do you think of it?"

The innkeeper was afraid to anger him further.

"A splendid stroke," he answered. "The captain could not have done it better, I'll swear."

"'Twas a pretty thrust. See how the wretch bleeds; his tongue will not wag any more in this world."

"Truly excellent. You are a master-piece."

"No man shall insult me with im-punity. Drag that carrion out! throw it into the old well in the garden! It will not be the first corpse you have put there, and you know it."

"Ah! he deserved his fate, for insulting a gentleman like you."

"Of course he did. The fool knew my temper, and should have held his peace."

"You promised to show him some sport."

"So I would have done," said the Dwarf of Blood. "The English boy we captured is in my power now, and I intend to throw him down the rocks in a barrel stuck full of knives."

The innkeeper smiled.

"By Our Lady!" he exclaimed, "that is worthy of you. I should like to see that."

Tito drank some wine with as much composure as if nothing had hap-pened.

Taking the body by the heels, the innkeeper dragged it out of the room.

It left a trail of blood as it went along.

"The reckless fool!" muttered Tito. "Oh! how I love to kill! To my mind, there is no pleasure that can compare with it."

Putting on his broad-brimmed hat, he quitted the inn, without stopping to say adieu to the landlord.

He walked rapidly back to the caves.

His mind was full of the startling news that the unfortunate Guiseppe had brought him.

As Possilippo was a prisoner in the Castle of St. Angelo, he would be tried and executed in due time.

He never expected to set eyes on his chief again.

There was one thing that puzzled him.

That Possilippo had a large collection of very valuable diamonds, he was fully aware, but he did not know where they were concealed.

The Dwarf of Blood was avaricious, and longed to possess the precious stones.

He determined to make a search for them in the caves.

As he climbed the winding path leading to the plateau, his ugly features were irradiated with a smile.

The sun was declining in the west, and the brigands were grouped outside enjoying the cool air of the evening.

"Comrades," exclaimed Tito, "I have extraordinary news for you."

"Are there any rich travellers expected to pass our way?" asked one named Giacomo.

"No. I am sorry to say our chief is captured."

"Possilippo a prisoner?"

"It is too true."

The brigands raised a howl of rage.

"I always told him he was wrong to go to the city," continued Tito; "the pitcher goes often to the well, but gets broken at last; but, my friends, I will lead you, if you will have me for your master."

"Yes, yes, Tito's the man," cried several.

"No, no!" cried the others, "let us have Giacomo."

"Put it to the vote," exclaimed Tito, "I am willing to abide by the decision of the majority."

"So am I," replied Giacomo. "Hands up for me."

The hands that were held up were counted carefully.

"Now for me," exclaimed Tito.

It was found that the supporters of the latter were more numerous than those of the former by two.

Accordingly the Dwarf of Blood was acclaimed as the leader of the brigands.

Giacomo seemed greatly chagrined.

He got his friends into a corner, and talked to them in a low tone.

It seemed as if mischief was brewing.

Tito, on the other hand, was jubilant at this popularity, and sent into the cave for some wine.

Now happened what generally takes place among a band of robbers when it loses its acknowledged and accustomed head—jealousy and discontent.

Giacomo was by no means satisfied at the election of the Dwarf of Blood to the leadership of the band.

He had only won it by a narrow majority.

Possilippo had kept these wild characters in hand by a judicious mixture of kindness and firmness.

If any case of serious insubordination occurred in their ranks, he did not hesitate to shoot the offender.

He fully understood the value of making an example.

It was a bullet first, and a few words of reprimand to the others afterwards.

When Tito had disappeared in the caves for the bandits to receive some wine, with which to drink his health, Giacomo gave free vent to his wrath and disappointment.

"Who is this misshapen imp that he should lead us?" he exclaimed. "I am as brave as he is, and have as clever a head."

Sarati had been watching what was going on.

He deemed it according to his interests to fan the flame of discontent.

For Tito he had no liking whatever, who had openly thwarted him in his designs against Ada.

With Giacomo he fancied he could get on better.

Whether this was so or not remained to be seen.

He had stabbed Septimus in his ungovernable passion, and he was determined to take the life of Ada if she would not be his bride.

For a time Tito had stayed his hand.

He felt a most bitter antagonism towards the Dwarf of Blood.

"Ha, ha!" he laughed, when Giacomo had finished speaking. "You are a man, but Tito, what is he? A caricature, nothing more."

"You speak the truth," replied Giacomo. "I will not follow him."

"Nor I! Nor I!" cried three or four of the brigands.

"Put a bullet in his back when he is not looking," Sarati suggested.

Giacomo shook his head.

"No," he rejoined, "I am what you have called me—a man, and I will not assassinate an old comrade."

"Then fight him for the mastery."

"Yes, that is better. I can handle a knife with anyone, and I will challenge him to single combat."

"Bravo!" exclaimed the brigands in chorus. "A fight to the death! *Viva! viva!*"

"As true as the sun ripens grapes, I will kill him."

"Giacomo's the man we want," they replied.

"Stick to your text," whispered Sarati.

Scarcely had he finished speaking, than the Dwarf of Blood made his appearance.

He carried a stone jar which contained two gallons of excellent wine, and in his other hand he held a tin cup, which was to be passed round from one to the other.

"*Viva* Giacomo!" cried the discontented brigands.

Those who had voted for Tito held aloof, looking on askance.

They saw that something was going to take place, though they did not know exactly what.

The Dwarf of Blood frowned fiercely.

"Why do you shout for Giacomo," he demanded, fiercely, "when you have made me your master, and I have brought this wine from old Bianca to treat you with?"

"Let me answer that question," replied the disappointed brigand.

"Mind what you are about."

"Oh!" laughed Giacomo, "do not think for a moment that I am afraid of you. There must be a struggle for the mastery. Fight me with knives to the death, and the victor shall be leader."

Tito snapped his long, elfin fingers.

"A fig for you!" he cried.

"Will you fight? If not, I shall wake you up by giving you a taste of my knife."

"*Santa Maria!*" yelled Tito, "the dog is showing his teeth."

"I am laughing at you, my little man."

"By all the saints in the calendar!" continued the Dwarf of Blood, "you will laugh on the wrong side of your face directly."

"That remains to be proved. Draw your knife," said Giacomo.

In a moment two knives flashed in the sunshine.

The brigands fell back to allow the combatants to have plenty of room.

Sarati folded his arms, and grinned sardonically.

"These men will kill one another," he muttered. "No matter if they do.

Possilippo is captured, and I shall have a free hand."

"Have at you," hissed Tito between his clenched teeth.

He made a thrust at his adversary, which took effect in his arm.

"Perdition to you!" shouted Giacomo, staggering back.

The Dwarf of Blood followed him until he reached the rock, and dealt him another blow.

This time Giacomo received it in the chest.

So quick and furious had been the attack that the unfortunate man had not been able to even defend himself.

He sank to the ground deluged in blood.

"I give in," he cried. "Mercy! Remember, Tito, we have always been good friends up to now."

"Yes," replied Tito, satirically, "I will give you mercy. Would you have had any upon *me?*"

"Let me live."

"You do not deserve to. Why, you cannot handle a knife with me. Indeed, you are a poor creature!"

Giacomo groaned in anguish.

"For Heaven's sake, forbear!" he whined.

The Dwarf of Blood laughed aloud.

"Ha, ha!" he said, "here's a joke, my merry men. Fancy a brigand talking like that."

Recollecting his early days, when he knew the consolation of religion, Giacomo crossed himself.

His lips moved as if he was offering up a prayer.

It was pardon for his misdeeds he was asking.

Well he could tell from the expression of Tito's face that he was doomed.

"By my faith!" chuckled the Dwarf of Blood, "this is better still, he makes the sign of the cross. Where is the latest addition to our band? Sarati, I think he calls himself."

At the mention of his name, Sarati stepped forward.

He was clever enough to recognise the fact that his man had lost the game, and could be of no use to him.

For this reason he was willing to do homage to the conqueror.

"My chief," he said, "I am here. What do you require of me?"

"I will honour you by making you the executioner," replied Tito.

"What shall I do with him?" asked Sarati.

"Throw him down the rocks."

Sarati bent over Giacomo, and took him up in his arms as if he had been a log of wood.

He walked to the edge of the precipice.

For a moment he stood still, then exerting all his strength, he hurled him into space.

Giacomo uttered a terrible shriek, which rang far and wide, finding many an echo in the rocky fastnesses.

The body struck a ledge, and bounded to another and another, until it fell into the valley beneath, horribly crushed and mangled.

Tito smiled grimly.

His wrath was appeased by the terrible way in which he had punished his enemy.

"Does anyone else wish to dispute my authority, or quarrel with me?" he asked ; "if so, I am prepared to meet him."

There was no reply to this challenge.

"Hurrah for Tito!" said Sarati; "he is the leader we want, and I, for one, am prepared to follow him to the death."

Shouts of applause burst from the throats of all.

"Drink," continued Tito, "we have a prisoner ; soon I will show you some sport."

"A prisoner?" echoed Sarati, who was ignorant of Jack's capture, "do you mean me? I am one of you."

"Peace," replied the Dwarf of Blood; "no harm is intended towards you, my friend."

"Who is it, then?"

"You will see anon."

Going into the cave Tito rolled out a large barrel capable of holding the body of a man.

Inside, the blades of two dozen knives had been stuck in the staves.

If a body were placed within it, and the barrel set in motion, the knives would soon hack it to pieces.

"What is that?" enquired Sarati, wiping away with some grass the blood of Giacomo, with which he was plentifully bespattered.

"I call it our cylindrical coffin," replied Tito, with a fiendish grin.

"Get in, and I will give you a ride down the hill."

Sarati shuddered.

"No thank you, I must refuse your kind offer.   Try it on your prisoner," he said.

"I mean to do so, directly."

"Upon my word, you should have been a butcher."

"That was my trade before I killed a man, and had to run for my life and join the brigands," answered the Dwarf of Blood.

"Excellent training.   Ha, ha!" exclaimed Sarati, forcing a laugh.

In reality, he was very nervous to think that he was in the power of such a cold-blooded monster.

The wine was handed round three or four times, and the swarthy faces of the bandits began to glow with excitement.

They were eager and ready for any villainy.

The figure of a man was seen coming up the path.

"Who goes there?" cried the sentry.

"Friend," was the reply. "Don't you know me? If you don't put your gun down, I will ask you for the money you owe me."

"Why," exclaimed Tito, "'tis our esteemed host of the 'Garibaldi.' Hey! what brings you here?"

"Business, as you may guess."

"State it at once."

"I have just received intelligence that a cart containing treasure for one of the banks in Naples will pass my house at ten to-night."

"Is it guarded?"

"By six mounted soldiers," replied the innkeeper.

"That is nothing ; an ambush will quickly dispose of them. Is the treasure in gold?"

"Silver and gold, I am informed," replied the innkeeper.

"Good," said Tito, "we will capture that cart, come what may. By all the saints, that will be the finest haul we have had for a long while."

"It ought to make all our fortunes."

"You shall not be forgotten. Will you stop and sup with me?" asked the Dwarf of Blood.

"Thank you, I cannot stop a moment," the innkeeper said, "I have some wine carriers at the inn, 'twas they who brought me the information."

"*Addio!* a thousand thanks."

Saying this, Tito shook his hand, the brigands gave him a lusty cheer, and he retraced his steps.

He was speedily lost to sight as he wended his way down the winding path.

"By Heaven!" cried the Dwarf of Blood, "this will be a fine chance.

Luck is in our way, my lads, to-day. More wine! more wine! finish up the jar."

This was quickly done.

"Now for our sport," added Tito.

"Who is the prisoner?" again asked Sarati.

"Mind your own business. What has it to do with you?"

"Nothing; but——"

"Cease prating; we captured him fairly. He was coming here to hunt us down. Is not that enough?"

Sarati was silent.

He saw that the dwarf had a disagreeable temper, which was aggravated by drink.

"I will not be talked to by anyone; least said, soonest mended," continued Tito. "A wise man keeps a still tongue."

He went to the entrance of Jack's prison, and rolled away the rock.

"Come out, you English dog," he exclaimed.

Jack did so immediately, looking handsome and fearless, though worn and very anxious.

"If I am what you call me," he replied, "you are an Italian hound."

He thought he was under Possilippo's protection.

Little did he dream that the brigand chief was in prison.

Sarati could scarcely believe the evidence of his senses when he beheld Jack Massey emerge from the prison.

He fancied his eyes must be deceiving him.

Another look, and he was satisfied that it really was his enemy, and his heart rejoiced to think that he was to be Tito's victim.

In a few minutes he would suffer an awful death, and all would be over with the brave English boy.

Sarati could not have devised an ending to Jack's career which would have suited his base instincts better.

"Look here," said Tito, whose eyes glistened like a snake's, "who are you insulting, I want to know?"

"You, evil-looking dwarf that you are," answered Jack.

"By Heaven! this is too much," cried Tito, stamping his splay-foot, and foaming at the mouth with rage. "You shall die!"

"Tell your master I want to speak to him."

"I have none. Possilippo is a captive; I am chief here. You will never see him again, nor will any of us, unless we go to his execution."

Jack turned deathly pale.

This news took his breath away, for he saw that he was in the power of a lawless and truculent brute, unworthy of the name of man.

The situation was very critical.

He was absolutely without a friend, and death seemed certain.

CHAPTER XX.

THE ESCAPE.

TITO saw the change in Jack's countenance, and grinned with delight.

It was a pleasure to him to see his victims cower and tremble.

Mental agony pleased him as much as did the spectacle of physical suffering.

Jack looked enquiringly at Sarati.

"Why do you not interfere on my behalf?" he exclaimed. "Will you stand by and see me murdered by these miscreants?"

"Do not appeal to me," rejoined Sarati; "I have no power to save you, even if I had the inclination, which, decidedly, I have not. Go and join your father in the spirit world."

"Your time will come."

"Not at your hands," sneered Sarati.

The Dwarf of Blood pointed to the barrel.

"Let me call the prisoner's attention to the knives," he said. "He will be put instde, and rolled down the incline, being cut to pieces before he reaches the bottom."

Large beads of perspiration gathered on Jack's forehead.

Was this terrible fate really intended for him?

He could not doubt it.

The first feeling of horror, however, gave place to one of intense rage.

He was beside himself with passion, and a feeling of madness took possession of him.

His blood boiled in his veins like molten lead.

In a moment his brain seemed to be on fire.

Rushing at Tito, he dashed out his left fist, giving him one of his terrible blows straight from the shoulder.

Tito spun round like a teetotum, then he seemed as if he were trying to learn a new dance, and finally he cannoned against Sarati.

They both fell down together.

For a brief space the dwarf was unable to recover himself.

The left-hander had struck him in the eye, and he saw as many stars as there are in the firmament on a bright night.

Jack was not satisfied with what he had done.

He ran at the nearest brigands and knocked two of them down like ninepins.

But the force of numbers told against him.

The remainder of the band, wondering at his great strength, fell upon, and, after a short struggle, bore him to the ground.

He was quickly secured by a piece of rope passed round his wrists.

When Tito got up, his face was dreadful to look at, so contorted was it with irrepressible anger.

"How dare you strike me?" he demanded. "*Diavolo!* you shall pay dearly for this. What was it he hit me with?"

"I used an Englishman's weapon, my fist," replied Jack, who was panting and drawing his breath with difficulty.

"It was more like a sledge-hammer than anything else."

"Only cowards, such as you Italians, use knives and pistols."

"You have struck your last blow," said the Dwarf of Blood, savagely. "I hate the English; it is a treat to kill one of that nation. *Peste!* how my eye aches. Hits like that one you gave me resemble kicks from a horse."

"I would give you another, if I could get hold of you."

"Bah! your time has come. You shall die!"

Tito beckoned to one of his men.

"Here, Milani," he continued, "just show this English John Bulldog how to crawl into that tub."

"I'd rather not," replied the brigand.

"It cannot hurt you. See, there is a space at the bottom for the body to rest on, where there are no knives. It is only when the rotary motion comes that the knives are felt. I ought to know, as I invented the infernal machine, and made it."

The barrel was lying about three yards from the edge of the precipice.

Its bristling knives reflected the sun's rays.

Milani, though reluctant, hesitated no longer.

"No joke," he said.

"What are you afraid of?"

"The cursed thing might take it into its head to get into motion, and then I should be nicely carved into tit-bits for dinner."

He laughed at his ghastly joke.

"That is impossible," replied Tito. "No one will touch it; get in. I want the prisoner to contemplate it, and realise what is going to happen to him in the few minutes which intervene between him and eternity."

"Ah!" said Milani, "it is easy to see that you understand the art of torturing."

"I ought to do so, when I have practised it all my life."

"Bravo! you graduated in a good school."

"I should think so," said the Dwarf of Blood, proudly.

He gloried in his acts of cruelty.

The brigand went down on his hands and knees as directed, and crawled into the barrel.

"Look!" said Tito. "You will observe, Signor Englishman, that he is as comfortable as if he had gone to bed; but soon, when you are in his place, the case will be altered. The knives will cut as the tub rolls. Ha! ha! There will not be much life left in you when you reach the bottom of the incline."

"You are a nest of vipers," replied Jack.

"True, that is just what we are—vipers—and you are going to feel our sting."

"Perhaps."

"Do you doubt my word?"

Jack Massey made no reply.

By a sudden jerk and an eel-like

movement he slipped from the grasp of the man who was holding him.

His arms were bound, but his feet were loose.

Quick as lightning he ran to the barrel.

Before anyone could stop him, he gave it a prodigious kick.

It rolled rapidly to the edge of the plateau.

Horrible shrieks arose from the inside as the knives began to cut the flesh of Milani.

For a second it paused on the top of the rocky ledge.

Then it careened over, and rolled down the precipitous incline.

Before he could turn round, a dozen hands seized Jack, and half as many knives were presented at his breast.

"Do your worst," cried Jack, "your death-trap is gone, and one of your number in it. I wish you were all there."

Fierce oaths and dire threats of vengeance sounded in his ears.

He expected every moment to be hacked to pieces.

Instead of that, Tito burst into a loud laugh, and standing on the extremity of the plateau, watched the tub roll down towards the valley.

He was intensely excited, and clapped his hands.

"Ha!" he yelled, "there it goes. What a bump that was! *Diavolo*! it has burst open, the body falls one way, the barrel another. What sport!"

Sarati touched him on the shoulder.

"You are forgetting your prisoner," he said.

"No, I have not done with him yet," was the answer; "but, I say, what a trick to play. I would not have lost the sight for a thousand *scudi*."

"The prisoner deserves death."

"I will attend to him presently. That sight, I tell you, was worth a thousand *scudi*."

Tito rubbed his hands and laughed with glee.

Turning to his men he added:

"Sheath your knives. The prisoner shall jump after poor Milani."

"Ah! that is better," muttered Sarati.

"What is that you say?" asked Tito.

The Dwarf of Blood had quick ears.

"Nothing," replied Sarati, "except that I would like to see it."

"Did you think I was going to let him off?"

"Not exactly."

"We shall have two executions instead of one, that is all," said Tito.

Surely, the spirit of the ancient Roman lived in this dwarf.

The Romans thronged to the amphitheatre of the Colosseum to witness the degrading spectacle of Christians and slaves torn to pieces by wild beasts.

So did the Italian revel in scenes of blood.

The brigands returned their knives to their belts.

They fell back, leaving Jack standing alone.

A look of sullen discontent had crossed their stern visages when they fancied, for a moment, that Tito was in a merciful mood.

Jack had killed one of their members, and they held that his life was forfeited.

He must pay the penalty.

"Now, Signor Englishman," resumed Tito, "I shall say one, two, three, and at the word 'three' you will be good enough to jump after Milani, whom you so kindly sent to announce your coming in the next world."

"I shall not move," replied Jack.

"Do you disobey my orders?"

"Push me, if you like, but I am not going to commit suicide."

"Oh! that can be done; look out."

The Dwarf of Blood advanced towards Jack, who, through his arms being bound, was powerless to protect himself.

His life hung on a single thread.

Only a miracle it seemed could save him.

He uttered a short but fervent prayer.

Just then Ada, who was anxious about the return of Possilippo, her only friend among the rude men, stepped out of the mouth of the cavern.

Bianca had been very kind to her.

She had furnished her with a pistol to enable her to protect herself against Sarati if he again attempted to injure her.

It was loaded in six chambers.

Directly she came into the sunlight she recognised Jack.

Her Jack—her sweetheart!

How her heart throbbed, and her bosom heaved!

Tears rendered her eyes misty, and she nearly fell to the ground.

This was no time for fainting.

She saw from Jack's face, and the general surroundings, that he was in some kind of awful danger.

What that was she could not tell.

It was her duty, however, to help him in every way in her power.

"Down you go!" shouted Tito, "no more nonsense."

Jack prepared for death.

He shut his eyes and awaited the push which was to hurl him down the hill-side.

With a wild cry Ada dashed forward and placed herself between the Dwarf of Blood and his victim, presenting her pistol at him as she did so.

Tito halted.

"Hold!" she exclaimed, her eyes flashing, "what would you do?"

Not being insensible to the charms of female beauty, Tito paused.

"Ah, my pretty one," he replied, "how is it that you are so much interested in him as to constitute yourself the champion of this boy?"

"I love him," was the simple rejoinder.

"It is quite a romance. Sarati brings you here, your lover follows you. Our poet, Tasso, would have liked to write about it, Dante would have been softened. Well, you are worthy of love. Give me a kiss, and I will let him live till to-morrow."

"On your word of honour?"

"Such honour as you can find in a brigand."

"Can I trust you?" asked Ada, tremulously.

"Until to-morrow my word holds good."

She turned her pretty, flushed face towards him.

The hideous dwarf took her in his arms.

Twice he kissed her on the lips.

She shuddered visibly in his hateful embrace.

But she had saved Jack for a time.

Giving her lover a significant look, she tripped lightly back to the cavern to seek shelter and consolation with Bianca.

Her heart was full to bursting.

How Jack came there she did not know, it was enough that she had saved his life for a few hours.

In that time much might be done.

Halting in the shadow of the doorway, she saw two men conduct Jack back to his prison.

He was unbound and thrust like a dog into a kennel, and the rock was rolled against the entrance.

She now knew where his place of confinement was.

Listening, she heard the Dwarf of blood say:

"His death is only postponed, my comrades."

"You surely would not be so mad as to spare him for the sake of a girl's pleading?" exclaimed Sarati.

"I wanted a kiss from those rosy lips."

"Be a man, and think of the business you have in hand for this evening."

This was an unlucky remark for Sarati.

"Do you think I ever forget such things?" retorted Tito; "by no means. We will start directly, and as this is your first outing with the band, you shall be in the front rank."

"What do you mean?"

"It is for you to lead the attack."

"Cannot I remain and act as sentry to the caves?"

"Certainly not; someone else will do that. Are you afraid, comrade?"

"Why, no," said Sarati. "If it comes to that, I am not afraid of anything, or anybody."

"You talk strangely."

"I am not well to-day," replied Sarati, as carelessly as he could.

"Good wine will cure you, and screw your courage up."

"Do you doubt my courage?" demanded Sarati, affecting fierceness, and tapping the hilt of his dagger.

"After your remark just now, I do."

"I allow no man to do that, but we have seen blood enough shed to-day. Giacomo and Milani, too."

"Oh, come," said Tito, "I will shed yours if you particularly wish to provoke me. I stand no nonsense."

It was not Sarati's intention to fight.

He had only attempted to bluster, and finding himself defeated in the effort, gave in.

"Enough," cried Tito, "we will test your mettle presently. Make ready, men. In half-an-hour we start to stop the treasure cart on its way to Naples. One man is sufficient to guard the caves."

Ada had heard all she wanted to hear.

With a beating heart she sought Bianca in the inner cave.

Her mind was sorely oppressed.

She longed to rescue Jack, and to get back to England, where she could have the shelter of her father's home.

Septimus was recovering, thanks to Dr. Pincio's care.

If there was no relapse, he would soon be well enough to travel.

She told the old Bianca all that had happened.

The woman did not appear to sympathise with her, or take any interest in her recital.

" Do you not hear me ? " asked Ada.

" I have ears for no one," replied Bianca in a choked voice. " If my tears had not been dried up years ago, I should be sobbing like a child."

" What has happened ?"

" My heart is broken. How can I interest myself in the fate of your lover, or in your own, when my son is lying in the prison of St. Angelo ?"

Ada was astounded at this news.

" When did you hear that ?" she asked.

" Only just now. One of the band told me Tito is master now," answered Bianca.

" Heaven help us ! Although I was afraid of him, Possilippo was my only hope."

" They will hang my son. I wish he had never been born."

" There is hope yet," said Ada ; " perhaps the information is not true. He may have friends who will aid him in his hour of need."

" You seek to comfort me in vain."

" Why so ? "

" My boy, whom I loved so much as to sacrifice position, honour, friends, everything for him, and to come to this place to lead this life, is doomed."

" You were foolish to do it."

Bianca looked at her vengefully.

" Tut ! " she cried, fiercely, " what does a girl like you know about a mother's love and deep devotion ? "

" Nothing, I admit."

" He told me that there would be no danger, as he should lead a double life—Possilippo here, Count Casati in Naples—that would throw the police off the scent. Then, again, this stronghold is impregnable. Thirdly, he said it should only last for a time ; he would retrieve his fallen fortunes in a few months, and we would quit this wretched place. Oh ! Holy Mary, how I have been deceived ! "

She crossed herself devoutly.

Poor mother !

Ada pitied her from the innermost recesses of her heart, but she had her own trouble to bear, and her mind was fully occupied in trying to divine how she could be of service to Jack.

The brigands were, all but one, going on an expedition that night.

Sarati was included in the number.

Assuredly she would never have such an opportunity offered her again.

Jack must be rescued at whatever cost to her own safety and well-being, but how was it to be done ?

That was the question.

Of a sudden, Bianca, who was standing up, uttered a cry, pressed her hand to her side, and fell back on a chair.

Her face became ghastly white, her hands were tightly clenched, her teeth firmly set.

Ada was dreadfully alarmed.

" Heaven help her ! " she cried, " the woman looks as if she were dying."

She ran to the table, got some water, and dashed it in her face.

In a few moments Bianca gasped for breath.

" Oh ! the pain," she said, wildly ; " my heart ! This news has killed me ! Air, air ! I cannot breathe."

With trembling fingers, Ada unfastened her dress at the neck.

As she did so, a canvas bag fell from Bianca's bosom to the floor.

Stooping down, Ada picked it up, and her curiosity was so strong that she opened it.

The bag was full of the most splendid diamonds.

This was the brigand chief's hidden treasure, which he had given to his mother for safe keeping.

No one would think of looking in the bosom of her dress for it.

This idea would not even have occurred to Tito.

Urged on by some irresistible impulse, Ada hastily concealed the treasure in her pocket.

It was lucky that she did so, for the moment afterwards the Dwarf of Blood entered the cave.

" What is this ? " he asked. " Bianca unwell ?"

" I fear she is dying," replied Ada ; " she complained of her heart, and went off in a swoon all at once."

" The air is full of death. If she goes, my little girl, you will have to cook for us."

Bianca sank to the ground, bleeding at the mouth.

"I am afraid," exclaimed the dwarf, "that the sands of her life are running out. She was a good cook, peace be with her. That, however, is not what I came here to tell you, my pet."

"What is it?" enquired Ada, growing uneasy.

"We are going on an expedition, and you will be left here, guarded by the sentry."

"Are you fearful lest I should escape?"

"I don't think that likely, but I always take precautions," replied Tito. "You showed me a pistol just now; be good enough to give it up."

This was the last thing Ada would have chosen to do.

She had no option, however, but to consent.

Reluctantly she presented him with the weapon which was her only means of defence.

"By all the saints!" he said, "you are a beautiful girl. If I were a marrying man, I should like to make you my wife; but I care not for wedded life. I should kill you in a fit of passion before we had been together a week."

Ada was very glad to hear this confession.

She had been afraid that he was going to add himself to her list of admirers.

"Have you any friends in this country?" he asked, after a pause.

"Alas! no," she rejoined. "I was brought to this place under a false pretence by my brother, who wanted me to marry his friend Sarati. Your prisoner, Jack Massey, followed to rescue me. Sarati knew Possilippo as Count Casati in days gone by; he asked the chief for shelter in his country house, not knowing his true character, and, to our dismay, we were brought here."

"Ha, ha!" laughed the Dwarf of Blood, "Possilippo is a sly dog; it appears to me that he had cast a loving eye on you himself. The chief, however, will not trouble you again, for the authorities have got a firm grip on him. You are Sarati's."

"I will die rather than be his," said Ada.

"Beware of him. I saved you once from his knife, and may not be able to do so again."

"As the chief, now, of these lawless men, you can let me go free."

"It is impossible."

"Do not say that; protect an innocent and friendless girl," replied Ada, in tears.

"I must not interfere," rejoined Tito; "all is fair in love and war. You might do worse than take Sarati for a husband."

"Never! I will die since you abandon me to my fate."

"Try and think better of it. _Addio!_ my child," exclaimed Tito.

With these words he left her alone with the corpse of poor Bianca.

She was veritably in a cave of death.

The lamp suspended from the ceiling burnt dimly, the cooking fire in the stove was out, and the vault, to her excited imagination, was peopled with ghosts.

Drawing the quilt from the bed, Ada placed it over the body of Bianca, thus hiding her awfully-contorted features.

Then she walked through the deserted caverns, and, looking out, saw Tito and his men descending the zigzag path.

Very picturesque they looked in the setting sun, with their plumed, broad-brimmed hats, their black velvet doublets, and trousers of the same material, gaitered up to the knees.

The solitary sentinel walked up and down the plateau, occasionally eyeing his companions.

Ada noticed a jar of wine on the floor of the cave.

Shaking it, she found it was nearly full.

An idea suddenly came into her head.

What if she could make the man tipsy, and send him to sleep on his post.

The brigands, she had noticed, were always ready to drink if they were afforded the opportunity.

Surely her exertions, added to Jack's, inside his prison, would suffice to roll away the rock at the entrance?

All the banditti were away but this one.

She might never have such a chance again.

Jack had to die on the morrow.

What her fate would be at the hands of Sarati, before long, she could easily divine.

Now or never was the time.

Taking up the jar, she summoned all her courage to her aid, and approaching the man, said, in her best Italian:

"In the name of the Virgin, good evening."

"Ah! my little lady," replied the brigand, smiling, "what have you there?"

"Some wine I have brought you, because you seem so lonely."

"My thanks are yours, for in sober truth, I am always troubled with an accursed thirst which I cannot quench."

"Help yourself," replied Ada.

"You shall not bid me twice."

He raised the jar to his lips and drank several deep draughts.

"By Bacchus, god of wine!" he cried, "you have done me a service. A dry round is very weary work for a sentry. I must be careful, though; if I went to sleep, and Tito found me so, a bullet would quickly send me to the other world."

"It is a poor heart that never makes merry."

"Quite so. I mean to enjoy myself, thanks to your kindness."

Ada smiled and retreated into the cavern.

Securely hidden from view, she watched the brigand carefully.

Her heart beat wildly.

Would she, after all, be able to rescue her lover, Left-handed Jack?

Placing his rifle on the rock, the brigand sat down beside it, and applied his lips occasionally to the jar of wine.

The man was naturally a drunkard.

He could not resist the temptation when it was offered him.

Gradually, as the sun sank lower and lower, and he made repeated applications to the jar, his eyes grew glazed.

His head nodded; he sang in a low voice the chorus of a drinking song.

Then his mood changed.

In a lower tone he murmured a hymn, as if his mind were reverting to the days of his youth, before he had steeped his soul in sin.

Finally he fell on his back and snored like a hog.

The brigand had arrived at his last stage of intoxication.

Stealing gently forth from her place of concealment, Ada seized the rifle, and hurled it into the abyss.

Going to the entrance of the prison, she whispered:

"Jack!"

"Who calls?" was the reply. "Is it really you, Ada?"

"It is," she replied. "We are alone, the brigands have gone to rob a treasure cart. I have stupefied the sentinel with wine. If we can only move this rock, we can both escape from this terrible place."

"Is Sarati with the band?"

"Yes, he is one of them, and was forced to go. Push from the inside, and I will endeavour to aid your efforts."

"Trust me for exerting all my strength," replied Jack. "By Jove, Ada, you are a splendid girl."

"Did not your heart tell you that I would die for you?"

"You shall do better than that—live for me."

"Make haste," cried Ada; "do not waste the time in talking. We never know when those horrid men will come back, or the sentinel wake up."

Jack set to work with a will.

He put his left shoulder to the rock, and pushed with all his might and main.

From the outside Ada helped him.

She pulled at the jagged rock till her delicate fingers were torn and bleeding.

The rock, though ponderous, was not so heavy as they had thought.

It gave way, moved a little, at last it rolled on one side.

Jack was free.

All through the efforts of his sweetheart he saw liberty before him.

His first act was to catch her in a firm embrace, and kiss her tenderly.

"How can I ever repay your devotion?" he asked.

"By saying nothing about it," replied Ada.

"I shall never forget it. I am astonished at your tact and bravery."

"The mouse helped the lion once when it was caught in the net, but we are not out of the wood as yet."

"That is true," replied Jack.

The sentry moved uneasily.

"Hush! down!" whispered Ada.

Her heart fluttered terribly, and her face flushed.

Jack sank on his knees behind the rock.

This manœuvre completely hid him from view.

So quickly had it been executed that the sentinel did not see him, though he opened his eyes and raised himself upon his elbow.

"Hullo!" he growled, "I thought I heard voices."

"You have been dreaming," replied Ada.

"Why don't you go and talk to Bianca, my pretty bird?"

"She has gone to sleep, and I am lonely in those dark caves."

"It appears to me I have been asleep also," said the brigand. "This won't do; 'twas this wine, I expect. Holy Mary! how heavy my head feels."

"Have another nap."

"If you will promise to keep a look-out, I will."

"I will do that with pleasure," answered Ada, readily.

The man reclined on his side again, his eyes closed, and he was soon fast asleep.

Luckily the danger that had threatened them was averted.

When the man's heavy breathing convinced her that the brigand was in the land of dreams, Ada beckoned to Jack.

He got up and came to her.

In his hand was a piece of jagged rock.

"You see, I was prepared for a tussle," he whispered, grimly.

She took his hand, and together they descended the winding path.

They were compelled to leave Septimus behind.

He was not sufficiently recovered to go with them.

Besides, he was in league with the brigands, and therefore was in no danger of his life from them.

They hoped sincerely that they were leaving the bloodstained spot for ever.

It was growing rapidly dark.

The early stars were glimmering in the far-off sky.

When the descent was accomplished and the valley gained, they breathed more freely.

They had to cross a wide plain before they gained the main road to Naples.

This was sterile, covered with pieces of rock, and nearly devoid of herbage.

No sheep or cattle were to be seen anywhere.

Not even a farm-house, a vineyard, or a labourer's cottage was visible.

The brigands had chosen their hiding-place with considerable sagacity.

Here and there were a few stunted trees that evidently did not thrive on the arid and ungenerous soil.

"Do you know the way?" enquired Ada, nervously.

"We must keep straight on until we reach the road. I remember that much, though it was dark when they brought me along," Jack replied.

"And then?"

"We shall come to the 'Garibaldi' inn, where I was captured; after that we have but to walk into the city."

"Do you think we shall meet Tito and his men?"

"Heaven forbid!" said Jack, "it will be all up with us if we do."

"Be careful, I beg of you," cried Ada.

They at length reached the main road.

The stars were now shining brilliantly in their setting of opaque sky.

The hearts of the fugitives were beating high with hope and anticipation.

But they were not yet out of danger.

CHAPTER XXI.

A CRUEL FATE.

THEY had not proceeded far before they came to a portion of the road which was rendered dark by leafy trees on each side.

Sombre shadows were cast athwart their path.

It seemed as if gigantic ghosts having fantastic forms were barring their progress.

All at once Ada uttered a cry, and sank on one knee.

"What is the matter? Are you hurt?" Jack asked.

"I slipped over a stone," Ada replied; "I fear I have sprained my ankle."

"Lean on me."

She tried to do so, but could not get up.

When he raised her, she fell down again, apparently in great agony.

"Oh! dear," she said, "I cannot go a step further. Whatever shall we do? Save yourself and leave me to my fate."

"Do you think I would be guilty of such base and cowardly conduct?" answered Jack.

It was indeed an embarrassing situation.

At that time of night it was not likely any vehicle would pass by on the lonely and deserted highway.

Jack thought he could carry her as far as the "Garidaldi" inn, but he gave up that idea when he recollected that the keeper was in league with the brigands.

The position was full of danger.

At any moment, the brigands, who were going to attack the treasure waggon, might come along.

Recapture would then be inevitable.

It was most unfortunate that such an accident should have occurred.

"Take my boot off," continued Ada, "it is the right one. I shall scream with agony if you do not."

Jack endeavoured to do so, but the sprained foot was so swollen that it resisted all his efforts to disengage it.

In his pocket he had a small penknife.

With this, after some exertion, he contrived to rip open the leather and remove it.

Ada breathed a deep sigh of relief.

"That is better; but, oh, Heaven! how I am suffering," she murmured.

"If I were to put you behind the wall under the trees for a while, would you be frightened?" asked Jack.

"Not at all. What do you propose to do?"

"I will hasten into Naples, get a carriage, and come back post-haste for you."

"That is an excellent idea," said Ada.

"I am only afraid of the brigands, but I should not imagine they would find you in this darksome spot."

"It is not likely; go, Jack. I will bear the pain as well as I can, and lie quite still until you come back."

"I'll do it, if you can't think of a better plan."

"Indeed, I cannot."

"That is settled, then," replied Jack.

He took her in his arms, got over the low wall which bordered the road, and deposited her on the ground.

No one could see her from the road, and high grass and the trunks of trees hid her from view on the other side of the wall.

An aged cypress waved its mournful branches over her head when the night wind blew.

Begging her to be brave, and bear her trouble gallantly, he kissed her, pressed her hand, and started off at a run for Naples.

He determined to lose no time.

Suddenly she remembered something of the utmost importance.

"Jack!" she cried, "come back."

He had not gone too far to hear her.

Instantly he returned, wondering what she wanted with him.

"I had forgotten one thing," said Ada.

"What is that?" asked Jack, curiously.

She drew from her bosom the canvas bag of diamonds.

"These are, I believe, the treasure of Possilippo," she replied. "I have heard that he converted all the money he got into diamonds."

"How did they come into your possession?"

"It is easily explained. An old woman who cooked for the brigands in the caves was his mother. The news of his capture caused her death, and the bag dropped from her clothes as I was attending to her. No doubt it was given to her for safe keeping."

"Ha!" cried Jack, "this is a valuable find, it will make our fortunes. I will lodge the jewels with a banker, in your name."

"No, in yours!" exclaimed Ada, generously. "If anything should happen to me, you will be provided for."

"Dear girl, what a kind heart you have."

"All for you, Jack."

He took the bag from her hands, and was sure, from the weight of it, that it contained stones worth an immense sum.

All that Possilippo, Count Casati, had toiled and sinned for was his.

Wishing her good-bye again, he once more started on his journey.

She listened to his retreating footsteps until they died away in the distance.

Then all was still as death.

She was in the midst of a frightful solitude, which was aggravated by the darkness.

But worse was to come.

An hour passed, during which she suffered intensely from her sprained foot.

Then she heard the tramp of several men, who were approaching her hiding-place.

"Halt!" said a harsh voice.

It was that of Tito, the Dwarf of Blood.

She recognised it in an instant.

Her heart seemed almost to stand still.

"This spot will do," continued Tito, "we could not have a better one for our ambush. Get behind the wall and kneel down. I will give the word to fire, when the cavalcade comes along with the treasure waggon. Aim true, every shot must tell."

The brigands obeyed these orders with alacrity.

They jumped over the wall, and one of them knelt down close to the reclining girl.

It was a wonder he did not touch her.

Ada scarcely dared to breathe.

It is easy to imagine the horror of her position.

Fortunately for her, the suspense did not last long.

Five minutes elapsed, and then horses were heard coming up the road, with the accompaniment of the grinding wheels of a heavy waggon.

She could see nothing, and remained perfectly motionless.

All the same, she trembled with anxiety, for she expected a terrible calamity to happen every moment.

The treasure waggon was approaching.

It had travelled from Rome under a military escort, for the gold and silver were the property of the government.

An officer rode slightly in advance, three soldiers were on each side of the waggon, and the driver sat on the box guiding the horses.

All were tired and jaded with a hard day's march, and looked forward eagerly to the end of their journey.

Entirely unsuspicious were they of their danger.

The officer in command of the detachment was well acquainted with the road, and had promised them a brief halt and refreshments at the "Garibaldi."

When they got within the ambuscade, Tito, who, with instinctive cunning had climbed up a tree, and was sitting on a branch, cried:

"Fire!"

A deadly fusilade was poured in upon the unsuspecting members of the cortège.

The Dwarf of Blood picked off the officer, who fell, mortally wounded, into the road.

Four of the saddles were emptied at the first fire.

The brigands quickly slipped fresh cartridges into their rifles, and the other two soldiers fell dead.

Their horses dashed over the wall and disappeared on the Campagna, wild with a sudden fright.

Strange to say, the driver of the treasure waggon had escaped unhurt.

Either the bullets had flown harmlessly past him, or nobody thought him worth shooting.

Yet he was the most important factor in the game.

When he saw the soldiers fall, he whipped up the two horses that drew the waggon, flogging them with all his might.

They responded gallantly to the urgent appeal.

It was in vain that Tito fired after them; they, as well as the driver, seemed to be bullet-proof.

Not a shot touched them.

The waggon thundered along the road, enveloped in a cloud of dust.

Tito slipped down from his elevated position in the tree.

His imprecations were fearful.

The treasure on which he had counted had slipped through his clutches.

He was exasperated beyond measure at this mishap.

It was in vain that he fired bullet after bullet in the rear of the retreating waggon.

It was soon entirely out of range.

Pursuit on foot was utterly useless.

"Malediction!" he exclaimed, bitterly. "Why did not one of you fools shoot the driver? This is a pretty go; we have had all our trouble for nothing."

The brigands looked blankly at one another.

Suddenly one of them uttered an exclamation.

"What is the matter with you, Veronesi?" asked Tito.

The man thus addressed was standing up under the cypress tree.

His eyes were cast upon the ground.

Something was evidently perplexing his mind.

"SHE TOOK HIS HAND, AND TOGETHER THEY DESCENDED THE WINDING PATH."—(See page 126.)

No. 9.

"My foot touched a body, captain," he replied; "as all the soldiers have fallen in the road, I can't make it out."

"Lift it up, and bring it here in the starlight."

"That is as soon done as said."

Veronesi stooped down and grasped the shoulders of Ada, for it was her arm he had trodden upon.

The movement caused her exquisite pain.

She gave vent to a shrill scream.

"Hullo!" cried Tito, "this is some mystery, 'twas a woman's voice. Your body is a very live one, my friend."

The brigand carried the miserable girl into the middle of the road.

Everyone crowded round him.

"Heavens!" exclaimed Sarati, when he saw her face, "it is Ada, whom we left in the cave."

"Our little captive, by all that is holy," said Tito. "How could she have escaped, and why was she lying behind the wall? Speak, child!"

Thus encouraged, Ada looked up.

"I ran away," she answered. "You were gone, and——"

"But the sentry, what of him?" interrupted the Dwarf of Blood, fiercely.

"I gave him wine; he slept."

"Asleep at his post! he shall die. The penalty is death! eh, comrades?"

The reply of the brigands was unanimous.

"Death, death!" they chorused.

Their rough voices found a sullen echo among the trees.

"Were you alone and unaided?" asked Tito.

"Left-handed Jack accompanied me," she replied.

"Confusion! there is nothing but bad luck for us," ejaculated Tito. "I had sworn to kill that boy in the morning. Pity I listened to you, and spared his life temporarily for the sake of a kiss."

Sarati had made no remark, yet he was furious with rage.

His rival had slipped through his fingers just when his end seemed certain.

It was almost more than he could bear, and everyone could hear him grate his teeth savagely together.

"Where is he?" demanded Tito.

"Gone to Naples," said Ada; "and if you injure me, he will make you render an account of your crime."

"Bah! we study nobody. We are above the law."

"Beware! your day will come."

"Silence, girl!" cried the Dwarf of Blood, shaking with suppressed anger. "Explain why we found you here alone, hidden behind that wall."

"I slipped on a stone and sprained my foot. I suffer greatly, and could not stand if this man did not hold me up."

She indicated Veronesi, who was supporting her.

"Ho, ho! you were stopped in your flight. What a joke. Your sweetheart hid you away, little thinking that we should find you. Ha, ha! the brigands have a keen scent."

He laughed loud and long.

When he had exhausted his mirthful mood, he continued his examination.

"Is Left-handed Jack coming back for you?" he enquired.

"Of course he is," replied Ada, boldly, but incautiously. "Do you think he is coward enough to desert me?"

She did not mean to get Jack into danger.

Yet that was the very thing she had done.

"Ho, ho!" laughed the Dwarf of Blood again, "you could not walk, and he has gone to get a carriage. I see. We will give him a hot reception, ha, ha!"

Ada was horrified.

She perceived the danger into which she had, unintentionally, brought Jack.

"What have I done?" she said, under her breath.

Tito caught the words.

"Sealed the doom of your lover," he rejoined; "he will not see to-morrow's sun set, I'll swear to that."

The tears coursed down her cheeks.

"Away to the hills!" shouted Tito.

"Stop a moment," said Sarati; "it seems to me that you have forgotten one or two things, Tito."

"What are they, pray?"

"In the first place, it does not look well to leave those dead soldiers lying about in the roadway."

"True, they shall be thrown over the wall. What next?"

"If Left-handed Jack is to be caught or killed, someone must stay here to do it."

"Good."

"Appoint somebody, then."

"Yourself," replied Tito, promptly.

"I!" said Sarati.

"Why, yes. You have a grudge against the youth, because he wants to take your girl away from you."

"Must I stop ?"

"Certainly ; I order you to do so. Have you anything else to suggest ?"

"Seeing that the young lady cannot walk, how are you going to get her back to the caves ? "

"That is a puzzle," replied Tito. "What a head you have, to be sure ! We must have her to keep as a hostage ; things are becoming serious with us. If I had captured the treasure waggon, I meant to have divided the spoil, broken up the band, and made a run of it to Rome, where I know how to enjoy myself. Suppose the soldiers are sent after us, what then ? "

Veronesi, who was an old man, smiled grimly.

"They will have to find us," he remarked.

"But what if they should do so ? "

"We must fight to the bitter end."

"Yes," answered the Dwarf of Blood, excitedly ; "that is what it must come to. I am ready to do my share of the fighting, for I love it."

He gave an order, and the bodies of the six soldiers, and that of their officer were hidden away behind the wall.

Two brigands crossed hands, joining their fingers together, making a kind of chair, upon which Ada was lifted.

She was instructed to put her arms round their necks and hold on tightly.

Then they raised her, and she travelled as comfortably as if she had been in a sedan chair.

Sarati, gnawing his lips with vexation, remained behind, walking up and down with his rifle on his shoulder.

"She shall be mine," he muttered. "I will kill her lover. Ha, ha ! he shall find a snake in his path to-morrow morning."

He halted and gazed over the wall.

His keen eyes took in, and noted well, all the surroundings.

" 'Twas here he left her," he added. "Well, I shall be in ambush ; a bullet from my rifle will soon lay him low, and if she will not then consent to wed me, she shall join him in the spirit world, and I will seek fresh fields. Bah ! I am not to be made sport of by a boy and girl."

He sat down on the wall and lighted his pipe.

There was a long vigil before him.

CHAPTER XXII.

LEFT-HANDED JACK AT WORK.

It was about eight o'clock in the morning when Jack arrived at his hotel in Naples.

He was terribly worn out with the efforts he had made to get over the ground as quickly as possible.

His spirit was such, however, that it supported him amidst all his trials.

He was naturally strong, and had a courage that kept him going to the very last.

Still, he was almost inclined to faint with fatigue when he entered the hotel, and staggered into the breakfast-room.

To his delight, he saw Dick Lambert at one of the tables.

"Taking it easy, Dick ? Nothing like it," he exclaimed.

Dick sprang from his chair, nearly upsetting the table in his haste.

"Is it really you, Jack, dear old boy, or your ghost ? " he cried.

"Not much of the unsubstantial about me," replied Jack. "Give me some breakfast, and try me."

"Are you hungry ? "

"Yes, and thirsty. I have had nothing inside my lips for hours."

"Sit down and eat mine," said Dick, "and tell me your adventures."

Jack took a seat, and while he was eating fish, flesh, and fowl, to the accompaniment of some delicious chocolate *au lait*, he unfolded his narrative.

Dick listened in wonder.

"You are another Ulysses," he remarked.

"Say a second Jason, for I have got the golden fleece."

"Let me look at the diamonds.'

"Not here," answered Jack.

The room was full of people, waiters were flitting about here and there.

To have produced the bag containing the precious stones in such company would have been to excite attention.

Perhaps it would have aroused suspicion.

In continental capitals it does not require much to bring about a visit from the commissary of police.

An arrest is made at once, and questions asked afterwards.

"You will go to a banker, I surmise?" said Dick.

"The first thing after breakfast," replied Jack. "I look upon these diamonds as lawful spoil; the sum they realise will be Ada's marriage portion."

"How will you account for their possession? If you cannot give a good account, they will be detained."

"I did not think of that."

"If you tell all, the government will claim them."

"By Jove! you are right," exclaimed Jack. "I will keep them in my pocket, come what may."

"Right; stick to them. I wish Ada had come with you."

"So do I, but it could not be done."

"Poor girl, how great her pain must be!" observed Dick, feelingly.

"True; but she can endure it without showing any weakness. You don't know the courage that she possesses. She is another Joan of Arc, or Miss Nightingale, or Grace Darling."

"It's easy to see that she is *your* darling," said Dick, with a smile; "but what are you going to do about sleep?"

"Do without it until the work is over. I will order a carriage directly, and fetch Ada."

He was confident that he would find her where he left her.

Little did he think that he would be doomed to disappointment.

Not for a moment did he dream that the Dwarf of Blood and his attendant brigands had got her in their power again.

He was lulled into a confident calm.

But he was destined to have a rude awakening.

"You are a man of iron," remarked Dick.

"I wish I were," said Jack; "of course, I am as frail as other mortals, but I try to hold out as long as I can. I persevere, and won't give in until I am compelled to, which I hold to be the great secret of success. You will come with me?"

"Most decidedly I will."

"If I break down, you must take the lead. Where is Sparks?"

"Gone to the Minister of the Interior, the Duke of Calabria."

"What for?" queried Jack.

"To ascertain if he will send a company of soldiers after the brigands. You have heard of Possilippo's capture, I apprehend?"

"Yes; but not the details."

Dick told him how the arrest was brought about.

At this, Jack was immensely delighted.

"Bravo!" he exclaimed; "you deserve the title of hero, for it was a clever, daring, well-executed piece of business."

"Don't flatter me," replied Dick. "What shall you do, as soon as Ada is able to go about again?"

"I shall return to England," said Jack.

"What about Sarati?"

"Oh! he can follow his own course; having taken Ada away from him, I fear him no more."

"And the brigands—will you not help the soldiers exterminate them?"

"Certainly not; let the government do its own dirty work," rejoined Jack.

Just then Sparks, the detective, entered the room, having returned from his visit to the Minister of the Interior.

His face was lighted up with a pleased expression, which increased when he saw Jack.

"Welcome!" he exclaimed, "I am glad you are come."

Jack shook hands, telling him all he had told Dick.

"Now," he added, "what is your news?"

"Excellent. The minister, after a lot of red tape and circumlocution business, has consented to send the soldiers after the brigands."

"That is good intelligence."

"All we wanted was a guide, and you will supply that deficiency."

"I can take you to the very spot; but it is a difficult stronghold to attack."

"Wait a minute," said the London detective, "we can discuss that presently. I have more of importance to inform you of."

"More?" echoed Jack.

"You will be surprised."

"Do not keep us in suspense."

"Possilippo has escaped during the night; the guards were posted as usual in all parts of the goal, but in some mysterious manner he contrived to get away."

"Confound it !" exclaimed Jack, "that complicates matters."

"Still," remarked Dick, "I do not see how it concerns us."

"The Duke is very angry," continued Sparks. "He has suspended the governor of the prison, and Signor Madia, pending an inquiry."

"What will the brigand chief do ? " asked Jack.

"Run away, I expect."

"Not he. I will wager anything that he returns to his cave in the hills."

"For what reason ? "

"Because he left his treasure there."

"Ah !" said Sparks, "you are right. By the way, there is another item of news I have omitted to mention."

"Rumour is busy," replied Jack.

"All I tell you are facts. Last night a treasure waggon, guarded by six mounted soldiers and an officer, was attacked on the Roman road."

"I knew it was intended."

"The soldiers were shot to a man, but the driver escaped, and brought the waggon safe into Naples."

"I am rejoiced to hear that the brigands were foiled," replied Jack ; "but my dear fellow, I can give you no more time. Ada is writhing in pain, she awaits my coming. I have wasted too many precious minutes already."

"You can rely upon my assistance," the detective responded.

Jack called a waiter, and ordered one of the hotel carriages to be sent to the door at once.

There was no time to be lost.

His heart flew out to Ada, whom he pictured to himself lying under the wall where he had placed her.

Waiting ! hoping ! watching ! Listening for the slightest sound.

That was what he anxiously thought.

The reality, however, was very different.

Stretched on a bed of pain, she was lying in the inner cave, from which the dead body of Bianca had been removed.

The brigands had lighted no fire, as they could manage without cooking if they wanted to, owing to their supply of tinned provisions and bags of biscuits.

No one attended to her, and she had made shift to bandage her ankle in the best way she was able.

Jack's heart, however, was beating high with pleasurable expectations.

In a short time an open, lightly-built carriage, with an awning over it to keep out the sun, drove up to the door.

Jack, Dick Lambert, and Sparks got in, and being told in which direction to go, the driver started.

As usual, in that lovely climate, the day was bright and clear.

Mount Vesuvius continued in a state of eruption, but, up to the present, there had been no volcanic disturbance.

Dense clouds of black smoke, accompanied by flame, ashes, and scoriæ, were cast up through the crater.

When they had got out of the precincts of the city, Jack's head sank back on the cushions, and he went fast asleep.

The strain upon his system had been too great.

Exhausted nature could not bear any more.

"Don't wake him," said the detective ; "I know the feeling. A few hours' sleep will do him a world of good."

"He will wake up like a giant refreshed," replied Dick.

"I am glad this affair seems likely to be settled, with the recovery of Miss Titmarsh," continued Sparks. "It is not worth time and money to keep up a hunt after that scoundrel Sarati."

"He is a brigand now, and the soldiers will deal with him."

"That is certain. They have started ; we shall overtake them directly, and I will have a word with the captain."

"What do you propose to do ? " asked Dick.

"I thought that you could conduct Miss Titmarsh back to Naples, while Massey and I waited at the 'Garibaldi' inn for the soldiers, to whom Massey could give instructions how to find the brigands' cave."

"By all means ; but do not let Jack take any part in the attack ; his life is too precious to be risked for nothing."

"I will see to that, and keep him out of danger," answered Sparks.

How true it is that man proposes, and Heaven disposes.

They little imagined what was about to happen.

CHAPTER XXIII.

SARATI'S LAST STAND.

THE carriage had not gone more than four miles along the road before it came up with a company of infantry belonging to the Italian army.

In their neat, green uniforms, and their hats ornamented with feathers, they looked gay and serviceable.

They stepped along in quick time to the music of a drum-and-fife band.

It seemed as if they were going for a march out, rather than to undertake a dangerous campaign against brigands.

Yet they were in heavy marching order, and every man carried sixty rounds of ball cartridge.

An ammunition waggon followed in their wake, with three provision waggons, and one water-cart.

The captain of the company walked by the side of his men, the band going in advance.

Sparks stopped the carriage when he reached the head of the company, and saluted the captain.

"I don't speak Italian," he exclaimed; "but I want to speak to you."

The captain bowed politely.

In a loud voice he halted his column.

The band ceased playing instantly, and the soldiers grounded arms.

"I think, sir," said the Italian captain, "there will be no difficulty about that. I was educated in England."

"Thank goodness," replied Sparks, "we shall get along easily now."

"My father intended me for commerce, and said that, with a knowledge of English and French, one could go over the world, but my tastes were for the army. What is your pleasure with me?"

"You are sent after Possilippo's band, if I am not misinformed, by the Minister of the Interior."

"That is the rather unpleasant duty upon which I am detailed," said the officer. "I assure you, sir, that I would sooner charge up to the cannon's mouth than perform such a disagreeable mission."

"We can give you some information respecting the brigands."

"Ah! that will be welcome, indeed."

"Where do you halt when you get near the hills?"

"At the inn 'Garibaldi.'"

"We will meet you there. Adieu, captain."

"Many thanks for your courtesy," replied the officer, as Sparks and Dick lifted their hats and the carriage drove on.

They did not stop again until they had passed the inn.

Not knowing the exact locality where Jack had left Ada, Dick thought it was advisable to rouse his friend.

He had some difficulty in doing so.

Jack was sleeping so soundly that he required a great deal of shaking.

"I say," he cried, "what is the matter? Can't you let a fellow sleep?"

"We have nearly come to the end of our journey," replied Dick.

"Oh! that is it; all right," said Jack, yawning.

"Pull yourself together."

"In a twinkling. Where are we? Oh! I see. Drive on, it is only a little further. I left Ada under that big cypress tree yonder."

The carriage moved forward again.

Nothing was to be seen in the road, which was as deserted as if it had been midnight.

"Stop," said Jack.

Again the carriage halted.

"Here is the identical spot," added Jack.

Scarcely were the words out of his lips, than a man sprang up from behind the low stone wall.

It was no other than Sarati.

He raised a rifle to the level of his shoulder, and took deliberate aim at Jack.

There was a sharp crack, a puff of smoke, and the bullet fled on its deadly errand.

Jack and Sparks were sitting side by side at the back of the carriage.

They offered a good mark for the ball of the assassin.

Dick Lambert was seated in front.

Consequently he was protected from harm.

Sarati had been waiting many hours for this opportunity.

At last it had come.

Much depended upon his aim.

If he shot his bullet home, he would be rid of his hated rival for ever, and Jack would not be able to betray the brigands' hiding-place.

It would have been better for him, however, if he had waited until Jack had got out of the carriage and stepped into the road.

Then he would have been surer of his quarry.

As it was, the driver saw the brigand, and although there was only one, his fervid imagination conjured the place full of them.

He expected to be killed every moment.

With a spasmodic movement he jerked his horses across the road.

This slight change in position altered everything.

Instead of Jack receiving the bullet, it struck Sparks in the chest.

The unlucky detective threw up his arms, and with a wild cry fell forward upon Dick's knees.

"Heaven help me !" he moaned, "I'm done for."

Jack was on his feet in a moment.

With the rapidity of lightning he drew a pistol, with which he had provided himself before leaving the hotel, and fired at Sarati.

The latter dodged behind the wall.

This manœuvre saved his life, for the bullet whistled harmlessly over his head.

While under cover he was able to load again.

Jack jumped out of the carriage.

He ran to the wall and also dodged down, effectually concealing himself.

Thus Sarati and he were each hiding, one at one side of the wall, one at the other.

But the Italian was not aware of Jack's proximity to him.

One brief glance had been sufficient for our hero to recognise his enemy.

He feared the worst with regard to Ada.

Yet, dearly as he loved her, he forgot her for the moment.

His mind was solely occupied with a fierce desire to have revenge upon the man he firmly believed to be his father's murderer.

He would kill Sarati, or the Italian should make an end of *him*.

It was Sarati's last stand.

A half-minute passed in complete silence.

Then Jack heard the man cock his rifle.

He was getting ready for renewed action.

Kneeling, crouching, eyes turned upward, pistol in hand, Jack was ready for him.

Suddenly Sarati sprang up.

He looked at the carriage, and an expression of blank dismay came over his countenance.

His prey had escaped him.

Before he had time to decide on what he should do, Jack rose to his feet.

His first impulse was to use his pistol.

On second thoughts he raised his fist and gave the cowardly Italian one of his famous left-handed blows.

It struck him between the eyes.

Sarati dropped his rifle, and fell on his back half-stunned.

In a moment Jack was upon him.

He snatched away his knife and the two pistols he had in his belt, hurling them from him.

Then he stood over the fallen ruffian, his revolver levelled at his head.

Dick Lambert had watched this proceeding with the utmost interest.

He gave one glance at Sparks.

The detective was dead.

Disengaging himself from him, he opened the carriage door and alighted in the road.

"Three cheers for Left-handed Jack !" he shouted. "Bravo ! old boy, I never saw anything better done in my life."

The coachman did not understand what he was talking about, but he clapped his hands and cried :

"*Viva* !"

Sarati moved uneasily.

His coal black eyes opened, and fixed themselves on the boy of whom he had made a deadly foe.

They were full of hatred and malignity.

"Lie still, you hound, or you die !" said Jack. "Where is Ada ? "

"Where you cannot get her," was the reply, with a stony look.

"Did the brigands find her ? "

"No matter. I know where she is and I alone can find her for you. Spare my life, and I will bring her here inside of six hours."

Jack smiled sarcastically.

"It won't do, Sarati," he said. "I know you too well. Not on your oath would I believe you, nor would I trust you farther than I could see you."

The Italian scowled.

"If I die, you will never see her again," he exclaimed. "Others love her as well as you and I."

"To whom do you allude?"

"Possilippo."

"What of him?"

"Bah! Do you think I am a child?" cried Sarati. "News travels quickly. The brigand chief has escaped."

"You know that?"

"Yes, I have seen him."

"It follows, then, that the brigands have recaptured Ada, and that she is in their power in the caves?" said Jack.

"Draw your own conclusions. All I say is this—kill me, and you will still have a formidable rival."

Jack was sorely perplexed.

For the present, Sarati held the key of the situation.

What was he to do?

"If I release you, will you swear to bring her to me, at this place, or at the 'Garibaldi' inn, before sundown?" he asked.

"Willingly."

Dick interposed.

"Don't believe him!" he exclaimed. "He only wants to deceive you to save his worthless life. It is all deception."

Sarati looked daggers at him.

"I only wish I had you alone for about two minutes," he hissed.

Jack had been growing weak through his love for Ada.

The warning note sounded by Dick strengthened him.

"No," he said, "I will not trust you. Let me question you about another thing. How did my father die?"

"By my hand," replied Sarati. "It was in a fair duel, however. We fought with pistols in his own room. You have heard how he wronged me in the past, I suppose?"

"I am sorry to reply that I have."

"Was I not justified in seeking revenge?"

"Tell me the truth about the duel, or I will shoot you on the spot!" cried Jack.

He was determined to get to the bottom of the matter.

Sarati was alarmed at his attitude.

He wanted to save his life at all hazards.

"If I make a clean breast of it, will you promise not to shoot me?" he asked.

"You have my promise."

"Your father and I arranged to fight a duel. I forced it upon him. Before the moment arranged upon for firing, I discharged my pistol."

"In that case, you are my father's murderer."

"I am; but he wronged me. For years I had vowed to have revenge, for years I had sought him, and at last my chance came."

Jack was justly indignant.

"Wretch!" he exclaimed. "You deserve to die, and you shall not escape me."

"Your promise—remember your promise."

"Did you not try to kill Septimus Titmarsh? I will have you tried for that crime, and also for being a brigand."

Ada had told him of the desperate wound Sep had received.

"Mercy!"

"I can have none on you."

"Let me go," whined Sarati.

"Never; you shall not escape the gallows."

"But this is a breach of faith."

"By no means," replied Jack; "I only promised not to shoot you, if you confessed all. Your life is justly forfeited, for you are a brigand."

"Forgive me!"

"When you are dead, not before," said Jack.

"Do you want me to do anything?" asked Dick, producing a coil of rope which he had brought with him in view of possible events.

"Thank you," answered Jack; "tie him up, neck and heels; he can cool himself here till I give him to the soldiers."

Sarati gnashed his teeth.

He saw clearly that it was all over with him now.

His career would be cut short in very quick time.

If Jack had spared him, it was only to give him to the soldiers, who would hand him over to the executioner.

Dick, in high glee, advanced to the prostrate man, holding the rope in his hand.

It was useless for Sarati to offer any resistance.

The pistol that Jack held covered him.

Yet the man was desperate.

He argued to himself that he could only die once, and that it was worth his while to make an effort to get away.

Would Jack's bullet be worse than the rope, preceded by a long imprisonment and a weary trial ?

He opined not.

As Dick Lambert neared him he jumped up, and leaping the wall, ran up the road like a hare.

For this contingency Jack was ready.

He fired two balls after him.

One struck him in the back, the other sank deep in the base of the skull.

With a plunge he fell in the dust, grovelling on his face for a few moments in the convulsive throes of death.

Then he was still and motionless as a stone.

Thus died the accomplished, but unscrupulous and bitterly vindictive Sarati, Count di Mora, one of the oldest of the Italian nobility.

"My father's death is avenged," said Jack, grimly. "I meant that the man should die on the scaffold, before a jeering public, but perhaps it is better thus."

"You cannot feel any compunction in killing such a scoundrel ; his life was justly forfeited over and over again ; besides, he shot Sparks," replied Dick.

"I am sorry for the detective," answered Jack, "though he was not a very bright specimen of his class, self-willed, conceited, ignorant, and a coward at heart."

"All he wanted was to make money, but he has made his last shilling, poor beggar."

"Tell the coachman to drive to the inn ; we will walk up and wait for the troops."

Dick did so, and Jack dragged the body of Sarati to the wall.

Slowly and sadly he and Dick followed the carriage to the "Garibaldi."

Ada was again in the power of the brigands.

Possilippo had escaped, and was, no doubt, at the head of his band once more.

Jack had all his work to begin over again.

But in this new campaign he had one great advantage.

The soldiers were at his back.

When the inn was reached, the keeper was not there, he being represented by his wife.

On being questioned she stated that her husband had been obliged to go on a journey.

Jack interpreted this to mean that he had gone to the brigands' stronghold, possibly under the orders of Possilippo.

Naturally the chief would want to strengthen his slender force as much as possible.

Giving the coachman some refreshment, Jack directed him to go back to Naples, and deposit the corpse of Sparks, the detective, in the public mortuary to await burial.

When he was gone, the boys sat on the verandah, sheltered from the blazing sun, ordered a bottle of light wine, and lighted their cigarettes.

"I omitted to tell you that I received a letter from Sir Dando Titmarsh, yesterday, when the mail came in," said Dick.

"How are things at home ?" asked Jack, moodily.

"Your barge-boy, Rumbo, as you called him, who turned out to be Sir Dando's heir, had a relapse and died."

"Poor chap ; that is better, though, than being an idiot for life."

"Sir Dando is very anxious about Ada and us. He is far from well, and states that he has made a fresh will, leaving all his fortune to his daughter. What with the brigand's diamonds, and that, Ada will be rich."

"If she lives," replied Jack, gloomily.

"We must succeed in rescuing her."

"I hope so ; but you do not know, you cannot imagine how strong the bandits' position is ; it will take a lot of storming."

"Can't we get at it from above ?"

"No ; unless, like flies, we could walk on the precipitous sides of the hill. Rather than surrender, I believe Possilippo would blow the caves up."

"That is bad," replied Dick, reflectively.

"They can fire down on us, and hurl huge boulders of rock they have collected on the plateau, while we ascend the winding path that leads to their eyry."

"Why not starve them out ?"

"They are well provisioned for a siege," answered Jack ; "their only weak point is water. They have a tank hollowed out of the rock, which fills when it rains, and, in the absence of rain, is filled by casks, brought by hand from a stream that runs through the valley."

"How long will that supply last them?"

"Not more than a week, even if they exercised the utmost economy; but, if they perish for want of water, the same fate will befall Ada."

"True; the case is full of difficulties," Dick remarked.

"I can't see my way at all," replied Jack, with a gloomy air; "but, by Heaven, I'll fight Possilippo to the last drop of my blood."

"By George! old fellow, I'm shoulder to shoulder with you as long as I can stand."

"The coil of the snake of destiny is tightening round the brigand."

"Yes; his sands of life are running low."

"I always thought it was a defect in his fastness," continued Jack, "not to have a way of escape if hard pressed."

"How do you know he has not?" enquired Dick.

"Of course, I do not know everything, but I suppose I should have heard of it if there had been one."

"That does not follow. He was not going to tell you everything."

"His mother, Bianca, who wished to befriend Ada, would have imparted the secret to her, I imagine."

"Would a fond and doting mother, who loved her son so much, have betrayed him? That is where your judgment misleads you."

"Perhaps I am wrong."

"Depend upon it, he knows a way out of the caves, by the side, or the top of the hill."

"If you think so," said Jack, "it will be a good strategic movement to post some soldiers on the summit; but how are they going to get up?"

"These Italian soldiers can climb like sheep. Tell the captain, arrange your plans carefully, leave no stone unturned, no loophole open."

"I'll do it, Dick; stick to me."

"Like a brick; haven't I always done so? I love Ada like a sister, and I will do all I can to rescue her."

"Advise me; my head does not feel very strong."

"It is the worry you have had to go through. Bear up, there is a good time coming. You have got the brigand's diamonds," replied Dick, with a laugh.

"That is a capital bit of business; but I would give them all for Ada."

"Of course you would; yet, I will wager that you will have both soon."

"Do you really think so?"

"Certainly. Keep up your pluck, and never forget that in me you've got a chum who would lay down his life for you."

Jack wrung his hand affectionately.

"I thank you from the bottom of my heart," he replied.

Their conversation was interrupted by the merry, spirit-stirring sound of the drum-and-fife band.

The soldiers were approaching the "Garibaldi Inn."

When they arrived they stacked arms, produced their rations, bought some wine, and reclining in the shade of the trees, enjoyed a rest they were well entitled to.

The officer, whose name was Captain Martello, had a long conversation with Jack.

He listened carefully to all the latter had to say about the situation of, and approaches to, the brigands' retreat.

With a pencil and a piece of paper he made a diagram.

"I have it all mapped out," he said, at length; "it is quite clear to me."

"When will you attack?" asked Jack.

"That remains to be seen. I shall invest the place to-night; to-morrow I will reconnoitre. Will you join my force as volunteers, you and your friend?"

"With your kind permission."

"I feel sure that your services will be invaluable to me."

"You honour me too highly," said Jack.

After this exchange of compliments, Captain Martello borrowed a horse from the stable and went for a ride to the hills, in order to survey the ground; and Jack took advantage of the opportunity to snatch a few hours' sleep in a chair.

The result of the officer's examination was that he despatched a messenger to Naples to request the Minister of the Interior to forward him a mountain howitzer.

This species of small cannon can throw a shell to a considerable height.

It was a good idea.

As the sun was declining, and the cool evening breeze setting in, the column marched for the hills.

Jack Massey and Dick Lambert walked by the side of Captain Martello, whom they found a very pleasant and well-informed gentleman.

They talked on the subject which occupied their minds.

Though they all agreed that they had a difficult task in hand, they hoped to be successful in the end.

CHAPTER XXIV.

THE BRIGANDS AT BAY.

IT was an immense relief to Ada when her captors arrived at the top of the winding path and deposited her on the plateau.

She was about to enter the caves and obtain some refreshment, of which she stood very much in need, preparatory to resting on Bianca's bed, when the Dwarf of Blood cried:

"Stop! If you were not Sarati's chosen bride, I would kill you for escaping; as it is, you shall live, and he shall deal with you as he pleases."

Ada made no reply.

"No doubt," continued Tito, "Sarati will soon settle accounts with your English lover, and so prevent him betraying us. If he does not, you shall die."

How signally he was mistaken, the events we have described in the last chapter fully proved.

"Before you seek seclusion," Tito went on, "you shall witness the punishment of the sentry whom you overcame with wine."

The wretched man was stretched in sleep on the rock.

It was now about two o'clock in the morning.

The moon, nearly at its full, was shining brightly.

Tito walked towards the sleeping sentry, and kicked him in the side.

"Dog!" he cried. "Wake up."

The brigand scrambled to his feet, looking round him in a dazed manner.

"What are you all up to?" he asked, stupidly.

"We have found you asleep on your post," replied the Dwarf of Blood.

"Well, yes, I admit that."

"You have allowed the prisoners to escape."

"Have I? Confound the wine. I never drank on post before. Let me off this time; it shall not occur again."

"No. I am captain now, and I will preserve discipline. Prepare to join those who have gone before you."

"Oh! if it comes to that," said the brigand, who, nevertheless, looked very pale, "I can die as bravely as any of you; but you may regret losing my services."

"How so?"

"I dreamt that the soldiers were after us, and that we were besieged in this place; the water gave out, and we were all dying of thirst. The tank is half empty, and we shall not have any rain yet awhile, by the look of the sky. I will go and fetch water from the valley for you, if you will look over this folly of mine."

"If I am thirsty, I will quaff blood," Tito replied. "Bare your breast; my knife is ready."

The brigand unfastened his collarless red shirt, and exposed his chest.

"What does it matter, a year or two, sooner than later? We all have to go the long journey. I discounted death when I became a brigand," he exclaimed.

"Are you ready?"

"Strike!"

The Dwarf of Blood raised his knife, and plunged it deep down in the man's neck.

Blood gushed from the wound; he staggered back, and fell headlong over the precipice.

Sick at heart, Ada limped into the caves, and hid herself in Bianca's chamber, where she ate some food and drank some wine, after which she threw herself on the bed.

No one came near her.

For some time she heard the brigands singing, cursing, and shouting, as they drank deeply and gambled with dice and cards.

Ada slumbered at intervals only, for the pain in her injured ankle continually awoke her.

Terrifying dreams racked her mind.

She was haunted with a dread that Sarati would kill Jack when the latter came to take her to the city.

The lamp, not being supplied with oil, flickered and went out.

It was intolerable, in her frame of mind, to be in the dark.

Getting up from the rough pallet bed on which she was lying, she groped her way into the outer cave.

The brigands were asleep, having exhausted themselves with their nocturnal orgies.

Emerging on the plateau, she saw a sentinel standing still, watching the grey dawn breaking in the east.

Clouds of mist, white and fleecy, were rising as if by the waving of a magician's wand.

To pass the sentry was impossible, and if she could have done so, her injured ankle would not have allowed her to go far.

Selecting a secluded spot, she sat down, watching the long expanse of plain beneath her.

She was very low-spirited, feeling that her sands of life were fast slipping away.

If Sarati got the best of Jack, she was to be given over to him by Tito, and the Dwarf of Blood had declared that if the contrary happened, he would put her to death, as a punishment for releasing the captive, who might do them so much injury by revealing to the authorities the exact position of their mysterious stronghold.

Take it either way, she thought it was a disagreeable prospect.

Two hours passed by, and the lonely, friendless girl sat like a statue, her tear-stained eyes carelessly watching the sun climb higher and higher into the heavens.

Presently she beheld the form of a man walking across the plain.

He approached the hills, and began to ascend the zigzag path.

Now she knew that he was some spy or messenger affiliated to the brigands.

If not, the sentry would have fired upon him and given the alarm.

As it was, the sentry simply went to the mouth of the cave and beckoned to Tito.

The Dwarf of Blood was just finishing his breakfast of bread and wine, having recruited his strength by a few hours of sound and refreshing sleep.

"What is it?" asked Tito. "Has our ally, Sarati, come back?"

"No," was the reply, "it is Frato, the innkeeper."

"Ah! mine host of the 'Garibaldi.'"

"The same."

"*Basta!*" cried Tito, while a look of vexation crossed his face, "he is ever a bird of ill omen."

"True; he never comes here but to bring us bad tidings."

"Yet," said Tito, "it is better that we should hear the news, whatever it is, than be kept in ignorance."

"You are right again; he is in the world, and we, in a manner of speaking, are out of it," replied the sentry.

The innkeeper made his appearance, bathed in a profuse perspiration, which showed that he had been hastening.

"Well, you infernal old woman," exclaimed the Dwarf of Blood, "what have you come to croak about this fine morning?"

"Matter enough," replied Frato.

"Speak out. If Vesuvius is going to burst the whole place up, I for one don't care, it will only be sending me to my future home a little earlier than I had reckoned on. Ho, ho!"

He laughed at his own irreverence; but Frato was not in the same mood, for he crossed himself devoutly.

"Heaven forbid," he muttered.

"What have you, or the likes of you, to do with Heaven?" cried the Dwarf of Blood, his eyes flashing angrily.

"No more than you have, but the word was familiar to my lips before I had the misfortune to be mixed up with your crew. But a truce to this. I wish to have no quarrel with you, indeed, it is no time for bickering."

Tito stamped his foot with rage.

"Fool!" said he; "come to the point. Tell me what errand brought you here, or I'll search your heart with the point of my knife."

"Don't be so impatient," replied Frato; "I have not had time to get my breath yet; besides, I am as dry as the inside of Vesuvius, and I know you keep good wine here, for I brought it myself."

"Not a drop of drink do you get until you've spoken."

"Well, then, prepare to be shot at," said the innkeeper, sulkily.

"Fire away ; I'm bullet-proof."

"That is more than Sarati was."

"Malediction ! is he dead ?"

"He is," answered Frato. "I have been on the look-out all the morning."

"How did he die ?"

"Shot by that young Englishman, who was captured in my house—Left-handed Jack they call him."

"Where is this Jack now ?" demanded the Dwarf of Blood, savagely.

"At the inn, awaiting the coming of the soldiers, who will bring a mountain howitzer with them."

Tito sprang half-a-foot in the air.

"Perdition !" he yelled, "are the soldiers coming to storm us ? "

"Undoubtedly. I saw them down the road, but there is yet hope for all of us," said the innkeeper.

"How is that ?"

"Possilippo has cheated his guards ; he is free."

The brigands had come out of the cave on hearing the voice of the innkeeper, who was a character well known to all of them.

"Down with the soldiers, and long live Possilippo !" they cried. "Hurrah for the brigand chief !"

The number of the brigands had been sadly depleted of late, and there were only ten of them to be seen.

But these were fine, stalwart, well-built, courageous villains, each capable of doing the work of two ordinary men.

"How do you know that our chief has broken prison ?" asked Tito.

There was a lingering doubt in his mind as to the truth of the innkeeper's statement.

"I have seen him," was the reply.

"Where is he now ?"

"Lurking in the neighbourhood. He informed me that he had a purpose in view, but what it was he did not explain."

"All I can say is, three cheers for the chief !" cried the Dwarf of Blood. "I am willing to serve under him as I did before."

"*Viva* Possilippo !" exclaimed the picturesque band of ruffians in a loud, approving chorus.

"Cheer heartily, my lads. If we have to die, why, let us perish fighting, with our faces to the foe," said Tito.

"I am with you to the last drop of my blood," remarked Frato.

"We shall want all the hands we can get."

Suddenly the quick-sighted dwarf noticed Ada sitting on a rocky lodge under the shelter of some flowering shrubs and mountain-ash trees.

"Ha ! my little traitress !" he added, "you now see a band of brigands at bay, and when in that condition, they are not apt to show mercy to anyone, least of all to one who has betrayed them."

Ada looked at them with lack-lustre eyes.

The hot, scalding tears had ceased to flow down her cheeks now.

She felt a dull, aching pain in her head, and her grief-stricken heart beat feebly.

"What do you wish of me ?" she asked.

"Step forward, if you please," replied Tito.

With a painful limp she did so, regarding her captors with a tired, weary air.

It seemed as if she wished that life's fitful fever was over.

She had little hope that Jack Massey would ever see her alive again.

"You have heard that Sarati has been slain by the hand of your lover, who is about to guide the soldiers to the fastness ?" continued the Dwarf of Blood.

"Yes," she rejoined, laconically.

"For that we hold you directly responsible."

"How can you justly do so ? "

"If you had not last night released our prisoner, this would not have happened. Your life is justly forfeited. What say you, comrades ? "

"Death must be her portion," said the innkeeper.

"Ay, ay ! blood for blood !" the brigands cried.

"You hear your sentence pronounced," Tito added.

Ada trembled visibly.

Apparently her last hour had come.

"It is not manly for armed men like you to kill a defenceless girl !" she exclaimed. "This will be a murder."

"Not so. Call it an execution," replied the Dwarf of Blood ; "but I will be a little merciful."

"*You* show mercy !"

"Hear me out."

"As soon should I expect the tiger

of the jungle to show mercy to its hapless prey," said Ada.

"Come, don't storm; listen to me. You shall have your choice of deaths."

"If I am to die, it is all the same to me."

"What shall it be: steel, lead, or hemp, the knife, the bullet, or the rope? Methinks that hanging is not a graceful way of quitting the world. A woman does not look well when she is dancing on nothing."

"It does not become you to joke on such a subject," replied the girl in a tone of rebuke.

"I shall decide for you!" exclaimed the Dwarf of Blood, "and I choose the pistol. Fall on your knees."

Ada bestowed an appealing glance upon him.

On Tito it had no more effect than has water on a duck's back.

Her beautiful and expressive eyes wandered to the assembled brigands.

Though not insensible to her charms, they were equally uncompassionate.

"Oh, Heaven!" she murmured, "it is to Thee alone that I must look for help."

The Dwarf of Blood grinned sardonically.

He bound her arms behind her back, and tied a white bandage over her eyes.

Then he retreated a few paces.

In his hand he held a seven-chambered revolver.

"I will bet," he exclaimed, "that I will kill her at the first shot."

"How much?" asked the innkeeper.

"Fifty scudi."

"I will take you."

"Done," said the Dwarf of Blood, "the wager is made. By Our Lady! I love killing women and children."

He raised his pistol, and levelled it at her.

There was an ominous hush.

Ada's livid lips moved as she commended her soul to Heaven.

It was an awful moment.

Some of the bronzed faces of the brigands blanched under the sun-tanned skin.

Yet not a hand was raised to save her.

What was the life of the pretty English girl to them?

A mere bagatelle, a shadow in their path, nothing more.

CHAPTER XXV.

POSSILIPPO'S ADVENTURE.

THE news of Possilippo's escape from the fortress in which he had been confined was perfectly correct.

Luckily for him, the brigand had met in one of his gaolers a man who had formerly belonged to his band.

This fellow was under many obligations to the chief, and preserved a lively recollection of favours received.

He had left the band to marry a peasant girl, who had stolen his heart during one of the bandits' predatory excursions.

Coming to the city he abandoned his former career, and obtained a situation as a prison-warder.

He determined to show his former leader that he was grateful.

In the night he opened the cell-door, conducted him into the yard, and with the pass-key let him out at the gate.

Possilippo lost no time in getting clear of the city.

If he were recaptured, he might not have such a chance a second time.

The man's name was Capri; he was about forty years of age, and a thin, wiry, active fellow.

"I have an idea," muttered Possilippo, "that I shall see that man again; it is my misfortune to drag men down."

In truth, Capri could not stop where he was.

When the prisoner's escape was discovered, he would be one of the first of the officials to be suspected.

Scarcely had the brigand spoken, than a hand was laid on his shoulder.

He clenched his hand and turned round.

Capri, hot, dusty, tired, stood before him.

"Capitano," he said, "the needle must fly to the magnet."

"My poor Capri," replied Possilippo, "it would be best for you to return."

"No, no. I must stay with you."

"My fortunes have fallen very low I fear that I shall soon end my career, for I will never desert my men."

"Nor they you. And I, as well as they, will die for you."

The brigand shook hands with him heartily.

"Be it so," he said, "we will die together. Come."

They walked on side by side until they reached the inn, outside which they met Frato, the keeper.

Possilippo instructed him to go to the caves, and inform his followers that he would be with them in the course of the day.

He proposed to remain in the neighbourhood for a time, to see what course the authorities would take in the matter.

After obtaining some refreshment, the chief and Capri retired to a wooded, shady spot near the road.

Here they waited for further developments, while the innkeeper walked towards Naples, saw the soldiers advancing, and reported progress to the Dwarf of Blood.

The sky became heavy and leaden.

It was streaked with flames of yellow-looking fire at times, as the eruption of Vesuvius became more marked and striking.

Now and again the earth trembled.

A sulphurous smell pervaded the air.

"There will be an earthquake," said Possilippo, "or I am greatly mistaken."

"What matters it?" replied Capri. "If the earth swallows us up, is it not a kind of natural burial, saving the expense of a funeral?"

"Jester! would you laugh at death in its most fearful form?"

"I have never feared it."

"Yet, life is sweet," answered the brigand chief. "It is those who, like us, sin against the laws, that make it bitter. I have longed for a better life, if not for my own sake, for that of my mother, but fate has been against me."

"Let us hope that better days are in store for you and all of us."

The brigand shook his head sadly.

"I entertained that hope once," he said; "but I fear that things have gone too far now. I can only die at the head of my men."

"Why not go away to parts where you are unknown?"

"For two reasons—I may say three.

First of all, I must protect my mother; secondly, she has my treasure—my diamonds; thirdly, my devotion to my men peremptorily calls me back."

"You are an extraordinary man."

"Somewhat out of the common, I admit," said Possilippo, with a complacent smile. "It would not do for us to be all alike, or else 'twould be a humdrum world indeed."

"That is correct," replied Capri. "Variety is the spice of life, and I must confess that I like a life of adventure."

"There you and I resemble one another. I love danger. My heart leaps and bounds when peril is in front of me; my blood becomes on fire, and my brain is in a whirl of delirious delight."

"That shows you were born to be a leader of men."

Possilippo made no answer to this remark.

There was little doubt, however, that if he had been an officer engaged in some important war, he would have risen to the highest rank in the army.

If not, he would have died gallantly on the battle-field.

Unquestionably, he was no common man.

His noble brow was clouded with dark, carking care.

Bitter thoughts flooded his active mind, which was always at work.

He reflected on his misspent life, and his heart became heavy.

There was nothing for him now but to carry on his career to the end, and that, it seemed, would be a sorry one.

All at once he heard the sound of footsteps.

"Hush!" he whispered.

"I will be as silent as the grave," replied Capri in the same tone.

"Someone approaches."

"I hear it."

In less than a minute, two tramps of the *lazzaroni* class made their appearance, clad in rags, and smoking cigarettes.

"Halt!" said one; "this seems a likely place to waylay a traveller."

"No better could be found," replied the other beggar.

"We will have gold."

"Ay, and blood, too, if need be!"

They sat down by the roadside, and sharpened their knives one upon the other.

Villainous-looking creatures were they.

Gaol-bird was written on their hang-dog faces.

Possilippo was unarmed, for he had had no opportunity of purchasing any weapon since his escape from prison.

And if he had had the chance, the want of money would have prevented him from doing so.

Capri was more fortunate.

He was the lucky possessor of a pistol, which he pressed into the chief's hand.

"Take it," he said; "you will do more good with it than I."

Possilippo grasped it eagerly.

"Thank you," he replied, "I shall know how to use it."

Another surprise awaited them.

A man, who was evidently a gentleman of position, was seen riding along on a coal-black horse, which looked like a charger in a cavalry regiment.

He was unsuspicious of anyone being near him.

Suddenly the horse snorted and reared, pawing the air as if frightened.

The sky became more overcast as the clouds thickened, and a profound calm reigned.

As for the heat, it was intense.

When the horse reared, the ground shook and slightly cracked, opening in the middle of the road.

A rumbling noise was heard.

The horse rolled over on his side, and the rider had only just time enough to alight from the saddle adroitly on his feet.

Now was the tramps' opportunity.

They rushed forward and seized the gentleman from behind, one rifling his pockets, while the other threatened him with a knife.

"Would you kill me, wretches?" asked the stranger.

"That is my intention presently," replied the ruffian with the knife. "Dead men tell no tales, and if I let you go, you might identify us."

"Help! help!"

"Hold your noise."

"Murder! help!" shouted the gentleman.

The *lazzarone* raised his knife.

At whatever risk to his own safety, Possilippo could not see the threatened murder done without making an attempt to prevent it.

He was determined to rush to the rescue.

Telling Capri to remain in hiding, he leaped over the wall that bounded the road.

In an instant he was by the side of the helpless man.

With a rapid movement he snatched the knife from the hand of the *lazzarone*, and drove it into his back.

The blade touched a vital spot.

With a horrible groan the footpad sank to the ground, which he dyed with his blood.

Seeing the fate of his companion, the other took to his heels.

He was quickly out of sight.

It was useless to pursue him, as he ran with all the fleetness of a hare.

Up to this time Possilippo had not enjoyed an opportunity of seeing the countenance of the person he had rescued.

With a quick turn the latter faced him.

Great indeed was the astonishment of the brigand chief to see before him the all-powerful Minister of the Interior.

It was the Duke of Calabria whom he had saved from destruction.

"You, Casati!" cried the duke.

"Or Possilippo, whichever your grace likes," replied the brigand, with a smile.

"How strange. I was actually riding in this direction to see if I could find any trace of you or your band."

"You have heard of my escape?"

"It was telephoned to me from the central office. I started soon afterwards. Who are those fellows who attacked me?"

"*Lazzaroni*. None of my band, I can assure your grace."

"I am glad to hear that. *Per Baccho!* you have saved my life, and I owe you a good turn for that."

"It is fortunate for me."

"Come, you shall not find me ungrateful; this is what I will do for you," said the Duke of Calabria.

He was in a most excellent temper.

The brigand listened, with great curiosity depicted on his face.

"Everybody in society liked you," resumed the minister. "It was a great shock to us all to hear that you led a dual life."

"I was driven to it by want of money," said Possilippo.

"We knew that you were a gambler and lost large sums, and that your personal expenditure was large."

"Much larger than anyone suspected."

"No one, however, suspected that

you were reduced to extremities. I have only to add that if you will give up this life, I will grant you a free pardon."

"Your grace is too good," answered Possilippo.

He was overwhelmed with gratitude at this unexpected kindness.

The Minister of the Interior had the power of life and death.

He could override a decision of the judges, and the brigand had not yet been either tried or condemned.

In short, the word of the Duke of Calabria was higher than the law of the land.

"You must go to some city where you are unknown, and make a fresh start in life," went on the minister.

"I should be glad to do so, but what of my band? I have nearly a dozen devoted followers."

"They must be exterminated. I will annihilate them all like rats in a trap," replied the duke.

He frowned darkly.

"The public will expect an example to be made of them," he added. "I must do something to regain the confidence of the people."

Possilippo looked depressed and downcast.

"I regret to say that I cannot accept your grace's pardon," he exclaimed.

This declaration profoundly astonished the duke.

"Are you mad?" he demanded.

"Allow me to disperse my band."

"Impossible! I can make no terms as to them."

"I will undertake that they shall cease to be brigands."

"Only to become thieves and murderers in the slums of the city," cried the duke, angrily.

"That is as it may be. Your police can deal with them," responded Possilippo.

"My dear Casati, you must listen to reason. You laid me under an eternal obligation to you just now; I want to serve and save you."

"Let us argue the point."

"Oh! certainly, if you wish it; my time is my own; but I warn you that soon it will not be safe for you to be seen on the high road."

"And why not?"

"I have ordered a full company of bersaglieri, belonging to the famous 91st regiment of the line, to march in search of you."

"So the soldiers are coming?"

Possilippo said, with a bitter smile. "I expected as much."

"You cannot stand against them long, if you refuse to agree to my terms."

"I beg your grace's pardon," the brigand replied, proudly. "If I had more men, I could defy the whole Italian army."

"How is that?"

"Because my mountain stronghold is really impregnable."

"Bah! you think so, that is all."

"You will alter your opinion when I have killed all your bersaglieri."

"Do not boast. It ill becomes a man in your position to indulge in such braggadocio," exclaimed the duke, much annoyed.

"Pardon me, I spoke hastily," Possilippo replied. "Let us look at the other side of the question."

"Well, how then?"

"Your soldiers will eventually kill me and my men. I shall die with a bullet in my heart, that is all," said the brigand, twisting his moustache.

"I am sorry that you are so obstinate; it is a pity, for you have sealed your doom. If the bersaglieri fail to take your stronghold, I will keep on sending soldiers against you until——"

"Enough!" interrupted Possilippo, "I thank you for your princely offer, but cannot accept it."

"Reflect!"

"My mind is made up, I will not forsake my men."

He caught hold of the bridle of the duke's horse, and assisted him to mount.

"Farewell!" he added.

With this word, which to both of them had such a melancholy significance, he vaulted over the wall, and calling Capri to follow him, disappeared among the trees.

In a few minutes they were walking over the plain towards the hills.

Freedom and pardon had been offered to the brigand chief.

He had refused both from a sense of duty to his followers, and had chosen death to life.

Capri was silent, but it seemed, from the expression of his face, that he was plunged in deep thought.

"You heard my conversation with the minister?" said Possilippo.

"Every word of it," was the answer.

"Do you not think I acted rightly?"

"You stood in your own light. I can only tell you that I would not have done so. What a chance to throw away."

"My honour is concerned in this matter. I wanted the pardon extended to my men."

"Ah! you asked too much. It is possible to open one's mouth too wide."

"I am satisfied, for I have the approval of my conscience. Say no more. We must prepare for a hard fight. If we can beat off the soldiers, I will disband my gallant fellows, for I am tired of the business, and now that the duke has taken the matter seriously in hand, we shall have no opportunity for future operations. My game is over."

Possilippo was undoubtedly right.

His career as a brigand must soon be cut short one way or another.

It was with a feeling of deep dejection, however, that he once more approached the winding path that led up to his stronghold.

What would the next few days—nay, hours, bring forth?

It happened that he arrived at the top of the path at a very critical moment.

Tito was about to shoot Ada, whom we left kneeling on the plateau, bound, blindfolded, wrapt in silent prayer.

In a moment he took in the situation.

Rushing between the Dwarf of Blood and his victim, he cried:

"Hold!"

Gnashing his teeth, Tito dropped his hand.

Ada was saved!

CHAPTER XXVI.

THE SIEGE OF THE BRIGANDS' STRONGHOLD.

PUTTING his pistol in his belt, Tito held out his hand to his chief.

"Welcome!" he exclaimed. "We have felt your absence deeply. You could not have come at a better time."

The rest of the brigands crowded round their chief, and were enthusiastic in their greeting.

Vivas rent the air.

"Comrades, friends, I thank you," said Possilippo. "I have always endeavoured to earn your confidence."

"And you *have* earned it," replied Tito.

"I will continue to do so to the end. Now, a word to you, Tito."

"As many as you like," said the Dwarf of Blood, carelessly.

"Did I not order you to protect this young girl?"

"You did."

"Why, then," asked Possilippo, "have my commands been disregarded?"

"Circumstances have altered since you left, capitano."

"Explain them to me."

Tito did so, relating how Ada, when he and the brigands went to intercept the treasure waggon, made the sentry intoxicated, and escaped with the English prisoner.

Then he narrated the finding of Ada with a sprained ankle, the return of Left-handed Jack to the spot where he had left her, and the death of Sarati.

"You see that she is a dangerous character," he concluded. "She has proved a traitress."

"Her love guided her," replied Possilippo. "We must make allowance for that."

"You condone a fault—nay, a crime like that?" asked the dwarf, whose eyes flashed with fury.

"She shall live."

"Give me your reasons. I have a right to ask for them, since you have overruled me."

"With pleasure," answered Possilippo, calmly.

"One word first," continued Tito. "Do you know that the *bersaglieri* are after us, and that this left-handed Englishman is going to lead them to our lair?"

"I am fully aware of all the facts; the girl shall be kept as a hostage."

"Ah! is that your idea?"

"Fool!" cried Possilippo, "do you not see that she is worth money? This English boy has influence with the police and the authorities."

"What a head you have!"

"If," continued Possilippo, "we are hard pressed, we can make terms, perhaps, on the condition of sparing the girl's life."

"True enough."

"Don't you see, dolt that you are, that we can put her to death, if we want to, at any time?"

"I did not think of that."

"That is your worst fault," said the chief. "You never will give yourself time to reflect."

"Admitted, my chief."

"With you it is always the tigered thirst for blood—you must kill. I wonder you did not become a hangman."

"Ah! that would have suited me well; perhaps I shall adopt the profession if I live to get over this trouble."

Possilippo took no further notice of him.

He unbound Ada, and removed the bandage from her eyes.

Then he gallantly raised her to her feet.

She was like one in a dream, though she had heard distinctly all that had been uttered.

It seemed too good to be true.

Possilippo had come back and snatched her from the brink of an abyss.

The chasm of eternal night had yawned before her.

She was to live, and be held to ransom.

Sarati could no longer conspire against her happiness.

He had passed away.

Jack—her Jack, whom she loved with all the fervour of her soul, was with the force that was going to attack the rocky fastness.

She was lifted from despair to hope.

"My little maiden," said the brigand, kindly, "fear nothing, for no harm is intended you; rely upon my word."

Tears of gratitude forced themselves into her eyes.

"Heaven will reward you for your goodness to me," she replied.

"Go inside. We shall have rough work presently. Bianca will care for you."

"Alas! she is no longer able——"

"What!" he interrupted. "Bianca gone!"

"She is dead. When the news of your capture came to her ears, she died of a broken heart, so suddenly, that I could do nothing for her."

Possilippo was profoundly affected.

"My mother dead!" he cried. "This blow is hard to bear."

His followers were greatly astonished, for they had never known, nor even suspected, the relationship that existed between him and the old woman.

"*Basta!*" said Tito, "that is bad. I sympathise with you, captain. I had a mother years ago, and she was very good to me."

"Where is the body?"

"We threw it on to some rocks; it did not roll into the valley, but no one can get at it, be sure of that."

"Fool! you have ruined me."

"How is that, capitano?" asked the dwarf.

"She had my bag of diamonds concealed about her person. I had hoped that a fortune was provided for me if I escaped from this life."

"Who would have thought it?" muttered Tito.

He was almost as much disappointed and chagrined as his chief.

High and low had he hunted for the coveted treasure.

It had been within his reach, and yet he could not find it.

Ada considered it advisable to be silent on the matter.

If Possilippo knew that she had secured his diamonds, and given them to Jack Massey, his ire would be roused.

He might recall his promise to be merciful to her.

Therefore she uttered not a word.

Possilippo recovered his composure by the exercise of a great effort.

He took Ada by the hand and led her into the inner cave.

"Take what refreshments you require," he said. "You know where they are kept; remain here, and you will be out of danger. Whatever happens, I think I shall be able to negotiate for your freedom. I do not make war upon women. Indeed, I long to quit this life."

"Why do you not escape while you can? The soldiers are not here yet," she replied.

"I owe a duty to my men."

"Let them disperse and go where they like."

The brigand hesitated before he made an answer.

He was evidently considering her proposition, which, indeed, was feasible.

There was yet time for them all to get away, and the soldiers would find the nest empty, and the birds of prey flown.

He took up a jar of wine and poured out a deep draught, which he drank.

"I am more than half inclined to adopt your advice," he exclaimed. "We might save ourselves, though the pursuit would be hot. Yet what could I do without money?"

"If you would go to Rome, hide there, and send me your address, I would promise, on my sacred word, to keep it a secret, and Left-handed Jack should forward you a handsome sum of money, enough for you to live upon modestly all your life."

"Would, you, indeed, do this for a blood-stained wretch like me?"

"Repent, live a new life."

"Remorse for the past would ever be gnawing at my heart."

"Seek consolation where comfort, hope, and pardon can alone be found," replied Ada.

"You talk like a saint. Would to Heaven that I had had you at my side when I was tempted to become what I am."

"It is never too late to reform."

"No, you are right; I shall call you my guardian angel. We will go. A few words to my men, and we will depart at once," said the brigand.

The tearful pleading of the girl had won his heart.

Visions of a better life rose before him.

He would work and endeavour to redeem the sinful past.

Yes, it should be buried in oblivion, and, like a phœnix rising from its ashes, he would be another man.

Ada clasped her hands ecstatically, so overjoyed was she at the success of her pleading.

His good intentions were nipped in the bud, however.

There was a dull, heavy, booming noise, which penetrated to the interior of the cavern.

Anyone who had been on a field of battle could tell that it was the report of a cannon.

Count Casati had, in his youth, been an officer in the army.

Early in his life he had been an ardent republican, and had fought with Garibaldi.

Later on he had seen service in a terrible battle in which the Italians were defeated by the Austrians.

He carried the scar of a sabre-cut, and the mark of a bullet-wound.

"Too late!" he cried, "the soldiers are upon us."

"Oh! do not say so," murmured Ada.

"Our retreat is cut off; there is no escape, save by the path."

"Are all my hopes destined to be crushed?"

"It's a fight to the death now. Farewell, little one, I must away."

With these words, Possilippo hurried to the plateau.

All hesitancy and weakness vanished in a moment.

The spirit, the instinct of a brave soldier dominated his mind, and like a spirited war-horse, he sniffed the battle far off.

On the plateau the brigands were assembled, looking eagerly into the plain below.

Captain Martello had marched as soon as the cannon was brought up from Naples.

Under the guidance of Jack, he had reached the spot in quick time.

To announce his presence he fired a shell.

This burst below the plateau, scattering a mass of shattered rock, which fell with a crash.

The soldiers were standing in double file.

Jack and Dick Lambert were by the side of Captain Martello.

Two artillerymen were reloading the howitzer.

"Keep cool, men," exclaimed Possilippo, "we must act on the defensive for the present."

"When they get the range," replied Tito, "they will make things lively for us. There is an ammunition waggon full of shells."

"They will soon get tired of firing."

"I don't know so much about that; their cannon will cover a storming party, and I don't think they are going to wait long either."

"Watch for the match to be applied to the fuse," said Possilippo, "then run into the cave for shelter."

"Look out, they are sighting the field-piece," shouted Tito; "this time they will get the elevation. I can see they mean to fight us at once."

"Yes," replied the chief, "it will soon be over."

He was right in his conjecture.

Captain Martello had seen the Duke of Calabria, and the Minister of the

Interior had given him strict orders to force the fighting.

The siege of the brigands' stronghold was not to last long.

It would not do for seasoned, well-disciplined Italian troops to be kept in check for any length of time by a few banditti.

"Retire, all of you," suddenly said Possilippo.

He remained standing like a statue.

His proud spirit would not let him look for safety.

All ran into the cave except Tito, who placed himself by his leader's side.

He grinned with a fiendish glee and rubbed his hands.

"We shall see some fun presently," he remarked.

"Why do you not seek shelter?" asked Possilippo.

"What you are not afraid of cannot terrify me."

"You were always brave, Tito."

"*Basta*! what is life? I hate the idea of growing old! let me die, if I must, but I want to kill first."

There was a hissing, whizzing sound.

The howitzer was fired a second time.

In this instance the shell flew over the heads of Possilippo and the Dwarf of Blood.

It struck the rock and burst, but neither the chief nor his lieutenant was injured.

"That is not bad," observed Tito; "they have the elevation now. Next time they will rake us finely."

"Wait and see," was the reply.

A movement was observable among the Italian troops.

Twenty-five men numbered off from their right, and Captain Martello addressed a few words to them.

They were led by a non-commissioned officer.

This was the storming party.

The men removed their caps, and gave a loud cheer.

After that they approached the zigzag path, and ascended it in single file.

"To the front!" exclaimed Possilippo.

His brigands came out of the cave with a downcast air.

The cannon had unnerved them, for they were not accustomed to that sort of warfare.

"Hurl down the rocks we have collected for that purpose!" continued the chief, "and if any soldier escapes, shoot him when he is near enough."

Setting to work, the men pushed the rocks, one by one, over the precipice.

One just missed the leader, and struck the foremost soldier.

He was knocked over, upsetting several others in his fall.

They were hurled to the bottom of the declivity, horribly mutilated.

The remainder persevered.

Then came retribution, as a shell burst in the midst of the brigands.

A number of them fell.

Possilippo was hit in the side, and sank to the ground.

"Curses on the cannon!" cried the Dwarf of Blood. "Charge down the path! Charge for your lives!"

The men, now only four in number, hung back.

"Cowards!" shrieked Tito. "Will you give in like this?"

He drew his knife from his belt, and, with madness in his eyes, descended the path.

In a few minutes he met the advancing soldiers.

A brief but terrible struggle ensued.

He killed four of his enemies before a bullet laid him low.

"I die! I die!" he screamed. "Flames flash before my eyes! Demons are coming to seize me! Mercy! mercy!"

Stepping over his body, the brave *bersaglieri* advanced boldly.

The remaining brigands lost all heart.

They fired their rifles in a hurried manner, and in a few minutes the soldiers had gained the plateau.

The position was carried at the point of the bayonet.

Not one of the brigands was left alive excepting Possilippo, who had fainted from loss of blood.

He looked so like a corpse, that no attention was paid to him.

The victors raised a hearty cheer.

This was answered from below.

The leader of the storming party had escaped with his life.

He carried an Italian flag, which he waved in the air.

This was the signal of victory.

As soon as it was seen in the valley, Jack and Dick started up the path.

They were followed more leisurely by Captain Martello.

It had been no business of theirs to do the fighting, which was the legitimate work of the regular Italian troops.

To engage in the conflict would have been foolhardy in the extreme.

How Jack's heart was beating!

Would he find Ada alive or dead?

When he reached the plateau, he pushed the soldiers aside, and rushed into the caves.

Ada, terribly alarmed, was on her knees, her face buried in her hands.

The explosion of cannon, the discharge of rifles, the cries of the wounded and dying, had nearly maddened her.

By her side was her brother.

Dr. Pincio was close by.

In her nervous agony she had taken refuge in the infirmary cave.

Septimus had so far recovered as to be able to walk about.

He was still weak, and the doctor told him that he would never be strong again like other young men.

Our left-handed hero rushed towards his sweetheart.

He was overjoyed to find her living.

For the worst he had been prepared.

Jack caught her in his arms, and pressed her to his breast.

"My love! my life!" he exclaimed.

She raised her tear-stained eyes to his.

"Oh, Jack!" she murmured, "is it all over? Thank Heaven you have come!"

"We have won the victory, dearest," he replied.

Her eyes closed, her head fell back.

She had fainted from excess of joy.

CHAPTER XXVII.

CONCLUSION.

JACK MASSEY, Dick Lambert, and Ada and Septimus Titmarsh, are back in England.

Sir Dando Titmarsh, recovered in health, received them right royally, and was never tired of listening to the narration of their stirring adventures.

Possilippo died of his wound, so that he escaped the executioner.

The goodwill of the Duke of Calabria was of no use to him.

Jack sold the diamonds which the brigand chief had accumulated.

Sir Dando acted as a father to him, and invested the money well.

The diamonds realised an amount which brought him in the splendid income of three thousand a year.

Jack lived in the old house, next door to Sir Dando's, where his father had died, and to which his mother had returned from the seaside in restored health.

He had determined upon the army as a profession.

Having a yearly income of three thousand pounds, he could afford to go into an expensive cavalry regiment.

Jack employed an army tutor—that is, one who prepares for exams., and worked hard.

We must now speak about Septimus Titmarsh.

Though he had recovered from the terrible wound inflicted on him in the caves of Possilippo, thanks to the skill, care, and nursing of Pincio, he was not well.

He was the victim of a constant lassitude.

What was very extraordinary, was that he had grown smaller on one side than the other.

He was wounded in the right side of the neck.

His right arm and right leg contracted several inches, so that he became uneven.

He was compelled to use a crutch to walk with.

His body shrivelled up also, and his face became emaciated, until he looked old and worn at eighteen.

With a singular perversity of reasoning, he set all this down to Jack Massey's account.

It was very unfair.

Yet he hated him more than ever.

To make up for the deformity which had grown upon him, he spent much money on dress and jewellery.

Thinking a change might do him

good, Sir Dando Titmarsh let his house at Windsor and took one at Brighton.

Ada went with Sir Dando and Sep to the seaside.

By the time he was twenty, Jack passed his examination with flying colours.

He was soon after gazetted as a subaltern to the crack cavalry regiment known as the Royal Dragoon Guards.

To his delight and surprise he found it was quartered at Preston Park Barracks, at Brighton.

He would be close to Ada.

He was ordered by the War Office to join his regiment in a fortnight.

That evening he received a letter from Ada.

She had seen his name in the pass-list, and wrote to congratulate him, being also anxious to know what regiment he was going into.

"We have a very nice regiment here," she concluded. "Poor Sep is quite intimate with some of the officers; he is always at the barracks, or driving about with them. He brought two of them to our house yesterday. Lord Goldenhurst, who was at Eton with him, and Subaltern Slavin, who says he knows you. The regiment is named the Royal Dragoon Guards. I wish you could get into it, we should be near one another then."

Jack laughed lightly.

"I *am* in it, and I am in *for* it, I expect," he muttered. "Two old enemies in the regiment, and one out."

All the same, he manfully made up his mind to do his duty as an officer and a gentleman.